I0717507

Published by GladEye Press
Interior Design: J.V. Bolkan
Cover Design: Iron Serif and Sharleen Nelson
ISBN-13: 978-1-951289-09-6 (trade)
ISBN: 978-1-951289-10-2 (hardcover)
Library of Congress Control Number: 2024930448

Printed in the United States of America.
10 9 8 7 6 5 4 3 2 1

The body text is presented in Adobe Jenson Pro, 11 point for easy readability.

Dragon of the Federation

Book One of the Heartstone Series

JASON A. KILGORE
https://jason-kilgore.com/

Springfield, OR

Dedication

For my children, Ben and Anna. May you live the fantasies you dream of.

REGIONAL MAP
The White Lands Federation, Peshilaree, and Surrounding Lands

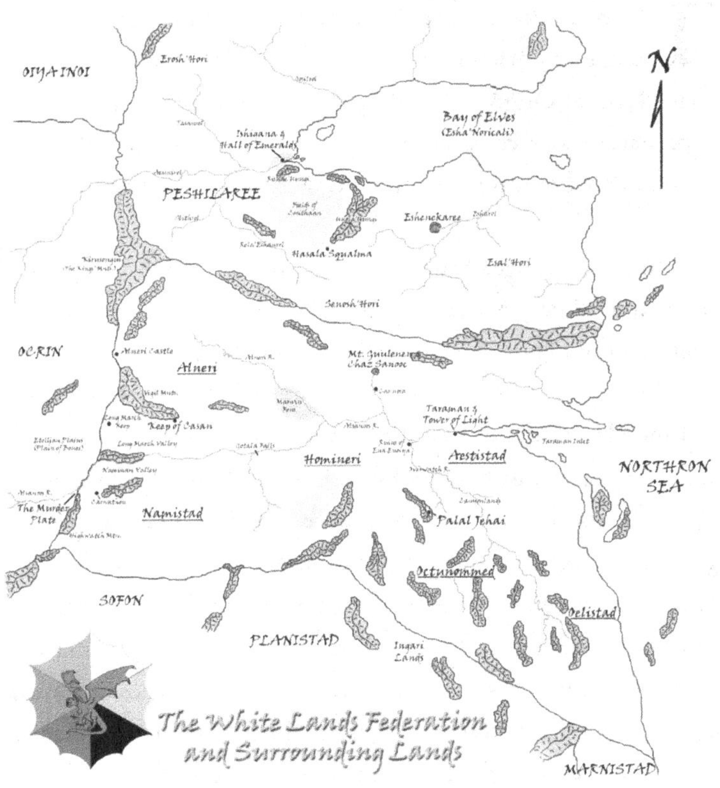

PROLOGUE
The First Drop of Rain

The twin moons were at their zenith, casting a silvern radiance onto the unfretted surface of Eshenakaree, elvish Lake of Origins. Brooding cliffs surrounded, imposing a supernatural silence upon the scene. A lone owl in the valleys beyond dared to utter a haunting cry, then its echoes fell mute once more.

On the east edge of the lake, where the ridges fell abruptly to make a valley at the lake's gravelly outlet, three figures stood waiting near a large, domed structure composed of a living, leafy membrane with ribs. One figure, the speaker of the elvish Hall of Emeralds, leader of Peshilaree, watched the stars intently, his staff leaning against his shoulder. Dressed in his most formal attire, the speaker's live, multi-flowered headdress stood out garishly against the dulling effect of midnight darkness. The light of the moons conjured an ultraviolet glow from the stamens and veins of the flowers and created a halo around the speaker's head.

Next to the speaker, scanning the hillsides with ecstatic eyes, crouched an elvish cleric, a *padgarun*. She held her broad-bladed spear at an acute angle toward the water. Long, dark green hair fell untamed across her shoulders and back.

Looming over them both, a dragon the color of dried blood raised its head and stretched its wings. Muscles as thick as tree trunks shook and popped under skin covered with scales the size and shape of imperial shields.

The dragon yawned, its lion-like roar shredding the solemn stillness. The speaker wheeled to face the dragon. "Have you no respect for the sanctity of this moment, Iron Dragon?" he said in the elvish tongue.

The dragon smacked his broad lips. "No. Let's get on with this." He smirked, briefly exposing rows of razor-sharp teeth.

"Look to the sky." The speaker thrust a staff toward the moons. Giant hornets perched on a hive at the fork of the staff moved in restless discomfort at the sudden jerking. "In moments the Millennial Starfall will come. As you surely know, it appears but once every thousand years, and only for a short span in the night. Tonight will be the fiftieth starfall since the death of Peshiluud. It is the signal for His rising." The speaker narrowed his eyes at the dragon. "So exercise patience, dragon, or you will have me to deal with as well."

The dragon huffed but said no more, choosing instead to examine a claw of his massive left forefoot. The speaker turned his gaze once more to the sky. "Has the Doom Empress yet moved her troops to the border of the White Lands Federation?"

"It is going as planned. I have taken care of everything," the dragon growled.

"And the Namistad traitor ... "

"I said I've taken care of it!"

The speaker was unmoved by the dragon's indignation. "Let us hope the Gold Dragon joins us, and such preparations are not necessary." The Iron Dragon grunted. The speaker pointed upward. "Behold!"

The padgarun and the dragon followed his gaze. First one, then another, then a score of shooting stars darted across the sky directly above. In moments the firmament was filled with fleeting shots of white and azure fire that drowned out the stars.

"Praised be the Creators," said the speaker. He looked down to the padgarun. "Phasgala, the amulet!"

Dropping her spear on the ground, the elvish cleric reached into her leatherine riding clothes and pulled out a clay amulet—a triangle surrounded by a circle. She stood, lowered her head to whisper a prayer, then reared back and threw the amulet as far into the lake as she could. It landed with a whispered splash and disappeared beneath the surface. She crouched again, then reverently touched her fingertips to her forehead then to the water's edge.

"It is done," the speaker murmured. "All great storms begin with a single drop of rain." He spread his arms wide toward the lake and spoke in an exuberant voice. "In moments our lord Peshiluud will arise and a new age will begin."

The storm of shooting stars still glowed upon the still surface of the lake when a shadow passed overhead. The shriek of a griffin steed betrayed its exhaustion and fear as its rider forced it to land next to the dragon.

The padgarun brandished her spear and approached the rider. "Ektibal!" the speaker said, calling the rider by name. He stepped toward the elvish mage, his brow furrowing in anger. "You dare interrupt us!"

"You must stop this insanity," Ektibal said, dismounting the griffin. His austere face showed little emotion despite the ire in his deep voice. His living, silkbark robes slid across the gravel as he strode toward the speaker, finger pointed at his leader. "Your obsession with the Triumvirate gods has gone too far."

"You're too late. We've just performed the summoning. Soon the world will be in flame, and elvenkind will resume their rightful place beside the true makers of this world."

"Elves have lost in nearly every war with humanity, right back to the time of your precious Peshiluud!"

The speaker made a flourish toward the shooting stars. "Yes, but now the Triumvirate will be unleashed, with Him at their command!"

"You'll doom us all to oblivion! I have taken steps to head you off."

The padgarun stalked toward the mage. The speaker narrowed his eyes. "What steps, Ektibal? How have you betrayed us? Even if I should disappear, others stand in my place to warn the White Lands and the Tower of Light of your attack. The Gold Dragon would stop at nothing to protect against an invasion."

The speaker chuckled. "Who would warn them, Ektibal? Your apprentices?" He pointed his staff toward the mage, its hornets leaning outward, ready to fly in attack. "Or perhaps you talk of my son, the Prince of Mirrors?"

The mage's eyes widened. "Yes, Ektibal. I know what you've been plotting. I have allies of my own. Even the prince, whose veins run with my own blood, cannot sway me from our holy goal." The speaker's jaw tightened. "If you do not stand with us, you will be destroyed."

"Kill me, and you will never see the Book of Alasar! Without it, your plan is ruined!"

"Kill you? There are fates worse than death!" The speaker shook his staff. The swarm shot toward the mage.

"*Chasanti al!*" Ektibal shouted. A force field slammed against the hornets, knocking them to the ground. He crushed one with a booted foot, then turned and thrust a palm toward the dragon. "*Gontor antali!*" he shouted. Instantly, a shimmering field appeared around the Iron Dragon. The dragon pushed forward, barely moving against the mage's *Hold* spell.

Phasgala ran forward, whooping and swinging her spear. At the last moment Ektibal turned and grabbed the spear. He thrust out a hand and pounded her chest, knocking her to the ground, breathless. The spear clattered to the rocks.

Ektibal turned back to the speaker, raising a hand to cast another spell. The dragon's clawed foot came down hard upon the mage, smashing him to the ground with a sickening crunch of breaking bones. Ektibal screamed as the dragon twisted his forefoot, breaking more bones.

"Fool!" the dragon growled. "Powerful though you are, your spells are no match for the indomitable energies of the Triumvirate coursing through me!"

One of the mage's arms was free, and he reached back behind him. Grasping a digit of the dragon's foot, he weakly uttered, "*Chrostia magnitosti!*" Instantly, the *Thunderstroke* spell emitted a deafening boom and shot a wave of white-hot electricity up the body of the Iron Dragon.

The dragon roared, falling backward, wings flapping in a spasm of pain. His howls echoed against the prominences of the cliffs. Coughing up blood, Ektibal raised to his arms and readied for another spell. The speaker backed to the edge of the lake. The padgarun got to her feet and stepped unsteadily toward the mage.

"Enough." The voice came from behind the speaker.

Suddenly Ektibal was lifted upright into the air, as stiff as a statue and rotating slowly. Blood ran from his mouth and down his chin and neck.

The speaker and the padgarun turned toward the voice. A dark figure soundlessly strode out of the water, his left arm and hand pointed toward Ektibal. He wore dark leatherine clothes. A laurel crown encircled his head of long, green hair, dripping with the holy water of the lake.

His eyes reflected the shower of stars like a mirror. Instantly the padgarun fell prostrate toward the newcomer. "Hail, Peshiluud!"

"*Ecaea Ecimii alu alleia*," the speaker muttered, then fell to his knees, arms outstretched.

The dragon's cries of pain died away as Peshiluud stepped out of the water. "Let us not war against ourselves," he said, looking down to the speaker, his face as serene as the lake he had risen from. Peshiluud's voice was a melding of three different voices—two male and one female.

The speaker did not look up. "My lord, my court mage wishes to obstruct your plans, and the plans of the Triumvirate, by passing crucial information to the Gold Dragon. If Ingal Jehai cannot be turned to our way of thinking, he may stand in our way. If we wish to attack the Tower of Light, they must not know our strategy."

Peshiluud slowly shook his head. "No, my speaker. Dragonkind are beloved of the Creators. They will serve their purpose in the end." The Iron Dragon rose to his haunches, grunting in pain, and gave a nod to Peshiluud.

Peshiluud looked back to Ektibal. The mage still hung unmoving in the air. "Your court mage is dead, speaker." Peshiluud released his spell, and Ektibal's body fell to the ground with a thud. "His wounds were too extreme."

The speaker flashed a look of anger toward the dragon, then he dared to look up at Peshiluud. "Ektibal was the only one who knew where to find the renegade spell we need, in the Book of Alasar."

"No," Peshiluud said. He raised his head to look out across the valley. "There is another. So says the Triumvirate." He turned and looked down at the speaker again. "Send a dispatch to the Gold Dragon at once. There is a code you must include on its surface, which I will give you."

The speaker dropped his head again. "My lord, anything you wish. Praised be the Creators! Praised be Peshiluud."

Peshiluud raised his face back toward the heavens. There, reflected in the curving orbits of his mirrored eyes, the Starfall waned and stopped, leaving only the glimmering stars and the glow of the moons. "Praised be the Creators," he repeated, and turned his gaze to the southeast, toward the Tower of Light, one of the three great towers of magic in the world ... and the Heartstones they protect.

ONE

Birth among Mankind

Ingal Jehai, Gold Dragon and ruler of the White Lands Federation, looked over the balcony railing of the South Birthing Room of his palace. He tilted his head in thought and swished his tail, the scales sliding across the stone floor with the sound of dry leaves.

In the room below, stretched out on a gilded cot, was a pregnant human woman surrounded by midwives and relatives. The woman, a pilgrim to his palace, moaned and strained to push the baby out.

Birth, the ancient dragon thought, is more than the beginning of a life. More than a biological function. It is an act of creation. A canvas no longer blank, like a painter's first brush stroke.

Ingal smelled the acidity of her sweat, the mild sweetness of her water. The birthing party, too, smelled of sweat—the kind that came with excitement, not exertion. And lingering in the room, faintly, were the smells of all those other women and babies who had passed through. No amount of scrubbing the floor tiles and marble walls could erase it.

"Just one more push, my lady," a midwife said.

The pregnant woman looked up at Ingal, eyes wet with emotion, and gave a wan smile, reaching a hand up toward him. He raised a hefty forefoot over the railing and spread his golden wings slightly, a sign of blessing to one who worships him as a living god.

The woman's smile broadened for a moment before giving way to pain and concentration as she gathered strength for one last push. Ushered by the midwives, the baby slipped out of her, wet and wrinkled, to the delight of all around the woman.

Tears streaked down the mother's face, and she smiled in exhausted relief as the baby cried. The small group of women sighed and attended to their various duties, seemingly lighter in mood. And the father, a stocky man with broad farmer's hands, massaged his wife's shoulders and kissed her wet brow.

No matter how many times he saw it, Ingal could not understand the emotions the humans experienced, though he would never admit it openly. Human newborns were so frail, so dependent. How could a parent delight in the exhaustive effort of raising such a frail and ignorant thing?

The umbilical cord was cut, and the child was carried to a nearby table for cleaning. Moments later the head midwife raised the swaddled newborn up toward the dragon as the birthing party bowed their heads. "A boy, my lord: Gentua Sa'Jehai."

Gentua would be the little boy's name. Sa'Jehai referred to the honor of being born in the presence of the Gold Dragon of the White Lands.

"May the child live long and healthy, and serve his nation with esteem," Ingal said, and gave his blessing again. As always, the pilgrims shuddered at the strength of his voice.

Ingal turned away from the railing and lumbered steadily down a wide corridor. He groaned. He felt his years, all 2,203 of them, in his joints as he walked, in his wings when he stretched them out, in the weight he had put on in recent decades. It had become steadily harder to read his scrolls and tomes, even with the broad magnifying glass presented to him by the dwarves of Sarsa. Flying was slower, and the deft aerobatics of his youth were now but a memory. Old wounds ached with changes in weather and the vast corridors of his palace seemed to grow narrower and narrower over the years.

A man stood patiently in the shadows of the broad hallway beneath a fluted archway. It was Metharcus, Ingal's chamberlain. Ingal knew he was there from the old man's quiet breathing, the fine rustle of his gray cloak, and the gentle scent of lavender that he always applied to himself for Ingal's benefit, so dilute as to be nearly undetectable to most humans.

"Good morning, my lord," Metharcus said, taking up step beside the dragon. He always whispered when he talked to his dragon lord. Ingal greatly appreciated that, as his sense of hearing was so much more sensitive than most humans realized. "A party of elves has arrived, griffin warriors headed by the Prince of Mirrors himself. They claim an urgent message."

Ingal nodded. "We will see them after the general audience this morning."

"Very well. I have a number of dispatches from the Ocrin border for you to review. Apparently more enemy troops have amassed along the north of the border near Alneri Castle. Another reported Ocrin troops in the south at Namistad." Metharcus paused to indicate a change in topic. "The Chief Minister of Planistad requests a reduction of trade restrictions. The high priest of Jonaatha requests your urgent presence in Taraman on matters of prophecy. Oh, and an Oelistad magistrate is holding a marriage in your gardens this morning."

Ingal sighed. "You seem troubled, my lord," Metharcus said. "Is it today's audience?"

Ingal didn't have the heart to tell his old chamberlain how tired he had grown of the day-to-day duties of ruling the White Lands Federation and the six nation-states that comprised it, Namistad, Alneri, Homineri, Aestistad, Octunommed, and

Oelistad. He chose to brush it over. "We are not troubled, *decauna*," he said, using the old Etollian word for 'friend', "only living in wonder at human reproduction."

"How so, if I may ask?"

"We have had this conversation before, Metharcus. But we shall bring it up again, for you were new to the household then, and only twenty-four years of age."

"Yes, lord. You must excuse me. At seventy-five, my memory is not as good as yours."

Ingal smiled. Another of Metharcus' subtle jokes. Like all dragons, Ingal had a flawless memory—not just of his life, but the memories of the last twenty forebears before him.

"Dragon reproduction is such a different thing from that of man, or most any other creature," Ingal said. "Perhaps it is for this reason that we cannot share the emotions that man has for newborns. Humans, in particular, are born in such a vulnerable state, and require such a dedication of energy and resources. It takes more than a decade for a single child to be reared to any degree of independence—a considerable period in a human's lifespan."

Ingal stopped walking and looked down at Metharcus. The light was better at this point of the hallway, and he saw the lines in his chamberlain's face. There were shadows and bags beneath his eyes, and a slack wattle of skin beneath his chin. Metharcus had thrown back his hood to reveal a mostly bald pate with silver hair on the sides. Thin skin stretched over his clasped hands like worn silk ready to rip, the knuckles as swollen as tree burls. Yet Ingal could still see features of the young boy from decades before. He wondered, were there signs of youth like those beneath his own sagging exterior? There was no one to see it in him, for only other dragons were as old as he—and the gods.

What a joy it must be for humans to relive youth through a child of their own loins.

"You have three children, *decauna,* who have grown and raised families of their own. What were your thoughts when your children were born?"

"My first thought was 'Praise be to Jonaatha for blessing us.'" Metharcus smiled in his patient way and considered the question a moment more before continuing. "But for me, giving life to a child is more than a blessing from my goddess, or even more than procreation, my lord. They grow and care for you when you are old, and help with the family work, but there is more. A child is a form of immortality, passing on what you have taught him, and carrying on your name and legacy. It is inheritance."

Metharcus sighed, then continued. "What makes the investment worthwhile is not the need for support or immortality," he said. "For me, it is no different from an artist creating a vast masterpiece in stone or paint. The love I feel for my wife, and she toward me, is put forth into our children, and their children. We have been blessed by Jonaatha to see them blossom, like the cherry orchards in the valley below, and ripen with the seasons."

Metharcus reflected another moment, with eyes fogged over in memory. "It is in expectation of this that we express our joy during the birth, my lord."

Ingal stood silent, considering these words. He looked back toward the balcony and revisited the look on the mother's face as she gazed upon her son for the first time. Perhaps, as Metharcus had suggested, she had seen not just the smooth round face of a newborn, flushed and damp from birth, but a vision of immortality, and the spark of creation.

Ingal scratched at the base of a horn. "An ancient philosopher of the Magnus Regnum once told us, 'Every child is a new world upon itself, shaped by destiny and experience, and by those who care for him.'" He smiled and looked down at Metharcus. "Exhausted as she is, this mother must feel like a god, giving birth to a new world of her own to be shaped as she wills."

Metharcus shook his head and gave a gentle smile. "With all due respect, my lord, it is the child who is the god, changing the world of his parents."

Ingal chuckled. "Yes. Perhaps this is more the case. Thank you, *decauna*."

Metharcus bowed slightly. Without another word, Ingal Jehai turned and continued down the passage with Metharcus walking by his side.

TWO
Torra Com Gidel

Torra called a halt and nearly retched when the wagon shuddered to a stop. Her driver and servant, Olos, a squat but strong man with a shaven head, leaned over and asked if she was all right, but she waved him off. She reached into a robe pocket and removed a small roll of waxed paper, then peeled off of it a thin layer of dried fruit pulp and herbs, medicine for her nausea and the cramping in her legs. For the last year she had suffered a mysterious illness that, in addition to those symptoms, caused spontaneous rashes over large parts of her body, requiring a special salve to calm them. She chewed her medicine absentmindedly and stared up at the sight in front of her.

They had just rounded a curve in the rutted stone road, the last in a long climb up Jehai Mountain. For two days they had strained the pair of horses to pull them foot-by-foot up the vertiginous, winding mountainside. This, after nearly a couple months of hard pace from Taxia, accompanied by three Taxin bodyguards that the Astronomer's Guild had hired to protect her on the long journey. Now they sat beneath the looming gates of Palal Jehai, the palace of the Gold Dragon, their final destination. A sheer cliff soared skyward to their right, and to their left, eastward, was some forty yards of open area and then a sudden drop of a thousand feet. Severe and blasted crags rose from distant valleys as far as she could see.

The gleaming walls of the gate were of a stone that the native White Lands people called bonerock. Unlike other such structures Torra had seen, the white walls were fluted, decorated with golden frescos of the dragon, and emanated both strength and beauty. The gates were metal strips and bars, but gleamed like silver, unlike the black or rusted gates of other citadels, and not straight bars, but curved and convoluted, a puzzle to the eye, forming the shape of a lotus flower if taken as a whole. Thin, white towers stood to either side of the gates, running the height of the walls to guardhouses where figures moved behind arrow slits.

Torra quickly cast a *Clean* spell on her robes, in expectation of being hailed by the gatekeepers. She shook her head in disbelief. After all those months of travel and sickness she was looking up at the entry to the Gold Dragon's palace grounds, home to one of the most powerful entities on Irikara. And to think Taenos hadn't believed the dragon even existed!

Torra chilled at the thought of Taenos. At twenty-two years old, every one of her female friends had married, and most had children. Taenos had been the only young man with whom she wanted a relationship. But when he discovered her magical studies, things took a turn for the worst. Like most Taxins, he felt magic was evil. And now she left him for the sake of magic.

This is my last chance to turn back, she thought, and a part of her wanted to. But Torra knew she couldn't. It was much too late for that. The embarrassment of her elderly mentor, Lanos Morikal, would be unforgivable. And Taenos—she'd never be seen crawling back to him!

A strong voice called down to them from the battlements, speaking Etollian. "Greetings, travelers. Identify yourselves and state your business at Palal Jehai, palace of the Gold Dragon." Torra grasped a Rod of Translation in her robe pocket, and the words came to her ears in her native tongue, Taxin.

Torra stood in her wagon seat, legs shaking and tingling from the sickness, and pulled her tan-colored robes close to her against the chill air. Her hand wrapped around the Rod of Translation. "I am Torra Com Gidel, Third Astronomer of Caranamere and envoy from the nation of Taxia. I have come to address the Gold Dragon in urgent matters of state."

The guard gave a signal to someone out of sight, and the gates swung soundlessly open to the bailey beyond. "Come inside where you will be inspected," the guard shouted, "then you will be guided to the palace and lodged. May your visit be fruitful, and may the Gold Dragon bless you."

Olos shook the reins as Torra sat down, and the party rode into the bailey. The gates swung shut behind them, and for many minutes they waited in a secure court, walls or gates on all sides, trapped, watched carefully by armed guards behind battlements and arrow slots. Guards in golden armor walked in, headed by a captain with a silver helmet, and briefly searched the wagon. Torra allowed them to look into each bag and box, but when they reached a nondescript iron chest, she held out her hand.

"That is for the Gold Dragon's eyes only. The contents are the reason for my visit." Scowling, the captain tried the chest anyhow, but it was locked.

"I have a letter from Lord Gaes, Regent of His Highness, King Halis III of Taxia, regarding the necessity of secrecy." She unfolded the letter from a pocket of her robes and showed it to the captain.

He glanced at the letter without reading it. "Very well, but one of our guards must stand over it at all times." Torra's three hired bodyguards shifted nervously, but she agreed.

The inner gates opened and they rode out. Beyond lay a cobblestone drive that curved around yet another bend of sheer cliffsides. Turning a final corner, the drive opened to immaculate gardens and lawns that seemed to defy the cold and high altitude.

The drive passed through a grove of aspen, then up onto a vast lawn ruled over by Palal Jehai, palace of the Gold Dragon. The palace lay like a snowy gem nestled amidst well-trimmed shrubbery, herbal gardens, and gnarled spruce and fir trees twisted by nature and man into shapes that appeared both tormented and pleasing to the eye. Resplendent in white and gold, a vast dome towered above all, topped with a golden spire. Building wings stretched north and south to either side, like the wings of a dragon. The sight seemed to Torra's eyes like a painting come to life, unreal and imagined. And somewhere inside was the great dragon himself!

Everywhere wandered noblemen and peasants alike, though the two castes did not appear to mix socially. Some talked in hushed tones, others seemed deep in meditation. Torra heard snatches of prayers to Ingal Jehai. Another drive separated off to the south where a large number of peasants were encamped. Often enough in recent days Torra had passed their sort on the road—pilgrims to the palace, there to worship the Gold Dragon and bask in his presence.

Torra could certainly understand. All of her life she had read about dragons. The Gold Dragon was purported to be the strongest of all, at least magically, able to cast the most powerful spells, and ruler of this nation of humans, by their choice, throughout the eons. As a child she spent many idle hours pretending that she was a companion to dragons, flying with them, playing with them, roaring at imagined enemies until townsfolk and family wondered about her sanity. But she couldn't imagine worshiping him. She was an atheist, after all.

Powerful, unique, and magical as he was, the dragon was an entity of flesh and blood, nothing more.

Her heart fluttered as they rode toward a circular courtyard surrounded by massive granite pillars. If the gargantuan entry doors were any indication, the dragon would be a fearful sight. She didn't know if she could face him.

"Aximdrac," Torra whispered, the name for the Gold Dragon in her homeland. A snippet of ancient dragon legend came to her then, read from a Taxin tome and passed down through the ages.

Aximdrac, the golden lord,
Dragon of the eastern land.
In his claws a flaming sword.
In his mind good will for man.

Despite the beneficence implied by the legend, there were other tales of Aximdrac, tales which exposed the dragon's more dangerous side:

And when King Crotos refused the dragon's command, Aximdrac flew in from the north with a storm, the Iron Dragon at his side. Threw the fire upon the guardhouse, burning to death all who bunked there. And into the palace Aximdrac burst, rending all who opposed him, until he reached the lord's chambers. There he stole away the lord and his wife and flew with them into the night, and all was lost.

The worst of those tales were thousands of years old, contrasting sharply with the newer tales more friendly to the Gold Dragon. And no citizens of this land gave any indication of injustice or violence at the hands of their ruler.

In many tales the Gold Dragon gave much-needed counsel and engaged in scholarly study, even in the halls of the Taxin Astronomy Guild. Some say it was Aximdrac who laid down the Twelve Tenets of Magic. She wondered, would he teach what he knows to one as lowly as her? Would he see in her the talent for magic that her mentor had seen? Share in her knowledge of renegade spells? Maybe even recommend her to the Tower of Light as an apprentice? Or teach her himself?

Torra shook her head. Stupid, she told herself. You're not a pretending child anymore! Stop building your hope. You're just here to deliver an important message. Nothing more. Why would an ancient and powerful dragon take note of you? And with the news you're bringing, how could he stop to consider you at all?

Torra's nausea had abated, but her legs were still cramping and tingling. She reached down and rubbed them as she looked up at the shining dome, now towering above her.

Olos drove the wagon into the palace courtyard and stopped before great, gilded doors, which were opened slightly to allow one person to pass through at a time. An ornate coach was parked nearby, dazzling white. Servants were busy unloading it, but its passenger was nowhere to be seen. From the north, toward what looked like the stables, came angry, raptorial shrieking. The dragon? Surely not. Palace servants looked up in alarm, but continued their duties as if expecting the outburst.

A palace footman in a white and gold uniform stepped from the doorway and bowed to them. "When will your Ingal Jehai hold his next audience?" Torra asked before the servant could speak.

"Noon, my lady," he replied.

"By the stars!" she muttered. She had precious little time to prepare. She hurriedly introduced herself, then said, "Please take me to my quarters immediately, help my servant with my belongings, and arrange for my presence at today's audience. I know it is short notice, but it is of utmost urgency that I address the dragon lord today!"

She glanced at the iron chest and felt the nausea rise again.

THREE

Birth and Death among Dragons

Ingal spent several hours presiding over the wedding of an Oelistad magistrate in the main gardens, blessing the masses of pilgrims at the palace entry, and listening to the pleas of the common folk. In times past he would relieve his ministers of these duties and thrill his worshipping subjects with personal appearances. It had been months, but today he forced himself to do so again. The act had once pleased him. As he feared, even attending to these menial rulership duties only tired him.

Now he was back in his private chambers for a break until the political meetings of the afternoon. Something about the coming audience worried him, like an advancing storm. War was brewing with the nation of Ocrin, but that wasn't it. War was something he understood, and Ocrin had always been held in check. No, there was something else. Was it the unexpected visit by the Prince of Mirrors, son of the elvish speaker? It was a rare event indeed for the elves to venture out of Peshilaree, especially those of the ruling family.

Like most of his chambers, this one was sparsely decorated. Other than the rare tapestry, he preferred blank walls. There were few tables, and only the occasional chair or bench for visitors or older servants to use. Works of fine art were placed in rare and unexpected locations—a painting, woodcarving, or statue had the best effect when you least expected to see them. Arras hung where light could gleam off gold threads or flamboyant dyes. He had his servants move them around from time to time.

For Ingal, his personal chambers were a place of escape from the rigors of rulership and the ever-present demands of magistrates and pilgrims. By the Treaty of the Six States, it was the role of the Gold Dragon to mediate disputes, control international trade, determine national budgets, and to hold together the six nation-states of the White Lands Federation— by force, if needed. But he saw his role as the champion of both nobility and commoner alike.

There was always a steady stream of pilgrims, at least when the weather warmed. Long ago his forebears gave up trying to dissuade them. They traveled from great distances, out of awe, or curiosity, or religious piety. They ventured to Palal Jehai to get married, deliver their children, or bathe in the streams that flowed through the palace gardens.

Since he was more powerful than any creature they knew, they seemed to feel that his power must be godly and his presence would somehow deliver unto them some of that power. It could really inflate a dragon's ego.

Attempts to scare the pilgrims off only increased their ranks. Besides, then there were more daredevil types who came to "challenge" him—and lose. So he capitulated, as his forebears had done, and simply accepted the fact that these people would come and worship him, and he played the role with as much humility as he could.

He thought again of the human woman and the birth of her child. He revisited the look on her face as she gazed upon her lord. Usually the women were afraid when he appeared at the balcony, having not expected him to appear, perhaps (for he attended only some of the births), or unprepared for his size or the aura of power around him. *This* woman had been so ... serene. Her dampened face was smooth, as if gazing upon some exquisite gem and seeing in its reflection the face of a queen. And her eyes were like the still waters of an elfin lake.

How he wished he could carve that look into marble and place it in every throne room, every nave, every court of justice—every high and mighty place in the world where the powerful forget the beauty of the lowly. Yes. And this is why he let the pilgrims into his palace, presided over their marriages, blessed their births. All for the rare and beautiful moment of serenity that he and his later generations could treasure in their mind for the next twenty thousand years or more. Why couldn't he find that serenity in himself?

What was the child's name, again? Gentua, yes, Gentua Sa'Jehai. Death and rebirth.

Ingal didn't want to think about that. He turned his attention aside, to the first thing he saw. He stood in his sleeping chamber, skirting the broad, shallow pit of warm mud where he slept each night. He longed for it now, as he did more often these days. The servants knew just the right consistency he liked, not so wet that it ran, but not so dry that it stirred up dust. And it was warm, kept that way all day and all night by steam pipes fueled by a fire and cauldron in an adjoining room. And the faint scent of lilac, too faint for the human sense of smell, lulled him toward the soft warmth of the sleep pit.

But he couldn't divert his attention to rest, not right now, and despite his best effort, Ingal's attention turned back toward the one subject he wanted to avoid.

He glanced across the room to an arched doorway and the broad corridor beyond. At the end, at the limits of darkness, were the gilded doors of the Egg Chamber.

He found himself lumbering that way, through the arch, down the corridor. Servants moved about Ingal's side rooms, mopping floors, carrying wood for the fires or flowers for the vases in the corners. Upon seeing the dragon round the corner, they immediately stopped where they were and lowered their eyes in deference.

Ingal smelled the servants' fear, heard them hold their breath. He ignored them. Most were used to seeing him in the corridors and attending to his needs. They weren't normally afraid if they had been in his service a while. No, their fear came from something else. They knew he never visited the Egg Chamber, and something about that frightened them. He soon stood before the gilded doors.

He found himself stalling and focusing more on the doors than the effort of moving beyond them. They were quite old, dating back more than seven thousand years to the time of his forebear, Tosem, and magically preserved. Each door was carved from a single slice of Lilim tree, as wide as he was, and transported from the Senoshhori highlands of Peshilaree, land of the Elves. The golden coating had been rubbed away where the doors had been opened and closed over the millennia, but they were still breathtakingly beautiful, depicting the Gold Dragon in battle and in audience. He would need to have them touched up again; it had been more than five hundred years since the last time.

Ingal wondered at his sudden impulse to come here. He hadn't visited the room in hundreds of years. He raised a forefoot to push the doors open, but he found himself unable, his forefoot only hanging motionless in the air. He dropped his foot back to the floor and fought the urge to turn and move back toward the sleeping chamber.

With a sudden thrust of willpower, he barked a *Word of Opening*. Instantly the doors flew open and slammed against the walls, their hinges shrieking in protest. The violent bang echoed off the chamber walls and past him down the corridor. Servants scattered as if blown away by a great wind.

The room was dark. With another quick spell, he commanded brands along the wall to burst into flame, their wild dance throwing shadows to the vaulted ceiling.

The tiled room was completely empty. There was no decoration whatsoever, no furniture, no indication of any special purpose—except for an ovoid depression dipping a couple feet down into the center of the floor, about as wide as a wagon. The depression was meant to hold the Dragon Egg.

Ingal saw in his mind's eye the moment of his birth, breaking through the stony shell and roaring up at the ceiling, "I am Ingal Jehai!" At once there was a flood of memory from previous generations, bewildering his newly formed mind for a moment. Then came the great triumph of being born.

But *his* birth had been different from those of his forebears. Along with the triumph was hidden despair, and he had roared another cry to the ceiling, wordless, powerful, and sad. He didn't know why the despair, but the feeling never really left. And after all these millennia, he still did not understand. He knew the despair was something of his, not passed on from his forebears.

At his birth, the room had been lined with priests and noblemen singing ancient songs in his honor, bidding him to break free and rule them. Braziers had burned mild incense. Rich tapestries were hung, showing the Gold Dragon's past glories. Servants came forth to clean him after he had come out of the egg, then they anointed him with oils and led him to the feeding chamber for his first meal. And now he remembered the death of his immediate forebear.

It happened every time: the memory of birth could not be separated from the memory of death, for there was no pause in the memory between the two. Rambanor Jehai had been one of the oldest Gold Dragons in his lineage—2,584 years old. Unlike most dragons, he had actually died a natural death, growing older, decade by decade, his scales falling off, his eyes clouding, his health failing. And yet, the Gold Dragon had stayed. Rambanor had felt a strong commitment to serve the White Lands, holding together the fragile Federation that he had inherited from his forebear, Samboria Jehai.

Rambanor had lived too long. Too old to make a difference anymore. Ingal did not wish that physical decay upon himself, yet he could see it beginning already. He was only a little less than 300 years younger than Rambanor had been at his death.

"I am Ingal Jehai," Ingal said, his mind momentarily back in the present, his voice whispering. But the whisper came back to him from the plain walls and the high ceiling, twisted by the echoes, and seemingly sinister.

He let his memories dwell again on his forebears. Rambanor had died quietly in the sleeping pit. But most of the others had died violently. His third forebear, Tasma Jehai, had been killed at the mere age of sixty-two, poisoned by a servant who had disagreed with his politics. It was a painful death, stretching out for days, with foam in the mouth, growing paralysis, and fearful visions of apocalyptic fires and the undead. Geniori, his sixteenth forebear, had been cut to death by millions of shards of glass, whipped into a whirlwind around him by a powerful mage. That had been more than twenty-seven thousand years ago, yet the pain of it still woke Ingal from a deep sleep now and then. But the worst death was that of his eighth forebear, Do Naimi. He had been lanced through the abdomen by a renowned knight of one of the Southern Empires. Yet great magic had kept Do Naimi alive long enough to be burned alive in a vast fire pit to torment him.

Immediately following the heart's last beat, the energy of the dragon—the dragon's very essence—forms a globe of intense light where the heart had been. And then, a fraction of a second later, an egg takes shape there from the energy, tougher than stone and magically protected. No weapon or force on Irikara could break the shell. And the egg grows, sometimes for only a few months if the forebear had been very old at the time of death, sometimes for a century or more if the forebear had been very young.

Of course, Ingal could not remember those moments after death, nor any time in the egg until just before hatching. These things were known only from the knowledge of others who witnessed them.

Long ago in his lineage, early in his vast memory, each dragon had to break his way through the shell at birth and then break through the remains of his forebear to get out. It was still this way with some other dragon lineages. But in recent generations, since the Gold Dragon had become protector and political minister of the White Lands, his egg had been retrieved from the remains and brought to the Egg Chamber, where it was lavished with attention, like a shrine, as it grew and neared hatching.

More memories came, but this time Ingal shook them off completely, groaning. Instead he thought yet again of the pregnant woman of that morning, and the things that Metharcus had said, and fixed his eyes on the far wall.

Metharcus' words came back to him. *We have had the great fortune of seeing them blossom,* the chamberlain had said, *like the cherry orchards in the valley below, and ripen with the seasons …*

It is in expectation of this that we express our emotions during the birth, my lord.

This may be true for humans, but not for dragons, Ingal thought. No human could live long enough to see a dragon "blossom." Those who had sung in his honor at his last several births did not have for him the same love they felt for their children. They sang out of respect, awe, or honor, but not love.

Because of the nature of dragon procreation, Ingal had no parents to cry in joy at his birth. There had been no lovemaking, or even reproductive organs for the act. And no one babied him, or groomed him in their image. He was born with all the memories of his last twenty forebears and all their accumulated wisdom. Though he was only a little larger than an ox when born, he was in minutes completely self-sufficient and able to protect himself as necessary.

Not like a human baby at all. No, death did not mean the same to him as it did to a human, and birth was a very different experience. How fragile and fleeting was the human life! How robust and lengthy could be a dragon's.

Ingal felt a chill pass under his scales as he looked back down at the Egg depression. Someday he would die again, and be reborn, in memory, through his offspring.

The thought of death seemed in one way relieving. At least he would be free of the reins of rulership. But there was something else—a thought rising up through the cavernous depths of his soul—telling him that things were changing.

That maybe the Gold Dragon wouldn't be reborn. That, like humanity, one life was all there was, and then there would be no offspring at all. The thought scared him beyond rationality.

Ingal tried to shake it off. No one could rewrite the laws of dragon biology, not even the gods, for there was no god of the dragons. Right? But the thought lingered, troubling Ingal for the rest of the day.

FOUR

The Stone of Lethori

Torra felt insignificant as she stood in the antechamber of the great audience chamber. The antechamber itself was as large as any audience chamber in Taxia. Gold Dragon statues clung to the vaulted corners of the ceiling, staring down at her with sparkling gemstone eyes. Beneath them stood massive double doors leading to the audience room, heavily reinforced with gold-leafed iron supports over naturally white wood.

A footman had come to her only briefly before to say that her attendance to the daily audience had been approved, though he could not guarantee that the Gold Dragon would call on her today. With haste, she had gathered herself, her servant, Olos, and the chest, and rushed to the antechamber to wait with the others. She told her Taxin bodyguards to stay behind. She felt it would be rude to take them into the presence of the dragon.

The crowded room hushed as the doors opened. Torra could not see much over the heads of the notables around her, but she felt more than saw the great expanse beyond the doors.

She was preceded into the audience chamber by figures of great power. Viziers from the six states of the White Lands Federation, with fine robes and miters reflecting their states' colors, jewels sewn into their vestments, and walking with an air of importance. Alongside were generals in gilded armor and gleaming sabers, stern-faced and strong, and an entourage of a dozen advisors and servants each.

Next entered renowned scholars, some of whom Torra had heard of, from throughout the Federation and countries beyond its borders to the south.

And then in walked a band of elves, a dozen of them from the land of Peshilaree, standing tall and lean with thick, forest-green, dreadlocked hair and skin that was an olive color with emerald blotches. They wore tough clothing that looked like leather yet moved fluidly as if filled with some form of gelatin. Among the party was a male of such stateliness and demeanor that Torra could not help but stare. He wore upon his chest a long necklace wrapped in cunningly worked silver and gold, a small, gilded mirror as its highlight. Stepping next to him was a very somber elf with his hair in a topknot tied with a beaded cord. Noticing her stare, he turned his dark eyes to meet hers, and she was held for a moment in their depths before she turned away. When she looked up again, he had entered the chamber, and in his place stood a female with wild hair and pale yellow-green eyes that burned with untamed fierceness. As the she-elf entered the audience chamber, she licked her lips, gripped her broad-tipped spear tightly, and looked across the room as if judging her next enemy.

Finally, an usher directed Torra and her party through the gigantic double doors of the audience chamber. Olos grunted as he lifted the iron chest and stepped forward, followed closely by the palace guardsman who had been assigned to stand over it.

She caught her breath as she entered. The cavernous audience chamber was perhaps one hundred yards in diameter and almost twice as high, supported around the sides by massive columns that soared to the topmost spire. There were no windows, yet the room glowed with a soft white light that left no room for shadows. Natural-looking veins of gold played in the seamless walls of bonerock.

The usher led her toward a position the center of the room near the visiting scholars. The viziers sat in high-backed wooden thrones ahead of her, three to either side of Torra, with their generals and entourages behind them. The elves stood in a cluster toward the back of the room.

There were more than a hundred people in the audience, yet the crowd was dwarfed by the size of the room to the point of seeming puny. Torra felt smaller yet, and her knees shook as she faced a wide, stone dais built into the wall at the far end, raised five broad steps above the bonerock-tiled floor. The dragon's throne.

Another broad set of doors at the back of the dais opened slowly and soundlessly. Torra held her breath, expecting the dragon to come looming out, but there came only a half dozen young pages, followed by ten men and women in gold-threaded white robes. The robed figures took equally spaced positions on the top step of the dais. Then a dozen palace guardsmen in bulging golden armor marched out the door and off to either side. Their faces were hidden behind winged helms shaped like roaring dragon maws. Finally, two heralds in gold and white uniforms and turbans marched through. They raised gilded ram's horns to their lips and blew long, resonating notes into the room, deep and primeval. The notes echoed off the walls and reverberated through Torra's spine, then died away.

The room grew silent, impregnating Torra's mind with a sudden awe of what was to come.

On the dais, a young woman with long, blonde hair, raised her arms and said in a clear voice, "Bow before the Gold Dragon." She and the other robed figures turned toward the back doors and knelt with heads down. The viziers bowed in their seats. The generals, scholars, and servants bowed like those on the dais. Only the elves remained standing. Torra and her party knelt, and all was silent again.

Then Torra heard it coming. Slow, booming steps. Strong and measured. She raised her head enough to look up through her bangs to the doors. A shape grew in the shadows of the corridor.

Torra's heart exploded in a staccato of hurried beats, and she couldn't breathe. Her legs and hands shook. Her eyes fixed on the coming leviathan. Some ancient impulse told her to run, but she gritted her teeth and held her ground.

And then the dragon stepped into the light. Its upraised head was as broad as a wagon, scales gleaming like a thousand gold coins around a grim, serpentine jaw. Its mouth was parted, showing double rows of jagged teeth. Golden eyes looked over the assembly with blazing glory. Upon its head were wide, webbed ears and a set of dull ivory horns. One horn was cracked and broken off a foot out from the dragon's forehead. The other extended at least three feet at its sharp point. Its feet stepped heavy upon the dais, spreading slightly as it put its weight down, showing thick, sharp claws hidden within like a cat's. The Gold Dragon was larger than she imagined, four men high from the ground to the top of its head as it walked on all four legs. Vast golden wings, webbed and veined like a bat's, were folded across its thirty-yard long torso and tipped with ivory spikes. Another thirty yards long, the tail rippled with muscles, as thick as an ancient oak, tapering to another ivory spike.

"Aximdrac," Torra whispered softly, voice shaking. The Gold Dragon turned her way at the name. Torra looked down.

The dragon spoke, his voice booming with unrepressed command. "I am Ingal Jehai, White Lands Dragon. We welcome you to our court."

At this cue the assembly stood again, and the viziers sat upright. An elderly man in a gray cloak emerged from the doorway and stood at attention behind the dragon.

The blonde lady who had spoken earlier introduced herself as Asamaya Sa'Jehai, Minister of Audience, and proceeded to announce each of the important visitors in the room to the Gold Dragon. The robed figures were all palace ministers, advisors to Ingal. She introduced each of the viziers and their states, and each of their generals. Next she announced the visiting scholars, a mathematician and a biologist from the Royal Aestistad University, in billowing green and white shirts, a young alchemist from the nation of Marnistad supporting himself with a cane, and two graying historians from the nation of Charin Saruza dressed in fine silken outfits.

Still in wonder of the dragon looming before her, Torra paid little attention to names. The elves were not mentioned at all.

And then Asamaya turned to Torra, announcing only what Torra had said to the gatekeeper. "My lord, I present to you Torra Com Gidel, citizen of the nation of Taxia, envoy from the town of Caranamere, and Third Astronomer of the center of magic known as the Astronomer's Guild."

The Gold Dragon's eyes widened, and he turned his head to look Torra in the face. Torra nearly fainted. Her heart raced, and the light in the room seemed to grow dim. She staggered a moment. Catching herself on unsteady legs, she bowed sharply at the waist as was custom in Taxia.

When she rose again, the dragon still regarded her with those blazing, wise eyes that never seemed to blink. The edges of his mouth moved up slightly, as if amused at her behavior. But then, she didn't know dragon mannerisms enough to tell for sure.

He regarded her a moment more as Asamaya said, "This concludes the visitors to your court for this audience, my lord."

A moment of silence passed as Ingal looked over the assembly. Finally the dragon said, "We shall first greet the envoy from Taxia." Torra caught her breath. *So soon?* she thought. *Am I ready? What about the others?*

As if reading her thoughts, one of the generals stepped forward, armored boots clanking on bonerock tiles. "Honestly, Ingal! War is coming. War! There is no time for triviality! We must ..."

"The general of Namistad has *not* been recognized," said the Minister of Audience in a stern voice. The dragon turned his head slowly, seemingly unsurprised.

Tall and lean, perhaps forty in age, the general had deep lines incised in his face from years of sun and weather, and short-cropped blond hair. He held a red-maned helm under his right arm, matching the red and silver of his ceremonial armor. Hanging from his hip was a burnished silver battle horn with a red tassel. He ignored the minister's chastisement. "Troops are building, my lord. Soon our western border will be overrun at Alneri. We must cancel the audience and focus ..."

"Silence!" The dragon stomped his foot. The boom merged with the echo of his voice. The general shut his mouth and narrowed his eyes.

"General Tasami," the dragon said in a deep and severe tone, "you will have your moment to speak, but it will be when we grant it to you. We guarantee that Ocrin will not strike us in the little time it takes to hear other issues. Now return to your position behind the vizier of Namistad."

"You dare chastise me like a child," the general said, low and unrepressed.

"Udullu, do as he says," said the vizier behind the general, his voice slithering through his teeth. His red-robed body sagged with the decay of advanced age. General Tasami locked his jaw, but he turned sharply and returned to his position behind the vizier's throne. There was a shared sigh in the room, and eyes glanced about as the assembly looked to each other for reaction.

The dragon shrugged it off and looked back to Torra. For the first time, she noticed many tarnished scales, lines beneath his eyes, giving them a touch of sadness, and a bent back. Fine scars crisscrossed his body, and there were missing scales. The horns were yellowed with age. This was a very old dragon.

"Torra Com Gidel of Taxia," the Gold Dragon said, "you may proceed."

Torra only managed to say "Um, ah," then gulped and looked down to the iron chest. The gravity of the situation sank in, and she gained control. She grasped her Rod of Translation.

"Lord Aximdrac, thank you for hearing me on such short notice."

The dragon interrupted, raising a hefty forefoot. "Please," he said in Torra's native tongue, Taxin, "address *us* as 'Ingal Jehai.' Aximdrac is a generic name for the Gold Dragon in the ancient tongue of your land, applying to all generations of our lineage." He paused a beat, then added, "And there is no need for your translation spell or device, for in this chamber all understand what is said, no matter the language spoken."

Torra felt blood rush to her face. She let go of the rod. "Sorry, Lord Jehai."

Ingal gingerly lowered himself to the dais, wincing slightly as his belly touched the cold tiles. Torra heard his joints pop as he laid down, sphinx-like, facing her. "It has been a very long time indeed since this court was graced by a Taxin astronomer. What brings you to us?"

Many times along the trip Torra had mentally practiced what she would say and do. She turned to Olos and said, "The bracelet." Watched by the palace guardsman, Olos bent to the iron chest and opened it just long enough to reach in and withdraw a faded red satin pillow. Red light pulsed from the depths of the chest, and then the lid was closed. On top of the pillow lay a sparkling silver bracelet with a single, large moonstone mounted in it.

Olos lifted the pillow and approached the dais, visibly shaking, but when he reached the steps he shook, transfixed by the dragon, and was unable to move forward.

"Asamaya," Ingal said, and the Minister of Audience gracefully stepped down to Olos and took the pillow and bracelet from him, placing it at Ingal's feet. Her servant stood a moment more, then turned and walked quickly back to his place at the chest, eyes down, shaking so badly she feared he would collapse.

When Ingal looked down at the pillow, Torra said, "A gift for you from his majesty Halis III, King of Taxia, and Colnos Com Dimb, First Astronomer of Caranamere."

Ingal bent his head closer and sniffed at the bracelet. He extended a claw and slipped the bracelet over the tip, holding it up to his eyes, squinting. "A woman's bracelet," Ingal said, "typical of Taxin workmanship. Perhaps a millennium in age? There's something very familiar …"

Torra remained silent. Will the dragon find the connection on his own? She glanced back to the iron chest.

Ingal's eyes widened. "Ah," he said, "How lovely she was, Irana, Queen of Taxia." He closed his eyes and took a deep breath as if inhaling a fresh draft of mountain air. "We hear again the brush of Quisha silk on Almanian carpets, smell the magnolia flowers left in her chambers, hear her hum the 'Song of Midday' as she walked by our side." He opened his eyes again. "It is a lovely gift, and the King and First Astronomer honor Us with it. It has been over a thousand years since last we visited your fine city. Queen Irana wore this bracelet as she hosted us at the palace castle while we studied with the court astronomer, Gamin Dolos."

General Tasami exhaled in annoyance, but the dragon appeared not to notice. Ingal tilted his head, and the slight smile that played on the edges of his mouth disappeared. He snorted. Torra knew he made the connection.

"But why bring this now?" Ingal asked. He looked back to the bracelet, then again at Torra. His eyes widened with alarm and he put the bracelet back down on the pillow. "This is no social call, is it, Com Gidel? Tell us you have no alarming news."

Torra took a deep breath. "According to our records, Queen Irana made a promise. As she wrote upon her deathbed, 'If the Stone of Lethori should glow, send this bracelet to Aximdrac as symbol of our danger, thus he may take action to prevent the destruction of us all.' We have kept her promise, Lord Jehai."

She nodded at Olos, and the servant reached into the chest again, pulling out a smooth, oddly shaped bundle wrapped in silk. Red light pulsed through the garment. Olos knelt heavily and unwrapped the bundle. He strained against its weight, yet held the parcel steady. In his hands lay a smooth stone, a foot and a half long and roughly ovoid and pitted as if all edges had been melted away. It alternated in color between a dull gray hue and a bright red glow.

Ingal's mouth opened, and he ran a long, thin tongue across the edge of a double row of jagged teeth, as he seemed to consider the situation. Struggling against a weight that seemed to defy the size of the stone, Olos placed it at the foot of the steps.

Torra continued. "Legend tells us that if the gods become angry at the world, the Stone of Lethori will glow as a warning. Yet we know not what is the cause of their anger. Legend hints at magic. What magic is being misused? My only speculation is that renegade magic has been used, for that has caused the stone to glow in ages past, but only briefly and dimly."

Ingal sighed and wrapped his tail around his right flank. "It is a long legend that follows the Stone of Lethori. It has its root in the destruction of the empire of Occultii, in distant times that predate even our long memory. The Great Destruction was an age ago, yet still the tale is remembered by a select few, and we shall here retell a small portion of it."

"Oh, please!" General Tasami cried. "This has little bearing on our current situation. Put the matter aside, Jehai, and let us get to the urgent military needs of the day!"

Ingal rose and extended his wings, hissing. He turned and looked past the general at the red vizier. "Vizier Janisim, you will control your general, or he will be expelled from the audience. The glowing of the stone is of serious consequence that will affect us all. His ignorance of its importance is no excuse."

The vizier put a hand on the general. Tasami returned to his position, slouching against his vizier's throne. Still looking toward the general, the dragon began the tale. "So long ago it was in the history of Irikara, the empire of Occultii is now but a myth on the tongues of man. Almost nothing remains of its accomplishments. Yet its borders stretched over an entire continent, even to these lands, and its impact was felt worldwide. No sea remained unsailed. No mountain obstructed its view. No land escaped its influence. No existing empire can now claim such a feat, nor in the nearly forty millennia since the Great Destruction which spelled the end of that land."

The dragon's eyes glazed over, and he seemed to stare through Torra. "It is said the empire of Occultii was built over the course of ten thousand years. A great land it was, surrounding the Emni Sea, and more powerful in the ways of magic than any land since. It was in that time that the three Towers of Magic were built. Many great artifacts, powerful and lasting, were created.

"It is said that nearly every man and woman learned the ways of the mage. No household chores were needed, for spells took care of menial labors. Magic was a way of life taken for granted.

"And great were the most powerful mages! With mere words they brought forth mass devastation or overwhelming beauty. Cities were built of their skill, and great temples, and beasts changed to serve their needs. All other empires of Irikara quaked at their name. It was then that the Towers of Light, Darkness, and Balance were made. The very powers of nature were at their command. Winds, rains, seas, earth. Even the gods were called to attention. No power seemed beyond Occultian grasp."

Torra remembered to breathe. Renegade magic! He was talking about Renegade magic. Spells so powerful and destructive that they drove the caster mad.

"The mages grew ever more vain in their power," Ingal continued, swishing his tail across the dais. "In their vanity they raised an army of mage-warriors such as the world has never seen, eight-hundred thousand strong! The Occultian suzerains opened a portal to the heavens using two renegade spells more powerful than any ever created before or since. Proclaiming themselves to be living gods of Irikara, they readied their army to march through to conquer the gods they had once worshipped.

"And then the gods had their vengeance. In less than a day, the skies opened, and fire and acid scorched the greatest part of Occultii. What had once been half a continent rich in harvest was laid bare and blackened, spoiled forevermore. Still desolate, we now call this the Great Wasteland. The beautiful Emni Sea heaved up and drained in hours, inundating many lands, and came to form the Meril Desert. And the coastal lands around it, where all the Occultian capitals had lain, were thrown up and destroyed, raised high to the clouds, erupting into a ring of snow-capped mountains. The army of mage-warriors was incinerated. The portal to the heavens collapsed. And the mages who thought themselves gods were taken away, forever in torment at the hands of the deities they had threatened."

A moment of silence passed as Ingal paused. "Fascinating, my lord, to be sure," said the red vizier, Janisim, bent and faded. Torra wasn't sure if his tone was serious or sarcastic. "But how could this tale possibly apply to us?"

The dragon did not look his way, but answered, "We are not the only ones in peril, but all of the world. Listen! The gods sent harbingers of doom, warnings to the survivors of the Great Destruction. The Stone of Lethori was one such harbinger, blazing to earth and burying near the ruins. When the astronomer Lethori touched it, he was taken to what he called the 'gods of the gods' and delivered a stern warning. Said they to him, 'If the stone glows, mortal, then you shall know the great energies of the world are misused again. Destruction shall follow the kingdoms of Irikara if the threat is not quelled.' Lethori went insane upon return, repeating the message again and again, traveling far with his message for years until he died."

Torra stared at the stone and its hellish red pulsing. Fire and acid! "And now it glows, and we are doomed!" she heard herself say.

"Doomed?" said Ingal. "Only if we fail to find the threat, Astronomer."

"Find the threat?" said another vizier dressed in white, an aged woman with golden jewelry, stern of eye and strong of jaw. "How are we to do this, my lord? Is there not the whole world to search? Are we to look for an army of mages, or one maddened individual? And who is to share in this burden?"

"It is not our burden," said General Tasami. "Let someone else attend to this threat, Jehai. This is an issue for the Towers of Magic to decide. The White Lands Federation has more pressing worries, such as hordes of warriors poised at our western border ready to race headlong from Ocrin into Alneri fields and towns!"

The dragon seemed unfazed and turned his patient eyes to the general. "Your concerns are noted, General, and not entirely unappreciated. But it is the duty of all men to preserve the powers they wield. Magic is not a force to be dealt with foolishly, but a necessity for the greater control of nations and the answering of the unknown. The coming war may seem of greatest need and wholly unrelated, yet we cannot discount the importance of the warning, nor even the possibility that the two are related."

"Related?" said Vizier Janisim, "Ocrin wields no magic, my lord, and its troops are ignorant of such things."

"Not true," said Torra. All faces turned to her in astonishment as if to suggest she had no place to speak, impudent in her reaction. But she steeled herself and added,

"Though Taxia does not border Ocrin, we know that land well. Ever does it threaten our nation through the land of Scroen, to our north. There have been reports of mages in the Ocrin army, but they are shadowy figures, inhuman. And …" Here she caught herself about to reveal her interest in renegade magic. "And I have reason to believe that these Ocrin mages are servants of a greater power, worse even than the Doom Empress."

"On what do you base these beliefs, Astronomer?" asked the red vizier, Janisim, leaning on a frail arm toward her. His voice hissed with repressed attack. Intimidated, Torra remained silent. "Secondhand reports?" Janisim continued. "Rumors? Tales told by frightened Scroens? Our spies have lived among the Ocrinians for years without word of such mages, or any other power." Vizier Janisim leaned back in his chair and looked away. "Foolishness."

The dragon only turned from one to the other, then added, "One never knows where the truth lies." He looked down at one of his advisors, a tall, robed man with a long, wispy beard. "We must contact the Towermasters at once. Other signs may be present."

Ingal looked back over the assembly. "Over the millennia, the stone has been passed from kings to mages, astronomers to peasants, conquered, lost, and found again. Yet through it all We have ever sought to preserve the legend, for the memory of man is brief, and even dire warnings are forgotten." Ingal stood and spread his wings. "Let us not forget, either, that the lives of men and even dragons are but seconds to the gods and hold little value." His voice grew deeper, and he pounded a massive fist on the dais floor. "We must find who is responsible for this magic who is challenging the gods—and crush them before they destroy us all and tear apart the very fabric of civilization!"

FIVE

Saber Rattling

Ingal looked around the room as he lay back down. The young astronomer clearly understood the importance of the Stone of Lethori. She was pale and shaking, as were the guards and servant with her. The visiting scholars still held confused looks, but seemed willing to listen. The elves were characteristically nonchalant.

But the viziers and generals? He knew them well enough, and they weren't moved by the importance of the stone's glow. Many were clearly impatient to get on to this little war with Ocrin which had not yet even begun. How many wars had there been with Ocrin in his lifetime? A dozen, not counting short conflicts? The war would come and go, and little would change. But the stone was a harbinger of dire consequence, a sign that the world's history could be changed in conflagration, and the White Lands, where magic is focused in the Tower of Light, would likely be the most impacted area of Irikara. How could he get them to understand?

"My lord," said Vizier Janisim. "I ..."

Ingal raised a forefoot for silence, then looked down at his Minister of Magic, Wu Tian Oso. The mage was now quite old, with a long, gray mustache trailing down to the collar of his gold-threaded robes. Hired through the powerful Tower of Balance, Wu Tian hailed originally from the land of Quisha far to the south. "Wu Tian," Ingal said, "please send word of the stone to the Tower mages. We must speak with the Towermasters at once."

Wu Tian bowed his dark-skinned head. "Yes, my lord."

The astronomer, Com Gidel, sat hard upon the now-empty chest. She blushed at the echo from it and looked down to the floor. She was an odd human, to be sure. Small and frail, young —perhaps twenty-five years—with large, green, childish eyes under short-cropped brown hair. Her behavior was a study in contradictions, competing between shy humility and bravado. As Third Astronomer of Taxia, she had been projected far beyond her peers. She had to be talented in magic and astronomy to do so. Plus, she had the bravery to travel farther than many adventurers.

And she knew magic, like most Taxin "astronomers." He felt it emanating from her, but it was almost hidden in an aura of untamed power the likes of which he had rarely felt from a human. With training, she could be a great mage indeed. One of the world's most powerful, even. It was so strong, in fact, that he could almost *see* the waves of energy coming off of her. He wanted very much to get to know this young woman.

"Com Gidel," Ingal said to the astronomer, "We shall meet with you again very soon." She nodded in acknowledgment, and Ingal looked over the rest of the assembly. "Now on to other issues. We shall hear the other scholars." The viziers again sighed in protest.

Asamaya Sa'Jehai stood and addressed the audience again, calling forth the other scholars. Ingal heard their requests in turn. All of them wanted answers to various academic questions: What does the dragon lord know of culturing traditional Ingari herbal remedies? How would he mathematically describe the rotation of the moons? Where could historical tomes of the Ja'Hazeel occupation of Etollia be found? Ingal answered their questions succinctly and ordered the relevant advisors to meet with them afterward for clarification.

With prior business finished, Ingal bid all but the viziers and generals to leave the chamber until the following day. The Taxin astronomer followed the scholars out, looking back at Ingal with a look of relief mixed with wonder.

The elves were last to file out. They knew they would get a private audience later, as was typical for elvish visitors. Their unannounced presence at the audience was part of the ritual, a form of introduction. They were still dressed in their riding garments of living leatherine. The group was headed by none other than the Prince of Mirrors, son of the leader of Peshilaree, with his silver torque and noble crest upon his slim chest. There were ten other griffin riders in his party, including a somber male with his hair in a topknot—a graduate of the famed Dendarin Academy—and a fierce female cleric, a Padgarun, with wild hair and a broad-bladed spear in her strong hands. She looked back to Ingal with eyes that seemed to gaze directly into Ingal's long-lived soul.

As soon as the doors were closed, General Odullu Tasami stepped boldly forward, his heavy boots clomping loudly upon the marble floor. Standing at attention, he said in a baritone voice, "My lord Jehai, it is my solemn duty to inform you that war is soon upon us."

Ingal slowly turned his broad head to face the general. "We don't believe we have given you leave to address us, General. You continue to tax our patience!" His tail thumped loudly upon the stone dais. The general scowled but remained silent.

Asamaya stepped to the front of the dais and announced, "The court will now hear the combined concerns of the Viziers of the White Lands Federation and their generals regarding the buildup of Ocrin troops at the western border."

General Tasami snorted in annoyance. "My lord, Ocrin has recently increased the number of troops stationed at the border. As of four days ago, the enemy forces may have numbered as many as twenty-thousand. Their ranks grow daily." The general paused in an obvious attempt to build alarm.

"Yes, General," Ingal said calmly, "We have heard this news already. It is alarming, but not unexpected. May we remind you of your reluctance to position your troops in the Long March Valley for training exercises? Now your forces are in position to defend the border. And forces from the other states have joined them for the 'exercises.' Do you think this to be coincidence?"

The general paused to consider Ingal's words, when a female voice interrupted. "My lord Jehai," the woman said, "you are indeed wise in your leadership." Ingal looked far to his right. The speaker was Entar Misaqi, Vizier of the state of Aestistad, white-robed and grandmotherly save for the hardness of her eyes. She glared at General Tasami as she said, "If we had not sent our troops to the west, Ocrin would have poured across our border by now."

"Misaqi," the general said brusquely, "we are quite capable of holding our own border, but we are quickly losing the advantage. If Aestistad had sent its share of conscripts and funding we would have already had the necessary number of troops in the valleys."

"What you consider our share is far more than the Federation Charter calls for, General!"

The general took a step toward Misaqi and pointed a finger. "You have refused to institute a draft just so your nobility can profit. Leave it to the vanity of Aestistad nobility to justify greed and cowardice."

At this point, other Viziers and generals stepped into the argument, defending one side or the other, until the chamber rang with raised voices and chaos.

Ingal glanced to the bracelet still encircling his right index claw. Again he remembered the Taxin queen. In early summer, her servants would come each morning to scatter fresh magnolia petals over her floor. Ingal wondered if the present queen was afforded the same beautiful gesture.

He looked to the stone, still sitting upon the edge of the dais, pulsing with a dim red glow. What dangerous magic was at work out there? Who works it, and why do the gods feel threatened by it?

Reluctantly, he brought his thoughts back to the moment and the noise of argument. He slammed a massive foot to the dais. The low boom brought sudden silence to the audience chamber.

"We are much too preoccupied with the distressing news brought to us by the Taxin astronomer to deal with petty bickering. Laying blame for perceived inequities will not lead us to resolution. Let us immediately return to the matter at hand and the preparations for war."

Vizier Misaqi bowed her head toward him from her chair. General Tasami quieted and stomped back to the side of his vizier.

General Rena Sa'Mellaq of Aestistad stepped forward from her place next to Vizier Misaqi. "My lord, I move to convene the War Council. Further, I believe it would be prudent to commit as many available troops as possible to the border of Ocrin."

Ingal nodded. "We agree that the Council should be convened in a timely fashion. Command of the coming battles must be organized. We request that we hold the Council in the Keep of Casan. Its location is much closer to the front, yet far enough away that we may be clear of immediate danger. Its battlements and audience dome have served us well in the past." The assembly nodded in approval.

The young, fair-haired Vizier of the state of Alneri, Harin Depal, in whose state the Keep of Casan was found, agreed as well. "Alneri accepts the request, my lord. The Keep will be prepared for the Council immediately upon my return."

Ingal nodded. "Thank you, Vizier." He looked back at General Sa'Mellaq. "As for the commitment of troops, a decision must be made immediately, subject to amendment at the War Council."

A doubt floated like a cloud at the edge of Ingal's mind, an odd feeling, as if he had missed a vital clue to a simple mystery. He couldn't help but wonder if it had to do with the stone, yet there seemed no connection. Something was out of place. Why would Ocrin attack now? But it was something else, something outside of Ocrin, that picked at his thoughts.

He shifted his gaze from person to person and thought about the issue. The generals leaned forward or raised their eyebrows, yet they kept silent. They were obviously eager for battle, and hungry for more men to gain the advantage. As it was, Ingal knew the White Lands had about twenty-thousand soldiers already at the border, highly trained and experienced. Another twenty-thousand or so could be rounded up from other parts of the White Lands Federation, mostly reserves of retired soldiers and young recruits, and could be ready within a few days' notice to march to join their comrades. If more were needed beyond that, tradesmen would be conscripted.

Ingal looked over to the Vizier of the Octunommed Highlands. "Hamab," he said, addressing the black-robed, wide-shouldered vizier. "Have there been any Ingari tribal raids across the border from Planistad in the last year?"

The vizier shook his thickly-bearded head. "No, my lord, the border has been quiet. But our priests have had dire visions of late. Visions of invading forces armed with magic. The Ingari do not seem to be what the visions have warned against."

Ingal nodded. Octunommed priests were rarely wrong with their prophecies. He next turned to Vizier Misaqi of Aestistad. "And have there been any attacks by Vinta pirates?"

"Naval captains have reported sporadic attacks at the northern fringes of our fishing territories, my lord," she said. "Other than that there have been no raids, nor any conflict with the Eastern Lands across the Northron Sea. I believe our naval fleet is more than capable of protecting the coast."

"And how many river-worthy vessels are available to sail up the Alsanoos River if necessary?"

"Other than a handful of battle barges near Taraman, a dozen river war boats can make it as far as the Alneri River. Four of those are small enough to go farther, almost to the border of Ocrin, but repairs will need to be made to the lifts at Gotala Falls."

"See to those repairs, Janisim, for your state manages those locks."

"Yes, my lord," replied the Namistad vizier.

Ingal bent his head in thought before speaking, scratching at his chin with a claw. He tapped his tail spike against the dais floor as he inventoried the nation's forces. That cloud at the back of his mind—Caution! There was something else! Why couldn't he focus on it?

"As for the commitment of available troops," Ingal said, looking back to the viziers, "we command that each of the states commit half their available reserves to the front. All others are to be held for contingencies."

"Half!" General Tasami swept a gauntleted hand through the air. "By the gods! Why would we need to hold back? Is it not obvious that we need as many as we can muster? We must commit them *all*." The general stepped forward and pointed a finger at the dragon. "What 'contingencies?' You heard for yourself there is no threat from the Ingari or any other enemy force besides Ocrin. You are not thinking this through, Jehai. Ocrin is a far larger nation, and the Doom Empress thinks nothing of forcing her population into fighting. We will be outnumbered in only a few days at the current rate!"

Ingal had a rising desire to leap from his dais and smash this greedy, power-hungry human once and for all. Heat rose up his neck to power the magical centers of his mind.

Vizier Misaqi stood from her seat to admonish the general, but Ingal raised a forefoot in a gesture for her patience.

"We need not explain our motives to you, soldier," Ingal said, getting to his feet. The general stopped his advance and lowered his finger, but he stood his ground. Ingal continued. "We have doubts of which we shall not speak at the moment."

Ingal looked to each of the viziers. "An envoy must be sent to the Ocrin capital, Zern, to state our concerns and receive their reply." Ingal looked to his Minister of Arms, Gona Emoch, who had once been general of Alneri. "You will represent us in this regard, Emoch. If this buildup of forces is merely an attempt to blackmail the White Lands, the Doom Empress' response should bear it out. Take with you ambassadors and guards from each of the six states." Tall and muscular with a thick, black mustache, Emoch bowed in response.

Ingal looked again to the viziers. "Step up reconnaissance of the border and communication with our spies in Ocrin. Increase production of food, mining, and necessary supplies and weapons for the armies in your respective states. And, most importantly, build your citizens' patriotism with messages of coming victory. Be confident that we shall win any conflict with Ocrin, for their tactics are predictable to us."

Ingal paused, yawning as softly as a dragon can. He was tired; time for his midday nap. Still looking toward the dais, General Tasami leaned to his vizier and whispered, "Stubborn, decrepit dragon." The corner of Janisim's mouth twisted in a sardonic smile.

Ingal pretended not to have heard. "We must call an end to the audience now. We have much work to do, and, quite frankly, the matter of war between Ocrin and the White Lands pales in comparison to the potential danger of the astronomer's news."

Ingal stretched like a cat, forefeet straightened down the dais steps, wings spread and quivering. Joints popped in his wrists and shoulders.

"Prepare the War Council," he continued, when finished, "and commit what resources are requested, including no more than half of your troop reserves. We will meet with you or your representatives again at the War Council, at the Keep of Casan, in six days. That is all."

Asamaya Sa'Jehai, Minister of Audience, rose and proclaimed, "All rise and bow to the White Lands Dragon." The assembly did as told.

Ingal handed the jeweled bracelet to a court page with instructions to take it and the stone to his study, then turned and walked back through the doors he had entered. He heard Metharcus take up step beside him, then the echo of the heralds blowing their exit call from the audience chamber. The entry party would leave the hall in reverse order as entered.

When the corridors echoed only to the sound of Ingal's ponderous feet, Metharcus asked him in his quiet way, "The Stone of Lethori glows. War is coming. The Prince of Mirrors visits our hall. What does it all mean, my lord?"

The sleeping pit called loudly to Ingal, and he knew he couldn't resist it this time. He shook his head. "We don't know, *decauna*, but we have a feeling that troubled times are upon us."

SIX

The Dreaming Dragon

A little boy asked, "Where do dragons come from?" Ingal was dreaming, and he knew it. His dreams always drew from the Memory, but events were switched around, with moments from different times and different forebears thrown together.

This dream had a little human boy in it, perhaps eight years old, looking up at him with wide, brown eyes, unafraid, while adults ran around him in panic. It was a scene from many generations before, when a forebear had landed in a village in present-day Maldurbia.

"Where do dragons come from?" the little boy asked again, as he had in real life.

Ingal couldn't answer at first. Did the boy want a place? No, more likely he meant it in an abstract way, as if asking his mommy where babies came from. He stared down at the child for a long moment before he finally replied, "Perhaps we come from the same place you come from."

"No," the boy answered. "My gods created me. What gods created you?"

"We merely exist," Ingal said. "We are of no god. We are of Irikara."

Then, the boy changed and the dream departed from the reality of Ingal's memory. The child's skin took on a rusted color, and his eyes turned bright red. In a much deeper and more powerful voice, the boy said, "You are wrong, Gold Dragon. I created you myself!"

Ingal awoke with a start. Through the haze of sleep he heard a deep howl echoing through the room and corridors, and then he realized that the howl was his.

Metharcus and a couple servants appeared in one of the two doorways, concern etched on their faces. "We are fine," Ingal said sleepily. "Call our bathers."

Metharcus turned to fetch the bathers, who were waiting in a nearby room. After a moment of snorting and stretching, Ingal headed out a doorway and into an adjoining room, trailing mud. The floor would be cleaned by servants.

The bathing room was larger than his sleeping chamber. In it was a deep pool filled with steaming water, just wide enough for him to enter, and long enough to accommodate his entire ninety-foot length. Sunset-tinged rays filtered down through a skylight and sparkled orange and gold on the current-swirled water.

Taking up an entire side wall close to the ramp entrance was a highly polished silver mirror, giving the room the illusion of being twice as large as it truly was.

As Ingal entered the room, a dozen young men and women filed in and took up positions along either side of the pool. These were among the most trusted of the palace servants. Each one held in his hand a long pole with a sturdy brush at the end. Metharcus walked to the head of the pool, a large scroll rolled under his arm, as Ingal walked down the ramp and slipped into the water, submerged up to his neck.

The servants lowered their poles into the water and began scrubbing. "The bath is scented with vanilla today, my lord," Metharcus said. "I hope it isn't too strong."

"Not at all, *decauna*."

Metharcus nodded and unrolled the scroll. "You are scheduled to meet next with a party of elves from Peshilaree, my lord, the Prince of Mirrors and his griffin riders. The prince says it is a matter of urgent concern. After that you wished to meet with the Taxin astronomer before your evening meal. There is also a wedding taking place in the gardens, if you should wish to attend, at sunset, for the Vice Admiral Tanoci of the Aestistad navy. Are there any other events you wish to add today?"

"No." Ingal gently lifted his wings out of the water, and several of the servants brushed them diligently. "And we will skip this wedding. We have research to do tonight."

"A number of communiqués have arrived today. Would you like to hear the list?"

"Skip the low-priority ones."

Metharcus rolled his scroll to the bottom. "There are a couple from your sources among the courts of Aestistad and Alneri regarding preparations for battle. The dispatch from your Namistadi sources has been overdue for two months. Two communiqués are from your spies in Ocrin. An additional dispatch is an urgent communication from the Hall of Emeralds."

Ingal jerked his head up, splashing water on a couple of the servants. "The Hall of Emeralds?" Ingal said. This was the seat of power of Peshilaree, led by the speaker of the hall. "Is the seal correct?"

"Yes, my lord. As far as I can tell."

Ingal tilted his head in thought. "Why would they send a dispatch to us when we are already meeting in person with the speaker's own son?" He tapped a claw against the bottom of the pool. "Ah. Did the Prince of Mirrors bring the dispatch with him?"

"No, my lord. It arrived by griffin messenger, separate from the prince and his entourage."

"This is highly irregular of the elves, Metharcus. We must read this dispatch immediately, before we meet with the elves."

Soon the scrubbing was over, and Ingal exited the pool, backing up the ramp. There he stood looking in the mirror as the servants used poles with firm sea sponges to first wipe excess water off of him, then dry him completely.

"Metharcus, please go and tell the elves we will be delayed. And have the dispatch placed in our study for immediate review."

"Yes, my lord." Metharcus gave a quick bow and walked out of the room.

~ ~ ~

Ingal's study was a circular chamber, with over-large tomes and scrolls filling the high shelves from floor to ceiling. Hundreds of glowing globes lit the room like daylight. The globes were not supported in any way, but floated over the dragon, bobbing slowly, but loosely held in place by unseen forces.

Ingal sat in the center of the study in a wide, flat depression, two steps below the rest of the room, carpeted with a tough layer of woolen rugs. He activated his magic center and waved a forefoot in front of his face, chanting, "*Mirosti colum miniscum, talen torunis.*" A fog developed in the air, coalescing into a flat, vertical structure that turned opaque, then reflective and shimmering like a sort of mirror. "I am Ingal Jehai, White Lands Dragon!" he pronounced to the mirror. "We hail the Tower of Light on urgent business."

He waited, expecting to see the face of the towermaster's representative, called the voice of the towermaster. But no one appeared. He repeated the hail. Still no one. Then the spell suddenly collapsed, cut off at the other end, and the mirror dissipated like a lifting fog.

Strange, he thought. He would try again later. The towermaster needed to hear about the Stone of Lethori.

Ingal turned his attention to other issues. He faced three great, oaken tables at one end of the circular depression. The table to his left was slanted, and on its surface lay three open books, each written in a different language and featuring complicated illustrations of stars and orbits. On the table to his right were various scrolls rolled and tied, stacked neatly in order of priority. And on the table directly in front of the dragon lay two objects: the Taxin queen's bracelet on its pillow, gleaming in the soft light; and a carved wooden cube, about twelve inches on each face, sporting a dizzying display of finely etched and gold-inlaid swirls and grooves. Over the tables hung a gigantic magnifying glass in a bronze frame, supported by a telescoping arm that could swing over any of the tables for easy viewing. It currently rested over the cube as Ingal studied the cube's surface.

Ingal felt a quick chill. He jerked his head up and toward the wall off to his left. For a moment it seemed that a shadow moved, but his eyes had barely focused. A split second later, there was nothing there but unmoving shadows and row upon row of books. There was little that a person could hide behind: some chairs and tables for visiting scholars, a decorative statue or two, some vases. A water clock next to the door clicked and splashed as it moved to the eighteenth hour of the day. He was alone in the study.

He turned back to the table in front of him. The cube was a dispatch from the elvish speaker, and its message was disturbing, to say the least. His earlier humor quickly faded, and now he was jumpy.

The surface of the cube hid words in Peshilarn, the language of the Peshilaree elves. He mumbled them to himself as he read a portion of the dispatch for the third time. "It is with sincere regret that the Hall of Emeralds requests of you an execution in my name. My son, the Prince of Mirrors, and his warriors, must not leave your palace alive, for they have committed an act of treason in the murder of the court mage, Ektibal, and plot to overthrow me. Do not listen to their lies."

Ingal sighed and shook his head. To think that the prince could murder a member of the elvish court! And to have the speaker ask for him to kill his own son? Such a thing was unprecedented! He felt much older now than earlier.

Ingal had met Ektibal on a number of occasions. Ektibal was powerful enough that masters of the Tower of Light gave him great deference. Many spells had he engineered. But, like other elvish mages, he had learned in solitude with his own master, and much would be lost with his death.

Political assassination was almost unheard of with elves, and now he would be drawn into the middle of it. Long was his relationship with the speakers, but trade between Peshilaree and the White Lands Federation had diminished in recent years. Performing this execution for the speaker would surely strengthen old ties both personal and economic. The elves had always been xenophobic, but time and again their support and knowledge had ended conflicts in the favor of the White Lands. He owed them for their support.

Once again, Ingal jerked his head toward movement off to the side. *We're getting jumpy in our old age*, he thought, but the feeling of being watched continued. He muttered a *Reveal* spell and turned to look at every inch of the room, but the telltale purple glow of any invisible or camouflaged person was missing.

"Yes. Old age," he whispered, but he kept searching. Nothing. He forced himself to again study the cube.

Ingal had left the doors to the room cracked a bit in expectation of a visitor, and now he heard two sets of footsteps in the corridor beyond. One pair belonged to Metharcus—a slow, irregular rhythm caused by the chamberlain's age and arthritis. The other pair was healthier, most likely female, and varying in pace as if she were nervous. This would be the Taxin astronomer, he thought, and watched the doorway for her arrival.

SEVEN

Celestial Message

Torra reminded herself to keep breathing. She was about to visit the dragon. The Gold Dragon! Her stomach knotted as she followed the shambling old servant, Metharcus. He had appeared at her chamber doors and bid her to follow him to meet the dragon, but would not explain the purpose of the private meeting.

Torra thought back to the audience. She had left feeling relieved to have finished her duty, yet it seemed to her that the dragon had been unimpressed by her. She was a bug to him, a drop in the endless river of years, right? What more could she tell an almighty and wise dragon that he wouldn't already know?

By the stars! Does this old man have to walk so slowly? She checked her steps and fell back away from Metharcus a bit. *Calm yourself, Torra. This is important. Calm down.* The Gold Dragon!

Metharcus slowed his gait. Looking past the chamberlain, Torra spied a wide pair of doors set in the side of the corridor. One door was ajar. *Just through there. Through there lies Aximdrac, and he wants to talk to me. Me! A private audience!*

They stopped at the doors, and Metharcus stepped through and stood at the opening looking in. "My lord," Metharcus said, "I have brought the Taxin astronomer, Torra Com Gidel, as requested."

The dragon replied, his voice deep and resonating. "Thank you, Metharcus. Show her in."

The old man turned, stepped out into the corridor, and gestured toward the room with a slight bow. Suddenly Torra couldn't move. The open door rose over her like a behemoth, alive with its own foreboding power. The space beyond seemed as alien as a portal to another plane, teaming with demons, celestials, and avatars.

Metharcus put a gnarled hand on her shoulder, smiling reassuringly, and gently urged her forward. Torra stepped through. Her eyes widened. The dragon was in the middle of a vast, round room, glimmering in the silky, radiant light cast by hundreds of small globes floating near the vaulted ceiling. A number of these lights separated from the rest and glided to the ceiling over her.

The Great Aximdrac lay in a depression behind three broad tables. The table directly in front of him held the pulsing Stone of Lethori, the bracelet on its pillow, and a sculpted cube made of some dark wood with gilded filigree. A massive magnifying glass loomed over the cube at the end of strong supports.

Torra jumped as the door closed behind her. "Please," Ingal said, and gestured to a seat at the table in front of him.

At first Torra couldn't move her legs. Then she steeled herself and walked the thirty or so feet to the chair, glancing around the room. She couldn't bring herself to look the dragon in the face again. Thick volumes lined all of the walls, and stacks of scrolls lay along the floor. Occasional artifacts of weaponry, pottery, and gilded finery, each worth a king's ransom, sat haphazard in the empty spaces like forgotten knickknacks.

Torra stopped before the chair and gave a rigid bow to the dragon. "Thank you for coming, Com Gidel. Please, have a seat."

"It is my awestruck pleasure," she managed to croak. Torra did as asked and sat looking at the table in front of her. Beyond it heaved the vast chest of the dragon.

Ingal was silent for many moments. The intake and exhalation of air through his nostrils were a bellows. His shield-like scales rustled and pulled across rough carpeting. Finally Torra glanced up at the dragon's eyes. The pupils flashed golden and sparkling.

"Good," he said. "If we are to get any useful information from you, you must first be unafraid to look *Us* in the eyes once in a while."

Torra felt herself blush. "Yes, my lord." She forgot to grasp her Rod of Translation, then realized that the dragon was speaking her native language—the noble form of it, to be precise.

The dragon looked down at the red-pulsing stone. "We wish to thank you again for traveling so far to deliver this important and pressing news about the stone, and for the gift of the bracelet."

"It is both a duty and an honor, my lord."

Ingal nodded and pawed at the bracelet, seemingly lost in thought. "Are you enjoying your stay in *Our* palace?"

Torra fought the urge to hyperventilate, forcing herself to control her breathing—a skill necessary for mages. "I just arrived, my lord, before today's audience."

"Hmm." He looked back to her. "Then *We* insist that you spend some time with *Us*. A month, perhaps. Such a long journey requires that the trip be worthwhile."

"It is worthwhile already, Lord Aximdrac." Too late she remembered his admonition to address him as Ingal Jehai. "Sorry … Lord Jehai."

"A name is an important thing," Ingal said. He tilted his head and looked her over. "We are known by many names around the world: Aximdrac, Or-Gan-Utcha, Sulunesa Khan, Sien Tsu Andrac, others. But *We* most often refer to *Ourselves* by the name given *Us* by our forebear before his death. *Ingal*, ancient Etollian for 'Winter', and *Jehai*, the name given many forebears ago by the Zhameel civilization, meaning 'Golden Nation.'"

"Why is it that you refer to yourself in the plural?" Torra immediately regretted asking. *Stupid! Who cares? Why do you always have to ask the first thing that comes to your mind?*

The scales to either side of Ingal's wide jaw tightened upward in a slim smile. "It is not an unreasonable question. The only time you will hear us refer to ourselves in the singular is when we introduce ourselves. I am Ingal Jehai. The name identifies only this generation of Gold Dragon—unlike *Aximdrac*.

"Think of elders of your species. They have lived what is considered a long life and cannot always remember at which point in their life certain events took place. True?" Torra nodded. "It is the same with us. Only, it isn't the year which we cannot instantly recall, though we are over two-thousand years of age. It is the *generation* that confuses us. Do you know how far back our memory stretches?"

She leaned forward in her seat. "No, my lord. How far?"

"Twenty generations, some thirty-thousand years. There is a lot of time in there, and generations, in which we could get lost in our memory. We might recall an event clearly, as we usually can no matter how long ago, yet we may not instantly remember whether it was Ingal who experienced it last year, or our last forebear, Rambanor Jehai, four-thousand years ago, or Nothos Drac eleven-thousand years ago, or Taliminovi thirty-one thousand years ago. Do you see?"

The casual recitation of eons of time boggled Torra. In her studies she was often amazed by books that were a hundred years old, and thrown by legends that dated back a thousand or two-thousand years. Now she was faced by a dragon who was at least that old, and could remember back thirty-thousand years. She simply couldn't conceive of such a vast time.

"I imagine one could get lost in such memories," she said, playing with the cuff of her robe, "like deranged individuals I have heard of, lost in past episodes of their lives."

"Well, we are not deranged."

Torra threw out her hands. "Oh no, no, my lord!" She felt her face flushing. "I didn't mean … "

"Of course not, Com Gidel. It is quite all right. We see the analogy and agree with it."

The dragon absently picked at a loose thread of the carpet with a foot-long claw. "Using the plural helps us keep things straight in our mind. There was a time, long ago, when the Amber Dragon began acting strangely. Reports came to us of violent outbursts and erratic behavior. We enlisted the aid of our dear friend, the Iron Dragon, and together we investigated."

Ingal sighed. "The first thing we noticed upon finding the Amber Dragon was that he referred to himself in the first person. It was a symptom of a deeper problem, and we learned the heart of it when we followed him across the lands in a state of chaos as he forgot who he was or even which millennium he was in. One day he would take on the identity of a particularly wise and beneficent forebear, helping nations and scholars, the next terrorizing the cities and countryside in search of enemies long vanquished by another generation, convinced that his foes were alive and hidden."

"What caused this? Is this common?"

"No, not common at all. Unique, to our knowledge. And as to the cause, all he would say was that he had looked into 'forbidden knowledge of the gods' or 'communicated with the imprisoned.' It was the ranting of insanity."

Ingal scratched at a loose scale. His eyes glazed over, and he seemed no longer to address her. "The Amber Dragon was very strong at the time, and near impossible for most men to engage. The towermasters wanted to step in and execute him, but we intervened, along with the Iron Dragon. We tried to counsel the Amber Dragon, heal his derangement, but he would not listen. For many months we and the Iron Dragon followed him, pleading rationality and attempting to cure his ailment with medicinal and magical methods. In the end, he destroyed a town and all of its inhabitants. It was up to us to put an end to the madness."

Torra couldn't believe she had never heard this legend. "You killed him? One of your own?"

"We and the Iron Dragon, yes, long ago. He was too much of a threat, to himself and all of civilization." The dragon winced. "When he was reborn, he remembered all of that life clearly, and it nearly drove him insane again. But he did not repeat his mistakes. He returned to referring to himself in the plural, and used magic and herbs to help forget that forebear and his 'forbidden knowledge.' He understood our actions, for the most part, and forgave us. Partly because of his experience, and because of his discomfort with the outcome, he left for lands westward, never to return."

All was silent again as Ingal was lost in thought. Finally, Torra asked, "Why have you called me here to your chambers, my lord?"

Ingal looked back to her. "There are two reasons, Com Gidel. The first is to explore you as a person, for there is a quality you possess which intrigues us. The second is to ask your help."

"Me?"

"Indeed, but let us explore the first reason. Magic is strong with you, Com Gidel, very strong. Yet the use of magic is outlawed in Taxia."

Torra looked down. "You are very perceptive, my lord. I … I learn in secret." She touched the Rod of Translation that her mentor had given her.

Ingal seemed to choose his words carefully. "So you are a renegade?"

Torra looked up in alarm. "You overestimate me. I am a renegade only in the sense that I study magic illegally, in my nation, as is true for all at the Astronomer's Guild. But I am not a *mage renegade*, my lord. Not the sort who would cast renegade spells!"

Ingal leaned closer to Torra. She smelled his hot, musky breath and felt the heat on her face. His eyes were each as large as her head, and close, so close, burning into her. "Yet you know of renegade spells," he said, eyes narrowing, "and you possess a wild magic in you, unharnessed and potentially dangerous. What do you know? Hmm? What spells have you seen? To call forth such vast powers could destroy entire cities, ruin countries, lay waste to armies. What do you know?"

"Nothing, my lord!" Torra wanted to run away but feared to turn her back in the escape. "I study their histories, search out knowledge. Nothing more!"

Ingal pulled back from her. His features seemed to soften. "You tell the truth," he said. "We are certain. You understand, no doubt, that we must rule out certain possibilities. We can read magic around you like you would see heat waves off a bonfire. You are born with a great talent for magic, yet your training has barely tapped the energies within you."

Whatever anxiety she had felt at the violation quickly melted away. The Gold Dragon said she had talent!

Ingal sat back and curled his tail around his front legs. "You say you study the histories of renegade spells, yet such knowledge is off limits to all but the highest mages in the three towers of magic." He looked off to a water clock to one side of the room. Its gears clanked and its water cups moved a notch.

"Oh no, my lord. I seek them out through legends," she said. "Though extremely rare in the course of history, these spells were witnessed by many at the time they were cast, for their power can sometimes be seen by entire populations. Control of the forces of nature, the disappearance of mountains, or the mass-morphing of entire armies into bizarre creatures—such things become the stuff of legends, passed down through the millennia. Sometimes the mages' names are known and passed down as well, and they can be traced. I have collected information of a great many of these ... "

Ingal raised a forefoot for silence, and Torra cut herself short.

"Please excuse us. It is a subject that must wait for another time. While this dangerous pastime of yours is a fascinating subject, Com Gidel, we diverge again from our purposes. There are many issues facing us tonight and the elves await an audience, so we must go on to other topics. The second reason we called you here was for help in deciphering an elvish dispatch for us."

"I don't know elvish, my lord."

Again, Torra felt Ingal probe her mind, but the feeling came and went much quicker than before. "Yet you can help us, nonetheless." He raised a forefoot and extended a claw to point at the cube on the table in front of her. "Do you know what this is?"

Torra leaned forward to examine the cube. Then, checking the dragon for approval, she picked it up for a closer look. It was about a foot wide on each face, lighter than she expected, and covered with fine, gold filigree on a black wood that, on the whole, presented an impression of geometric symmetry. One face featured a golden circle amongst the swirls.

"It's beautiful," she said, putting it back on the table. "Such fine craftsmanship. It's of an unfamiliar wood, and the curious swirls on its surface are like no design I have ever seen. Is it elvish?"

"Indeed, but it is not meant as merely a work of art." He looked down at the cube through the magnifying glass. The floating globes descended toward the table as if sensing the need. "This is a dispatch from the elvish kingdom of Peshilaree."

"A dispatch?" She looked closely at it again. "Are all elvish messages so elaborate?"

Ingal tilted his head closer to the cube. "Only the ones which have a purpose of utmost importance, or which could fall into human hands. The elves are untrusting of other species as a rule. Most humans would see this as a work of art, and treasure it, not realizing that it contains a message in the swirls and sparkles."

"What does it say?"

Ingal frowned. She backed up, fearing she had said the wrong thing. "It is distressing news," he said, "but we do not believe it would be appropriate to share with you. However, there is a part which we are having trouble deciphering. Look here." He gestured with a claw to the top face of the cube.

Torra stared a moment at the massive, yellowing claw, then turned her attention to the cube.

"The part to which we refer is, we believe, a star chart."

Torra leaned forward to look more carefully. Suddenly, the claw inches from her face held less interest. "I don't see it."

"Pick up the cube and hold the face with the circle up to the light." Torra did as asked. Ingal continued, "Tilt it slightly such that the designs on that face sparkle. Do you see the points of light?"

"No, I … Yes!" On the cube were golden sparkles outlining at least one constellation that Torra recognized.

Ingal rearranged his legs, groaning at the exertion, and ripping through a portion of the carpet where his rear claws had hung up. "We have studied this pattern for over an hour as the elves from today's audience await us. We are well-versed in the art of astronomy, having studied even with your own predecessors in years past. A number of our forebears have written detailed texts on the subject and charted the paths of constellations over the millennia. Yet, though the patterns are familiar somehow, we cannot decipher this chart."

Torra studied the chart for many minutes, and Ingal seemed patient, settling down into a more comfortable position with his head upon his front legs. She touched one, then another of the constellations as she recognized them. But the third …

"Ah ha! I believe I know the pattern."

Ingal raised up. "So soon! Are we a fool of a dragon, then?"

Torra looked away from the cube and up into Ingal's eyes. "I mean no disrespect, my lord, I just meant … "

Ingal chuckled. "We praise your abilities. Please, tell us."

Torra blinked, then smiled. She turned back to the cube and placed it under the magnifying glass with the star chart facing upward. "If you look in this corner of the face you will see that these stars outline the constellation of Corbilla, the Griffin, and the other constellation is of Mantalla, the Bear. See? Here is the cub at her feet."

Ingal nodded. "Yes, that much we recognize already. Curious that they chose two predators. What of the third?"

Torra's eyes widened and she raised a finger. "Ah! Here is the tricky one." She looked back to the cube and moved her finger across the cube face. "If you draw an imaginary line diagonally from this corner to the other, everything across the line seems out of place with the constellations I just pointed out, right?"

Ingal nodded again. "Go on."

"Well, imagine if you were the gods, looking down at Irikara from the heavens. You would be looking through the constellations at us. Here," she said, tracing the circle on the cube face, "our world is represented by the circle. Now, if you were looking through the constellations from the heavens … "

"We understand, now," Ingal said, peering closer through the magnifying glass and squinting his eyes. "The constellations would be a mirror image of what we would see. How clever!"

"And there is only one constellation featured there, my lord, in mirrored form. An odd one that few people know, seen only from the far southern lands."

The smile faded from Ingal's lips. "Yes," he said, rising away from the magnifying glass. "We see what it is."

Torra sat up as well and finished her thought, saying, "My lord, it is Corthos … the Dreaming Dragon."

EIGHT

Execution

Ingal stood amidst fifty palace guardsmen in the corridor leading to the back doors of the audience chamber. Called the Dragon Guard, or *Jehai Nassium*, they were the most skilled warriors the White Lands had to offer. The men and women lined the walls like so many stacks of plated gold, with shiny halberds and strong, curved falcata swords at the ready. He knew another twenty five guards were forming behind the front doors of the chamber, as well.

"My lord," Metharcus said, "is this necessary? We've never before had problems with the elves."

"Not for a very long time, *decauna*," Ingal said, staring at the closed audience chamber doors in front of him. "Not for a very long time indeed. But we have many worries right now, and we haven't time or energy to investigate. If the speaker of the Hall of Emeralds asks of our honor to execute his son, then we must entertain the idea."

"It is extreme, my lord. And based only on a dispatch."

Ingal turned suddenly and glared at his chamberlain. Metharcus looked down in humility. "It is not for you to question us on this matter, Metharcus!" Instantly, Ingal regretted his harsh words. The old man was always a true advisor, more so than the men and women on his advisory council. But it was out of place for Metharcus to question him in front of other staff.

Ingal looked back up at the doors. This task was not an easy one, and he had misgivings. Dimly, he realized that there must be something else going on. He had carried out political executions before without such nagging doubts. It could not be coincidence that the request was made just as the Stone of Lethori was delivered and war was about to break out with Ocrin.

Another thought clouded his mind. These dozen elves were among the best warriors in Peshilaree. There was a real possibility that they could defeat him in battle.

His legs trembled a moment before he gained control. It was very slight, and as he looked around he didn't think anyone else noticed. For a brief moment, a memory flashed through his mind of his last forebear breathing his final, wheezing breath.

"My lord," the captain of the guard said at Ingal's other side. "All guardsmen are in place and ready for your command."

Ingal nodded. "Do not proceed until we give the signal by throwing open the doors. The elves cannot know of your presence until we are ready."

Guards opened the broad double doors, and Ingal moved forward alone onto his dais. The doors closed behind him.

The elves formed a loose group in the center of the chamber. Some sat in the high-backed seats that had earlier been occupied by the viziers. The Prince of Mirrors lay across one of those seats, legs draped over a chair arm. Like his warriors, he still wore his riding garb. The only thing that distinguished the prince from the others was the gilded mirror amulet hanging around his neck. Another elf, a Dendarin graduate with his hair in a topknot, stood beside the prince in somber guardianship.

The elves looked up at the dragon, but those who were seated did not rise, and none bowed. Such was the typical attitude shown by elves. Formality was a thing to be conjured for special occasions—*elvish* occasions—and absolute.

This time, Ingal found the lack of respect annoying. He took his place at the edge of the dais and remained standing. The sunlight was long gone, but the room was still decently lit. Long ago the Prince of Mirror's own grandfather cast a permanent *Light* spell on the chamber as a gift for the dragon's valiant deeds for Peshilaree.

Just then Ingal smelled the cinnamon-tinged scent of elvish blood, and quickly scanned the group. There was one more individual than that morning, a male whose arm was heavily bandaged. He had lost his left hand. But before Ingal could inquire about it, he first had to start the audience in a manner consistent with elvish ritual.

Ingal raised his right forefoot and chanted in the language of Peshilarn,

> Granted be the right of trust.
> Granted be the right of truth.
> No time is long
> If the court is true,
> And all gifts given are from the heart.

At this the Prince of Mirrors finally stood, raised his hand to the dragon, and replied,

> Our trust is in your hands.
> Our truth is in your tongue.
> Long is the hour
> For true hearts to share
> When our heartfelt gift is ourselves.

The elves spoke their own fluid language, which was instantly translated by the room.

Ingal did not sit, as was typically required in elvish courts. The prince showed his confusion with a slight twitch of a dark green eyebrow and remained standing as well, leaning against his chair.

Ingal continued in Peshilarn. "You have a badly injured man, prince. Should he see one of our priests?"

"That will not be necessary, dragon lord. One amongst us is a cleric." The prince glanced to a wild-eyed elvish female with long light-green hair coursing in tangles over her padded leather armor. She was the only one wielding a leaf-bladed spear. Ingal recognized her as a *Padgarun*, a woodland elf shaman warrior from the wilderness of Peshilaree. Known for going berserk in battle, the Padgarun were the main reason Peshilaree had rarely been invaded. They answered to no one except their own 'spirits of nature.' Not even the Speaker of the Elves could command them.

"May we ask how he was wounded?" Ingal asked.

A young male, stern of face, leaned over and whispered in the prince's ear. His hair was pulled into a topknot and tied with a lapis-beaded leatherine strap, designating him as a graduate of the Dendarin Academy. Such graduates were highly sought for their political savvy.

The prince paused, then carefully replied, "I think it more prudent to tell you later, Ingal."

Ingal nodded. "Very well. And who is your advisor, if we may ask?"

"This is Rethuud. He is a cousin to me as well as political counsel and bodyguard."

Ingal gave a nod to Rethuud, who responded in kind, adding, "Jehai."

He focused back on the Prince of Mirrors. "You are missing warriors, prince, if you flew with the usual contingent. Has something happened of which we should be aware?"

The prince glanced to his advisor. "Again, Lord Jehai, this is a topic for another time."

Ingal huffed. Had they been attacked by their own people? Traitors, fleeing from the speaker, perhaps? "We see." He shifted his weight. "Tell us, what brings you and your warriors to our court?"

"We come with warnings. There are plots against the White Lands Federation, my lord. Plots that run deep into history and implicate entire civilizations."

"Oh?" Ingal tensed and swished his tail. The warning of the Stone of Lethori flashed through his mind. "These are serious accusations. We know of no threat from Peshilaree." The prince started to speak, but Ingal broke him off. "On the contrary, We received a very interesting dispatch from your father just this morning." The wild-eyed Padgarun tensed.

The prince tilted his head in concern, his brow furrowed. Ingal took a step down the dais toward the prince. A number of the griffin warriors grabbed the handles of their weapons. The Padgarun woman, too, tightened her grip on her spear, pointing it toward Ingal, but her eyes were on the Prince.

"Your father told us you assassinated the court mage, Ektibal, and that you wish to overthrow your father as speaker."

"Not true!"

Ingal stepped down to the chamber floor. "Tell us, prince! Why do you wish the speaker's death?"

The griffin warriors pulled together to shelter the prince, weapons drawn. The advisor, Rethuud, stepped in front of the prince, his hand upon a rod at his side. The Padgarun warrior took a stance at the prince's side.

"Ingal," the prince said, waving his guards out of the way, "the speaker," he paused as if to find the right words, "is not well. He worships strange gods and speaks of ancient legends. I believe it was he who ordered Ektibal's death."

The warriors became more agitated, shifting and looking at each other. The Padgarun, in particular, tensed and licked her lips, eyes flashing back and forth between Ingal and the prince. The prince ordered his men to sheathe their weapons. Reluctantly, they followed his orders.

Ingal did not back off. "And why, exactly, would the speaker wish to have his own court mage murdered?"

The prince sighed and reached to his mirrored amulet, rubbing it nervously. "It has been many years since my father trusted me with matters of national security. He now refers to me as a 'pagan', excluding me from matters of state; all such matters now revolve around his newfound gods. So there is a lot of which I am not aware. Plans are in motion. The more I have investigated, the more I see the tendrils of those plans infiltrating every facet of Peshilarn society, and societies outside of Peshilaree. It is the plot against the White Lands and the Tower of Light that has prompted ... "

Suddenly, the Padgarun woman screamed with animalistic intensity. Ingal watched as, wide-eyed and seemingly aflame with anger, she plunged her spear through the prince's back. The leaf blade slipped through his torso and out his chest with a sickening rip. Ingal and the elvish warriors had hardly reacted before she withdrew her weapon and ran for the front audience doors.

Ingal came to his senses and swept a forefoot through the air, shouting a *Word of Opening*. The doors to the chamber flew open at both ends of the room, revealing row upon row of palace guard, who ran inside.

The Padgarun woman never slowed. She ran straight at the waiting guards at the front doors. Before they could level their halberds at her, she screamed again and slashed her spear in a wide arc and through the throats of three of the guards, jumping over their slumping bodies and into the fray beyond.

By now the prince had fallen limp to the floor, but Ingal didn't tarry. Wings fully unfurled, he leapt into the air and over the elves to the front doors. Roaring "I want her alive!" he reached over the heads of the guards, slicing his arm on their weapons. He just missed grabbing the Padgarun.

It was hopeless for Ingal to continue pursuit. The corridor was crowded with confused palace guardsmen, armor clanging and halberds knocking, trying to turn and run after the woman without injuring each other in the process. If he charged forward he risked killing his own men. The woman, meanwhile, killed two more men and fled toward the front of the palace.

In his fury, Ingal craned his neck toward the elf and roared. The contingent of guards from the rear doors had run into the chamber and formed a ring around the elves. The elves, meanwhile, had taken up a defensive formation around their fallen leader.

Ingal went back to the elves and beckoned them to move aside. They raised their weapons, ready to strike, but some sign was given, and they reluctantly made way for the dragon. Surprisingly, the Prince of Mirrors still clung to life, lying in a spreading pool of his own blood. Blood gathered in the corner of his mouth. The prince's advisor and bodyguard, Rethuud, wide-eyed in apparent disbelief, cradled the prince's head in his lap.

Ingal leaned his head close to the elf lord. "Prince," he said, "tell us why your cleric has done this."

The prince swallowed hard, seeming to want to say something, but only succeeded in choking on his blood. Rethuud motioned for Ingal to move away, but the prince stopped the warrior and swallowed hard.

"The speaker," the prince managed to say. "The speaker is insane. Strange gods." The prince choked again and clutched at his chest, his body shaking. "He intends to invade … week … Ecemii." The prince coughed in a bloody spasm, trying to speak, then gave up and reached a hand to a belt purse, withdrawing something in his fist. Just then, his body quaked, tensed, then fell limp.

A mournful sigh passed through the elvish warriors as they leaned in to gaze upon their fallen leader. Many of them murmured in surprise, whispering the name "Phasgala" in shocked and hushed tones.

Ingal reached a claw down to the prince and unwrapped the fingers of his fist. In the dead prince's hand was a clay pendant —a hollow circle with a triangle touching the inner edges.

The audience chamber was silent. For whatever reason, the prince had been killed, Ingal believed he hadn't deserved to die at the treasonous hands of one of his own warriors. There was no doubt, now, that an elvish conspiracy brewed in the Hall of Emeralds.

Still caressing the prince, Rethuud gazed in the direction of the fleeing assassin. He looked up at the dragon with wet eyes and asked in a level tone, "What are your intentions, Jehai? Wish you still to execute us like our fallen prince?"

Ingal turned and walked toward the exit, moving through a line of palace guardsmen. "We have not decided," he said without looking back. "For now you must wait here until our guards have captured or killed your cleric. Then we will make a judgment."

NINE

Phasgala

Torra sat in the North Wing Library, an old astronomy tome open to browning pages, but she hardly paid it any attention. All she could see were the dragon's golden eyes. Was the private audience only an hour ago? Less? He had asked her for advice. A *dragon* had asked *her*!

Torra looked through one of the wide library windows to the flourishing gardens, open to allow the blossom smells of highland summer, then past the gardens to the snow-capped mountains beyond.

She thought back to her last visit with Master Morikal, her old mentor. "You're lucky to have this chance," Morikal had told her. "I have spent my long life lost in the ways of the academic mage, traveling no farther than the borders of our country. Take the chance while you are young, live for the adventure, and serve a higher power than your own ambition."

She turned a page of the tome. *The old chamberlain has it good. To serve Ingal and share in his wisdom! If only I could be so fortunate.*

A deep and angry roar echoed through the vast corridors of the palace. Torra stiffened. The Gold Dragon! No doubt about it. The power of his roar chilled her blood. For a moment she thought only of running and hiding, but as the echoes of the roar dissipated, curiosity made her edge slowly toward the door, only to stop in her steps at the clanging of metal on metal from down the hall, the shouting of orders, and, over the sound of battle, a woman's vicious shriek—not of terror, but of victory, full of raw, murderous energy.

But the sound of fighting faded quickly as guards ran past the library door toward the palace entrance, where she had stood that very noon. *The elves! Ingal said he was going to talk to the elves.*

A movement caught her eye outside the library window. The fierce she-elf Torra had seen at the audience was now running through lush green grass and immaculate topiary ahead of a band of tromping, gold-armored palace guardsmen. Her glaucous eyes burned with violence, full of victorious confidence. Emerald hair flew behind her like a tempest of angry wasps.

As Torra watched, two fleet-footed guards caught up to the elf. But with a swing of her broad spear and twist of her body the elf sliced through them both in a single stroke. The blade cut cleanly and deeply through armor and belly flesh. The guards crumpled to the ground.

The she-elf hardly slowed. She spun again. This time she reached a hand down into a pouch bobbing at her side, withdrew a brown, palm-sized globe and threw it at her pursuers. The globe splattered on the faceplate of a guardsman, splashing a light green liquid over the guard's head and on those around him. The guard fell to the ground, writhing and screaming with his hands to his helmet, struggling to pull his faceplate off.

Torra ran right up to the library window to get a better view of the elf warrior's progress, but the she-elf disappeared through the ornate doors of the royal stables, slamming them shut behind her. The guards arrived steps behind, but the doors were already barred. They ran around the sides of the stables to other entrances.

Torra allowed herself to relax a bit. The elf was surrounded, trapped. But in a hail of splinters, the stable doors crashed outward, raining shards upon the guardsmen there. The elf warrior rode upon a giant, winged beast with the head and wings of an eagle and the body of a lion. A griffin! Large lion's feet with cruel, curved talons stomped and ripped the guards. The griffin snapped at one guard's shoulder, crushing bone and armor, then ran to lift off, flapping madly. One brave guard grabbed onto the beast's reins. With a shriek from both rider and mount, the griffin flew eastward over the lawn, and the lone guard let go and fell to the trees before he went too high.

Ingal! Torra thought, and threw open the window. Was Ingal the target of this warrior? Where was the Gold Dragon?

For many long minutes Torra watched from the library window as the palace guards secured the area. Awestruck pilgrims were ushered inside. The first pair of fallen soldiers were turned onto their backs, their roaring dragon helms taken off, showing faces soaked with sweat and grimacing in pain. Their chest plates were removed to reveal evil, bloody wounds and exposed intestines.

One young guard's eyes rolled with panic and pain, his breathing shallow, mouth gaping for breath. Then, suddenly, he shuddered and fell still, eyes open. A comrade by his side tried in vain to rouse him.

Torra had never witnessed someone die, much less death at the hands of violence. She put a hand to her mouth. Tears welled in her eyes as the man's arms were crossed by a fellow guardsman. Priests arrived, and one immediately set to prayers over the deceased soldier.

The other guard clung to life, one hand clutching his sword, the other the priest. Yet his face was resolute, an experienced warrior. He clearly understood the enormity of his wound and was prepared.

The guard who had been hit by the globe now lay on the ground moaning. His face was a mass of melted skin and, in places, exposed bone. His eyes were missing, the gaping holes where they had been were now melted shut. A palace attendant threw water onto the man's face. Torra looked away.

And then, the dragon stepped into view from the right. In the sunlight his body glowed with the radiance of true gold, massive and powerful. Torra's heart skipped a beat. Ingal was unharmed as far as Torra could see. He looked in the direction of the elf's flight as guards pointed. His wings unfurled. He crouched as if to leap into flight. But then he looked down to the wounded guard and to others who had sustained less threatening wounds. None could look Ingal in the face.

Ingal relaxed and folded his wings. He raised his head in a noble stance and stepped to the guard with the gut wound. Ingal spoke in soothing tones of honor and victory, and of loyal service. He called the guard by name, reaching down with a wide forefoot and spreading his wings in blessing. The guard extended a shaking hand to touch the forefoot and smiled despite the pain. In moments, he died in the shadow of his master.

Ingal set off after the elf, leaping into the air with vibrant sunset oranges and reds reflecting off his golden scales before he disappeared around the cliffside.

Torra waited in the library for hours, watching patiently from a stiff wooden chair that she had dragged to the window. Once in a while she spied the chamberlain waiting in the shadows of the courtyard for his master. The bodies of the slain guards were carried outside and placed in a row, palace priests chanting prayers over them. Torra shook her head. What good were prayers for those who were already dead? What good were prayers at all, for that matter? The day a priest pulled forth from his pocket some material evidence for the existence of souls would be the day she would consider believing in such nonsense.

In the hours of waiting, Torra's arm began to itch—the latest spot of skin irritation from her illness. She reached to her robe pocket and withdrew a small bottle of salve, applying the herbal remedy to the affected area. She then ate a small strip of dried herbs to take the edge off of a rising nausea.

The night had long since cast its shroud on the mountains by the time Ingal finally returned, cruising in like a dark shadow from above and swooping into the courtyard.

The great dragon shook his head at his chamberlain without saying a word and lumbered inside.

TEN

Reflection

Both moons were full, and their lambent glow lent a ghostly quality to the semicircle of pillars around the front courtyard. Ingal sat toward one end of the courtyard, nearest the front doors to the palace. The pillars around him were taller than he was, and the massive stone slabs they supported made a continuous border, almost meeting at the far end from the palace entry as if they were two arms embracing all who visited. His forebear, Rambanor Jehai, had placed the stones himself four-thousand years before. Countless earthquakes later, none had budged.

Ingal started to look down to the courtyard surface, but quickly diverted his attention back up to the heavens.

The moons were rarely full at the same time. Ingal's ninth forebear, Tlakm Osmi, had calculated that the event happened once every twenty-five years and forty days, according to the Etollian calendar. Ingal's own calculations, though, showed a change over the millennia of about a day less every six thousand years.

Science aside, Octunommedian superstition stated that when both moons were full, disaster would strike the land. Ingal did not subscribe to such silliness. But tonight made him wonder.

With a sigh, he looked down into the courtyard. Off to one side were seven human forms lying on the granite surface, draped with white shrouds. A chill breeze rustled the sheets, tauntingly flipping up corners to show bloody skin or dented armor. Placed beside the bodies were the still-shiny weapons that the guards had wielded so ineffectively against the Padgarun.

She fled north-northwest—back toward Peshilaree. He had followed the few telltale signs of her flight, but the business of running the nation forced his return to the palace. *Another time,* he thought.

Ingal had known each of the guardsmen by name. As they had died away from their villages, custom demanded that the bodies lay outdoors overnight so that their souls may find their way back home. Two of their living comrades stood at attention over the bodies.

Additionally, the Padgarun had seriously wounded six others, including a guardsman who had been blinded and disfigured in the face, and another who had his shoulder crushed by the griffin, resulting in amputation of his left arm.

And what was the elvish reaction? The elves had refused to be led to the holding chambers, nor would they part with the prince's body. They threatened to fight to the death lest they be allowed to leave. The only thing Ingal could do was give them food and water and magically seal the audience chamber against their escape, making the central chamber of the palace a massive holding cell, heavily guarded outside. Fine. It would be enough for overnight.

Ingal groaned and looked eastward through the pillars. Despite the late hour, pilgrim campfires burned about four-hundred yards away. From their camps came the distant rustling of people packing their belongings. Little wonder. Word of the attack had spread quickly, and they wouldn't want to stay for any further violence.

As Ingal looked back, the guardsmen's shrouds stood out from the darkness around them. Ingal blamed himself for their deaths. Oh, he could lay the blame on others easily enough. The elvish cleric, most notably. She had done the killing. Or the guards themselves. They had been ill-prepared, having seen little action in years outside of the occasional squabble among pilgrims. More importantly, he could blame the captain of the guard for failing to adequately train them.

But Ingal knew the onus was his alone. *He* had opened the doors with a *Word of Opening*. The sight of forty guardsmen with halberds and swords at the ready would have halted any normal warrior. *He* had underestimated the Padgarun. She was berserk, fighting by reaction alone and driven by the need to flee. She would have escaped or died trying, and neither was preferable. *He* should have kept the doors closed and captured the elf himself, thus saving the lives of these seven guards.

But then the other elves might have killed her themselves, and attacked him, too, if he stood in their way. Treachery was as good as suicide among the elves, though it had hardly ever happened.

Why had she done it? Ingal scratched at a loose scale on his chest as he thought. The speaker wanted the prince dead, he thought, that much was clear. But the speaker has no dominion over the Padgarun. The cleric-warriors answer only to the spirits of nature. And she had been one of the prince's own griffin warriors.

He heard the whisper of the front palace doors pushing open behind him, and Metharcus' tired voice say from inside, "You may proceed." Then came the soft padding of slippered feet as the doors closed again. Light steps and the rustle of fine cloth suggested the person was a female in a summer dress or fine robe —nobility, and she was alone. Except for Metharcus, the servants had all been dismissed for the night, so it must be a visitor to the palace. The astronomer? No. These steps were soft and regular, refined.

"Good evening, Vizier," Ingal said.

The person skipped a beat in the rhythm of her steps. Ingal was right. Entar Misaqi, Vizier of Aestistad. Now he smelled the remnants of her perfume. Attar—essence of rose petals.

"Good evening, my lord," she responded.

Ingal turned to look. She was dressed in a silk sleeping robe of exquisite workmanship, an import from Quisha or Inlai'chi'a, far to the south. She wasn't wearing her miter, but the robe was white, the state color of Aestistad, with dark designs.

Vizier Misaqi walked to Ingal's side and looked over at the shrouded bodies. *Why is she here?* he wondered. *A need to comfort us? She has before. Or out of curiosity?* "We take it you heard the news, Entar."

"Yes, my lord. I heard you roar, as I'm sure everyone in the palace grounds had. Soon after, my handmaiden came to me with a tale of a runaway elvish warrior attacking guards in the corridors, though she did not know why the elf had attacked." Entar looked up at the dragon. "Are these seven the only casualties?"

The only casualties! Ingal thought. *Only!* He wanted to lash out at her, shout, *How many does it take to be important?* But he closed his eyes and forced calmness on his voice. "There was one other."

"Who, my lord?"

"The Prince of Mirrors. The assassin was a warrior of his—a griffin warrior. Do not ask us why, for we do not yet fully understand."

Entar nodded, rubbing her arms to warm them. "Elves killing elves. I have never heard of such a thing."

"Indeed. It has been many centuries since last we heard of it. Longer, in the case of nobility."

The two of them stood in silence for many moments. He saw the stunted trees of the hillsides above rustle with wind gusts. Clouds were rolling in, blotting out the moons. Vizier Misaqi shivered violently in her thin robe.

Ingal moved to stand over the vizier, motioning for her to stay where she was. He formed a partial wind block for her so that his radiant heat could warm her.

"It is cold here in the mountains at night. What's on your mind, Entar? More than tonight's events with the elves?"

Entar sighed and seemed to consider her words carefully. Her breath froze in a cloud of confusion as she spoke. "Why would Ocrin choose to take the offensive now? The Treaty of Long March Keep is still in effect; they have no right to attack. And, though meager, trade with them has picked up in the last year. All indications pointed to increasingly good relations with them."

Ingal nodded and watched the guards turn and pass each other behind the bodies. "The Treaty of Long March Keep is nearly a hundred years old, Entar. Mankind has a short memory. As for increased trade and productive relations, this would not be the first time Ocrin has put up a false front before attacking. It is meant to put us off guard; they have used that tactic many times in the past. Zerna, the first Doom Empress, wrote it into her text, *Command of Generals*, nearly seven thousand years ago. Her influence is still felt in modern Ocrin politics." Ingal let out a grunt of amusement. "The current Doom Empress surely has an ancient copy of the book in her library."

"But what would they hope to gain? Land? They ruined much of Alneri and Namistad in the last war. And if their goal is to move farther east than that, to more fertile land, or even to the coast to gain access to the sea, they would fail miserably. The White Lands Federation would throw every man, woman, and child at them before we allowed that!"

Ingal could not answer. Ocrin's intentions were no clearer to him. "Whatever their motives are, Entar, fear not. We have the forces to confront them. Likely they are only testing us, or pushing for some compromise in their favor. All of the states must work together to project a united front. This will give us maximum leverage when Ocrin finally announces its terms."

The Vizier nodded and remained quiet. Ingal's assurances were necessary to rally the troops and unite the viziers, but he didn't believe his own words. Entar Misaqi's analysis was accurate, he thought; Ocrin was gearing up for something more than skirmishes or threats, with no clear motivation or goal. Yet Ocrin was doomed to extremely heavy losses if they expected to take even one state of the Federation. If Ocrin actually succeeded, they could never hope to hold it more than a year or two. They had no allies to aid them, other than some trade with the far north. Did they possess some secret weapon? New magic? A pact with their neighbors, all of whom had traditionally opposed them? Not likely. Ocrin simply had nothing to gain from war with the White Lands.

Entar said, "You should know that General Tasami has made rounds since the audience." She looked up at him as if to judge his reaction. "He has met in secret with several viziers and most of the generals. He is attempting to dedicate more than half of the troops without your knowledge."

"It is to be expected. Likely he is acting at the behest of Vizier Janisim."

"So far I have heard no statement of support from the others, though he knows better than to let me know how they stand."

Ingal looked down at Entar Misaqi. The state of Aestistad and its viziers had always been supportive of the Gold Dragon. They should. Ingal and his forebears were the sworn protectors of the Tower of Light, and the tower was the foundation upon which the state of Aestistad rested. But Entar looked away from his gaze and tensed.

Ingal narrowed his eyes. "Your support is always appreciated, Vizier. There may have been no statements in support of Tasami, but was there any in opposition?"

She paused almost imperceptibly. "No, my lord."

"Not even from you, Entar?" She didn't answer.

The dragon shook his head and snorted. Janisim and his general were thorns, to be sure, power-hungry and contradictory. But Ingal had to admit that Janisim was a crafty politician, and Tasami was excellent at military strategy, if he could control his temper.

The fact, that even Entar Misaqi had been swayed by the general's argument said a lot. The need for more troops could be argued easily. Numbers counted.

Ingal wondered how he could possibly convince the viziers to hold troops back. Tell them the truth? That he had a gut feeling of dread? His gut feelings were usually correct.

"Vizier, as we said, it is important that we show a united front. Janisim and Tasami are welcomed to make their arguments, but they must be reminded that we are the final authority. We understand the need, but you must trust us. No more than half of the available units can be sent to the front. We command it."

"Of course, my lord."

Thunder rumbled to the east, probably too low for the Vizier to notice, and Ingal sensed a decrease in air pressure. A storm was moving in fast. If Ingal knew anything of the weather, there would be further storms in the coming days. As if in answer to the coming fury, wolves howled from the valley below. They were soon joined by a pack to the north, in the Canyonlands.

Ingal grew concerned about the coming storm; the bodies would need to be moved to a covered area. He was about to give orders to the guards when Entar diverted his attention.

"This trouble with the elves reminds me of something odd I saw when last I visited the Tower of Light."

Ingal looked down at the woman. "Oh? Tell us."

"I was at the tower," Misaqi said, "to meet with the Master of Resources regarding the tower's purchase of grains and meats from Aestistad, and renegotiation of their use of the Port of Taraman. He had escorted me up to the twentieth level—higher than I had ever been in the tower—and we were waiting outside of an audience room. One of the upper tower lifts was out of service, and the mages were forced to use a stairwell to get down to our floor."

Ingal shot her a look of concern. "The lifts never fail! It would take a contrary magical aura of great strength."

Entar shifted her legs and toyed with her collar, then chose to continue. "A group of master mages, including two Council Mages, stepped out of the stairwell and walked past us. High-level mages are always very stern-faced, but these were especially concerned—even fearful—by the look in their eyes. The object of their concern was a tall elf walking with a confident air in the midst of their group."

She paused, seemingly lost in thought. Ingal waited. "I have seen my share of elves, lord," she continued, "but this one was most bizarre. He was dressed in mage's robes, which I have never known an elf to wear. He carried a satchel with him, filled with mages' books by the look of it.

She pulled her arms tight to her breast and looked out over the darkened mountains. "This elvish mage turned to look at me, but it was clear he didn't realize I was there. His eyes held a hidden emotion, a moment of fear, then it was gone when he realized my presence. He turned away, and the group passed by."

"When was this?" Ingal asked.

Entar tapped her finger to her lips. "Just after the Feast Day of the Prophet Demesqua, three months ago.

"And I was able to hear a bit of their conversation as they passed," she continued. "The mages muttered something about 'an elf with mirrored eyes.'"

Thunder rumbled again. Entar shivered violently once more. "I must go inside, my lord. I cannot endure the cold any longer."

Ingal nodded. "Of course, Entar. Your company has been much appreciated."

She pulled her robe close to her and stepped away from Ingal. "Thank you, my lord, for your assurances regarding the conflict with Ocrin. Aestistad has faith in your leadership."

"We will talk specifics in the morning, Vizier." He tried to put on a smile for her. "Until then, we promise no more roaring to distract you." The vizier smiled and gave a short bow. She glanced at the dead guardsmen, then padded back inside the palace.

The breeze picked up as chain lightning lit the sky. The thunder was much closer this time; the storm was approaching quickly. Ingal ordered the guards to carry their fallen comrades to the north portico for the rest of the night, lest the bodies be rained on. More guards arrived to help as lightning flashed and illuminated the surrounding mountains. They finished moving the bodies just as the first drops fell. Soon only Ingal was left standing in the courtyard.

Ektibal, Ingal thought. This elvish mage could only be Ektibal, court mage to the elvish speaker. Only he would be powerful enough to command the attention of the tower mages and disrupt the lifts. But why? Why would he be there? Did it have something to do with his assassination? And what is this about "mirrored eyes?"

There came a distant hum from the east, which quickly grew until it sounded like an army of horsemen pounding the ground in full gallop. With a vengeful force, a wall of rain reached the palace grounds in windblown sheets. Deafening, it slammed into the granite courtyard. Thunder rolled with it, long and loud. Yet Ingal remained standing where he was.

"My lord!" Metharcus yelled from the doorway behind him, barely audible over the deluge. "The hour is late! The weather is unbearable! Come in, my lord! Come in!"

But Ingal paid little attention. Lost in deep meditation, he stretched his mind to recall a very ancient poem from the most distant edges of the memory, some passing lyric or bit of verse from tens of thousands of years before.

A portion came to him slowly, though he could remember no more of it. He muttered it to himself as he gazed up at the flashing clouds and falling rain.

"Guardians of Nature since first light.
Mirrored eyes to see the way
Reflected stars when in the night
Reflected sun when in the day."

ELEVEN
Shadow

Morning came, and Ingal had slept little. The globes of his study had glowed through the night as he searched his library for ancient legends. Now the floor was littered with antiquated tomes of arcane languages, scrolls so fragile that they started to crumble in his claws, and books paged with imprinted films of precious metal to help them survive the millennia. A few had sat on the shelves unread for many hundreds of years.

Still there was no answer to his dilemma. The words from the night before repeated themselves again and again in his mind. He recited aloud, "Guardians of Nature since first light. Mirrored eyes to see the way … "

And all night there had been that feeling of being watched.

"Old dragon!" Ingal said to himself and yawned loudly. His eyes felt as if they had been scoured by a sandstorm. Hips and shoulders popped as he lifted himself up from his reading area. He twisted his neck and cracked the vertebrae there, cringing, and groaned at the papery rustle of his scales. The muscles of his rear legs ached from leaping at the Padgarun cleric the night before.

Ingal looked down to the elvish cube and the menagerie of priceless books. He thought again of the feeling of being watched. "Metharcus," Ingal called. The doors opened a crack, and the chamberlain stepped through. He looked as haggard as Ingal felt. "Tell the captain of the palace guard to post a sentry on the study until we return."

"Yes, my lord," Metharcus rasped, his voice as dry as autumnal leaves.

"We know you are tired, my friend, but there is much to do this day. Call our bathers. We must refresh our senses before attending the memorial service. Once in the water, we shall tell you of other errands we need run."

"Of course, my lord."

Ingal bid Metharcus to go and make ready and waited for the sentry to show. He turned around and examined the study for a moment. A shadow in a corner by a bookshelf. Did it move? Had it been there a moment earlier? Anger mounted in his weary heart. With a sudden thrust of energy he reached up and grabbed a globe and threw it to the far side of the chamber. Its path curved oddly through the air as it tried to right itself. It smashed into the far wall with a shower of blue-white sparks.

No monster revealed itself. No nightmare loomed from the sudden light to wage battle. Instead, the slowly falling sparks created an army of gleefully dancing shadows before they sputtered and disappeared, leaving only the book-cluttered floor and empty air. If a wraith had been there, it was lost in myriad chaotic shadows from the sparks. Ruining a light globe had succeeded in nothing outside of expressing his paranoia.

Ghosts? he wondered. *No. Senility. We're going senile, just like Rambanor in his last days, seeing specters in the faces of old friends, and hearing demons in the corners. We can't go through that again. Not again! We had never believed we would live this long again.*

For many long minutes he stood there, head down, unwitting victim of the memory. He heard Rambanor's itchy scales drop off, one by one, saw his vision dim, felt his teeth ache. And yet senility had come only at the last for his forebear. Each generation was different; perhaps senility had come to claim his mind sooner.

When Ingal heard the steps of the coming sentry, he put on a noble face, closed the doors from the outside, and made his way to the bathing chamber.

TWELVE
Dedication

Nearly everyone still at Palal Jehai had gathered in the south gardens for the guardsmen's funeral. From pilgrims to viziers, they stood in quiet conclave around the steps leading up to the palace's south entrance where the bodies of the dead guards had been laid for display. The only sound was that of the wind and the mournful, rhythmic chanting of the priests.

Torra sat on a bench in the shade of a maple tree away from the throng. She had put away her Rod of Translation, choosing instead to hear the lamentations of the priests in their native Etollian, missing the meaning of the words and hearing them as simply a soothing song. Her servant and bodyguards stood a close distance away.

Understanding the prayers only reaffirmed her atheism. *What are gods, anyhow?* she thought. *If they exist at all, who's to say they are any more godlike than a parent is to a small child, or a child to a family dog, each in turn seeing the next as some great and unquestionable entity with powers beyond their own? Superstitious nonsense. The world is governed by natural laws and energies that can be manipulated. Gods, if they exist, are merely entities of a higher order, better able to manipulate those energies.*

Torra winced as she shifted in her seat. Her joints were stiff today, and the rash on her arm itched. She reached into her robe pocket and withdrew some of her herbal fruit strips, popping one into her mouth and chewing. *Tired,* she thought. *Dreams* of the rampaging she-elf had kept waking her the night before. The crazed, emerald green eyes. The flying hair. Ferocity and determination etched into every inch of her murderous body.

The priests joined together in a common chant. The priestess for Jonaatha, Goddess of Light, raised her hands to the sky. The priest for Onogoth, God of Darkness, lowered his hands toward the ground. And the Priest of Dramath, God of War, pulled a symbolic sword from its sheath and cut his own scarred palm, letting the blood dribble onto the clean, white sheets of the fallen guards. Other priests and priestesses she could not identify performed similar rites as they chanted.

The congregation of onlookers chimed in for part of the chants, speaking in concert with the priests. Ingal's old chamberlain was among them, eyes closed, one shaking hand outstretched toward the bodies, the other grasping a holy book.

This has been a trip of a lifetime, to be sure. She was an alien here, accustomed to different tongues, different foods, a different way of life altogether. And yet, every year that passed took her farther from those she knew at home, too, as she delved ever deeper into the ways of magic. Before long she would be like her mentor, Master Morikal, old and well-versed in magic, but so used to a life of hiding his talents that he rarely left the guild compound anymore.

Torra pictured herself returning to Taxia and the Astronomy Guild, telling her fellow guildsmen about the trip while seated around the great banquet table in the main hall. The long trip there and back. A rampaging she-elf. Viziers and generals. And, of course, a personal audience with the great Aximdrac. Gold Dragon. Ancient ruler of the White Lands Federation. Protector of Man.

She sighed. When all the stories were told, and she had bathed in the light of fame until that light died down, then what? Back to the mundane life of an academic, continuing her apprenticeship in magic, and looking forward to what? Protecting Taxia with her magic? A land that outlaws the very spells that protect it in times of need?

And then there was Taenos. She missed his strong embrace, wide shoulders, dark eyes. Captain of the militia of Caranamere. He was her first love. But when he learned she was a mage …

The south entrance doors opened, and the priests fell silent. Torra grasped her Rod of Translation. Ingal's advisors filed out one by one to stand in order along the edge of the portico. The last to emerge was the Minister of Audience, who announced, "Bow before the Gold Dragon!"

The congregation did as commanded. Torra stood at the sound of the coming dragon. She watched in awe as he emerged from the darkness of the corridor into full sunlight. Huge and majestic, his golden scales sparkled and shifted with his movements. He stepped to the edge of the stairs and looked out over the funerary attendees.

"I am Ingal Jehai, White Lands Dragon."

Ingal looked out over the hushed crowd, then down at the shrouded bodies. "Dangerous times have once again come to the White Lands, and thus to our palace as well. This morning we gather together to observe the passing of those who have given the ultimate sacrifice guarding us against those dangers. We knew them each by name. We presided over the birth of three of them, and they bore our name as their own.

"With great responsibility comes great danger. These brave men and women understood the dangers they faced, and they rose to the responsibility of defending their nation and its leader against those dangers.

"The White Lands Federation once again faces a confrontation with our neighbor, Ocrin. If war breaks out, as is likely, many more of our brave men and women may give their lives for the freedom of their countrymen. And with the elves, We can only guess at their motives, but that part of the story is surely not finished." He raised his voice. "Sacrifices will be asked of all of us. We must each do our part to end the conflict quickly and efficiently, whether we fight at the ravaged front lines, or whether we stay here, in our warm homes and productive fields toiling away for their sake."

Torra's heart beat faster at the mention of war. In this land where magic was open and freely used when needed, where the Tower of Light was located, no less, what role could a budding mage like her play in the fortunes of nations?

Ingal's voice grow somber, and he assumed a dreamy look. "Over the millennia we have known many a valiant fighter for freedom. Most died at the tip of a weapon, agonized and alone, but confident in the honor of their passing. A precious few ended their lives with the peace of old age. Deep in our memory is inscribed each of their lives.

"Most have fallen away from the memory of mankind, lost to the winds of time. Their tombs, large and small, glorious or humble, lay forgotten and crumbled. The songs sung in their honor are now numb on the tongues of the living. Their languages go unspoken. The glorious empires they protected have no remaining borders. But on the dust of those dauntless bones we have built new empires, new languages, new honors for the living."

Torra reeled at the vast span of time Ingal so casually mentioned. *Imagine,* she thought, *the accumulated knowledge in the mind of a dragon!*

Ingal flared his wings and raised a forefoot in blessing. "We commend the souls of these fallen heroes to the waiting presence of their gods. Their deaths were not in vain, for their service to their nation was honorable and will be remembered and cherished now and long into the future in the memory of the Gold Dragon."

THIRTEEN
An Aging Friend

When the funeral ended, Ingal turned and stepped back into the palace. He stopped in the dim, sterile corridor, empty except for Metharcus, and waited for the chamberlain to close the doors and catch up to him. All other attendees were expected to walk with the bodies to the funeral pyre behind the palace.

Forcing his mind off of the service, Ingal turned his thoughts to the matter of the elves. Their emotions had probably cooled by now, and they would be receptive to discourse.

But what if the elves were violent? He had, after all, told them that he considered carrying out the speaker's request for execution. Now their leader was the prince's bodyguard, Rethuud. Because he was a Dendarin graduate, he was likely a sly fellow and would plan an ambush if he felt negotiation would not be successful. Ingal wondered how he could garner the support of this Rethuud if the elves tried an ambush.

They would have to appear the winner, Ingal thought, however slight the victory. Rethuud's training in strategic thinking would require him to demand the upper hand before discourse could be successful. Ingal wondered how far he could let Rethuud go? To the edge of his own death?

Ingal started walking again. "You have made the provisions, Metharcus?"

"Yes, my lord," Metharcus replied, breathless from the effort of closing the doors and catching up. "A draught of elderberry wine, a dozen cones of cedar incense, and an eight-foot by four-foot roll of fine-woven, living silkbark cloth have been placed just outside of the audience chamber. The cloth has been growing for five years and has lost much of its flexibility, but I imagine it should do."

"And the guards are ready?"

"Yes, my lord."

Ingal nodded. "Very well. Thank you for acting on such short notice."

Ingal glanced down to Metharcus and noticed him holding his chest and shuffling. The man's breathing had increased rapidly. Ingal stopped. He smelled a panicked sweat from the chamberlain. "Metharcus, are you ill?"

Metharcus caught his breath and leaned against the wall. His hand clawed at the fabric over his heart for a moment as sweat beaded at his brow. A moment later he seemed to relax. "I fear a man of my age is not prepared for the events of the last twenty-four hours."

Ingal felt his concentration ebb. With a groan, he let it go and turned all of his attention to Metharcus. "Decauna, you serve us well. We cannot ask more of a loyal subject. But you must guard your health. You are useless to us if you are overtaxed."

Metharcus gave a wan smile and lowered his hand from his heart. His breathing slowed. "My lord, I fear you are correct. I am not the young man I used to be." He looked up at Ingal. "And you aren't the dragon you used to be." He pointed a finger at the dragon and shook it. "I still know you better than anyone living."

Ingal found himself smiling at the old chamberlain scolding him as if he were a little child. "Is this so, *decauna?*"

Metharcus stood away from the wall without support. "There was a time when you would have spent a few moments after such a speech reflecting on your words. Not this 'let's get on to other business' nonsense."

Ingal's humor faded. "There are more pressing issues to attend to."

"And last night," Metharcus continued, ignoring Ingal. "Once upon a decade you would have left the prince's side with a roar and run through the corridors after that assassin, chasing her off into the night and thundering to Peshilaree and back before you would let her go."

Ingal snorted in defiance and raised his head to the ceiling. "How dare you chide us! Are you calling us a coward, Metharcus?"

Metharcus waved his hand. "Not at all! Can't you realize what I'm saying? You're getting old, like me, and like me you've stayed too long in these drafty halls growing frail. You busy your free moments by blessing pilgrims and taking naps. You spend your days and nights hearing viziers and generals whine to each other, reading dispatches, and turning your mind from one bureaucracy to another."

Metharcus put his hand to his chest again and paused to catch his breath. Ingal reached a forefoot to the man to steady him, but Metharcus pushed it away.

The old man pointed toward the doors. "You need to get out there! Out beyond the valley. Find the Iron Dragon and stretch those tight wings like you did in all those adventures you reminisce about. Go find that assassin yourself and teach her a lesson. Get to the war front and bust some Ocrin heads. Fly! Fly before you get old in the head and crumble like your threadbare tapestries."

Ingal tightened his muscles. "Do not lecture us, old man! What do you know of growing old compared to the lives of dragons? We were here feeling stiff and ancient long before …"

"Oh, don't give me that 'older than stone' speech again! Old is old, no matter if you're a ten-year dog, a sixty-year human, or a three-thousand-year dragon! Your joints ache, your back stoops, and you start acting as if the weight of the moons was on your pitiful shoulders. I know what it means to feel old!"

Metharcus steadied himself on the wall again. Ingal sighed and shook his head. More important issues needed addressing, and time was limited.

"I know what you're thinking," Metharcus said. "We don't have time for this, right? Better start considering it now before your heart hurts and you find yourself out of breath." Metharcus stopped a moment to breathe, and then, with a shaking finger and squinting eye, he continued, "And don't tell me I'm not the one to lecture you. Who are you waiting for? Your advisors, who are busy scheming against each other? The pilgrims who worship you? Those quarreling politicians and generals? Some other dragon you see once every century or two?"

Ingal shook his head and replied in a drone, "Yes, Metharcus. We guess you are the one to tell us."

But a memory flashed through Ingal's mind of the Iron Dragon, Tellonta, telling Ingal's forebear that he was too old to lead his people against a powerful foe. Rambanor Jehai was 2,900 years old. "You'll crack up in one good dive," Tellonta said playfully. "Your muscles will fail you, and you'll hit the ground. Then who'll protect your precious White Lands Federation? Better to fly slowly so you don't overdo it, dear friend, and let me do the fighting for you." And with that the youthful Tellonta had launched himself over a cliffside in full dive. Ingal smiled.

The Iron Dragon had a way of knocking some sense into him. Metharcus actually had a lot in common with old Tellonta, in that regard.

Metharcus breathed deeply and stood straight. "As you said, those guards died protecting their nation and the dragon who rules it. But only you can protect your vitality."

Ingal smiled. "No, *decauna*. We have you to protect it as well."

Metharcus gave a crooked smile. He turned and continued down the hall with Ingal at a slow pace. "We were serious, Metharcus. You should take time off and rest. See a priest about your heart. We have worked you too hard."

The chamberlain nodded. "My days are numbered, and soon you will not have me around to argue with." He looked to the ceiling and raised his arms. "Like those guards, I will join Jonaatha and bask in her holy, healing light." His face sagged, and he lowered his arms. In the dim torchlight of the corridor, the shadows cast on his aged skin made him a paper shell of his long lost youth. "You should find a replacement for me."

This episode with the heart was enough to convince Ingal. Sadly, it was getting to be that time. How many chamberlains had come and gone? "Of course. Do you have someone in mind."

"No, my lord. My children know much about my duties, but they do not wish to fulfill the role. Only my daughter, Minia, was interested, may she rest in peace. There are others who could run the palace staff, but there are few who have what it takes to advise you the way I do."

Ingal looked down at the man as he walked, flaring his nostrils. "And what exactly does it take?"

Metharcus flashed a look of incredulity. "Forthrightness, of course, and an excellent sense of timing and organization. It takes an old fool like myself not to be overcome by awe in your presence; no one who is awestruck can give you a straight and honest answer when you need it."

Ingal agreed. The only servants who fit the criteria were nearly as old as Metharcus. He needed someone young enough to last many decades, yet wise, and willing to look a dragon in the eyes.

"We shall think on this."

Metharcus nodded. They walked in silence for a few minutes until Metharcus stopped at an adjoining corridor. "As you suggested, I shall take my leave for the day, my lord. Please forgive me for my moment of raving. This matter of the killing of guards has me a bit melancholy, and I am an old fool."

"Old 'fools' are often the wisest counsel." Metharcus bowed slightly, turned, and shuffled slowly down a side corridor toward the servants' quarters.

Ingal watched with wistful pride until Metharcus turned a corner. He saw in his mind's eye a dozen identical scenes over the life of the chamberlain, each scene replaying further back in time with a slightly younger man, ending with a spry youth. He found himself envying Metharcus, but he wasn't completely sure why.

The old human is right, he thought, tapping the spiked tip of his tail against the granite tiles. We've grown old. Enough self-pity. Time to take matters into our own, leave for a bit of adventure. Dedicate us to our vitality.

But first, there were important matters to attend to.

FOURTEEN
Rethuud

Ingal approached the front doors of the audience chamber. Thirty guards stood at attention, weapons at the ready in case the elves attempted an escape. But escape was impossible, as the doors to the chamber, both the front and rear, were magically sealed. There were no other openings. Ingal had earlier sensed little magic on the elves, so they had no hope of countering his spells and breaking through.

Off to the side lay a roll of silkbark cloth, incense, and a large bottle of wine on top of an ornately carved marble bench.

"Report," Ingal said to the lieutenant in charge.

The lieutenant stiffened. He was young, with dark hair and eyes, new enough to hold his breath in the dragon's presence, trying to suppress his fear. "We've had no contact with the elves, my lord," the lieutenant said, his voice breaking.

"Very well. We will be going in. But there are some important directions that you and the others must follow."

"Of course, my lord." The lieutenant shifted uncomfortably and glanced at the doors. "Shouldn't we wait for the Captain of the Guard and the other guardsmen?"

"No need," Ingal said. "The elves should not pose a challenge for us. Now do as we say. You are not to enter unless we are in dire need. Stay only at the opening to the chamber. If we are attacked, enter the chamber and engage the elves, but under no circumstances are you to *kill* any of them—even in self defense—unless we explicitly order you to. Understood? We need their cooperation."

The young lieutenant nodded, paused to lick his lips, then turned and passed the command on to the others. The guards formed a perimeter around the doors, with Ingal in the center. When all was ready, Ingal barked a *Word of Command.* The doors slowly swung inward.

Ingal saw only one elf in the room, the wounded one he'd noticed earlier, sitting now in one of the high-backed chairs about forty yards away, watching Ingal with sullen eyes. At his feet lay the dead prince.

Ingal looked around the chamber. Nearly a dozen elves were missing. None hid behind the remaining chairs or along the walls. The rear doors to the chamber were still shut.

He said, "Lieutenant. Where are the—?"

A cry echoed from above. Ingal looked up. Elves dropped from their perches over the doorway and onto his broad back, stabbed with their swords. Some were deflected by scales. Others plunged through the skin.

Ingal reared up and roared as the pain engulfed him. Guards ran forth and surrounded the dragon, engaging the elves who fell. But the guards could not reach the elves high on Ingal's back. He thrashed his wings, throwing off a couple more attackers. He reached back with his head and gnashed at the warriors. He couldn't reach them with his teeth even if he tried. At a command, they twisted their blades. The pain blinded Ingal, and he reared again, roaring to the ceiling, thrashing to throw them off of him, but they had him. One move and they could paralyze him.

Death! he thought, and grew suddenly weak. *Death is coming.* He found himself fearing not the pain, but the end of it, when all would grow distant and he would fade out, again, as his forebears had. And the darkness would come, until the offspring would relive, would relive the end of him.

"No!" he yelled. A spell came to him, a powerful shock of energy which would kill all in the room on or around him. Guards. Elves. But he had no choice. He had to save himself. Had to preserve the White Lands. He opened his mouth to chant it.

Then came a sound. It was a low thrum, and with it came the prickling of magic—great magic. He recognized it instantly, and was afraid. The sound was at his neck.

"Call off your men," a voice said in Peshilarn behind his head. It was the prince's Dendarin graduate, Rethuud. "Call them off now, or I'll kill you."

Ingal's mind cleared. If Rethuud meant to kill him, he would have done so already. The pain of swords in his back was excruciating, but the elves had avoided the deadly spots. They wanted to wound only, to force his hand with pain.

"Do you recognize what I hold to your neck?" Rethuud asked.

"It is Ascareth, the Baneblade of the East," Ingal answered in Peshilarn. "We know it well, and its bloody history. Ascareth's blade is a dimensional rip. No earthly substance is immune to its cut."

"That includes your neck, Jehai. Now stop your men and escort us out of here to the griffins, and we will be on our way."

Ingal gingerly looked around him. Two of the elves were wounded, but still able to fight. In contrast, three guardsmen were dead or seriously wounded. The young lieutenant lay unmoving among them, eyes frozen open and looking at Ingal, mouth agape. The air was thick with the scent of human and elvish blood. "Guards," Ingal commanded. "Withdraw and form a defensive perimeter."

The guards stopped their attack and backed away, forming a loose circle around the dragon and elves.

"Good," Rethuud said. "Now take us out of here."

"No."

"Do it or you die."

"If you kill us, our guards will obliterate you and we both will lose. You know that as well as we do." But Ingal was not sure. The remaining elves might well be able to defeat the guards, especially with the baneblade, Ascareth. The elf did not reply.

"What if we give you what you wish?" Ingal asked. "Where would you go? Peshilaree? You would be killed just as surely as your prince was. You are outcasts."

"Outcasts we may be!" Rethuud said. "But we have allies. We know what you do not."

Ingal shifted his weight but stopped abruptly as he felt the gravitational warp of Ascareth at his neck; the hellish energies of its infinitesimally thin blade pulled at his scales like a magnet.

"You realize that the speaker is a great and long ally of ours?" Ingal said. "Refusing to execute you threatens our relationship with him and all of Peshilaree."

"Thus I have a sword at your neck."

"Yet we have the power even now to carry out his wish, at great sacrifice. You would not stand a chance against us."

"You're bluffing," Rethuud said. But the pitch of his voice betrayed his doubt.

"We choose not to kill you—yet—for we have lingering concerns. Clearly a conspiracy has exterminated your prince. We came to the chamber for questioning, not battle."

"No questions. Take us out now!" There came a popping sound, and Ingal realized that Ascareth had sliced into scales. The guards eagerly closed their circle. His heart thumped as he waited for the pain, but the sword had not cut deeply enough to contact flesh.

Ingal thought quickly. "We cannot allow your whole party to leave, but there is a compromise we can offer in which we both benefit."

Rethuud paused before speaking. "What do you suggest?"

All was quiet in the chamber as the guards and elves stood in attentive defense. Ingal heard the drip-drip of his blood onto the marble floor at his belly. The guards rustled nervously, their armor scraping as they positioned themselves to spring.

A humanoid shadow moved along the base of the wall on the far side of the chamber. Ingal wondered if he was seeing things again. No, this was real. But he chose to ignore it, given the urgency of his predicament.

"First answer us this question, Rethuud: Is your prince responsible for the death of Ektibal, as the speaker accuses?"

"The accusation is false, Jehai, just as he said."

"What was the nature of this attack against the White Lands Federation."

The sword caused his scales to sizzle. This time it hurt as it cut into the skin. He detected the burnt-hair smell of his scales searing. "Perhaps I could tell you more *after* you release us. What is your 'compromise?'"

Ingal watched the shadow move along the wall, then it disappeared. Ingal forced himself to focus on the negotiation.

"We shall release your men and the body of your prince, but only after *you* accompany us to Peshilaree. We intend to investigate the assassination and this invasion plot ourselves—

with your help. If we should find the prince to have been guilty, and the mention of the invasion false, then we will kill you and order the death of your men. And if we should fail to return at all, they die also. But if we investigate and find that he is proven true, we will release your men and the prince's body back into your custody."

Rethuud gave a scoffing huff. "You expect me to fly with you to Peshilaree? Whatever for? Why not go alone?"

"Because you have the most stake in convincing us, and you are the best positioned to find out the information we need."

"And how do you know I won't lie to you?"

"We would know," he said, then an idea came to him, "but we believe we may be able to bring along another. An …*unbiased* observer, if you will. A mage we have only just met."

"Very well, but I have conditions of my own."

Ingal flipped his tail. He considered denying the request, taking a hard line. It was usually the best approach to controlling the elves. But if he was to have a trusting rapport with this useful contact, he must be willing to give-and-take. "Name them," he said.

"You must allow me to bring along four of my men … "

"Two. No more."

Rethuud paused. "Fine. The second condition is that you perform the Dirge of the Elf Lords on the prince. If he has been accused of treason, and a Padgarun murdered him, then he will be denied that last respect."

Ingal scowled, but it was a show; he had anticipated this request. "We have seen it performed only once, ten forebears in the past. And it is a very powerful spell. There is no guarantee it will work."

"But you agree to do it."

"Yes. Now kindly remove Ascareth from our neck, and the swords from our back."

Rethuud deactivated Ascareth and gave an order. The other elves removed their blades. Ingal winced as they were withdrawn.

In moments the two forces had withdrawn. The elves formed a defensive line toward the dais, the palace guards, and Ingal toward the main doors.

"One more question, Rethuud," Ingal said. "Your Padgarun cleric, Phasgala? What do you know of her? Why would she carry out the assassination?"

Rethuud tensed at the Padgarun's name and looked down. *They must have been close.* "She served with us for nearly a decade. She was as loyal to the prince—and to me—as any of us were. Or so we thought. I don't know why she acted the way she did."

"The Padgarun do not serve the speaker," Ingal interjected. "She and the speaker would have to have a common reason."

Rethuud shook his head. "I do not know the common reason. Once we are on our way to Peshilaree I will tell you more of what I do know."

"Very well." Ingal turned toward the doors, but then looked back. "Shall we send our priests to attend to your wounds?"

"No," Rethuud said. "Your priests will not touch us!"

Ingal gave a dry chuckle. "They would surely do less harm than your own cleric!" He turned back to the doors and exited, the guards walking with him, dragging along their dead and wounded comrades. "We shall return within a couple hours to perform the dirge." After guards carried in water and fruit for the elves, Ingal closed the doors and magically sealed them.

Without being able to walk through the audience chamber, he would have to go the long way to his quarters. Each step sent searing pain through the wounds on his back. Blood dribbled down his flanks to smear a trail on the floor tiles. The palace priests, and the cleaning staff, would have their work cut out for them.

His mind turned furiously. The War Council would meet at the Keep of Casan in only five days. Five days! It gave little time to crack the elvish conspiracy. Add to that a shadow creature lurking in the palace, *maybe*, defying identification—unless he was senile. And somewhere in the world, he remembered, magic threatened the gods. *Could it be related?*

Ingal cursed at himself. Things had nearly gotten out of control in the audience hall. Too complacent! But he had gotten what he wanted. Rethuud would accompany him to Peshilaree, but would he cooperate? This Rethuud was shrewd, and far more reactive than the typical graduate of the Dendarin Academy. Ingal swore to himself not to underestimate him.

He groaned against the thought of three more guardsmen dead. Their comrades had dragged them out of the audience chamber. There would be more shrouded bodies in the palace courtyard tonight, and another memorial service tomorrow. But he would deliver no speech this time. Time was running out, and there was much to do. They would have to be remembered alongside their brethren.

~ ~ ~

Ingal refused to see visitors as he recuperated, including the viziers. Instead, he dictated letters outlining his commands for the viziers and their generals regarding wartime preparations and battle strategy. This finished, Ingal allowed himself a troubled rest as the priests worked to close his wounds and heal them. The healing would only be partial, for the wounds were deep and would take time, and the priests had used much of their energy by consecrating the dead guards.

At least they hadn't cut his wings, he thought.

"Metharcus," he said. "Prepare our travel vest. We shall be flying to Peshilaree tomorrow morning."

Metharcus appeared drawn and eroded. Like the rest of the palace staff, he had refused rest, physically and mentally, as the standoff had raged in the audience chamber. But his eyes glimmered with sudden excitement.

"I'm glad to hear you have heeded my advice, my lord. But do you think it wise to travel in this condition? Give it a few days, at least."

"There is little choice, *decauna*. Time is short, and every day lost is another gained by our enemies. Nations may depend on it."

"Then I beg you to take guardsmen with you."

"Our guardsmen know not the art of griffin riding. Or would you have them ride us like a donkey?"

"I do not trust the elves. We would all feel better if you had more protection."

"We will keep a close eye on them, Metharcus. But I worry more for you. Get some rest. Delegate the packing of our vest to subordinates. Have servants and guardsmen care for the elves who are held behind. Visit with family in our absence."

Metharcus nodded. "As you wish, my lord. As you wish." But Ingal knew he was lying.

~ ~ ~

That night Ingal approached the audience chamber doors once more, shifting his weight uneasily as he walked against the pain.

Guardsmen lined the hallway and rushed in as Ingal opened the doors, forming a wide, lethal circle around the waiting elves and the bodies of their fallen. The prince's corpse lay in the middle of the circle.

Supplies were carried in. Soon the prince's body was placed on the ornate bench and lightly covered by green silkbark cloth. Cedar incense burned. A bejeweled goblet of elderberry wine was ceremoniously passed hand to hand for each of the elves to drink. A guardsman held the goblet to Ingal's mouth and poured the last bit over his serpentine tongue.

Torches were lit, and soon shadows danced like wraiths across the high walls. Ingal watched them, wondering if a true wraith slithered amongst them. Yes, he decided, he was being watched by one at that moment.

Ingal forced the shadows out of his mind and focused on the prince. More spell than song, the Dirge of the Elf Lords was the most ancient rite of the elves, and possibly the world. It preserved the bodies of elvish speakers, princes and princesses, and other high nobility and warriors for millennia, before their bodies were placed in Eshenakaree, the lake where the elves believed their species originated. It had been this way since the very first speaker, Peshiluud, died. *This* prince, however, would have to be consecrated on a marble bench until his name was posthumously cleared.

All grew quiet. Ingal reached back into the memory and pulled forth the words of the dirge. He stood high upon his rear legs, chest tight, wings and arms outstretched in a fearsome display. The pain in his back dissipated. He activated the magic region of his mind and began to sing.

In perfect Peshilarn, Ingal's voice rumbled and fell in that ancient elvish song of noble death and rebirth, starting slowly then building into a booming rhythm that pounded at his chest. As he built to the climax, so too did the magic build in power, flowing through him in warm waves to the prince, preserving the prince's body with ancient energies from deep within Irikara. The walls and torches dimmed as the body sparkled with a popping blue mist.

The elves joined in the singing, slowly at first, then as one voice, scaling up and down at the dragon's lead. Many lowered their swords and raised their heads to the ceiling. Their eyes glossed over. It seemed to Ingal that the energy of the spell permeated them and filled them to the point of overflowing. Soon the very stone seemed to echo back the accompanying voices of all the elvish nobles who had passed away in days of yore.

Yet the elves kept their swords drawn, and Rethuud's eyes never left Ingal.

FIFTEEN

Triumvirate

Ingal laid in his mud bath and tried not to move. His usual procedure upon lying down was to roll in the mud and warm his whole body. But the herbal poultices stuck to his wounds would come off if he did so. Disturbing the priests for new ones would tax their patience—they had the souls of the dead guards to pray for.

He tried to relax and breathe in the gentle scent of lavender from the mud, soothe himself in the warmth. But the pain in his back kept him from meditation.

Elves! he thought. Not for many generations had the elves bothered him or his forebears so. Normally level-headed, they typically …

Ingal jerked up. The shadow creature. He sensed it before seeing it, like the change in pressure before a storm. The magical energy it emitted was almost strong enough to see. It stepped out of a corner of the room, walked along the wall like the two-dimensional projection of a man. Skulking no longer, it strode boldly along the wall to stand directly before him.

Ingal stared at it for a long moment and wondered if he dare acknowledge what might be a figment of some emerging senility.

With a grunt, Ingal sat up, wincing. He might as well humor this delusion. "Yes, shadow, we see you. Your reasoning is unknown, and your trespass unwelcome. We will fight if necessary. Make known your purpose!"

The shadow creature bowed. Before Ingal could grasp the concept of a respectful shadow, the wraith broadened, taking a muscular shape. It became three-dimensional, stepping out of the wall. Quickly its features colored, as if a veil were thrown off. A man—a warrior—stood before Ingal where the shadow creature had been.

Ingal tensed and activated his magic center. This was a Shadow Emissary—a nonliving projection used by gods and other powerful entities to interact with living mortals.

The warrior was tall for a human. Dark black skin. Slim face. His body rippled with muscles half-hidden by a bronze chest plate and a wide, red and white silk sash across his shoulder. Thick legs were bare above sandals. At the warrior's waist hung a sheathed broadsword over a red and white striped tunic. A tall, conical hat, red and white and encircled with bronze about the base, sat upon his head like a statement of control for all to see. Silk coursed down from the back of his hat to lie over his shoulder in a ripple of ironic serenity. It was a ruler's hat. An ancient ruler from …

"Inlai'chi'a," Ingal said. "We know you. Noc Ang Soon. You died millennia ago."

The warrior gave a slight nod and took two steps forward. Ingal could not smell him, nor hear his footsteps. The thought of senility reentered his mind. But power loomed there, threatening to explode from the confines of the warrior's corporeal form, power enough to twist reality. It froze Ingal's legs to the spot, caused him to rear his head back in respect, yet there was something vaguely familiar about the sensation.

"No, Gold Dragon, you are not imagining this." The warrior's voice was that of the long-dead Noc Ang Soon. Deep. Gruff. Speaking the language of Eshnigara, now long forgotten by mankind.

Ingal blinked. Whatever this creature was, it was trying hard to fool him. "Come no closer. State your purpose or be gone."

"I am your Creator, Gold Dragon. Do you not feel it?"

"No," he lied. He certainly felt *something*. "We feel only the bother of one trespassed against." Ingal quickly went through his list of psychic spells that could be used to attack someone in mental contact, *Mental Shield*, *Terror Probe*, *Psychic Whip*, others, but no spell he knew could counter the strength of magic emanating from the entity. In fact, it would probably take a renegade spell to have any effect at all.

It held up a broad hand to the dragon. "It is not trespassing when all of the world is ours to control. I am one of three gods who created this world. We are the *Triumvirate*.

"Time is short, Gold Dragon. You clearly recall the human form I have taken. Do you remember the purpose for which he fought—the purpose for which he died?"

Ingal glanced through the open doorway. No servants were present to witness. "Noc Ang Soon led his fledgling nation against the land now called Quisha, to which they had once belonged."

"Why?"

"For freedom from the Quisha Emperor." A memory emerged, and Ingal added, "They wanted control."

"Of what?" the entity said. It looked up to the ceiling in concern, but Ingal saw nothing there. "Answer quickly."

Ingal frowned at being commanded, but something clicked in Ingal's memory. He now remembered. He decided to humor the entity. "They wanted control of the renegade magic discovered in the bowels of Irikara." Even as he said the words, Ingal could not recall the outcome of the war, save that Noc Ang Soon's army was victorious. The final events were forgotten! This distracted him even more than the trespasser. Never before, in all of the memory, had he or his forebears failed to recall something of such obvious importance.

"Yes," the entity said, clasping his hands. "You have forgotten the event. A creature with an unerring memory has forgotten. Do you think it coincidence? But it is not I who erased it. I will remind you. The wild magic they sought was gained and cast by the very warrior whose body I now possess. But it was not the first that his people had wielded it, was it?"

Ingal anxiously swished his tail through the mud. If he pounced, the entity would not have time to draw his sword. But something told him that nothing physical could control it, and this memory problem was compelling. "No, not the first time. Their most ancient myth told of a guru who had discovered the magic and performed miraculous deeds."

The entity looked again with concern toward the ceiling. *Why?* Ingal wondered. The god grimaced, his brow tightening as if hit by a sudden arrow. But his voice still seemed untroubled. "And why had the magic been hidden?"

Ingal thought back into the memory. Very ancient, the recollection came slowly. "The gods," he answered. "The gods had hidden it, because … "

"The *Outer* Gods, who stole the world from us. The ones worshipped by the world in place of us. They hid the magic because the magic was untamed, out of their control." The warrior tightened his fist. "Do you remember?" The entity looked intently into the dragon's eyes.

Something changed in Ingal's mind, and he tried to shake it off. There was a hole there in the memory, a void of forgetfulness, odd and unwieldy.

A mental spark set forth a flood of recollection as if water were poured in from above to fill the void. And the memory rushed in. His tenth forebear, Bimin Wang Onoc, nearly twenty-thousand years before, stood upon a vast battlefield littered with torn bodies and shattered war engines. Corpses of man and beast burned and obscured the sun with their foulness. There came a flash across the battle plain. The smoke glowed a brilliant blue-white. Chain lightning rippled through the haze close to the ground. The dead and dying around him jumped and quivered as electricity shot through them. A man stood at the epicenter, legs and arms spread wide. Raw power coursed uncontrolled over his tensed body. *Noc Ang!* The warrior's face was an impossible mask of anguish and victory, seemingly mindless with incomprehension.

And beside him stood a form. "We see now," Ingal said. "It was *you*, wasn't it? We sense your energy. *You* were with Noc Ang that day. *You* were the giver of the magic."

The entity smiled. "No, Gold Dragon. I *was* the magic."

The ceiling shimmered bright white over their heads. The entity looked up and, grimacing, seemed to will the light to fade away.

"What's happening?" Ingal asked.

"The Outer Gods do not approve of my presence here. We have little time to talk."

"Why have you come?"

"I have come to remind you of your heritage," the entity said. It shifted shape. The large, strong form of Noc Ang Soon melted away and shrunk. It reformed into the shape of the small child Ingal had dreamt about the day before. In the boy's piccolo voice it said, "I have come to remind you of what has been lost, and what will be regained. The wild magic is my life force, and the life force of the world. It is *of* me. It is *of* all three of us, the *Triumvirate.*"

"And what do we call *you.* Do you have a name?"

"We are nameless—for now. The Outer Gods have forbidden our names to be communicated, erased them from memory, but we will soon overcome their restrictions. Irikara is ours, as a work of art is that of a sculptor or an artist. We created the dragons, the elves, the dwarves, and all things material. But control was lost to the Outer Gods." Here the entity looked up at the ceiling. "Control must be regained. Our names remembered."

"And who created the humans?"

The boy smiled mischievously. "I must know your loyalties, my child. I created you. I can destroy you. But my love for you demands mercy. You are special to us."

Light again flashed through the ceiling, unbidden and now unchallenged by the entity. A rip of white luminance. The ceiling parted, and Ingal saw through it like a portal to the heavens, filled with nebulous reds and blues. But the entity gritted its teeth and reached a clenched hand toward the opening as if willing it to close.

"Seek out the Iron Dragon," it said, again morphing into the form of Noc Ang. "He knows the truth. It is for him to convince you. The wild magic is back, my child. Soon it will be back to stay. The battle for Irikara has begun!"

"And if we cannot remember this wild magic again?" He backed away from the portal.

The entity looked at Ingal, his eyes flashing myriad colors, his body warping and fading. "There is one here who can help you, Gold Dragon, a scholar of the stars, a mage in touch with our presence."

The entity reformed to a Shadow Emissary against the wall, and was briefly joined by two others, monstrous and looming at its sides. Strings of pulsing electricity shot between them and the ceiling like an exchange of weaponry. A flash of light. Blinding. Ingal looked away.

When his vision cleared, Ingal found the room empty. No strange lights. No Shadow Emissaries. Nothing but a scorch mark on the wall. The vast energy of the entity slowly drained away, leaving Ingal deep in thought. Who or what had he just seen?

Were we just visited by a god?

SIXTEEN

Invitation

Once again Torra stood outside the great audience chamber. The doors loomed over her like mammoths, and the little dragon statues watched her from the ceiling corners of the foyer. She scratched absentmindedly at the rash on her arm.

The last time she stood here she had been accompanied by about a hundred others, the viziers and generals, the scholars, and the elves. Now she stood alone in this large chamber save for a dozen guards lining the wall, scrutinizing her with glistening eyes half-hidden in the shadows of their frightful gold masks.

Through the doors she heard the muffled yet powerful voice of the dragon. Torra had been packing to leave when the page came for her. The palace was too dangerous. She had done her duty and delivered the stone. Now it was time to go. Even her Taxin bodyguards told her so. Only a warrior could feel capable of dealing with dragons roaring, guards slashing, and elves running about cutting people open and dissolving their eyes with globes of acid. She shuddered.

What could the dragon want with her now? Deciphering another dispatch from the elves? Astronomy advice? Surely not advice on magic!

The broad doors opened slowly and soundlessly. Across the vast space of the audience chamber lay the Gold Dragon on his dais. His advisors were stepping around him, exiting the chamber through the doors in the rear of the chamber.

"Come in, Com Gidel," the dragon said.

Torra's heart turned a summersault in her chest, but she found her feet moving forward. The doors closed behind her.

She halted. The tiles at her feet were stained umber from half-cleaned blood. She quailed at the sight, wanting to turn and run back through the doors. The smell of iron lingered in the air, mixed with a heavy, burnt cedar incense and an unexpected tinge of cinnamon.

"We apologize for the state of our audience chamber, Torra," Ingal said. "Please. Come forward away from the worst of it."

Torra stepped around the stains toward the dais. By the time she stood before Ingal and bowed at the waist, the advisors had left her and the dragon alone in the chamber.

The dragon studied her. His eyelids drooped from fatigue. He moved sluggishly, wincing as if pained, and a thin patch of scales at his neck was burnt. To meet with her in such a state must surely indicate something larger than advice on star charts. She lowered her eyes and waited.

Ingal snuffled. "There is an odd smell of sulfur about you, Com Gidel, very faint. Why do you carry sulfur here?"

Torra blinked back surprise. "Sulfur? No sulfur, my lord."

"Hmm," said the dragon, and sniffed at her. Torra took a step back, wondering if she had annoyed him. Should she have apologized anyhow? Why sulfur?

The dragon narrowed his eyes as he examined her. "You have a rash developing on your arm."

Torra looked down at her arm and noticed a redness near her wrist. It was the mystery illness. "Oh, that!" She thought fast for a less-alarming excuse than the disease she suffered. "There was a plant I brushed up against a couple days ago as we started up the mountain. Just a reaction to it."

"Ah," Ingal said, seeming to relax. "You should have our priests look at it before it spreads."

Ingal's face grew more serious, if such a thing was possible for a dragon, and his voice took on a more solemn tone. "There is a time in each generation of dragon when the world turns on its side, and all things that seem in balance topple. Now is such a time, Torra." Ingal leaned forward and placed a hefty forefoot on the top step of the dais. "We feel it in the air, taste it almost. Wheels are turning that will decide the fate of nations. The Stone of Lethori indicated it to be so, and now we see indications of it."

Torra couldn't think, couldn't move. The strength of Ingal's words boded some horror she could not fathom.

"Since last you met with us," Ingal continued, "we were visited by a very powerful entity, perhaps a god. Have you ever heard of a trio of gods called the 'Triumvirate'?"

Torra blinked. The Gold Dragon was asking her about religion? "I'm not sure I'm the one you should ask, my lord, for I am an atheist."

The dragon reared back his head. "An atheist?" The solemnity in his voice suddenly vanished. "Surely you have seen priests heal the wounded."

The sudden shift in topic caught Torra unawares. "Yes," she said, trying to focus, "but in each instance they have also applied herbs or medicines which, on their own, can explain the subject's recovery."

"Priests do more than heal, Com Gidel. They bless the needy, prophesize the future, and interpret the wishes of the gods."

"And who can dispute that the needy would not otherwise have had good fortune," Torra replied, "or that the prophecies are at best broad interpretations that could be applied to every occasion, or that the wishes of the gods are mere delusions?"

Ingal laughed, strong and echoing, yet tinged with relieved joviality. "Our advisors debated for nearly two hours about this and came to no conclusions. None had heard of the Triumvirate, but they all took our word seriously. And now we meet with you, a scholar from a distant land who questions even the word of a dragon!"

Torra lowered her eyes. "I mean no disrespect, my lord."

"No, no. No disrespect at all, Com Gidel. No offense was taken." Ingal gave a quick chuckle. "Your skepticism is refreshing in a palace where nearly everyone takes our beliefs as seriously as scripture—literally in many cases." The Gold Dragon grew serious again. "But we have diverged from the question. Have you heard of a trio of gods called the Triumvirate who claim to have created the dwarves, elves, and the dragons?"

Torra thought for a moment before saying, "There are at least a couple of cultures that believe in a trio of supreme gods: the Marshdwellers of Ocuulnuz, and the Lion Men of the plains west of Alman. But their creation myths, as far as I know, don't explain species or cultures besides their own. There are other cultures which do, but in those cases there is either a single god or a pantheon of gods numbering more than three."

Ingal dipped his head in thought, a foot-long claw tapping at the dais step. "Ah!" Torra said, raising a finger. "There is one possibility that I had nearly forgotten."

Ingal looked back to Torra. "Yes?"

"The elves, my lord."

Ingal shook his head. "The elves believe in a number of invisible nature spirits, which they call *eshenae*, or 'spirits of the world.' There is one for every species of living thing."

"Yes," Torra said. "But there is something else. Something I read one time." She concentrated, saw again the gray, bound tome in Master Morikal's library, gazed once more at the bookworm-eaten pages. She saw the relevant pages clearly in her mind. "An explorer who visited the elvish land of Peshilaree remarked that there is a type of wildland elvish cleric called a *Pagarn*, or *Padina*, or something like that."

Ingal's eyes widened. "*Padgarun?*"

"Yes, that's it! The explorer wrote that they worship different gods than the other elves, ancient gods that predate modern elvish beliefs. Gods of natural forces. The Padgarun were exceedingly xenophobic, and shared little with him, but he believed that the ancient gods were a trio, for each ritual performed by the Padgarun that he secretly witnessed was performed in three steps. Those elves even bore a symbol representing their gods—a triangle within a circle."

Torra stopped short as Ingal scraped his claws across the bonerock tiles—a high, piercing screech. She almost bolted as he gritted his razor-sharp teeth and hissed, head down in concentration.

"My lord!"

Ingal seemed to compose himself, then looked back to Torra. "Do you know what a Padgarun looks like, or how one acts?" he asked.

"No, my lord."

"It was a Padgarun that attacked and killed our guards yesterday."

The she-elf!

"I saw her from the north wing library," Torra said. "I saw her kill those guards."

A sadness briefly clouded Ingal's eyes. "We must learn more about this Padgarun religion. How is it we could not have known?"

Torra scratched at her wrist. "I'm glad I could be of use to you, my lord. But I'm afraid that religions are not my expertise. Surely you have advisors more qualified."

"In many ways, yes, yet in two hours' time they were unable to tell us even this bit of information." Ingal paused and watched Torra a moment before adding, "What *do* you consider to be your expertise, Com Gidel?"

"I know magic, to some small extent compared to the Tower mages, but I would have to say, astronomy."

Ingal shook his head. "You know much about that field. Of this we have no doubt. But it is not your expertise, for there are many, many scholars around the world who share in it and are more advanced, we think. No, your *true* expertise is your knowledge of renegade spells."

Torra took another step back. "Indeed I know a lot on the subject, my lord. But again, surely there are mages in your sphere of influence who are more knowledgeable."

"We are afraid not, Com Gidel. Our Advisor of Magic, Wu Tian, knows little of renegade spells, and the great towermasters have not replied to our hails. Even experienced mages around the world disdain speaking or writing on the subject for fear of running afoul of the masters of the three Towers of Magic. We must take advantage of the resources We have on hand. It falls on *you* to advise us, for now."

A curious look came over the dragon's face. Torra wasn't sure, but she thought it was a mix of amusement and curiosity. He was being careful, that much she was sure of.

She said, "Earlier you referred to my interest in renegade spells as a 'dangerous pastime.' In what way can it be of use to you, my lord?"

Ingal sighed and shifted his weight, wincing as he moved. "In your studies of renegade spells, have you ever associated one with the lands of Quisha or Inlai'chi'a?"

Torra calmed her mind and concentrated on the issue. "There are two, my lord. The more recent deals with a tale that is told in Inlai'chi'a about a mage who summoned a tsunami to wash away a coastal town. It was his revenge upon a university of magic located there which had opposed his experimentations in creating life. Everyone knew it was he who cast the spell, but none were strong enough to challenge him. In the end it was his concubine who caught him. After making love, she tied him to his bed and gagged him so that he could not utter a spell. At this point mages from the Tower of Balance came and punished him by freezing him in a glacier high upon Wontu Mountain. The spell, *Tsunami*, is now in the keeping of the Tower of Balance."

To her astonishment, Ingal seemed completely ignorant of the tale. It was a common story as far as renegade spells go, and yet the dragon tilted his head and widened his eyes in a look of rapt attention.

"The second is much older," she continued. "To my knowledge, the only remaining source of the tale is what is engraved on the wall of an ancient monastery in western Quisha."

She continued, "Back into the fog of time, the land of Inlai'chi'a had once been part of the Quisha empire, but the discovery of a 'great magic' had allowed them to break free and declare independence."

Ingal tightened his muscles and leaned forward, aquiver with such sudden excitement that Torra feared he would lunge upon her. "Please. Please continue," he said.

Torra continued slowly, her eyes on Ingal. "A renowned warrior had searched for and found some ancient, great magic buried in the deepest caverns of the world. Upon coming back to the world of light, he announced his find and raised a massive army against the Quisha emperor. Civil war ensued, culminating in a final, massive battle. When all seemed lost, the warrior cast his magic."

"And what spell was it?" Ingal asked.

"Whatever name it possessed has since been lost to time, to my knowledge. But its effects were undeniable. All enemies were obliterated, vaporized in a massive blast of energy, while his own soldiers were left unharmed and his dead soldiers were resurrected to fight again. The great warrior, however, went insane. Unable to tell friend from foe, he was on the verge of casting the spell again and annihilating everyone. His own generals killed him before he had the chance."

Ingal bowed his head in thought.

"One other thing, my lord," Torra continued. "The tale says that the Gold Dragon was at that final battle, and was untouched by the magic. Was a forebear of yours truly there, and you play a game of ignorance with me, or was this even before *your* memory?"

Ingal sighed. "The Gold Dragon was there, Com Gidel, and we remember things before and after that battle. But the memory of the renegade spell was not in our recollection."

"I don't understand," Torra said. "I would think something such as this would surely be memorable for you and your forebears."

"You would think so," Ingal said, "but it seems we have a weakness. We remembered the spell only today, when we were visited by a god of the Triumvirate. He called it 'wild magic'. Yet even now the recollection fades from the memory, as would all memories of renegade spells, it seems. Thus we called you here for this private audience. You see, not only do you know more than most mages about renegade spells, but the Triumvirate actually mentioned you when they visited us."

"Me?"

"You can help us, Com Gidel. We need your aid to remember, for this 'wild magic' is now a necessary issue."

Torra could barely breathe. Had the Gold Dragon just asked her to serve him? Truly? "I will do what I can, my lord."

"Excellent. We leave for Peshilaree tomorrow."

Torra hesitated a moment. "By 'we', do you mean only yourself, or am I to go with you?"

"Why, you're going with us, of course. You cannot very well advise us from a distance of hundreds of miles!"

Torra looked at the tile floor. A drop of dried blood lay near her feet. "I don't think I can do that, my lord."

"It is a chance for knowledge, Com Gidel, and adventure. Journey with us and the elves, Torra, and you will forever be grateful for the experience."

"With elves?"

"Yes. Three will accompany us, flying on griffins."

Torra heard again the she-elf's murderous cry echo through the corridors, saw her slashing at the guards, witnessed the griffin bite through a guard's thick shoulder plate.

And the melted face.

Torra coughed and backed quickly toward the door. "You … you have the wrong woman. I can't. I'm not made for that."

Ingal rose and stepped quickly down the dais. To Torra it seemed as if he were lunging toward her, angry at her refusal. She slipped on the tile floor and landed on her back onto a bloodstain. She yelped and rushed back onto her feet.

"I can't!" Torra walked hurriedly to the doors. Was he following? She increased her pace. "I can't!"

"We leave at dawn from the front courtyard," Ingal called to her, still at the dais steps. "It is an opportunity of a lifetime, Com Gidel. Don't let the adventure end so soon, Torra!"

"No!" she yelled, reaching the doors and swinging one open with a grunt. Globes of acid. Melting. Face melting. *The elves won't get me!*

She ran through the doors past stunned guards. Then she was in the corridors near her room, tan robes fluttering, shoes clopping double time on bonerock tiles. She had to pack. She had to leave this place. Leave right away.

SEVENTEEN

Summons

Two hours had passed since the Taxin, Torra Com Gidel, had refused Ingal's invitation. Had he misjudged her? She was timid, but he sensed a certain boldness at her heart. If the elves were involved with the Triumvirate, and if the Triumvirate was aiding them with "wild magic," he could certainly use her knowledge of renegade spells.

Ingal lay in his study with his head facing the elvish dispatch. He had ordered the light globes to continuously circle him, slowly, creating a swirling light pattern that glittered and danced on the golden swirls of the cube's filigree lettering.

On the table to his left was a stack of petitions from magistrates, noblemen, and pilgrims. Nearly all were from the state of Alneri, desperate pleas for more troops to protect them against the growing numbers of Ocrin warriors at the border there. Exactly how many were on the border with Alneri? His spies there were missing, or at least had failed to report in, and the numbers of troops quoted in the petitions varied greatly.

The state of Namistad also bordered Ocrin, and some reports stated that Ocrin forces were stronger there. Yet why were there so few petitions for help from that state?

And now the viziers were begging for the chance to meet with him again about war plans. Somehow this cube seemed more important than the possibility of war with Ocrin.

"It can't be coincidence," he whispered. "War is looming. Mysterious gods. The elvish speaker requests the murder of his own son. Then the prince's assassination by a Padgarun. What is the connection?"

Ingal closed his eyes and thought back to his encounter with the Triumvirate god. What had he said about "wild magic"? It was fading fast. His infallible memory was failing. He was a dragon, damn it! He was a creature of magic, yet the most powerful magic was beyond his recall?

He slammed a fist against the study floor, rattling the tables and causing the pile of petitions to roll off and scatter across the carpeting, coming to rest among the mess of books from his studies the night before.

Guardians of Nature since first light. Mirrored eyes to see the way. Why couldn't he remember where that verse was from? "What in eternity is going on?" he roared.

He calmed his mind, meditated for several moments, activated his magic center. The mages of the Tower of Light should have answers. He waved a forefoot in the air in front of him and chanted, *Mirosti colum miniscum, talen torunis.* A fog developed and coalesced into the Council mirror. As he had before, Ingal stated to the mirror, "I am Ingal Jehai, White Lands Dragon. We address the Tower of Light." He waited. As before, no one answered. No face appeared. He chanted again, this time addressing the Tower of Balance. Still no answer. He repeated it once more for the Tower of Darkness. Finally he gave up and negated the spell.

Ingal shook his head. He needed answers. All three Great Towers of Magic refused his hails. His advisors were useless. Com Gidel wouldn't help him.

He lowered his head and raised a forefoot. At the command, the globes stopped circling and returned to their usual places over him. He sighed and looked around at the jumble of books along the walls. It seemed there was only one way he could get the answers he needed. It was time to summon Azartial.

~ ~ ~

Night fell before Ingal gathered his strength and cleared his mind. He ordered all his servants away for the evening so that his personal quarters were empty of life besides him. No witnesses. No one to get hurt.

When he was ready, he rose from his place in the study and proceeded down the corridors, past the audience chamber doors, past the sleeping chamber, past the egg chamber. He came to a set of double doors. They had been hidden a thousand years before, but repeated use over the millennia had rendered them easily visible. He reached out and traced a symbol upon their surface with a claw, and they opened soundlessly. He lumbered through and down a darkened ramp beyond, closing the doors behind him with a swish of his tail.

With a Word of Command, braziers along the walls burst into flame and settled into a steady glow. A broad cavern unfolded before him, a chamber he thought of as the Treasury. This was the oldest part of the palace; this cavern predated the building and was home to the Gold Dragon long before humanity knew of the cave's existence. Flame light wavered on argent goblets, jeweled finery, and gold-encrusted weaponry along the walls. Works of art lay stacked and organized in aisles. Some objects glowed of their own accord.

But Ingal was not interested in this tonight. He moved down an adjoining corridor and came to a solid bronze door. It took more than an arcane tracing or a Word of Command to pass through. The unique spell of opening was long and complicated before he gained entry. After passing through, he locked the doors behind him with a similar spell. This was the most secure room in all the palace—perhaps in all that part of the world.

Braziers lit, Ingal entered another large cavern, completely bare except for a series of circles and runes upon the floor. This was the Conjuring Chamber.

Composing himself, he sat in the middle of the largest circle. Using a large stylus of chalk, he made some final touches to the design on the floor, drawing details and mumbling a Protection spell. Then, clearing his mind, he began a long incantation, allowing his voice to slowly grow louder, from a murmur to a whisper, whisper to speaking voice, speaking to shouting, shouting to roaring. The vocals were complicated, contrapuntal polyphonies ranging from bass to contralto, with entwined harmonics that strained his lungs to the edge of asphyxiation.

The cavern around him transformed outside of the circle. The walls disappeared behind blue and red fluorescent clouds that roiled around the circle as if blown by tempest winds. Multicolored lightning flickered in those clouds, pulsing with Ingal's words. Half-shadowed figures of beasts and men came and went in the clouds, never completely corporeal.

The magical energy was like a lighthouse in the haze of other dimensions, calling other entities to it like moths to a flame. Typically, beings of great power would leer through the glowing haze. Gods, or demons, or others that defied description. If Ingal lost concentration for even a moment, they could enter the circle and tear him apart, or worse, enslave his mind.

Oddly, the entities were missing this night, but there was a deeper energy, far more powerful, as if whole pantheons of gods watched from a distance. That concerned him even more.

With a final shout, Ingal finished his spell. The room grew suddenly silent, no echo. The swirling, glowing clouds outside the circle made no sound, no physical wind, as they whipped past him.

Speaking the ancient language of dragonkind, Draconii, Ingal commanded, "Come, Footman of the Ether. Appear before us, for your name is Azartial, and you are a servant of the Draconii forever!"

Through the clouds emerged a demon, formed like a very slender, almost snake-like dragon, but at best, a fifth the size of Ingal. Slick blue flames dashed over its body. Thin, amber-colored wings stood out at right angles like dagger blades. The anger it emitted was palpable even from the safe confines of the circle.

"What do you demand of me, Gold Dragon?" The demon's speech was meltingly smooth. "Why do you again bother me?" Azartial tested the circle by poking toward Ingal with one of his talons. The air over the edge of the circle sparked blue and white where touched. The demon jerked his forefoot away in pain and ran a blue, serpentine tongue over the digit to soothe it. "Can't you solve your own problems?"

"A question you will answer," Ingal said. "Who are the Triumvirate?"

Azartial's eyes gleamed in secret mischief. The demon grinned, but he nervously picked at his scales. "There are questions not meant to be answered, mortal."

Ingal tightened made a fist. "But answer them you will, demon. Who are the Triumvirate?"

The demon suddenly looked back into the mist. Ingal sensed it too. Someone of great power watched from the other plane. When Azartial turned back around, his eyes were wide, his nostrils flared, and his slim wings quivered. "There are powerful obstacles. Gods interfere."

"Who are the Triumvirate?" Ingal insisted. Allowing distraction could be seen as weakness. "What wild magic do they wield?"

"You ask too much," Azartial said, taking a step back, seeking to disappear into the mists.

"You will do as we say!" Ingal Jehai roared. He pounded his forefoot on the floor and shouted a one-word spell, "*Chrostia!*" Lightning arced from the circle and coursed over Azartial. The demon screamed in agony, high and piercing, animalistic. The shrill cries matched the demon's thrashing. The flames on its body danced chaotic with the spikes of electricity.

Ingal stopped the punishment and watched intently as the demon returned to a submissive posture, glaring at the dragon with eyes full of murder.

"Answer our questions … Now!"

The smoothness of the demon's voice had vanished. "I would call you a bastard if the term had any relevance to dragons." The demon hissed like a snake, then said, "Those you call the Triumvirate were the first, the Makers of your pitiful world." Then in a whisper, "It is forbidden to call them each by name." The demon cringed, glancing madly into the mists behind him. "They had great power, but they were divided, foolish. The other gods conquered them and drove them into obscurity, imprisoned in the energies of the world they created."

The mists flashed red and blue, and the demon abruptly stopped speaking. A low rumble shook the room.

"How?" Ingal asked. "How are they imprisoned?"

Azartial gritted his teeth, eyes darting. "They are weaker than stone. I dare not say more."

"Say it!"

The mists flashed again. The unseen entity was exerting its power. The demon shuddered and growled. "I will not say more."

"You will! What do the Triumvirate have to do with the elves of Peshilaree?"

Azartial whined and rolled his eyes, cowering from unseen forces. "Answer us!" Ingal's mind was clouding with fatigue. He could not keep this up much longer.

Azartial looked back to Ingal and cringed, whispering, "It is better to ask what they don't have to do with the elves." Then, in a softer tone that even Ingal had a difficult time hearing, Azartial added, "If the elves have their way, the names of the Triumvirate gods will be spoken aloud within days, by he with the mirror eyes." He leaned forward, almost touching the field. "They are the elves, just as they are you."

Mirror eyes! Ingal thought, remembering the lyric he had remembered. *Mirrored eyes to see the way.* He was too exhausted to force the demon to explain this riddle, and Azartial seemed unable to say more. Fatigue washed over him, but he tried to project a strong appearance. Azartial knew more, he was sure of it. But Ingal knew he would have to offer some sort of enticement or protection to the demon before Azartial would tell more.

In a rumbling voice, he said, "We have command of entities far greater than you, servant! Go forth and discover more. We will call on you soon for information. Tarry too long or inform anyone of your mission, and you will pay a price too horrible to mention!"

"I'll see you soon, Gold Dragon." Azartial smiled, his fangs showing, and backed into the clouds, disappearing.

Ingal restated his incantation, backwards, starting at a roar and slowly decreasing in volume until he merely murmured, the clouds disappearing as he did so. It took all of his concentration to pronounce the syllables correctly, subtly, until finally the mists were gone, the air was normal, and the cavern around him returned to its original dimness.

Ingal's breath rattled in his throat. His mind fogged. He found it difficult to keep his head raised.

But he was not finished. Another spell to unlock the bronze doors to leave, then again to relock them when he exited.

Once outside and indeed finished, Ingal collapsed to the floor in a heap, uncaring for the cold, hard stone or the damp air. One blink, then another, and he fell into a deep, dreamless sleep.

EIGHTEEN
Indecision

For the third time that morning, Torra stood at the window of the north wing library looking out to the front courtyard. Earlier the shrubbery had cast long shadows from the sunrise. Now they stood in luminous morning light.

She scratched at the red splotches on her arm, then pulled out the little bottle of salve. The itching went away with its application.

Torra remembered Ingal's words. *It is an opportunity of a lifetime, Com Gidel. Don't let the adventure end so soon.* Master Morikal had said nearly the same thing about this trip. *Live for the adventure,* her old mentor had said.

There had been no sleep the previous night. Finally she had given up and found her way to the library window before dawn, stretching her cramping legs. She had watched the courtyard all morning, traveling back and forth from her chambers in indecision. She was packed to leave for Taxia within an hour of her last audience with the dragon, but she stalled. "I'll wait until dawn," she had told her three Taxin bodyguards, but dawn came and went. Then she had sent Olos on an errand for fresh spring water for the trip, then for new saddlebags. But when he returned she still found herself postponing.

The chance to travel with a *dragon!* Ingal had said he would leave at dawn, but he had not shown up at the courtyard. Had he left by way of another entrance? Had she missed him, or would she still have a chance to catch him?

If, that is, she wanted to join.

She turned and looked out over the lawn. A patch of dead grass marked the spot where the acid globe had landed after bursting upon the guard's face. Dried blood still darkened grass blades where the other guards were slashed. The stable doors were missing.

Torra grimaced. *Melting*, she thought. *Face melting. Elves. She-Elf.* She heard again the warrior's unnerving scream of victory.

There was no way she'd travel *with* elves, to an elvish land, to look for *that* she-elf. What had Ingal called her? A "Padgarun" cleric? What sort of cleric could kill so coldly? Weren't clerics supposed to heal people? The elves always held a mystical, noble reputation with her people, though mythical in Taxia. How wrong that reputation had been!

So what now? she asked herself. *What's next if you don't go? Return to Taxia? Admit to Master Morikal that you turned down a dragon, were afraid of elves, and refused the chance of a lifetime? How many times have you dreamed of this chance, Torra?*

She took a deep breath and ran a hand across a shelf of books, absentmindedly caressing the rough, aged bindings. She wasn't a coward! Time to march back to the chamberlain and deliver the message. "I'm going," she said aloud, startling herself. She looked around the library, but it was empty. She gathered her robes and walked boldly out the library door and turned toward the dragon's chambers.

But she stopped. The shaking intensified. Her eyes widened. Seemingly without command of her senses, she turned and ran back to her chambers.

NINETEEN
Departure

Ingal awoke slowly, still tired from the summons. He gradually became aware of the dimly lit, earthen corridor in which he had collapsed. He had no idea how long he had slept.

He groaned. The side of his broad head was wet with drool. *Hardly royal*, he thought. His joints were stiff from sleeping on the floor. Cold. Headache. He was getting too old for such powerful magic. "This'll be the death of us."

Ingal took several minutes to yawn and stretch his body. His neck cracked painfully. Alone and unabashed, he reached up to his side with a rear leg and scratched himself like a dog.

Ingal closed his eyes and composed his mind. The summons replayed itself in the memory, the statements made by Azartial about the Triumvirate.

They were the First, the Makers of your pitiful world.

They are weaker than stone. I dare not say more.

They are the elves, just as they are you.

Riddles. Riddles. So many riddles.

Sighing, Ingal walked back through the trophy chamber and up the secret ramp to his quarters. His mind turned back to the day's only goal: leaving the palace to fly with the elves to Peshilaree. He would need to bring along many books to research these mysteries and compensate for the memory's recent failings. Too bad the Taxin wouldn't come along.

But first he needed to bathe and have his travel vest put on. His stomach rumbled loudly, too, but he had no time for his weekly meal.

Speaking the necessary unlocking and locking spells, he walked through the cellar doors and toward his sleeping chambers.

Before Ingal had walked twenty yards he spied a servant. Eyes wide, she shouted behind her, "I found him!" Voices echoed from down the corridor. Blushing, the servant turned and bowed low. "My lord," she said, "the chamberlain has suffered a heart attack. He is in dire need."

Ingal thought back to Metharcus' heart problem in the corridor the day before. He took a deep breath and forced himself to speak rationally. "Have the priests attended him?"

"Yes, my lord. But they are spiritually weak from attending to the dead and wounded from the last two days."

Ingal nodded. "We will go to Metharcus' chambers at once."

Other servants joined them as they wound through the corridors. Exhaustion ringed the servants' eyes.

They passed the palace Solarium. Ingal stopped abruptly. Light blazed through the broad solarium windows at a very steep angle. It was long past dawn; he had slept until midday! He groaned and whipped his tail in irritation. The elves would not be pleased with his tardiness.

Let them wait, he thought.

Ingal rarely visited the servants' quarters. They had a part of the south wing to themselves, with hallways too small for a dragon of his size to enter, except for the chamberlain's chambers. Ingal's forebears had planned it that way, since servants needed a place away from the lord of the palace. As chamberlain, it was up to Metharcus to rule there, yet be accessible to the Gold Dragon, so the chamberlain's chambers adjoined a large corridor.

Half a dozen servants, mostly family members, were clustered around Metharcus' chamber doors. Seeing Ingal, they bowed low and backed away. Ingal bent his head down and peered through the doorway.

Metharcus lay on a settee, arms draped over his chest. The old man's chest rose slowly and shallowly, his mouth parted slightly. A thin sheet lay over him like a prelude to a shroud.

Metharcus' wife sat to one side of the bench dabbing a dampened washcloth to her husband's blanched brow. Marna was thin and frail with silver hair pulled back into a bun. She looked over at Ingal, moving slowly as if in a dream. She did not have the mind or will to bow, but only watched him zombie-like, eyes wide with hardly-suppressed fear that had nothing to do with him.

Ingal turned to look at an attending priest. It was the priestess of Jonaatha, Goddess of Light. Her white robes softly rustled as she walked to the doorway.

"What is his condition?" Ingal asked.

"He will survive, Ingal." The priests reserved the term *lord* for their gods. "Jonaatha will be refused this good soul today —may her glory shine." She placed her hands across her chest, like a corpse at burial, as she spoke. "But we cannot expect a full recovery."

Ingal nodded and looked back at the chamberlain. "Very well. Do your best, but we must leave today for an important mission. We trust in you to keep him well."

Metharcus stirred at Ingal's voice. "My lord? What are you still doing here? Was your vest not packed?"

Ingal chuckled. "Still thinking of our best interest, Metharcus! What should we ever do if you retired?"

Metharcus gave a wan smile but did not answer.

"We are going soon. We do not expect to see you so fatigued when we return. Understood?" Metharcus blinked an affirmative. "The priests will see to you until then. Get well, *decauna*."

Metharcus nodded weakly. "Fly away, you old dragon. Pick a fight or two for me."

Ingal smiled and stood away from the doorway. He looked over at the small cluster of servants. To one of the higher ranking ones he said, "We will bathe, now, and then we shall have our vest fitted before leaving. See to it."

~ ~ ~

An hour later Ingal had taken his bath, been dried, and was now having his travel vest put on him in the audience chamber.

It took a dozen strong servants to heft the vest straps around his wings and torso and latch the massive bronze buckles at his back. The vest was made of thick, tanned elephant leather. Gold studs lined the edges. Six pockets, each as big as a man and pulled tight by leather straps, lay on his chest and belly. Ingal felt the bulk of the items within them: reference books, maps, and a gift or two for the speaker.

The servants finished their work and moved their ladders away, breathing heavy. Ingal thanked them and left the audience chamber toward the front doors.

Minutes later he stepped into the afternoon sunlight. It felt to Ingal as if his steps were lighter, his breathing easier, his sense of purpose more profound. He couldn't wait to stretch his wings and take to the sky. There would be a nice, easy tailwind for part of the day's journey at this rate, though he regretted he could not fly as high as he wished, for the sake of the elves. They would need to make good time to reach Chaz Sanooc, where they would stop for the night. Dark clouds loomed to the northeast. The storm would catch them by evenfall if they lingered.

In the courtyard before him were three griffins and a score of palace guards, mostly armed with halberds to keep the griffins at bay.

He hated griffins. It was in his dragon blood. They snapped their huge beaks at their handlers, straining at the iron-reinforced leatherine straps and flapping their wings. The beasts smelled like a concentrated mix of horse sweat and chicken dung. Their shrieks hurt his ears. Their unintelligent eyes rolled in their feathered heads whenever he was near. Worst of all, griffins shed copious dander to which Ingal was allergic.

Ingal began to regret his decision to bring the elves along, then he sneezed. The vast roar that resulted sent the griffins into hysterics of flapping and shrieking, and it took many tense moments for their handlers to get control again.

The commotion attracted the attention of nearby pilgrims, gathering a safe distance away, oohing and aahing. Ingal had nearly forgotten his duties. Yearning to leave the griffins, he turned and walked to a garden dais close to the worshipers.

By the time Ingal arrived, the pilgrims had long since bowed, knees and heads to the grass. He took his place upon the dais, composed himself, and looked down lovingly on his worshippers. "You may stand."

They did as told, rising slowly and gazing at the dragon's legs and chest with wide eyes. One woman rushed forward with a basket of dried fruit, apricots and apples by the smell of it, and placed it at Ingal's feet with shaking hands. He rewarded her with a smile and nod, and tucked the basket away into a vest pocket. Other pilgrims threw flowers to the dais.

Ingal raised his head to a noble angle. "It is Our pleasure to thank you for your patronage. In moments we leave Palal Jehai, and it may be quite a while before we return." He spread his wings fully and raised a forefoot to the onlookers as a blessing, and they bowed their heads. "We bless you for your dedication to us, to your states, and to the White Lands Federation." Given the trauma of the last couple days, he decided to go a step further. "Please accept our gift to you."

Ingal recited a quick incantation as he pointed a claw at each of the pilgrims. With a flash of golden light there appeared at their feet a small hazelnut wrapped in a thin, blue ribbon. It was a spell he had designed, but rarely used. "Plant this near your town square. Nourish it as you do your country, and you will reap threefold the harvest each season. May your journeys home be swift and gentle."

The spell had merely teleported the nuts from a stash inside the palace, but the pilgrims didn't know this.

With a flourish of his tail, Ingal turned and went back the way he had come, followed by cries of thanks and honor from the worshippers.

By the time he returned to the courtyard, the doors had opened again and the elves were escorted out under heavy guard. Rethuud led, followed by two of his strongest warriors, and they whistled to the griffins. The griffins shrieked in excitement and burst from their handlers, running up to the elves and bending their broad heads to loving elvish hands and soft whispers.

"Rethuud," Ingal said, "as per our agreement, you and your two companions are released into our custody. But please remember that your other warriors are hostage to our mercy."

Rethuud turned his attention from his mount and looked Ingal square in the face. "I remember, dragon, and I will keep my part. We will fly with you to Peshilaree and assist you, if indeed we can, in uncovering the conspiracy. When I have found the answers you seek, my part is over and my warriors will be released."

The elves quickly mounted the griffins' leatherine saddles and took the reins. At an elvish command, the beasts flapped their wings and ran headlong through the palace guards, taking to the air with a few clumsy strides and snapping at the humans along the way.

Ingal sneezed again, scattering guardsmen. *Damned griffins.* He stretched his wing muscles, wincing at the pain of his back wounds, and took a couple of deep breaths. With a grunt, he leapt high into the air and gave several strong wing beats until he reached a height where he could dive toward the valley, build speed, and then catch up to Rethuud. His wings were very tight; he needed to fly more often.

He was about to dive when he heard a hail from below.

"My lord! Wait!"

Ingal glanced down. Now distant, he saw a form in tan robes standing at the palace entrance waving its arms.

Ingal turned in flight and swung low over the courtyard.

"My lord," Com Gidel yelled up at him, "I've changed my mind. Take me with you, if you wish." She raised a leather pack. "My adventure hasn't yet ended!"

Ingal chuckled to himself and circled the courtyard once more before landing.

TWENTY
Dragon's Passage

Torra's heart leaped as Ingal landed in a gust of wing beats in front of her. Was this truly happening? He stood tall, gleaming bright gold in the daylight like a portal to the sun, seemingly more noble now than the last time she had seen him. He wore a gigantic leather vest around his torso like those worn by the horsemen of Taxia.

She dug a fingernail into her thumb. The mild pain of it seemed to confirm the reality of the moment. "We have not made provisions to transport you, Com Gidel," Ingal said. "No one rides the Gold Dragon like some horse, and we will not carry you in our claws, for it would fatigue us and possibly harm you."

Have not made provisions … Torra lowered her head. How could she have been so damned indecisive? "I understand, my lord. I should have taken the chance when I had it."

Ingal gave her a sly look, then glanced back toward the northeast. Torra spotted three figures in the distant sky, disappearing around the mountainside. *Are those the elves? On griffins?*

Ingal turned back to her. Was he smirking? "All is not lost, Com Gidel. You may come with us, but you may find the accommodations uncomfortable."

Torra looked up, eyes wide with hope.

Ingal reached to his vest and searched a pocket. He pulled out the pilgrim's fruit basket, a couple of large books, and a bag of scrolls from the top left chest pocket, then ordered a servant to return the documents to his study. "These books and scrolls contain information regarding renegade spells," he said to Torra. "With you along, We may not need them."

May not need them? Torra wanted to unroll the scrolls and find out more, offer to carry them for him, but the servant stole them away.

Ingal leaned down so that the vest pocket reached the ground, opening it wide with a claw. "Climb in, if you wish to come along."

Torra blinked. "In there?"

"Hurry, now. We haven't time to waste. We suggest you go in feet first. And don't forget the fruit basket. You may get hungry."

She nodded. Grabbing the basket in one hand and her travel pack in the other, Torra stepped to the vest, ducking low to avoid Ingal's neck. Heat emanated from Ingal's body as if she stood next to a wood stove.

By the stars, I could touch him! I can touch a dragon! And then she did, reaching a shaking hand up and running it along the scales where his neck met his chest, feigning the need to balance herself. The scales were rough, like raw lumber, and shaped like the leaves of a catalpa tree—sharply pointed toward the bottom, quickly widening and rounding near the top. His mighty heart beat through natural armor.

Then her hand met Ingal's vest. She knelt and got onto her hands and knees and backed gingerly into the pocket. The leather was surprisingly soft and yielding.

"Hang on," Ingal said, and before she had a chance to position herself, he quickly raised upright. Torra slipped to the bottom of the pocket in a lump, and all went dark as the top of the pocket closed. She grunted and struggled against Ingal's movements in an attempt to right herself. The pocket smelled acrid-sweet, like vinegar. Dragon sweat?

The dragon's words were muffled by the leather as he asked, "Are you all right in there?" There was a hint of humor in his voice.

Torra stood, her ankles twisting on the bottom seam of the pocket. She reached her hands up through the opening and pushed her head out into the air. The pocket was just tall enough to fit her. A memory flashed into her mind of her brother, Nickos, carrying a pet mouse around in his shirt pocket at age ten. "Fine. Fine," she replied to Ingal. "Feeling somewhat miniaturized."

"Good. Then we're off."

Before Torra could catch her breath, Ingal leapt high into the air. Torra yelped as the ground fell away, then Ingal threw out his wings and flapped several times. Each wing beat bounced her around as they rose at least a hundred feet into the air. And then he soared over the lawn, eastward, and plunged over a cliff edge into the valley beyond, only to rise even higher on a thermal and turn northward. She yelped as he swooped and turned.

Looking back and to her left, the palace diminished to the size of a playhouse—an impossible spot of vert and regal bonerock amid the desolation of granite cliffsides and rugged, clinging trees. The gatehouse to the grounds lay off to their left as the palace grounds fell behind a curve in the mountainside.

Her head spun. "By the stars!" she cried. "Do you wish to kill me with such acrobatics?"

"Acrobatics?" Ingal said. "You mean *aerobatics*, like this!" He folded his wings and dove again, twisting his body and rolling. Torra screamed. The valley whirled around her in a blur. Her hair whipped about her head. Then Ingal threw his wings out again and righted himself. Now they raced along a whitewater river, so close that she felt spray on her face. Suddenly the river dropped away in a thousand-foot waterfall to a lush valley bottom far below, and they were soaring again.

"Oh! I'm going to be sick!" Torra yelled. She coughed up bile, somehow managing not to vomit.

Ingal tilted his head to his chest so that he could just see her. The smile at the edges of his mouth faded a bit. "Apologies," he said. "That was childish of us." He chuckled, nonetheless, and looked back up. "It has been a long time since we gave such a ride. We promise, no more aerobatics if we can help it."

"I would appreciate it." Torra breathed deeply and closed her eyes. The wind froze her face and rushed past her ears like a torrent. Somehow she had always imagined flying and tumbling like a bird would be freeing. Now all she wanted to do was retreat into a pocket that smelled of dragon sweat and … apricots?

"I fear I have smashed some of the fruit in your basket," she said, "but the smell has been somewhat improved."

Did the dragon smile? "The fruit was a gift from a pilgrim."

"You're lucky your pocket doesn't now smell of human waste, the way you fly me about!"

Ingal flapped his wings some more, slower now than before, seeming to catch more of the frigid air. They rose high out of the valley. Looking ahead, Torra could just make out the three griffins ahead to the north.

Torra repositioned herself, but she didn't dare move too much for fear of slipping out to her death. As it was, she lay face downward at the distant features, darting over the hillsides and river like an arrow shot from a longbow. She reached into a robe pocket and pulled out a large handkerchief, which she carefully wrapped around her head and face for some meager warmth.

Torra's head and gut were settling. From her pocket she also retrieved a strip of her medicinal herbs and popped it into her mouth to relieve the nausea. Ingal did not speak, seeming to exert himself to catch up to the elves, so she made herself as comfortable as possible and lay still, closing her eyes. The sounds were deafening: rushing wind, the deep thump of Ingal's wings catching the air like sails snapping in the wind, Ingal's mighty, beating heart, and the rumble of his lungs and belly through the vest.

Perhaps a quarter hour passed before she heard Ingal speak. "So many times we have flown this way over the millennia! Yet the beauty of the Highlands still astounds us."

Torra opened her eyes and looked ahead past Ingal. They were higher than she had ever fathomed, higher even than the birds would fly. The griffins were now close enough to see their wings flapping and the form of their elvish riders.

She looked around at the scenery. Jehai Mountain curved away to their left, westward, in a graceful, tree-covered series of hills and vales. A thin column of gray stone, jagged at the top, stood at the top of one of the farthest mountaintops.

"What is that tower?" she yelled over the wind.

Ingal looked to the left. "No need to speak so loudly, Torra. We can hear you fine. That is what is left of Hoc Embarn, the westwatch tower of a nation that once existed here, called Zhameel Methu'um. They were occupiers of this land for five centuries, invaders from the far east across the Northron Sea. Ten thousand years ago, the tower was a marvel of engineering, awesome to behold."

Again Torra was amazed at Ingal's seeming disregard for the vastness of time. She pictured the travel map she had used in her journey to Palal Jehai, and tried to name the geography below her. The river they flew above was the Dragon River. The valleys and hills slowly fell eastward to the Canyonlands, at the bottom of which rushed the Overwatch River. In the afternoon sun, the creeks that fed it sparkled star-like through brief openings in the oaks and elms. Gray and brown cliffsides rose over the vales, stately in their timelessness like giants watching the world pass slowly by.

The crack of earth that defined the Overwatch River turned northwest in its majesty, then came out of the canyons to flow northward ahead of them. There the land flattened into the vast Alsanoos River valley, darkening from verdigris to olive, interspersed with pale green meadows.

Torra gasped. Far to the northeast, nearly invisible in the mist of distance, was an incredibly tall white spire against dark and brooding clouds. It stood far above anything else, tapering from the ground to the tip, easily a thousand feet high.

"Is that what I think it is?" Torra asked. "Is that the Tower of Light?"

Ingal looked toward the spire. "Indeed."

Torra remembered the drawings she had seen and the texts she had read. "Can it be true what I have read? That it is as high as a mountain, yet the stone walls are thin enough for light to pass through? That mages from all over the world congregate there in great throngs to study their art and trade their knowledge? That it glows at night like a great beacon to the world?"

"All of this is true," Ingal replied.

Torra gulped back her emotion. "I've heard the interior is completely open from top to bottom—a vast and seemingly limitless hall lined with balconies. But at the bottom, where you enter, is the Heartstone."

"Yes," Ingal said, "the Heartstone."

"Have you … of course you've seen it."

Ingal chuckled. "Yes, we have been to the tower countless times. The Heartstone is three times our height when we stand, tapering like a cone, and as smooth as glass. It is made of bonerock, like the tower itself, and emits a bright white light that illuminates the entire tower day and night."

Torra tried to picture it. The ink drawings she had seen surely did not do it justice. "How old is the tower? Were your forebears there to witness its building?"

Ingal shook his head. "It has stood for longer than our memory. It is said to date back to the Occultiian empire, when magic was strongest in the land. It was built in one piece, constructed with song—the voices of choirs of mages and enchanted lyres—over the course of a hundred years. If our forebears were there to take part, we do not know, but we would not be surprised if dragons were an integral part."

Torra sighed and tried to picture herself at the base of the tower, looking up at its incredible height, glowing white walls, and elegant minarets, as throngs of singing mages put the finishing touches on its construction.

For many long minutes she stared off at the tower in a daydream. Then the spire slowly disappeared to the darkness of distant stormy skies.

Ingal tilted his head downward and to the left. Torra followed his gaze to the ground. Below, a thin road curved through the jagged mountainside. The Dragon's Passage. Torra had previously traveled up the passage, southward, to Palal Jehai.

Ingal suddenly dipped lower. Torra saw where he was looking. A couple of coaches rushed at reckless speed down the road, northward away from the palace. The one in front was painted bright red, the other white, and piled high with trunks, and several hundred yards behind the red one. Ahead and behind each coach rode patrols of mounted guards.

"Com Gidel," Ingal said, "we will be going down for a moment to visit with the vizier of Namistad. There is an issue to be resolved."

"Are you landing?" she asked, realizing too late the touch of desperation in her voice. "May I get out for a bit?"

"Very well. But we have not the time to linger. Hold on."

Ingal swooped down in tight circles toward the curving road. The trees rushed up, and Torra gripped the lip of the pocket with white knuckles. Ingal flew ahead of the caravan and swung around to the ground, wings outstretched and beating faster, to touch down lightly on the rutted road with a small hop.

Last year's oak leaves skittered away from his wing beats, flying up from the undergrowth and circling each other in miniature tornadoes before separating and softly landing amongst the bowed limbs of stately oaks and the gleaming white, cruciform blossoms of dogwoods peeking out from the understory.

To either side of the road stood ancient, weathered statues of the Gold Dragon, looking northward down the road away from the approaching caravan. Flecks of gold film still clung to the innermost crevices. Moss grew in the shadows, but the exposed bonerock was bright white.

"Behold the Pillars of Jehai," Ingal said. "'Wisdom' and 'Strength.'"

One statue stood tall, up to Ingal's shoulders, with the countenance and poise of a thoughtful mediator, wings to the sides. One forefoot clasped an aged tome. The other rested on a scepter of rulership.

The second statue lunged forward, eyes full of fury, teeth bared, forefoot outstretched with claws extended, wings widespread. The other forefoot grasped a massive scimitar.

"I remember them from my journey up the mountain," Torra said as Ingal leaned down to let her out. "Who made them?"

"A sculptor now forgotten by his grandchildren's grandchildren."

Ingal was bent over with his head nearly to the ground, helping the shaky astronomer out of the pocket. At that moment, the caravan rounded a corner and came within view. Leading the forward guard was a man in bright red armor and winged helm riding a gray stallion, a large, silver horn swinging at his side. Torra recognized him as the general from Namistad who had raised such a fuss at the first audience. Tasami, was it? Expecting him to speak, Torra grasped the Rod of Translation in her pocket.

The general raised his hand, calling a halt to the guards and coaches, then said to Ingal, "I thought *I* was the one who was supposed to bow, Jehai!"

Ingal groaned and unceremoniously pulled Torra from his pocket, then stood upright. Still unsteady from the flight, Torra wobbled to the "Wisdom" pillar and supported herself against one of the statue's legs.

The general did not bow, but merely nodded with a shallow smile on his slim face, nor did he remove his helm. The other guards, seemingly unsure what to do, gave half-hearted bows. Ingal appeared to ignore the slight.

"We will address Vizier Navi Janisim of Namistad," Ingal said to the caravan.

A servant dismounted the seat of the red coach and opened a side door. Aided by a footman, the elder vizier stumbled out and walked unsteadily with the aid of a gnarled wooden staff to stand beside his general. The red miter on his head bent far forward of his stooped body, seeming to stay attached to Janisim's nearly bald pate by nothing more than the man's will.

In the background sat the Aestistad coach. The vizier of that state poked her head out of the coach to watch. Vizier Janisim looked up at Ingal. The old man's gray eyes swam over red lower eyelids that hung loosely as if peeled away and stretched. Despite his age, there was a sparkle in his eyes that betrayed some mischievous secret.

"We are on our way to the Keep of Casan, my lord," Janisim said, "as urgency requires. But it honors Namistad that you should stop to address me. How may I help you, my lord?" Despite his weary appearance, Janisim's voice was silky and measured.

"It has come to our attention that your general, Tasami, is fomenting dissent amongst our leaders."

General Tasami's eyes narrowed. He shifted nervously on his mount but remained silent.

"What sort of dissent, my lord?" Janisim asked.

"We gave strict orders that each state was to send no more than half of its troops. Yet rumor is that he is circumventing our order and urging other states to do the same. What are your state's intentions, Vizier?"

"*Intentions* are wondered all around." Janisim gave a secretive smile. "Namistad is, of course, in complete compliance with your mandate, my lord Jehai, and with the Federation Charter."

"It is much appreciated, Vizier. See to it that you stay in compliance. The Federation may well require its reserve forces against unseen threats. We shall see you again at Casan. You may continue on your way."

Janisim smiled wryly and remained where he was. Ingal frowned. "Is there something else, Vizier?"

"Perhaps you wonder why we ride at such a maddened pace? It is difficult on old bones."

Ingal whipped his tail. The spike at the end scraped a line across the worn path and dug into the soil at the tree line. "We had imagined you were eager to get to the border to organize your troops against Ocrin."

"Indeed, Lord Jehai, but something has happened to increase our haste." Janisim emitted a quiet cackle. His eyes flashed dangerously. Suddenly his face twisted into sarcastic sorrow. "Oh, I'm sorry, my lord. Did you miss the messenger from Alneri?"

Ingal blinked. "What messenger?" Torra stepped forward, no longer leaning against the statue.

"Perhaps you were too busy chasing elves?" Janisim said. "Or did you wish to rendezvous with your good, close friend, the Iron Dragon?"

Ingal tilted his head. "He is indeed a friend to us, and to the White Lands Federation." Ingal pointed a claw at Janisim and raised his voice. "Do not speak ill of him, Vizier, for the Iron Dragon helped us form your nation from the ashes of Etollia."

Janisim leaned toward Ingal. "Yet now he is helping to return it to ashes."

Ingal lowered his forefoot. "What do you mean?"

Janisim slumped and caught himself on his staff. He let forth a long and painful bout of rheumy coughing before regaining his breath and stature. Ingal sighed in seeming impatience.

The coughing fit had removed the attitude from Janisim's voice by the time he spoke again. "The messenger has ridden hard, and passed us on the road ten minutes ago. The Iron Dragon has attacked Alneri Castle. It lies now in smoking rubble. After only a short attack, using some sort of powerful spell, not a wall was left standing. An entire battalion of soldiers lie dead beneath, along with the lord of the castle, his family, and nearly all of the castle staff and guards."

Ingal slowly shook his head, speechless. The vizier continued, "The Alneri border is now greatly weakened." He narrowed his eyes at the dragon. "Perhaps you knew this was coming? Hmm?"

"No." Ingal's eyes narrowed, and he took a step toward the man.

Janisim seemed unfazed by Ingal's posture. "Perhaps this is why you withhold troops, half the hands to fight? You have strong ties to the Iron Dragon, who has attacked our own flesh and blood." The Vizier took a feeble step toward the dragon and pointed his staff at him. "And now our spies in Ocrin tell us of a link between the enemy and the elves. There have been noble elves seen in the foul capital. And they have attacked your own palace guard and wounded *you*! Yet isn't it interesting how you travel with them now to their land even as the nation you lead is headed into war!"

Ingal thrust his head close to the vizier and stared him in the eyes. "Do you dare accuse us of treason! Treason against the very nation we lead? A nation that our forebears formed? Men have been executed for far less!"

Janisim shrugged. "You had best think rationally about your words, Navi Janisim!" Ingal reared up, roaring. "War with Ocrin is of great importance, but other dangers hang over the White Lands this day, and over all of Irikara! Tend to your troops as you have been ordered, and we will attend to more weighty business.

"And as for this messenger," Ingal continued, "We have doubts about his worthiness. Until we can verify the news, you are not to discuss it. The Iron Dragon has always been an ally. Tellonta's aid in the security of this nation has been demonstrated time after time, countless, for generations of his lineage. Even if he actually did this thing, he must surely have sane reasoning for his actions."

Janisim seemed unaffected. "As you wish, Lord Jehai." He bowed slightly, which was as low as he could without falling, then turned and slowly returned with his footman to the coach.

Ingal glanced at Torra. The look in his eyes frightened her, a mix of anger and confusion.

General Tasami let out a long, deep laugh. He looked to Torra with dangerous eyes that flashed with mock humor. "See the mighty dragon and his little pet! Careful, Taxin, you aren't the only one he's got in his pocket!"

Ingal stepped closer to the general, who held his place despite his mount's head-shaking and sidestepping. Ingal placed a claw upon Tasami's breastplate and slid it down the metal. The claw incised a deep gouge in the steel, screeching loudly. Tasami's face grew red as he gritted his teeth and stared Ingal in the eyes.

Ingal said, "Be on your way, General, and watch your tongue better than you watch your politics."

Tasami spat, turned, and spurred his steed into a sudden gallop past Ingal, followed by his soldiers. Soon the rest of the caravan thundered by, each person bowing to Ingal as they passed.

When, moments later, the white coach passed, Ingal acknowledged the vizier of Aestistad by saying, "Good journey, Misaqi." Vizier Misaqi gave a bow but remained silent as she passed, averting her eyes.

When the caravan had passed, Torra looked up again to Ingal. He hardly seemed to notice its passing, deep in concentration, clenching and unclenching his claws, face twisted in anger.

Torra looked again to the "Strength" pillar. The statue seemed diminutive compared to its living counterpart. A stone forefoot reached down-road with claws extended, cracking at the tips. Gold specks burned in the pupils. Its mouth was pulled back, baring sharp rows of teeth, roaring in silence. Yet it seemed now as if the statue reached in vain to stop the caravan thundering down the mountainside, wasting its fury on the careless breezes.

Torra scratched at her arm and looked back to Ingal. "My lord? Are you all right?"

"Yes." But he did not elaborate. He merely leaned down and opened the pocket for Torra to enter. Reluctantly, she went to him and crawled in, quickly arranging herself to the most comfortable position. "Hold on," Ingal said without emotion.

With a massive leap, Ingal beat his wings heavily and thrust himself northward along the valley.

Torra watched as they passed over the caravan again. This time General Tasami looked up at them, his teeth showing white through a leering smile.

TWENTY-ONE
Flying with Torra

Ingal flew hard, pushing his muscles to their limits. Each wing beat propelled him faster, farther, but the strength of it could not ease his mind.

What was this about the Iron Dragon? he thought. *Tellonta, destroy Alneri Castle? Preposterous!*

Their forebears had worked together to build the castle a thousand years before. He consulted the memory, and saw again the Iron Dragon carrying huge granite stones in his claws, guiding them into place for the humans, cleaving trees with the Gold Dragon and hauling them to be shaped, then lifting the rafters into position. Bit by bit, they had worked together with the Alnerians to finish the castle and insure the stability of that region.

His wings burned. His back, where the muscles met, was tight and knotted, threatening to fatigue. His thighs ached from holding up his legs. He could dive, release the strain and fly up again, but a part of him longed for the pain, stretched it as far as it could go. The burning of his muscles matched the simmering frustration of dealing with the vizier and his general, and the confusion around the Iron Dragon.

No, Tellonta could not have done this thing, he thought. Tellonta's forebears had invested too much into the White Lands. And physically it was impossible. Alneri Castle was no small fortress. Destroying it would have taken days, weeks, for one dragon. Even fire, spreading throughout, could not destroy the castle. Magic? No. Tellonta was never that powerful, nor any of his forebears. It would take a renegade spell of great energy to level a castle of that size.

"My lord," Com Gidel called out. Ingal's flight was so fast and furious that the astronomer's voice could barely be heard above the rushing of the wind. "My lord!"

Lost in thought, Ingal heard the astronomer as if from a distance, took a deep breath, returned his thoughts to the moment, slowed his flight.

Ingal wasn't sure how much time had passed since Dragon's Passage. Half an hour? The flourishing land below had changed, grown lighter, even pale, with outcrops of bright white bonerock popping up here and there. The Dragon's River poured into the Overwatch River, swirling in miniature, white-capped maelstroms.

The griffins were in sight again, a few miles ahead, so Ingal slowed even more and allowed himself to glide.

"Yes, Com Gidel?" Ingal finally replied. He realized he was panting from his exertions. "What do you want?"

"What happened back there? What was that all about?"

"It is complicated."

"Movement of armies. Dragons destroying castles. I'd say it certainly *is* complicated!"

Ingal stretched out his legs. They were cramping.

"And this Vizier Janisim," Torra continued. "He and his general—'Tasami' was it?—they don't seem to respect you much. Why keep them around? Why not replace them?"

"It's not that easy." Ingal paused. He could see the elvish riders and smell their foul griffins. He pushed up to a higher altitude, out of the griffins' backwash. "Each state is semi-autonomous, as agreed to in the Federation Charter, which our forebears helped broker. We can make commands regarding the entire federation, particularly in regard to military and economic considerations. But each state is in charge of their officials and much of their local concerns. We can only make recommendations. As much as we despise those two, we must recognize their abilities and authority."

"They don't seem so able to me, not if they address you in such tones."

"Though he is awash in graft, Vizier Janisim is well-loved by his people, and he runs Namistad very efficiently. General Tasami is even less appealing to us, yet his abilities as a strategist and commander of troops is renowned, and he has powerful connections. They have done well to guard the White Lands Federation against Ocrin. Tasami, in particular, is a maverick, but his gruffness is out of concern for the well-being of Namistad, we think. We must tolerate those two for the time being."

Com Gidel was quiet for some time, and Ingal turned his attention to the northeast. The Tower of Light was visible through a break in the storm clouds. A thin projection, white with bonerock, the tower dimly lit the storm clouds near it. It projected up from the center of Taraman, capital city of the state of Aestistad.

"The tower," Com Gidel said. "How magnificent."

"Indeed. We find ourselves wondering what the mages know of this mission of ours. They do not reply to our hails. Has the towermaster knowledge of the Triumvirate? What does he know of the Stone of Lethori and its glow? What are they hiding that they cannot speak to us?"

Com Gidel shifted in the vest pocket. "Surely they are as concerned as we. The fate of the world is in their hands as much as yours."

Ingal nodded, adding, "If not more." The elves shifted to a northwestern direction, and Ingal followed. A favorable wind allowed him to do more gliding than flapping. He needed the rest. "We would like very much to talk to the towermasters. A visit to the Tower of Light is warranted. Yet we have a feeling that this trip to Peshilaree will reveal much. It must be our current focus."

They were entering the Alsanoos River Valley. The great river lay to the north, sparkling in the early evening sun as it ambled eastward to the Taraman Inlet and the Northron Sea. Outside of the towns and farmlands below, the land took on a white sheen: large, widespread bonerock outcrops, salt licks, and white sandy patches along the rivers and streams. The meadows were filled with milky-white wildflowers and blooming shrubs. Even the wildlife was white, to a large extent, or even albino. Such coloration, or lack of it, was the namesake of the White Lands, extending far up the Alsanoos to the Namineri Valley.

"If you will pardon my ignorance, my lord, why is it that we follow these elves? It is my understanding that they attacked you and did you bodily harm. It was these elves who killed your guards. Yet you fly with them to their land. In what way can they help us find those who abuse the magic and anger the gods?"

"There is a conspiracy among the elves, Torra. The Prince of Mirrors, heir to the throne of Peshilaree, was assassinated in our very audience chamber."

"And the assassin escaped," Com Gidel added, her voice trailing off.

Ingal remembered back to the wounded and dying guards, and the funeral. "Yes. The dispatch you examined was from the Speaker of the Hall of Emeralds, the prince's father. It asked us to assassinate the prince for him, and the prince's warriors."

"His own son! I had never imagined elves to be so barbaric."

Ingal looked toward the elvish warriors. "When it was apparent that we refused to kill him, the assassin did it for us."

"So the assassin was planted by the speaker."

"It would seem, but that would be surprising since the Padgarun do not take orders from the speaker; they are beholden only to their spirits. We still hold in our palace the rest of the prince's warriors, unharmed—for now, until we can determine if the prince was guilty of having murdered the elvish court mage, Ektibal."

"So these elves flying ahead of us," Com Gidel said, "they are helping to uncover the conspiracy? For their prince?"

"That's the agreement. Their leader is named Rethuud. But as you may surmise, we are not interested in Peshilaree only to find justice for the slain prince."

"You feel that the conspiracy is linked to the Stone of Lethori, don't you? Oh!"

At that moment Ingal hit an air current which dropped them dozens of feet in an instant. Ingal regained control, but his back and wings ached. "Apologies." He continued, "The clue to the link came with the dispatch."

"Was it something the speaker said?" Com Gidel asked.

"It was the star chart that you helped us with. Do you remember the constellations?"

"Yes. To one side of a block face were depicted the constellations of Corbilla, the Griffin, and Mantalla, the Bear. To the other side was a mirror image of the constellation of Corthos, the Dreaming Dragon."

"Why do you think the speaker would include those?" Ingal asked. He had his own idea, but he wanted the astronomer to figure it out for herself.

"Symbolism, I suppose."

"Of what?"

Ingal felt Torra move in the vest pocket, then heard the dim sound of munching. "Corthos might be an allusion to you, my lord."

"Good! Good! We believe this as well. Continue."

"Given that the elves ride griffins, I might assume that the constellation of Corbilla signifies the elves' involvement."

"Indeed."

"But what of the other, Mantalla?" Com Gidel paused to consider, then added, "I just can't imagine what it would symbolize."

Ingal reached up with a claw and scratched his head at the base of his right horn. "Mantalla may signify Ocrin, as the symbol for Zern is an attacking brown bear. If this is so, then we cannot yet understand in what way Ocrin may be involved. Of what use is it to Ocrin that the prince is assassinated? And why would the speaker reveal it in this way? Vizier Janisim alluded to reports of elves in Ocrin's capital, Zern. But why? The two nations have been enemies in times past."

Com Gidel was silent. Ingal added, "We have diverged from the main issue."

There was only the sound of the wind for a moment, then Com Gidel gave a jerk of recognition. "Ah, yes. The link between Peshilaree and the Stone of Lethori. You said it was something in the dispatch."

"You gave the answer yourself." Ingal paused, but Com Gidel did not respond. Ingal continued. "When asked about the symbolism of the constellations, you brought up the presence of Corthos, the Sleeping Dragon, and how it was in mirror form, as if the gods were watching us."

"Indeed, that is what I supposed."

"So the speaker may have suggested we were the object of godly observation. Well, don't you think it strange that the speaker would suggest we are being watched by gods *before* we were visited by the Triumvirate? And why would he care? On the surface it seems to have nothing to do with the purpose of the dispatch—the execution of his son."

The astronomer was quiet, seemingly pondering the issue. "And there is another thing you do not know," Ingal continued. "Upon the prince's death, We saw in his hand a pendant shaped like a triangle surrounded by a circle."

"The gods of the Padgarun," Com Gidel said in a rush.

"Interesting that we should be visited by both a Padgarun and the Triumvirate within a day of each other."

Storm clouds were moving in from the east, but with a good tailwind, Ingal figured they could still fly another hour or two. Inwardly, he cursed the griffins and their slow flying. He typically flew twice their speed, even at his age. Flying so slowly was at best boring, and at worst, it threatened to drop him from the sky. And unless he found an upcurrent, it actually took more effort. So he tried to think of it as practice for having not flown long distances for many months.

"You haven't asked me why I changed my mind," Com Gidel said.

"About coming along? Doubtless our speech had convinced you: the chance for adventure, the gaining of arcane knowledge, and such."

"That was part of it. But I remembered something. When we had last spoken in the audience chamber, you had mentioned this trip to Peshilaree. Upon hearing the name, I recalled an ancient legend, but quickly forgot upon seeing blood stains on your floor. I panicked and lost my train of thought. Only this morning did I remember again."

"And what was this memory, so strong as to overcome your fear?"

"A renegade spell, my lord."

Ingal missed a wing beat, caught in an unplanned turn and dip, then returning on course. "Go on, please."

Com Gidel continued, "There was an ancient legend about the downfall of the land of Occultii. I cannot remember it as well as I would like, but I do recall how the ancient mages of that land could conjure a dimensional gate and travel to another plane of existence."

"Indeed," Ingal said. "This most powerful of spells was, in the end, the downfall of their empire."

"Well, the legend stated that the knowledge was forbidden, renegade, after the fall of Occultii. But there were actually two spells, cast by different mages or teams of mages."

Ingal knew he had heard this somewhere before, but just couldn't recall. Was this another instance of renegade spell forgetfulness? "Go on," he said.

Com Gidel shifted to a more comfortable position. "The original *Dimensional Rift* took a great deal of magical energy to open, days of chanting by many mages. Only a handful of mages have ever been powerful enough to do it on their own. The opening took so much energy that the mage would not be able to conjure the strength to widen it. The infinitesimally small rip would seal up again."

Greatly excited, Com Gidel spoke quickly now. "So another renegade spell, and an experienced mage, would need to do the widening. Well, my lord, the legend said that all copies of the *Rift Widening* spell were destroyed, to prevent man from threatening the gods again, except for one copy—the Book of Alasar. This copy was passed to the elves of Peshilaree for safekeeping."

Ingal blinked. "In Peshilaree?" He had expected that it would be found in one of the towers. The other spell, *Dimensional Rift,* was destroyed by the Tower of Balance.

Com Gidel said, "As the legend states:

> The Pysont Guards were left alone
> Beside the ruined altar stone.
> They closed the Book of Alasar
> And took it to the elvish throne.

Yet I do not know who the Pysont Guards were."

Immortal humans, Ingal wanted to say. Cursed with immortality by the gods who destroyed Occultii, as witnesses to their power. Most went mad, but they all still lived, and Ingal's forebears had met a couple. "It doesn't matter," Ingal said. "Suffice it to say that they survived the destruction."

"So last night I consulted my notes," Com Gidel continued, "and I found some of the verses. One of them actually made reference to the elvish mage, Quintominel, who received the Book of Alasar:

> Into the hands of Quintominel
> The Pysont placed the cursèd spell.
> 'All the world may be destroyed
> If you fail to guard it well.'"

Ingal felt the mage was getting carried away with her enthusiasm. "Torra, this is very interesting, but we are afraid it has little relevance to the mission at hand. Even if the renegade spell is still in Peshilaree, it would be too much to try to search it out. We are among the greatest mages of this age, yet even we cannot open a dimensional portal to be widened by it. So the *Rift Widening* spell is likely of no use to anyone."

Com Gidel did not reply, remaining quiet for many long moments. Fearing he had offended her with his lack of enthusiasm for this renegade spell, Ingal added, "But, if we find sign of it, and there is little delay, we can search for this spell of yours."

"Thank you, my lord. It would be of great interest to me."

"For now, though, it looks as if the elves are about to land. Their accursed griffins need a rest. Let us join them on the ground." With that, Ingal began his descent.

~ ~ ~

Ingal was pleased with the elves' choice of resting spot. They were in a meadow, almost perfectly round, reasonably flat, and about two hundred yards in diameter. A thin stream curved through the middle of it, gurgling softly. Small, thin shrubs popped up here and there, leaves pale green and bark white in the light of late afternoon. The elves had settled on the other side of the stream from Ingal and stood watching him as the griffins dipped their beaks into the water, chirping like chicks.

As Ingal landed a fair distance away from the elves, Rethuud pulled his warriors close to him in a circle near the stream, then all bowed their heads, arms out, palms up. He muttered an elvish prayer, then the elves chanted a word in unison and went about eating and drinking.

Ingal leaned down, and Com Gidel tumbled out. Long after Ingal stood back up, the mage lay face down on the thick grass, breathing deeply.

"Are you all right, Torra?"

"Yes, my lord." She raised her pale face to the dragon but quickly averted her eyes. "I lie flat upon the earth, yet still I feel the sway and dip of flight! Or is it that the earth heaves?"

Ingal chuckled and looked beyond the meadow. His humor gave way to somber reflection. Gigantic statues stood on the margins looking inward, grim warriors or kings, frowning down upon the party as if in judgment. The bonerock had weathered to the point of smoothed edges and eroded facial features, and many of the statues had tumbled to their sides, cracked or shattered. Some were half-obscured by tangled vines with small, maple-shaped leaves. Beyond, mounds rose from the earth, interspersed with tumbled walls made of huge stones. And in the distance lay low hills, steeply sloped and tapering to a point, overgrown with the same pale shrubs and bracken.

"Where are we?" Com Gidel asked.

"This was once a powerful city, Ena Enoiya, religious center of the ancient land of Enot." He pointed beyond the circle. "Those mounds were the bases of magnificent temples to their gods. And in the distance, there, buried beneath soil and shrub, are the ziggurats from which their priests ruled the land. The meadow we stand in was once a place of competition, a killing field of bloodstained sand where great warriors fought for the glory of their empire and the excitement of the spectators."

"Lovely." The mage gained her footing and stretched.

Ingal sat on his haunches and stared into the distance. "They were an ancient race who had inhabited this land long into the mists of time, but their own barbarism ended them more surely than any invading army. Their last king was convinced he could defeat a foe far larger and stronger than him in one-on-one combat. He was wrong. He died on this very spot."

Com Gidel stood still and looked to her feet as if the ground would slide out from under her.

Ingal turned his attention to the elves, speaking Peshilarn. "Hail, Rethuud! Your flight was short, and storm clouds quickly approach from the east. We must be off."

At the sound of Ingal's voice, the griffins raised up from the stream and snapped in his direction, fluttering their wings.

"Indeed, dragon, this is so," Rethuud replied. "But the griffins are not used to such altitude. And, I might add, you seemed to have a problem keeping up."

Ingal scowled. "We had business at Dragon's Passage." But Rethuud had already turned to his mount and started adjusting his saddle straps. Ingal continued anyhow. "If we make good time, we may be able to reach Mount Guulenen before the storm."

Rethuud only nodded as he finished the straps. The other elves bent to the stream and filled their drinking gourds. Ingal also bent to the stream and filled his mouth, gulping loudly before rising up and wiping his mouth with a forefoot.

Off to Ingal's right, past the edge of the ancient arena and down a gentle slope, was the Overwatch River. By this point the river had calmed and widened, though faster than might be expected for its width. Flowing northward, it gurgled softly as if exhausted by its rushing course through highland vales and the Canyonlands. Meadowlarks called their notes into the daylight and flitted between rushes. A rain-scented breeze played along the shoreline.

The moment conjured Ingal's memory, and he saw again the ancient warships of the Enot with their bright red, square sails and armored sides upon the river, ready to throw grappling hooks and rush aboard Aelian or Etollian trade boats.

"It is time to go again, Com Gidel."

"So soon?" Torra paused a moment longer, eyeing the vest in trepidation, then returned to Ingal's pocket and climbed in.

As Torra got situated, Ingal saw in his mind's eye the gladiatorial ground as it had once appeared. The statues had stood without erosion, grim and horrible to behold, drenched in the blood of human sacrifices. Red banners waved upon every pole as thousands of Enots lined the arena to watch, cheering their king, crying out the names of their gods. Tlakm Osmi, Ingal's ninth forebear, had stood opposed to the King of Enot only steps away from where Ingal now stood.

Magic was banned in the arena. Tlakm had been very old by then, as old as Ingal was now, so the king had underestimated him. The fight had been long and bloody, claw, tooth, and blade. The king's skills were impressive for a human, but in vain. His death spelled the end of his ancient culture. With Enot out of the way, surrounding kingdoms unified into one large empire, Etollia, a third larger than the White Lands Federation was now.

Time and again, though, Ingal and his forebears wondered if the ends had justified the means. Unifying the kingdoms had brought peace and prosperity for nearly a thousand years, but the cost had been the extinction of an ancient, if bloody, civilization. Most of the survivors fought to the death rather than spread to the winds. It took only three generations for there to be nothing left of the Enot other than ruins. *Sometimes, extreme sacrifices are necessary*, he thought.

"I'm ready, my lord," Com Gidel called.

Now mounted by the elves, the griffins flapped across the meadow and up into the sky. With a sigh, Ingal gathered his strength and leapt into the air, unfurling his wings and flying northwest after the elves.

TWENTY-TWO

Gogonith

An hour's flight from Ena Enoiya, Ingal and company flew over the Alsanoos River, upstream, loosely following its undulating, northwesterly path. Unlike the clear, rushing Overwatch, fresh from melting alpine snow, the Alsanoos moved with regal slowness, pale with White Lands silt. Herons and geese frequented its banks. Occasional fishing boats and villages dotted the edges as hardworking men cast their nets and hauled their catches onboard. Some looked up as Ingal's shadow passed, standing in awestruck observance or bowing low.

Ingal looked over his shoulder to the east. The storm front was quickly catching up with them. A dark curtain of torrential rain spanned the height between black clouds and the obscured land beneath. He figured they had little time to reach Mount Guulenen before the front engulfed them. Ingal didn't mind the weather, but the conditions would be unfortunate for Com Gidel or the elves and unbearable for the griffins. The beasts didn't have the will for it. Already they grew impatient with their elvish masters, pulling toward the ground and flying erratically.

He flew closer to Rethuud, trying to ignore the griffin stench. "We must hurry," Ingal said. "At the pace we keep, we …"

Ingal stopped and stared off into the distance. A dark blot was silhouetted against the gloaming western sky. Rethuud turned to look, then quickly shouted a command to his warriors. Before Ingal could react, the elves dove at full speed toward the riverbank below.

Dazed, Ingal turned to follow, but thought twice and watched as the griffins made a hasty landing on the bank. The elves threw themselves off their mounts and pulled the beasts into the forest.

"What is this?" Ingal said aloud. He looked back to the shape in the sky. His eyes widened and a smile crept over him. "Ah! A dragon."

"Really, my lord?" Com Gidel said, clearly excited by the prospect. "Can you tell which one?"

Iron, he thought, for he could just make out the shape of the horns and body, but then his smile faded. *Why would Rethuud hide from Tellonta? They wouldn't yet know of Alneri Castle.*

Ingal remembered the wounded warrior who had accompanied the elves during the audience, and their numbers had been less than expected. *But why would Tellonta attack the elves?*

"Torra, you need to hide. Get down in the pocket and make no sound or movement."

"My lord? But this is an amazing opportunity! The chance to see two …"

"Do it. Now!"

She did as told. Ingal reached to his breast and insured the pocket was securely closed, hoping she would get enough air.

The Iron Dragon quickly narrowed the distance. He was flying at an unexpectedly fast clip against the wind, his wings and body standing out from the light orange sky behind. Glimmers of dull red flickered from the reflecting scales of his flanks and head. In moments they were close enough to call to each other.

"Tellonta," Ingal said in Draconii. "Greetings. It has been well over a century!"

The Iron Dragon answered, his voice deep and rumbling like thunder rolling. "Your eyes deceive you, Ingal Jehai, or have they grown dim with age?"

Ingal blinked in confusion. This was indeed the Iron Dragon, for his scales were the color of rust, his body was long and slender, and his thick horns curved back like a ram's above his piercing red eyes. But this dragon was smaller than Tellonta, faster, and …

"Younger," Ingal said. "You are not Tellonta, but his young offspring!"

Com Gidel jerked in his pocket.

The Iron Dragon smirked. He was close now, and the two dragons circled each other in a wide orbit. Judging by his size, Ingal figured he was only about a hundred years old.

Ingal followed tradition for a first meeting between dragon generations, stating with solemn air, "I am Ingal Jehai …

"Dragon of the Federation," the other finished. "Gold Dragon. Yes. And I am Gogonith."

A great sadness suddenly washed over Ingal. When last he had seen Tellonta, the dragon was aging but healthy. "How sorry we are that Tellonta has passed. As you well know, he was a dear friend of ours. It is our hope that we can continue the friendship We have enjoyed for generations. What calamity was it that took the life of your forebear? Age? Battle?"

A dangerous gleam flashed across Gogonith's clear eyes. "No. It was not battle, nor was it age."

Ingal waited a moment for Gogonith to continue, but the Iron Dragon only circled, silent. "What was it then?" Ingal asked. "An accident? Is it that you wish not to remember?"

"Tellonta is dead, Gold Dragon. Does it matter why? He gave his life so that I may rule in his place."

Ingal almost forgot to beat his wings, but not because of the news of Tellonta's demise. "*I?* You said *I?*"

"Is it really so shocking, Ingal? I! Me! Myself!"

"Do you not remember the Amber Dragon? Do you not remember the symptoms of his insanity?"

Gogonith laughed, booming. "The Amber Dragon was weak. *Is* weak. Yet it hardly matters anymore. I am different from him, now, as you will be."

Ingal caught a gust, and then another, from the east. Thunder rumbled from the ominous clouds quickly approaching. "Different how?" He tightened his brow. "By a desire to destroy castles?"

Gogonith chuckled deeply. "You are a ruler among rulers, Ingal. You know well that sacrifices must be made for the greater good. Alneri Castle was a sacrifice. There will surely be more sacrifices to come."

"Sacrifices! So the rumor is true! Our forebears *built* that place together. What justification could be made for this horror?" Ingal closed the distance of their orbit. "Our trust goes back generations, Iron Dragon. Be careful!"

Gogonith's smile faded. He looked away for a moment toward the east, then down to the river. "It is in friendship that I come, Ingal." He looked back to Ingal and met eyes. "You must trust me. There are reasons that you are not aware of."

Ingal exhaled and allowed another gust to push him away a bit. He narrowed his eyes at the Iron Dragon. "Gogonith is a foul name—an *Ocrin* name. But we are willing to listen, for those of your lineage have always proved trustworthy allies."

"The name was chosen, Ingal, by my predecessor, and I choose to keep it." Gogonith paused, seeming to collect his thoughts, before continuing. Thunder clapped to the east.

Lightning illuminated the clouds from within and flashed off of the dragons' gold or rust-red scales. In minutes the storm would be upon them.

"There is a great movement afoot, Ingal. A movement to restore something lost when the world was young, to bring peace back to its people. And magic, Ingal, magic for every elf, every dwarf, even every human. It is a movement to make you and me and all of dragonkind a greater part of that magic, able to change all of civilization, not just one group or one state or one nation. It is up to us, you and me, to make it work."

Ingal scowled. "Your notions are ridiculous, Gogonith. Not every elf, dwarf, or human is wise enough to use even the simplest of spells. Do you not remember the tale of Occultii? How they misused the magic they were granted? Even if such power were possible, what would give us the right to use it?"

"You underestimate yourself, Gold Dragon. It is up to us how we would use it. Who better? Dragons live longer than nearly any other entities on Irikara, with memories going far beyond the limits of mankind's legends. Why, where would the other intelligent species be without us to guide them? Generation after generation, we remind them of ancient evils so they may not repeat them, counsel them in times of emergency, guide them as no other scholars can. They fear us, respect us, name their children and institutions after us. Our images and reputations fill their art and their tales."

The storm was nearly upon them. Ingal dimly felt the first windblown droplets. Gogonith asked, "Has the Triumvirate contacted you yet?"

Again, Com Gidel jerked. This time Gogonith's gaze moved to Ingal's vest, but quickly returned to the Gold Dragon's eyes.

Should we feign ignorance? Ingal wondered. *No. The Iron Dragon knows us too well.* "Yes, we were contacted. But we know not what is wanted of us, nor who they truly are, nor even the nature of their desires. And we have only been contacted by one of them, who came via shadow emissary, then disguised as people we have known. He remained nameless, and said only that they created the world, and us, and have implied a connection with renegade magic. He told us to search you out."

Gogonith grinned. Lightning flashed again from the boiling black clouds, accentuating his young muscles. Thunder clapped immediately, deafening. "So many mysteries, Ingal. And yet the answer has been there all along, from the dawn of this world, vibrating beneath the surface of every particle, running along every current, flowing with every magic spell. It is in the lightning, the wind, the rain, the very sound of thunder.

"They did indeed create this world. They took from their own essence and used that power to build Irikara. And from the mud of that beginning they covered the land with water, and trees, and all living creatures. Raised mountains, carved rivers, gave currents to the sea and the sky. Then they exerted themselves even more. One created the elves, another the dwarves. And the third—Ingal—the third created us. He was the most powerful, just as *we* are the most powerful among mortal creatures. We were so mighty that the others grew jealous, so he made only twelve of us, and it has remained so since. Only twelve dragons, Ingal, at all times. No more. No less."

"And mankind?"

"What of them? They are slaves, mutants, created by dwarves, *of* dwarves, for a war no longer fought. They are weapons that have turned on their wielders. But there is room,

Ingal, for your precious humans in the new world, for they are of Irikara, too."

There came a sudden blast of wind and flash of lightning, followed quickly by rolling thunder. Then the storm hit them, engulfed them, tumbled the two dragons in a momentary chaos until they righted themselves. They faced against the wind, hovering side by side, carried aloft and in place by its force. Chill rain hit their faces and ran over their bodies.

"Crazy! None of this makes sense, Gogonith!" Ingal yelled above the fury. "You know as well as we do that there is no credence to it, for there is no legend, no memory, and no worshippers of these so-called gods. Your tale of humanity is ludicrous. They fool you with parlor tricks and ridiculous tales!"

"You are blind, Ingal! Blind because you have not been touched by them. If you were touched, you would understand. *I* was touched, and now I see the truth of it! When they trusted me, read my loyalty, they gave me a gift that surpassed anything the other gods could offer!"

"What, Gogonith? What could possibly buy off your sanity? They lie to you!"

Gogonith smiled, showing rows of gleaming white, deadly sharp serrated teeth. "They do not lie, old friend, for I have seen it myself. The gift was *complete* memory."

"Complete? We already have complete recall—twenty lives worth."

"I did not say 'complete recall'. I said 'complete memory'. Not of twenty generations, but of ALL generations."

"*All* generations?"

"Back through time, to the very *creation*. I see in my mind the *first* sight of the *first* Iron Dragon, smell his first smell, taste his first taste of flesh. I feel the air on his skin when he was born, still wet from the first egg, and the sight of the other eleven dragons, all hatching around me, including *your* first forebear. If I concentrate, I can remember *everything*, every moment of every lifetime of the Iron Dragon lineage, over a thousand generations! When I put the memories together, I perceive with my infinite knowledge, trends the likes of which you cannot even conceive: the movement of continents, changes in species, entire races come and gone and transfigured from one form to another by the actions of nature and gods and even humans. And most of all, I see now the history of the Triumvirate. How they created and ruled, offered peace and prosperity. How they were thrust down and made nameless by throngs of lesser, invading gods who cared not at all for the world except for their own ends.

"The Triumvirate was imprisoned in the very fabric of Irikara. It is their essence we call forth with magic. Renegade magic is from their heart.

"Now is their chance to escape imprisonment, for they are more powerful than before. Soon they will once again reveal their long-suppressed names. And they want *us*, Ingal, to lead the triumphant return! Their essence, their most powerful magical energy, will guide the way.

"What do you say, Gold Dragon? Will you pledge your loyalty? Will you join me in this, our most important adventure together?"

Though it still buffeted him, the storm had faded away from Ingal's consciousness. Now only the vision of Gogonith remained, hovering at his side, smiling broadly with wide, excited eyes. His tilting wings and bobbing body suddenly flashed and burned blue and white with static. The Iron Dragon was half Ingal's size, for he was very young, yet Gogonith emitted such power as Ingal had never known. If the Triumvirate held sway over every wind and every drop of water, they seemed to lend to their prophet all the charisma and energy they could spare at that moment.

And Ingal hovered transfixed, held by the awe of the moment, speechless. The thunder pounding around him gave testament to the emotions spinning through his mind. But he had to keep rational. Where were his priorities?

"And what of Alneri Castle, Gogonith? You still haven't given us a reason for its destruction. We feel this is the heart of the issue, for your motivations will likely stay constant."

Gogonith groaned and rolled his eyes. "I thought I was clear on this, Ingal. Must you be so attached to such a small population? They are only a handful of humans."

"Hundreds," Ingal corrected.

"Handful, hundreds, thousands, what does it matter? You have to see the long picture, Ingal. You have to see that this is not the issue of one nation or one state. Haven't I said this? Sacrifices, Ingal!"

"How many are too many? Just where do you draw the line?"

"I draw the line far beyond that, to be sure. When it is all said and done, there will be hundreds of thousands of dead. More."

"Hundreds of thousands! We weep even at the possibility! How could we not? How could *you* not?"

"Did you weep for the Enot when you destroyed them?"

Ingal growled. "That was totally different!"

"Was it?" Gogonith asked. "Was the stability of your land worth it? Wasn't it more peaceful after they were gone?" Ingal remained silent.

"The wars of gods are not fought in a day, Ingal, nor even in years. Each move of the grand game is the work of generations. Yet this is a surprise attack, of sorts."

"And just who are you, or *they*, attacking? You say they are escaping a prison imposed by 'invading gods,' yet why would it require the destruction of Alneri Castle? Alneri Castle is not an obstacle for any worthwhile god!"

Gogonith smiled, slow and sly. "Before I answer, I must first have your loyalty, Ingal. And the Triumvirate must trust you. You are the Creator's offspring as much as I, but wayward children must demonstrate their love before they are taken back into the family. Will you join us, Ingal? Will you help bring the Triumvirate back to their rightful place?"

The wind picked up even more. Rain and sporadic hail pounded at Ingal's eyes, but he ignored it. Ingal shook his head. "No." Raised his body. "You're disturbed." He let the wind push him away. "You're beyond control!"

Gogonith rushed after him. Together they were thrown westward by the tempest. Gogonith flew very close, nearly touching wings with Ingal as the lightning flashed around them.

"These are not sacrifices, Gogonith, but human lives! Give us a good reason first before we decide to join your fool's errand! Or leave us!"

"Why? So you can return to your mud baths? Do the humans still bathe you, Ingal? Still do they anoint you with pretty-smelling oils and kowtow at your feet? Feed you? Schedule your day? Is that what it's all about to you?"

"Of course not. Yet we have a duty, a duty to the White Lands Federation. We must use our powers wisely, but too much power would be disastrous, for no one is wise enough for it. Not you. Not us. There is a reason we are not gods ourselves!"

"But we can be, Ingal. We *can* be gods ourselves. There is so much more than one nation at stake, here, or even one species!

I cannot say it enough. It is about the *world*! It is about the Creators having their rightful place!"

"You're insane, Gogonith! They have twisted your mind and fed you lies to corrupt you. It has made you foolish and vain!" Ingal flew high into the clouds, yet the Iron Dragon followed.

"Leave us!" Ingal said. "Consider yourself banished from the White Lands! We will have no part in your insanity, and we will defend the White Lands against any further attacks! Do not force us to fight you!"

Gogonith reached out and swatted at Ingal's tail, taunting. "Or what, Ingal? You haven't a tenth the power I do! If I can destroy Alneri Castle with my voice, then what defense could you offer?" He grabbed Ingal's shoulder and dug into it with his claws.

Ingal roared and twisted his body. His claws ripped into Gogonith's wing. Together they plummeted with the rain toward the ground far below.

Gogonith screamed and gnashed his teeth. Claws dug into Ingal's vest and ripped open a breast pocket. Books and bags tumbled out and fell away.

Torra screamed.

Surprised, Gogonith let go. Both dragons regained their balance and swooped away from each other.

Torra!

Ingal flew into the storm, seeking distance between him and his opponent. He felt his vest. Torra was in a different pocket. He had to get her to safety. But Gogonith followed.

"Go your own way, Gogonith," Ingal cried out, "and trouble us no more. Be gone!"

"I'm sorry, old friend, but if you will not join me, then you are an obstacle to my success! Your life will be the worst of the sacrifices!"

Gogonith chanted, powerful magic that made Ingal's entire body tingle. Quickly Ingal cast a *Word of Safety*, and a thin shield of energy enveloped him. He folded his wings across his chest and dove.

Not quickly enough. The air warped around Ingal and exploded. Flames. Burning. The world tumbled out of control. Roaring, *his* roaring. Burning scales. Burning vest. Pain blinded him. He fell head over tail.

Instinctively, Ingal reached out with his scorched wings. The world stopped tumbling. He landed hard into the river with a mighty splash.

For a moment there was only calm and the sound of bubbles. Soothing cold. And then he was above the surface again, splashing, roaring, throwing himself ashore.

Around him fell rain in blowing sheets. Above, a shadow passed against darker clouds.

Ingal reached into the breast pocket and gently pulled Torra from it. She was limp but breathing. He placed the mage into the woods and, in the same movement, ripped an elm tree from the bank by the roots.

"If enemies we are, then you'll feel our wrath!" He swung the tree over his head and smashed it against the bank with all of his strength. With a thunderous crash the trunk split and splintered. Ingal ripped it apart with his claws and wielded a great length of the trunk, tapering from the roots to a sharp tip.

His magic center swirled in sudden activity. "*Ominum tes gorup tackard!*" Ingal chanted. With a whoosh the shattered trunk ignited in blazing white flame like a burning sword in Ingal's grip.

Gogonith dove from the heights, claws outstretched.

Ingal leapt aside and took to the air, slapping Gogonith in the flanks with the flaming trunk. White flames flashed where it hit and clung to the Iron's scales like burning tar.

Ingal needed height, so he beat as hard as he could to gain altitude, flaming trunk outstretched. Gogonith followed close behind. Too quick. He grabbed Ingal's tail and yanked him back.

Ingal turned and slashed with the trunk, but he missed. Gogonith pulled himself to Ingal, chest to chest, too close for Ingal to use the flaming trunk. Rows of razor-sharp teeth bit deep into Ingal's neck. Claws ripped into his sides.

Ingal pulled his neck free and raised his legs under Gogonith. Claws outstretched, he kicked at the Iron's belly, felt scales give way and flesh tear.

Both roared. Unable to fly properly, they fell earthward, kicking and gnashing, and slammed into the forest below. Tree limbs cracked and splintered. Trunks shattered. Bits of bark and leaves flew around them as their wings thrashed.

Both were shocked by the impact, falling off each other and shaking their heads. But Ingal came to first. With a roar, he grabbed the flaming trunk and leapt onto Gogonith, sat upon his chest, raised the trunk point-down over his head with both arms.

Gogonith chanted a spell, but Ingal plunged the trunk deep into his foe's belly.

The Iron Dragon screamed, mid-spell. Disrupted, the spell reacted chaotically; conjured lightning shot out of control from his foreclaws, igniting the forest around them. Drawn to the energy, natural lightning shot from the clouds above, danced around the struggling dragons like an electrified cage. Ingal ignored it, twisted the flaming trunk deeper into Gogonith's belly. Flames exploded from the wound, blinding white and wild. Gogonith screamed high and long and thrashed for release.

With a mighty heave and roar, Gogonith threw Ingal aside and leapt into the air. Incredibly, he ripped the bloody, flaming trunk from his abdomen and threw it into the forest. Flying heavily, he fled west with the wind.

Ingal got up to follow, but he fell exhausted against the shattered trees, wet, burned, and lacerated, with the forest in flames around him. He watched the Iron Dragon retreat into the dark sky.

"Gogonith!" he screamed into the wind and rain. "We curse you *and* your gods! Do you hear?" He gulped down blood and raised a clawed fist to the west. "No more sacrifices. No more, unless it be your own!"

TWENTY-THREE
Chaz Sanooc

Torra floated in a dark haze. There was pain here, pain that touched every part of her, yet seemed somehow separate and unimportant. A heavy beat, slow and reverberating, pounded through the darkness, coming and going but always regular. And voices. Voices in the darkness. First deep and threatening, then lighter, seeming to come from nature like the wind through trees. Still she floated, and in the dark nothingness that was her world she smelled smoke.

The smoke evoked a memory. A fireplace. She saw in her mind's eye the face of her mentor, Master Morikal, watching her with old eyes filled with laughter and wisdom. "That's my girl," he said, puffing on his pipe in his study and nodding to her. "Now concentrate. Use your mind. There! Like that. Did you feel it?" She held her hands aloft again and stated the words, and in her palm formed a ball of calming blue light. She laughed, and the ball floated away toward the corner of the room, into the darkness. She followed it with her eyes until it was the only thing she saw, and then it, too, faded away, and the memory ended in darkness.

Someone touched Torra's arm. A man spoke, but she did not understand. Her head and body ached. It was hard to take a breath. She moaned, cold and soaking wet, lying on her back. Nausea. There were so many ills that she could hardly take note of one when another would butt into her consciousness. The person spoke again.

Torra opened her eyes. It was nighttime. Beside her stood a figure with piercing eyes that glittered in the light of the moons. His hair was up in a topknot, dark-colored beads decorating the strap at its base. This was one of the elves, she realized, probably the one Ingal had called Rethuud. She crawled backward but stopped when he didn't pursue. Where was Ingal? How did she get into the forest? And then she remembered the encounter with the Iron Dragon. Gogonith. The fight. A massive boom followed by sudden darkness. She had heard and understood the argument to that point. She shivered at the implications of what they had said.

Torra and Rethuud simply looked at each other, surrounded by a dark and silent forest. The only sounds were the quiet murmur of water and a distant crackling. She reached into her robe and grasped the Rod of Translation. Finally Rethuud said, "You feel pain, mage?" in broken Etollian, running his hands over his body to simulate feeling for injuries. He probably thought she was a White Lands native. She nodded slowly, untrusting and unwilling to reveal her ability to understand and speak his language. He reached to a pouch at his side. Remembering the Padgarun and her pouch of acid spheres, Torra drew back and started to get up, but Rethuud pulled forth a sheet of some organic material and took a quick nibble at a corner, then gestured toward her. She didn't respond, but he tossed it to her and said, "Eat. Feel better."

When Rethuud backed away she reached out and picked up the material, sniffing at it. It was a thick and spongy leaf, like magnolia, but smelled pungent like rosemary. Her stomach rumbled at the thought of food, and the scent was good. She took a nibble, sinking her teeth through a thin, outer skin and into a warm gel at its center. It tasted like grilled beef mixed with dill. Within minutes she had downed the whole leaf. The pulp was warm in her stomach, and that soothing sensation spread through her torso, cutting away at the pain and nausea. "*Granaldelum* leaf," he said, then he bowed his head and muttered a quick chant.

Smoke wafted through the air. Looking behind her toward the crackling, Torra saw distant orange flickers of a forest fire. She looked back to the elf, but he seemed unconcerned, busying himself with a pack lying against a tree. The forest was quiet again save for the distant fire and the occasional rustling of some large animals in the forest just downstream—probably the griffins, she figured.

It suddenly occurred to Torra that she was alone in a strange land, her protector was gone, and her only companions now could be an elf she didn't trust and his two warriors, wherever they were. Should she try to sneak away? What was surely the Alsanoos River was off to her right. She saw the sparkles of moonlight on its slow-flowing surface. Could she swim across? The pain in her chest told her no. Simply standing up would be painful enough. And outside of her novice magic, she had no weapons of any sort with which to protect herself. She had no choice but to cooperate with Rethuud and his warriors.

The other two elves soon came into view, silently slipping through the forest and out of the darkness from the direction of the fire. One held a large book and a bag in his arms. Both reported to the first elf in hushed tones too low for Torra to hear. When they finished, they stood and watched her with eyes that reflected the distant flames behind her.

Torra was about to speak when the elves turned to look toward the river, cocking their heads. Then she heard it too.

Distant splashing and sloshing. The sound grew louder, getting closer.

The elves moved quickly. Rethuud drew a sword hilt from his waist, muttered a command, and a long, thin shaft of shimmering light projected from it where the blade should have been. The other elves drew swords. Each took up a position behind a tree, and then Rethuud motioned for Torra to do the same. She did as instructed and waited, listening to the ever-closer sloshing.

To be sure, this was the sound of something very large in the river. A dragon? Her heart pounded. Was it Ingal, or Gogonith? What had become of them? Sweat beaded on her forehead. Had Gogonith heard her in Ingal's pocket? Was he coming for her now?

Torra had hoped the dragon would pass by their position, unknowing, until he could be identified. But when he got almost close enough to see, the griffins started squawking and rustling nervously. The dragon paused momentarily, then moved again until its bulk obscured the river within a stone's throw. The elves leaned forward ready to rush at it. Then the dragon sneezed.

"We smell you, Rethuud, and your griffins." It was Ingal. "Put away your blade, for we feel Ascareth's power as well. We do not look for a second fight this night."

Rethuud whispered another word, and the shimmering shaft of light disappeared. The elves relaxed somewhat, but the other two did not put away their swords.

"Ingal!" Torra called out. "You live."

Ingal stepped out of the river, snapping tree limbs as he came forward. He grunted as he moved his bulk forward toward her. When his entire length was out of the water and standing before Torra, he looked down at her and knelt. "We are glad you live,

Torra," he said, his voice low and pained, a monotone. "We could not find you where we left you."

Something was wrong. Torra concentrated as she had with Morikal and muttered the words of a *Light* spell. She held out her hands, and from them came a white light that grew in intensity until all before her stood awash with light. She gasped, and the light faltered a moment before she regained control.

A dozen lacerations oozed blood from Ingal's legs, wings, head, and tail. Red tissue bulged from a vicious bite wound at his neck, blood trailing from it down over the vest. The vest front was shredded over Ingal's heart, and the pocket there had been completely ripped away. All over Ingal were charred and melted scales as if he had plunged through a devastating fire.

"By the stars!" she muttered.

Ingal looked at Rethuud. "The Iron Dragon may still be alive, but you need not fear him, for now; he is gravely injured. Still, we must move on to Mount Guulenen at our first convenience." Ingal sagged and grew quiet.

"You are not well, Jehai," Rethuud said in Peshilarn. "We must bind your wounds."

"With what, Rethuud? In Mount Guulenen we will find healing elixirs and other materials we need."

"Here," Torra said, taking off her outer robe. "Use this on that neck wound."

Ingal nodded, lowering with a groan until his neck was near the ground. Working together, Rethuud and Torra tore the robe into four wide strips and wrapped it around Ingal's neck. The wrap barely reached around, but was sufficient to staunch the bleeding.

"We must leave right away," Ingal said.

"There is one more matter, Jehai," Rethuud said. Ingal sighed, but nodded for him to proceed. "From our position in the forest," Rethuud continued, "we were unable to understand what was said between you and the Iron Dragon. But we saw much of what went on, even during the thunderstorm." Rethuud gestured to one of his warriors, who brought forth the book and bag. "We found a number of items in the forest lost when your vest was damaged. It was then that we found your human companion."

"We thank you, Rethuud, for your thoughtfulness." Ingal took the book and bag and placed them in another pocket. "Our highest concern was for Com Gidel's well-being." He sighed heavily and closed his eyes a minute before continuing. "You were not surprised by Gogonith's behavior, were you, Rethuud? You had an injured man back at the palace, and the number of your warriors was not as large as expected. Your immediate reaction to the presence of the Iron Dragon confirmed our suspicion. Your party was attacked by the Iron on your way to visit us, correct?"

"Indeed," Rethuud confirmed.

"We had asked your prince at our audience why the warrior was wounded, and, after hearing advice from you, he declined to say. Why would you hide this significant news from us?"

Rethuud shifted his legs and placed his hand near the hilt of his magic sword. "Your alliance and friendship with the Iron Dragon is well known. The moment was tense, as I sensed that something was wrong. I advised my cousin, the prince, as such. I was proven correct only minutes later when you announced our forthcoming execution. Suggesting to you that your friend and ally was responsible for unprovoked violence would have weakened our ability to negotiate a favorable outcome. You would not have believed."

Ingal closed his eyes and gingerly rubbed his head with a burned forefoot. "You may well have been correct, Rethuud. The moment was tense, indeed. But, combined with news we received when we stopped at Dragon's Passage, We would have better known what to expect from the Iron Dragon and taken action to prepare."

Torra's *Light* spell faded away, leaving the party in darkness until their eyes adjusted. Rethuud leaned against a tree. "We did not know why the Iron Dragon attacked. It took great skill and strategy for us to outmaneuver him and arrive at the palace. Our histories bear no warnings against the Iron Dragon, only good deeds, often together with your lineage. What has changed? What information do you have that you have not shared?"

Torra had heard and understood everything said between the dragons, aided by her Rod of Translation. Ingal surely knew that, for he gave Torra an eye to keep quiet, saying to Rethuud, "The fair Tellonta is dead, and has given rise to Gogonith. Gogonith is insane, having destroyed Alneri Castle. We cannot trust him and must consider him a danger to all societies with which he comes in contact."

"Just as the speaker has lost his sanity," Rethuud added. "Given the timing of his attack on us, and the prince's mission to visit you, it cannot be a coincidence."

"We agree. We must stay open to the possibility of a conspiracy that goes well beyond the elvish court, including Peshilaree, Gogonith, and even Ocrin."

Torra noted that Ingal did not bring up the issue of the Triumvirate gods or the powers they had bestowed to Gogonith.

Rethuud tilted his head and raised his chin, looking as if he had something important to add, but remained silent. Ingal seemed to sense it as well, watching him with expectant eyes. But when Rethuud failed to say anything, Ingal appeared to grow faint again. This time he closed his eyes and lolled his head to the point that both Torra and Rethuud took nervous steps toward him, but Ingal stirred again and insisted they continue their journey.

Moments later they took off, with Torra riding again in the now blood-soaked pocket. It was still preferable to riding with the treacherous elves and their monster steeds. Her eyes constantly strained against the darkness to see if Gogonith had come back, but saw only emptiness and the ghostly outline of hills below. They flew north away from the Alsanoos, following a lesser, meandering river that Torra could not name. Small, moonlit villages dotted its banks, surrounded by fields.

Ingal's flight was erratic and slow, dipping now and then, growing lower to the ground until, every fifteen minutes or so, he called a halt and landed in glades for a few minutes until able to continue. Each time his breathing grew more uneven, wheezing and wet.

The second moon had crossed the zenith by the time they approached a lone mountain poking up through the forest, far upstream from the nearest village. Its stark, rocky sides stood in contrast to the lush forest around its foundation. In the dim light of the moons Torra saw rolling hills in the distance beyond.

Ingal flew to the base of the mountain. Here lay the source of the thin river, pouring forth from a great opening. When they had flown close enough to hear the water, Ingal said, "Before you lies Mount Guulenen, source of the Cannosa River. Inside lies Chaz Sanooc, 'Cavern of Light' in the old tongue."

Ingal landed clumsily, straining to keep upright beside the rushing river. Torra tumbled out as soon as she could and stood watching as Ingal knelt to the gray, smooth stone of the riverbank to rest.

She took a moment to stretch her sore body, breathing deeply the cool night air. There was a chill from the river that washed through her, refreshing her, and she rubbed her raw eyes. Looking into the forest, the dim moonlight revealed looming shapes which at first she took to be something monstrous, but soon realized they were massive sarsen stones, arranged in a regular pattern, some toppled, and hidden amongst the trees.

The elves had been circling the mountain, waiting for Ingal to catch up. When they landed nearby, Ingal righted himself with a groan and groped his way along the wide, stone riverbank to the cavern entrance. The elves did not follow.

"Come, Rethuud," Ingal said. "You and your warriors must stay in the cavern tonight."

"It is forbidden," Rethuud protested. "Mount Guulenen is *asmanguulee*, a site of ancient evil."

Ingal's voice grew stern. "You have no choice. We wish to keep you close, and the Iron Dragon may yet return. We insist."

Rethuud clenched his teeth, but gave no further argument.

Ingal turned and continued to the cavern. Torra and Rethuud followed, with the other elvish warriors pulling along the reluctant griffins. The party walked slowly in Ingal's steps in a somber parade, with the river to their left. The opening yawned over them, ready to swallow them whole, its edge ragged like broken teeth, and then they were engulfed in shadow.

Ingal's shambling steps fell silent. "Cast your *Light* spell again, Torra, if you would be so kind."

Torra did as asked, but this time the light was feeble. It was enough, though, for them to make their way through the cavern to a back wall. The gray stone there was sheer and slick. Ingal raised a forefoot to the wall and pressed against it, lowering his head and closing his eyes. "*Costmen oc stookal ast,*" he murmured, almost humming the words. He lowered his forefoot and stood silent.

A moment passed, leaving Torra to wonder if the spell had failed. Then the mountain shook and groaned. Small stones and dust fell from the ceiling. She and the elves looked around for shelter, but Ingal remained still. The shaking increased, and just when Torra thought the roof would cave in, Ingal suddenly raised his head and shouted, "*Docem!*" The wall in front of him split evenly down the middle, and the halves separated, sliding apart, grinding stone upon stone. Dim light streamed out. The mountain grew silent as the doors stopped.

Torra gasped. Beyond the doors was an arched passage, wide enough for fifty men to walk abreast. Its walls were fluted, bedecked with gold and silver along the rims that reflected the light from within, but Torra could not see beyond Ingal's shambling bulk to its source. The party entered. A whispered word from Ingal closed the entrance behind them, shaking the mountain as the doors slid shut. The sound of the rushing river did not fail, only dimmed, growing strong again as they walked slowly down the passage.

Suddenly, the corridor opened up into a vast, oblong cavern, perhaps three-hundred yards long by one-hundred yards wide, and fifty yards high to the top of the vaulted ceiling. By some arcane magic the walls glowed of their own accord, a soft white light, and had wide flutes that became indistinct as they rose to the arched heights. Numerous white and orange stalactites of various lengths clung to the ceiling, with matching stalagmites beneath them, but this was no natural cavern. Skilled hands or amazing powers had carved it out eons before, shaped its features, and leveled the stone floor. The sound of rushing water echoed throughout.

Torra stood in awe, mouth open, before she realized that Ingal had continued lumbering forward, steering off to the right toward massive double doors halfway down the cavern. Over the door, supported by stone beams, were displayed two gargantuan weapons so large that only a dragon could wield them. One was a scimitar gleaming silver and gold and sporting a chain-wrapped grip. The pommel was shaped in the likeness of a snarling, fanged beast that Torra had never seen before. The edge looked as sharp as any human's sword. The other weapon, crossing the scimitar at its blade, was a battle scythe. The scythe's blade was almost as long as Ingal, curved like a half moon. The long handle was oddly crooked and corkscrewed and made from a dark wood that Torra could not recognize. The weapon was solidly made, but devoid of further artistic design. Both weapons showed signs of hard use, with nicks in the blades and handles, and signs of carbon scoring as if they had been set ablaze.

Rethuud stood emotionless looking about, then muttered in Peshilarn, "*Ecaea Ecimii alu alleia,*" before Torra could grab her Rod of Translation.

"What did you say?" she asked, now grasping the rod.

"I said, 'May the Great Ones rise again.'"

She watched Ingal's progress, and asked Rethuud off-handedly, "And who are the Great Ones?"

"It is just a saying." Rethuud took a moment to order his warriors to take the griffins toward the sound of the river. After they had passed, walking down the cavern toward her left, Rethuud turned back to Torra. "The Ecimii are all of the leaders and heroes who ever existed in Peshilaree, going back into the depths of time to the very first speaker, Peshiluud. When they died, their bodies were preserved through great magic and placed in Eshenakaree, the sacred lake of our origins, where they sank to await the call of our gods."

"When will this be?"

"It is a myth, nothing more." Rethuud was now wholly distracted and walked away to attend the griffins.

"Ecimii," Torra whispered. She caught up with Ingal. "My lord, what is this place? Did you make it?"

Ingal shook his head. "It was here long before our memory. Our forebears found it by chance, many generations ago." He paused, catching his breath, then continued onward. "It is of dwarvish excavation. But when or why they did so is a mystery, or even how they came to be here, for there is no way to the Deeplands that we have found." The dragon's eyelids drooped, and he slowed his progress to the point of almost stopping again.

Torra asked, "Is there anything I can do for you?"

Ingal seemed to shake off the fatigue and continued forward. "Please try to make yourself comfortable, Com Gidel. There are a few pieces of furniture at the far end of the cavern, and some stores of food. We are going to seclude ourselves into the side chamber. You and the elves may at times hear a great commotion. Under no circumstances are we to be disturbed, no matter how horrible the sound."

"Yes, my lord." Torra looked back to the elves. "But must I stay with … *them?*"

"You will be fine, Torra."

Torra wanted to say more, but Ingal was clearly in a state beyond conversation, and he had reached the double doors. Here Ingal pushed them open, revealing a wide, round chamber beyond stacked with books and artifacts around its walls.

"Remember, Com Gidel, we are not to be disturbed." Torra nodded, and Ingal went inside, closing the doors behind him. After a quick chant from inside, the doors shimmered with a blue light—magically locked—and Torra was alone again with the elves.

TWENTY-FOUR

Vitanomicon

Ingal collapsed to the floor. Had he projected a strong enough appearance? He could not allow the elves to see signs of weakness.

He moaned, lightheaded, and looked to the other end of the room. The round chamber was a bit larger than his study at Palal Jehai, with a large mound of compacted earth in the center—his sleeping mound. On the other side of the mound lay his salvation. Along the far wall stood a long, curved table with various flasks and elixir bottles. Next to it were rows of tall shelves stacked high with thick tomes and scrolls.

He knew well the extent of his internal injuries. Faintness threatened to overtake him. If it did, he wouldn't wake. He shook his head. Fear of death forced him to rise up on shaking legs and lumber, step by painful step, to the end of the room.

By the time he navigated past the sleeping mound to the table, his vision had doubled and grown cloudy. He couldn't hold his head up. His back sagged. But the fate of the White Lands Federation lay in his ability to save himself.

"Old dragon." If he had been younger, he thought, faster, more agile, he could have taken Gogonith without a problem. Maybe now was his time. Better to go now than the fade into senility. Like Rambanor. His mind slipping, body failing, unable even to chew, until he died in a helpless heap in his sleeping pit. Pitiful. But now wasn't the time to die. Others depended on him.

He threw a forefoot to the table surface. Glass containers shattered. Priceless potions spilled across the tabletop and splattered onto the floor. He closed his claws around a crystal phial as tall as a child, dust-covered and filled with a light blue liquid—a Potion of Healing. His vision dimming, Ingal snapped off the sealed cap and poured the contents down his throat.

All went dark. Dimly he felt himself slump to the floor. Death was near, and oblivion. He knew the feeling well. What would his offspring remember? He knew the answer. The offspring would feel all that Ingal felt, then the darkness would grow silent of thought. A flash of golden light, a rush of generations of memory, and suddenly the offspring would be in the egg, seeing crimson through the fluid and shell and hearing the muted sounds of those in the Egg Chamber at Palal Jehai.

No. Not the Egg Chamber. *This* room. And the offspring would burst forth, shout his new name, and find himself in this lonely, cold chamber, alone. Perhaps a decade will have passed. The doors would still be locked, and unlocking them, he would find the corpses of Torra and the elves mummified in the cavern beyond, for they could never escape alive without him to open the cavern entrance. The elves held at Palal Jehai would be executed. And war in the meantime could destroy the White Lands Federation—at least.

The healing potion worked slowly, soothing his throat and stomach, then spreading out to warm his internal organs. Energy grew like a forgotten dream, but only enough for Ingal to regain consciousness and return as much ability as he had when he entered. Then the warmth faded. He opened his eyes and sighed. Looking to the elixir table, Ingal saw nothing that could aid him further. He was no priest, and there were none within flying distance—even if he *could* fly in this condition. There was one more possibility.

Ingal turned to the shelves to his right and reached to the top. Scrolls and books tumbled to the floor in a cloud of dust, but he found the one he needed. The scroll was made of velum and sealed with rare saps from woods now extinct in this region.

This was the Vitanomicon, the renowned spellbook of healing. The recipient of its powers would be brought to full health and vitality, as if in the prime of life, as long as warmth remained in his body. But its healing arts came at great risk. Upon its casting, the recipient of its powers would be completely vulnerable, both to the spirits who came to heal him and to any entity of the outer planes powerful enough to entrap and possess his soul. The power of the spell would attract them. Ingal had to take the chance. Already the Potion of Healing was failing him.

Ingal cracked the Vitanomicon seal. The scroll unrolled before him. On its face was a stippled drawing like a misty cloud, below which were ancient writings dating back to before the time of Occultii. Ingal knew the words, and while he could still see, he started the incantation.

Thick and guttural, the words rolled off his dragon tongue. The drawing moved. The mists on the scroll surface shifted, clumped, and changed from a dull gray to sullen orange. They expanded, growing to the scroll edges and brightening. As Ingal continued to read aloud, the mists suddenly shot off the page with a thunderclap and turned vibrant orange and red, quickly filling the entire chamber until the walls and shelves were obscured as if in flame. Ingal felt an ethereal wind rising, soon rushing, past him, and the din of it overpowered his voice as he raised it in competition. He shouted the final words.

The flames stopped dancing. The wind stilled. All grew silent. Then movement slowly began again, softer, and the blaze became misty and revolving. Ingal lay exhausted on the floor, breathing heavily. It was as if he lay in the center of a candle flame, untouched by the heat. His energy failed him. He was at his most exposed now, helpless.

From the swirling mists emerged the vaporous forms of ghosts, *planar wraiths*, with miniature electrical storms where their eyes should be, and widespread arms that pulsed with the same hellish energy. First a few, then dozens came forth, moaning, encircling Ingal's hefty frame. His vest unbuckled and fell away. At some unseen cue, the wraiths fell upon him and ran their warm limbs over his scales. Ingal couldn't move, paralyzed by the wraiths. They dipped lower and passed though his body like fire through a split log. He gave in and closed his eyes.

Moment by moment, they poured over his wounds. The pain subsided. The wounds began closing. Ingal lay there, devoid of time's passage. It could have been minutes or hours, yet the wraiths continued working their energy through him.

And then came a change. The wraiths did not falter, but there was something else—someone else—in the room with him. He opened his eyes. The color of the mists shifted to include flecks of cerulean and jade. Off to his right, along the wall, a figure emerged from the clouds. Slender. Amber wings. Blue flames shimmered around a serpentine body and merged with the swirling red mists.

Azartial. Demon dragon. Footman of the Ether. Servant of the Draconii.

And there were others in the mist. Gods peered through the fire, like pillars of light or darkness. Many, many gods, struggling for space like a crowd of children around a confectioner. They were masked by the flames, shimmering and brilliant just beyond sight. Raw power radiated from them as if from an inferno, warping the mists before him. He was but a sapling in the eye of a hurricane.

"Azartial. Be gone!" Ingal said, trying to make his voice as commanding as possible. "You have not been summoned. Leave us!"

Unabashed, Azartial stepped elegantly across the floor and into the midst of the wraiths roiling around Ingal. The wraiths ignored the demon dragon, passing through him with no apparent effect. With each step, the demon's talons clacked against the stone of the floor.

"Good to see you again, Gold Dragon. And what convenient timing, too."

"You must leave us! We have not summoned you."

"No, but you are at the edge of *my* realm now, so to speak. I may come and go as I please." Azartial's words slipped easily from his mouth. "Funny how you should expose yourself so soon after tormenting me, hmm?"

Ingal tried not to show his fear. He knew full well what Azartial could do to him in this state. "It is your duty to obey us!"

Azartial jabbed a talon into Ingal's side and ripped open a gash. Ingal roared in pain. When he came to his senses again, the wraiths had fallen upon the wound to heal it.

Azartial laughed and threw back his head. "Ironic, isn't it? I could kill you now and it wouldn't make a difference. You cannot die while the wraiths attend you. I could subject you to torture, paining you to the edge of dissolution, and always the wraiths would repair it until you were completely healed. Why, I could torment you to infinity if I chose, couldn't I?"

Azartial pointed and lightning shot from his body to Ingal. The world momentarily disappeared from Ingal's sight as his body jumped and pain arced through him. He came to moments later, his limbs twitching. He took a deep breath, then his sight restored. Azartial was laughing again.

A gleam came over Azartial's eyes as the smile faded. Whispering, he said, "I could even possess you, if I cared to exert myself."

Ingal gritted his teeth and growled. "We will have retribution, Azartial. We have powers that rival yours. You will be no match when we emerge from the wraiths."

Azartial chuckled as he walked around to the front of Ingal. He paused a moment, calmly reached an arm back, then sliced open Ingal's forehead with his talons. Ingal roared again. He ground his jaws and glared at the demon as wraiths fell upon the wound.

"Oh, Gold Dragon, does it hurt? One must sometimes endure pain in the short term for benefit in the long. Remember that." Azartial squatted and looked Ingal in the eyes. "But playtime is over now. I did not come to torment you—solely."

"Get to the point, then! Why have you come?"

"To benefit myself, of course." The flames flared over Azartial's body. "Lucky for you, it will benefit you as well, and that little kingdom of yours. I have, of course, fulfilled my obligations from your summons. I come with answers to your earlier questions."

Azartial paused to gloat. Ingal looked beyond him. The gods just outside the mist ring seemed to step forward, their features tantalizingly beyond clarity. One, a female clothed in shimmering golden light, raised a hand in salute. This was surely Jonaatha, Goddess of the Light.

Ingal looked back to Azartial. "And how will it benefit the gods watching us?"

Azartial's smile faded. He did not answer. Instead, he said, "I have seen the future, Gold Dragon. One *possible* future. As Footman of the Ether, I alone have access to the Nexus. There, I can see all possible futures and pasts. Your lives are like gleaming rivers to me, coming together and moving apart as your lives intertwine.

"By sharing information with you, working together, you will save your land and all of its people, and I will be released from my eternal service—temporarily."

"Tell us this information then, and let us decide its value." Ingal shuddered as the wraiths dove into his neck all at once, concentrating their healing efforts on the bite wound. His neck seemed on fire.

"First, a history lesson," Azartial said. "Something you won't find in any historical tome or your precious memory." His flames died low, and he seemed to settle into a more comfortable position. "So listen carefully!

"Irikara was created by the Triumvirate," Azartial began, "and initially they were bound together by oath. Each populated the world with a sentient species of their creation. One created the elves to rule the surface, another created the dwarves to rule the underworld. And the third created the dragons to oversee the peace. Together, the Triumvirate sheltered their world from the Outer Gods, and the separate species existed in peace and spread across the world.

"Untold ages passed, but the peace did not endure. In time the dwarves grew tired of the darkness and rock, coveting organic riches as well. Eager to please his creations, the dwarvish god formulated a plan. Dwarves were not made to survive on the surface. So he stole the form of the elves from the elvish god and taught the dwarves to mutate their own kind. Generations passed, and those dwarven lineages who were chosen for the Transformation grew taller and leaner, more fragile, yet dexterous. Hair covered much of their body against the chill of snow and burn of sun. A new race emerged, which the dwarves called *humoncuum*: Humanity."

Ingal shook his head. "The Iron Dragon had spouted such insanity to us."

"Not insanity, Gold Dragon. Enlightenment. If you don't believe me, look to these gods for confirmation." Ingal looked up, and Jonaatha nodded, as did others.

Azartial continued, "The Transformation took place without the knowledge of the other Triumvirate gods, the elves, or the dragons. At the given time, armies of humans were moved to the mouths of caves and caverns all over the world, some specially made for the purpose, where humoncuum warriors were positioned to strike. *This* place was one of those striking points." Azartial gestured around him. "One of the first locations humans emerged onto the surface, where they would come to dominate."

"Nonsense!"

The demon continued, "This was the start of the Dawning Wars, a conflict that lasted thousands of years. Driven forth by their dwarvish masters, the humoncuum struck hard, catching the elvish lands by surprise and annihilating vast regions. The elves struck back with powerful magic and a subrace of their own to delve into the underworld."

"And the dragons?" Ingal asked.

Azartial chuckled. "Ineffective as always! Eager to keep the peace, fighting between each other, they compromised away their advantages until there was no eminence left, though some figured out how to take advantage of the battles to grasp the power for themselves."

"*Your* opinion, We think."

Azartial ignored him. "The war raged. Seeing the perfidy of the dwarvish god, the other gods struck back. Soon Irikara was devastated. Vast lands were sunken or raised. Entire continents were wiped out in a stroke. Earthquakes. Volcanoes. The heavens rang with explosions that filled the skies from horizon to horizon."

Azartial leaned closer to Ingal with hardly enough room for the wraiths to pass. "In their fighting, the Triumvirate forgot their duties, and the other gods, the 'Outer Gods', stepped in and took control, saving the three gods from themselves. The Triumvirate was overpowered and rendered like fat. But the Outer Gods showed mercy in the end. Irikara was part of the Triumvirate. To separate the trio from their creation would have destroyed the world, so the Triumvirate was trapped in the substance of Irikara, their energies dispersed throughout. It was as if they were imprisoned in the shell of their own corpse."

Here Azartial drew his snout within an inch of Ingal's face. Ingal felt the singe of the demon's blue flames on his nostrils. Azartial looked into Ingal's eyes and whispered, "And to trap them within Irikara, the Outer Gods erected three great stones upon the surface—locks, if you will—made of special stone which acted to dissipate the Triumvirate's energies."

Ingal's eyes widened. "'They are weaker than stone' you had said."

"Indeed!" Azartial backed away. "Now I have been given leave to speak, and you see the truth."

"The Heartstone of the Tower of Light!"

"Yes!" Azartial's flames leapt up. "And its Heartstone counterparts in the Tower of Darkness and the Tower of Balance. The Towers are centers of magic, but only because they are closest to the Triumvirate's energies. The Towers are vessels for the locks—or the Heartstones."

"And thus, if the Triumvirate wishes to escape … "

"They must destroy the Heartstones," Azartial finished. "Destruction of any one Heartstone would restore great power to the Triumvirate. Destruction of any *two*, and they will escape. Do you hear me, Gold Dragon? Losing one would be a major loss. Lose two—total catastrophe. And the Outer Gods would do anything to prevent that. *Anything*. Even if it means destroying the world entire!"

Thus the warning of the Stone of Lethori, Ingal thought. He lay in silence as the wraiths continued their work, and Azartial appeared to wait for the information to sink in. Finally Azartial continued. "But there is more that you must know, Gold Dragon." Azartial stood and walked a broad circle around Ingal.

Ingal had regained most of his energy and was nearly healed. He readied himself to pounce upon the demon. Yet he remained immobilized by the wraiths. He looked back to meet Azartial's eyes. "What else?"

"When the Triumvirate realized they were at risk of losing control of Irikara, they banned together their quarrelling forces. The Outer Gods counterattacked with warriors of their own, the Celestials."

Here the gods around the periphery of the mists faded away. In their place, tall beings appeared, bathed in robes of white energy and hair that burned with a golden fire. In their hands were long, argent swords that shone like starlight. But their faces were featureless save for a gaping, dark mouth that took up half of their faces.

The Celestials, Ingal thought, eyes wide. *Swordsmen of the gods.*

"They stand ready to attack again, Gold Dragon. But it is up to you to bring them."

"Bring them?" Ingal said. "Here? To the material plane? We would need a portal of immense power. No such portal has been made since the fall of Occultii, with two great renegade spells. *Dimensional Rift* was destroyed, and *Rift Widening* is useless without first creating the rift. It is not possible."

"And yet success depends upon it," Azartial said. "You will find a way. I have foreseen it. Bring the Celestials to Irikara, Gold Dragon, or the Heartstones *will fall*, along with the Towers that guard them."

The Celestials faded away into the mist. The planar wraiths were slowing, searching for further wounds and finding few. Azartial stood to leave.

"Wait," Ingal said. "How do *you* benefit from sharing this information? Why would you be temporarily released from your eternal service?"

Azartial smirked. "Call it a sabbatical of sorts." He winked. "Now I must leave you, Gold Dragon. You have work to do, and you must find a good tailwind, for there are already forces gathered, ready to strike. Farewell. We shall meet again soon enough!" Azartial turned and leapt into the orange and red mists in a flash of blue flame.

The wraiths finished their duties and, without ceremony, disappeared into the mists as well. Ingal was suddenly released from his paralysis, and the mists died away, folding back into the scroll, dimming, and coming to a stop in the bland ink of the drawing.

Once again all was silent.

Ingal stood and peered at the scroll for long moments trying to consider what he had seen and heard. But his stomach rumbled. It had been more than a week since last he ate. He took a deep breath and realized the boundless energy that now coursed through him. No pain. He examined himself. His body was clear of wounds. Even the scars of centuries past were erased from the scales. He reached up and touched his horns, but the broken horn had not regrown. No matter, he thought, and turned to the doors.

With sudden vitality, Ingal shouted an *Unlock* spell and burst through the doors. Heedless, he ran toward the river opening in the cavern, scattering elves and griffins with a roar, and leapt into the cold waters. He swam underwater to the outside of the mountain, emerging with a massive splash into the morning sky to hunt for prey.

TWENTY-FIVE
Murals

After Ingal locked himself in his chamber, Torra looked around the cavern. Across the cavern from the chamber doors was carved an opening to the river. The floor jutted out over the rushing water like a dock. Around the dock were projecting arms of stone that seemed to reach toward some invisible ship. Yet Torra could not imagine a vessel that could either make its way underwater from the outside, or emerge from the subterranean river, and then dock.

The elves had taken over the river area, but Torra managed to convince the scowling Rethuud to move the griffins away for her to clean her garments in private in the cold waters. She had hardly wrung out the excess water and dressed when the griffins broke from their lackadaisical guards to chase her away, snapping and flapping at her until she had cleared out of the area.

Sounds came from Ingal's chamber. There was moaning, chanting by Ingal, and the rush of wind, then all went quiet again. Still eyeing the griffins, Torra went to the doors to listen, but all she heard was a low moan. She called out to him, but there was no response.

She sat at the doors until she started to nod off, when from the chamber came pained roars, shouts, and angry voices. There was definitely someone else in there with Ingal, but it didn't sound human, and she could not make out what was said even when she used her rod.

All went quiet again—a pregnant, ominous silence. Torra backed away. The doors burst open inches from her, and Ingal rushed through the cavern in a blinding flash of sparkling gold, roaring, and dove through the elves and their mounts into the river with a massive splash.

Terrified, the griffins ran headlong around the cavern in a cloud of feathers, squawking and flapping, knocking themselves against walls. It was all Torra could do to avoid them in their crazed attempts to escape. It took a very long time for the elves to regain control of the griffins, shouting and cursing in Peshilarn, and twice as long to calm the beasts.

What got into Ingal? Torra wondered, attempting to catch her breath. The vision of the mighty dragon crashing through the doors replayed in her mind, and she dimly remembered a quick scream. The sight had terrified her as surely as it had the griffins, but there had been something else—yes— a thrill. Excitement. From the proximity of such raw and gargantuan power. The chamber returned to calmness. She had no choice but to wait again.

Once the griffins were under control, the elves huddled into a corner of the chamber. As they had done back at the meadow of Ena Enoiya, Rethuud pulled his men into a circle and chanted a solemn rite, then broke up and removed a large bundle from a griffin saddlebag. Inside the bundle was a leafy plant that resembled cabbage. Breaking the plant into portions, it exuded some sort of white cream from the thicker veins. They ate the plant then, slurping at the cream with a special zeal. Torra grimaced and headed the other direction.

At the far end of the chamber were some low tables, a couple of shelves, and a settee large enough to lie on. The shelves held small, wax-sealed jars of candied fruit and vegetables, and a pack of salted and dried meat of some kind. Torra sniffed at the meat and, deciding it was palatable, gnawed at a strip of it. It was tough and gamy. She wanted to sleep, but she was cold from her damp clothes, and the room was too brightly lit. Sullen, she watched the elves from the settee.

Her head ached. Her eyes were dry. And her heart fluttered again. The rash on her skin had spread and was now itchy to the point that she couldn't keep herself from scratching it. She reached to get the salve from a pocket of her outer robe and realized that the robe was no more, ripped in half and made into a bandage for Ingal. She frowned at the thought of it soaked in blood and still containing the only medicine she knew could soothe her condition—the herbs and the salve. She pulled her knees to her chest and laid her head on them, closing her eyes, and fell into an uncomfortable numbness of the mind.

~ ~ ~

Torra startled awake to find Rethuud standing over her. She hadn't realized she had fallen asleep, and quickly tried to compose herself. How long had she been asleep? Holding a blanket toward her, Rethuud said something in elvish before she could grasp her rod.

"What?" she asked.

Rethuud looked at the rod in her hand, then repeated, "I didn't mean to surprise you. You were shivering. Here, put this around you."

Still half-asleep, Torra accepted the blanket, and wondered why Rethuud was suddenly trying to be so friendly. The blanket was thick, like leather, and warm. She started to place it around her when she gasped and dropped it. "It moved on its own!"

Rethuud picked it up and said, "Of course. It is made of leatherine," as if that could explain it to her.

Torra stared at it. "I don't understand. It's alive?"

Rethuud looked down and nodded. "You are not familiar with elvish ways." She shook her head. Rethuud continued, "Unlike humans, elves find it sacrilegious to employ the corpses of any living thing: cotton, wool, leather, or any meat. We eat certain plants, but only if they have been blessed. Blessing our food was perhaps the most common of our Padgarun's duties."

Torra shuddered at the mention of the Padgarun assassin. She scanned Rethuud's belt for acid spheres.

Rethuud seemed not to notice, saying, "Our clothes, blankets, and saddles, therefore, are made of living material, an organism we call *resketa* which can be grown to any form we wish. Humans call it *leatherine*."

"That's all right," Torra said. "I would rather wear … corpses. No offense."

"Try to think of it as a warm pet." He offered the blanket again.

Torra shivered. Finally she reached out, took the leatherine blanket and put it around her shoulders. "Thank you."

The blanket squirmed slowly and settled over her body, clinging slightly and conforming to the shape of her arms, shoulder, and back. It pulsed slightly. A momentary fear washed over her that it would crawl over her head and smother her if she let down her guard. She fought the impulse to throw it off, choosing instead to bear it and put on a smile for Rethuud's benefit. The blanket was warm, at least.

Rethuud paused a moment, looking over his shoulder, then sat beside her. Torra scooted a short distance away, immediately regretting her rudeness. Yet the elf seemed somehow more civilized up close, more "human", she thought. But the obvious differences dispelled the moment: the cruciform pupils and jade irises of his eyes, the green hair, and the thin lips on a wider than expected mouth.

"Who are you, exactly?" Rethuud asked. Torra answered him, briefly, with her name and title. "Why are you with Jehai?" he continued.

"I'm wondering that myself." She shook her head. She tried to snap out of the attitude. *What should I tell him?* she wondered. *Probably nothing about renegade spells.* "He just wants me along to … advise him on magic."

"Then you must be a powerful mage indeed! When you were unconscious in the woods you cast a spell in your sleep—a blue sphere of light. And later a *Light* spell."

Torra snuffled. Had she cast a spell she had dreamt about. That could be dangerous! "You overestimate my abilities." She instantly regretted exposing her limitations, and quickly added, "I am nothing compared to Ingal."

"Yet Jehai would seem to think otherwise." Torra did not answer. "You are not of the White Lands, are you?" Rethuud asked.

"I am from Taxia. It is a land far to the southwest, below Ocrin, west of Sofon."

"Then he must think highly of you indeed to have summoned you from so far away."

"It's not quite like that," Torra said. *Summoned. Ha!* "It's a long story."

Rethuud blinked and nodded and did not pursue the topic. Instead, he asked, "What happened in there?" he pointed to the chamber.

"I don't know any more than you, I'm afraid. But I'm glad it seems to have healed him."

Rethuud looked away, and an uncomfortable silence enveloped them. "Did you know the Padgarun cleric well?" Torra asked.

Rethuud reached to his hair and repositioned the lapis lazuli beads there. "Yes. Phasgala was with me and the prince for almost a decade."

"A decade! Such treason!"

Rethuud winced. "It is a conspiracy which would seem to defy even the loyalty we shared. Phasgala was quick to anger, but she never failed in her support of us. She saved us time and again from threats we have faced together over the years, and stood by us in political disputes. If her goal had been to assassinate, she could have done so countless times. And she was … so much more than a warrior."

Torra scratched at the rash on her arms and thought about her next words. "If we should find Phasgala again, and she attacked, could you kill her if you had to?"

Rethuud turned suddenly, his eyes wide and angry. "She must have had her reasons! Must humans always jump to violence? A rational being would first try to find her reasoning."

Torra leaned away from him. Yet, surprised by her own words, she asked, "And if her reasoning is flawed?"

Rethuud's anger flared, then wavered. Doubt clouded his eyes. His mouth seemed to search for words, and then he turned away and slumped. "Have you never loved?"

Torra blinked back surprise. "I'm sorry. I didn't … It was insensitive of me." *How could anyone love such an animal?* she wondered. "I didn't know."

"No one knew." He turned back to her and drew a deep breath. "Jehai does not know. Consider it our secret. Agreed?"

"Of course." Torra looked down and rung her hands, feeling as if she should reciprocate. "I was in love, too, back in Taxia. Taenos was his name. But he … didn't understand me." She looked back to Rethuud. "Most Taxins think magic is evil."

"It is, sometimes. Even love can be a weapon in the wrong hands." Rethuud stood and tightened his sword belt, seeming to recompose himself into a more professional stance. "We have a request of you. The light in this room prevents rest. The griffins must have sleep if they are to continue. Can you cast a spell to dim the light until Jehai returns?"

Torra needed sleep as well. Somehow dimming the light would be a great improvement, but she doubted she had the ability. A couple hours before, she would have been too suspicious of any elf to humor such a request after what she had seen and heard at the palace. But if Rethuud had wished to harm her, he had at least a couple of opportunities to do so. Given Rethuud's odd confession, she was even beginning to trust him.

Torra thought over the spells she knew. "Let me see what I can do." She stood and placed the leatherine blanket on the settee. "But I'm tired. It may not cover a very large area." She quieted her mind and raised her hands. Torra chanted the *Darkness* spell, slow and steady. Her hands became obscured by a dark haze that spread over her body and into the air around her. Rethuud stepped back, but then allowed it to envelop him. She faltered, and the haze retreated back to her.

The spell wasn't working. She was too tired. Master Morikal had admonished her to try harder on this incantation, but it had been too much for her.

Torra forced her breathing to become regular, inhaling and exhaling in a slow, steady rhythm. She relaxed her eyes, face, and shoulders. She remembered Morikal's meditation lessons, and thought of the still surface of undisturbed water. The fatigue and aches faded away. She trilled her voice, and visualized a drop into the still water, vibrating with her melody. She raised an octave and let her voice fill her mouth, creating a richness in tone that felt incredibly natural, above her usual ability.

Suddenly it was if a back door in her mind was thrown open. Magical energy burst forth into her consciousness, and she threw back her head with the power of it. Shadows jumped from her body in a wave of intensity that spread darkness to the other side of the cavern.

Torra fell to the floor gasping, feeling the energy surge through her into the room like gale through a tunnel. Then the energy slowly dissipated, trickled, and stopped altogether. That door in her mind closed.

It was pitch black. Or had she gone blind from a botched spell? The sudden darkness made the cavern floor seem colder and the echoes louder. She caught her breath and tried to stand. The griffins squawked against their handlers.

"I'm impressed, mage," Rethuud said, "though it is more than I had desired."

Torra raised up, disbelieving. The entire cavern! She had expected, at best, a darkness sphere of merely thirty feet or so. The effect she had conjured was nothing less than miraculous for a mage of her limited experience, more befitting of a Tower mage, and a high one at that.

Unadjusted to the darkness, Torra's vision perceived dim patches of colors around her. She rubbed her eyes. But the lights grew. Soon the colors were bright enough that she could make out Rethuud's features. Turning, she saw that the lights emanated from the walls of the cavern.

Humanoid shapes formed on the walls in greens, blues, and reds, and within minutes brightly colored murals stretched over the walls of the cavern around the cavern's entire circumference.

Torra hardly believed what she saw. She walked silently down the cavern gazing at the walls. She knew of no spells to do this. Incredibly vivid colors danced along images of blocky, hairless dwarves in plate armor, lithe elves, and savage humans. Most of the murals depicted battle, especially between the humans and the elves. Dwarves wielded spikes and hammers. The humans had swords and knives. Elves dressed in living garments defended themselves with spears and clubs. Driven by the dwarves' command from cave openings, the chainmail-clad humans seemed all too eager to thrust their weapons into their elvish foes, slaughtering them with a gore that defied the seeming gaiety of the colors. The elves fought back, but many retreated into the woods with apparent cowardliness, shielding their eyes from the gaze of their attackers.

Seeming to command the elves was a male elf with emerald-green hair and silvery eyes. He stood tall and proud, and was clearly the focus of many of the dwarves' ire. Standing over him was the shadowy, looming shape of a goddess, seeming to will her energy to him with a face full of wrath toward the dwarves. Behind them both was the image of a mountain lake. Dead elves were being lowered into its waters.

At the other end of the cavern from that image stood another pair of entities: a female dwarf with golden armor and armed with a long, sharpened pole. Her eyes glowed red, and her blocky face exuded confidence. Behind her was the tall body of a god, wide-shouldered, gold-skinned, and larger than any other figure in the murals. He looked like a gargantuan version of a dwarf, and held a commanding hand over his heroine. Behind them lay a deep, crystal-lined chasm where dead dwarves were being laid.

Over Ingal's chamber door, half-hidden by the giant battle scythe, loomed a third god, dragon-like. This third god appeared in shadow like the elf goddess, but covered in stars, and commanded over a dozen different-colored dragons illustrated on the doors. All but one of the dragons averted their eyes from the battles, as if in shame or avoidance.

And over the river opening was the glowing form of an ovoid craft made of metal, gleaming silver. From a door in its side issued forth ranks of humans, with dwarves commanding them from behind.

Torra recalled what Gogonith and Ingal had said high over the Alsanoos River. *And Mankind?* Ingal had said. *What of them?* Gogonith had answered. *They are slaves, mutants, created by dwarves, of dwarves, for a war no longer fought.*

When she had finally finished walking along the walls, Torra returned to the center of the cavern and gawked in silence. Questions raged through her mind. Who made the murals? How old were they? Could the stories they told possibly be true? Were these gods the Triumvirate? She closed her eyes and tried to clear her mind, and calm was restored. When she opened her eyes again, she saw the murals as a whole. It dawned on her that they portrayed a one-sided account: the valiant dwarves driving humans to a victory over the evil elves.

She was joined by Rethuud. "This is nonsense," he declared. "Don't believe the lies it tells."

"How do you know they are lies?"

"Elves are not a cowardly species, and humans …"

"What? Humans aren't strong enough to rout elves?"

Rethuud gritted his teeth, then spurted, "Humans aren't dwarvish slaves."

Torra scratched at her arm and cleared her throat. "But who is to say that these things weren't true when these murals were made?"

"Peshilarn legends are extremely ancient. None mention such an improbable war."

Torra sighed. "I don't totally believe them, either. But most lies contain a kernel of truth. And after a lifetime of researching, I can say with certainty that ancient legends have a finite lifetime, no matter how important they were. Even the elves could forget events as major as these, given eons of time."

Rethuud shook his head.

Torra pointed toward the elvish goddess. "Is that lake the one you called Eshenakaree, where your Great Ones are placed when they die?"

"It appears so, though I know not who the goddess would be, or her hero."

"She is surely one of the Triumvirate."

Rethuud turned to look at her, concern on his face. "The Triumvirate?"

Torra realized too late that Rethuud had not been told. "Nothing. Never mind." She looked back toward Ingal's chamber.

"Tell me. Do you know something about these figures?"

"No." She told the truth, after all, as she was unsure herself. "When Ingal returns, perhaps he will have answers."

But Ingal did not return for quite some time. The elves and griffins huddled together near the main entrance, and Torra lay on the settee with the leatherine blanket. Eventually she managed a troubled sleep.

She was awakened by a mighty splash at the river opening, and a deep gasp. Again the griffins went into a panic, but were quickly gathered under control.

"What has happened here?" Ingal said, stepping up to the cavern floor. "Why is it dark?"

Torra moved forward and explained the situation, with the elves standing nearby.

Ingal lightly shook the water off of his body, then gazed around the room, shaking his head in amazement. "In all of our long generations, never has the light of Chaz Sanooc been extinguished." He looked down at Torra with wonder. "Thus, we have never witnessed these murals. How long has the cavern been dark?"

"Three or four hours, perhaps. It was more than I intended."

Ingal looked back to the murals, then again at Torra. "It is just as remarkable that *you* had the power to do this. Consider it, Com Gidel! This is no small cavern, and you have defeated a magical light that has shone *at least* twenty-seven thousand years without faltering! And you extinguished it for three to four hours so far without it coming back."

"Yes, my lord. I didn't know I had the ability. But the energy suddenly flowed at the right moment."

Ingal pointed a foreclaw at her. "We sensed a great power in you, Com Gidel. With the right training, We believe you could one day rank among the most powerful of the world's mages." He swept a forefoot through the air. "This is only the first of your great feats."

Torra felt her face flush. "Thank you, my lord."

Ingal walked around the room, stopping often, and lingering most at the depictions of the gods. Even in the dim light, Torra recognized concern etched over his features. At the sight of the elvish hero, he muttered, "Mirrored eyes to see the way."

"What did you say?" Rethuud asked. The Gold Dragon only shook his head.

Ingal did not explain what he saw in the murals, or answer questions posed to him by Torra or Rethuud, stating only, "We must not jump to conclusions."

The darkness began to break by the time Ingal made it around the room, the light rising slowly like a dawn. The colorful murals dimmed until they were almost gone, and the room became lit as before.

Torra studied Ingal. The gold of his scales gleamed like jewelry, with hardly a scar left. All of his recent wounds were healed. His eyes were clear, and the ivory of his horns and tail spike shone bright white. He was magnificent to behold.

"We must research in private," Ingal said, "and consider what we have seen." He turned back to his chamber, saying to the party, "Try to get more rest. We will leave for Peshilaree in an hour or so."

Torra walked with Ingal to his doorway, leaving Rethuud back at the river. "We hope the elves did not mistreat you in our absence, Torra," he said as low as he could.

"Not at all, my lord. Quite the opposite, in fact."

"Good. We yet need them, and must foster good relations."

"Where did you go, my lord?"

"Even dragons have to eat, sometimes." Ingal glanced away sheepishly. "But we also took the opportunity to scout out the Peshilarn border. There are many elves patrolling by griffin and on foot." Ingal entered the side room without her, closing the doors after him.

Once the doors closed, Torra stood a moment studying their surface. The last faint vestiges of the mural were still evident there, blurred to a pale ghostly outline. One by one, the depicted dragons faded away to plain stone. She raised a hand over the last remaining dragon—the only one who dared witness the battles—and traced a finger over its golden glow until it vanished.

TWENTY-SIX
Conspiracies

Sitting and trying to meditate on his sleeping mound, Ingal struggled to make sense of what he had learned.

Azartial's words had been troubling—beyond belief even: three gods created Irikara and then fought amongst themselves for control, pitting their respective species against each other. Humans and dwarves battled elves, and dragons failed to keep the peace. The murals only added strength to the demon's credibility. And then, trapped in the energies of their world for eons by outside gods, the Triumvirate now sought to escape imprisonment by destroying the Tower Heartstones.

Ingal had consulted all the books there at Chaz Sanooc, but none shed light on the situation. He slammed a fist to the sleeping mound, throwing up a small cloud of dust. The thud of forefoot to earth echoed through the chamber like the closing of a tomb door.

He desperately needed to contact the great Towermasters. As he had back at Palal Jehai, he once again cast the *Counsel* spell, creating a wispy mirror in the air in front of him. "I am Ingal Jehai, White Lands Dragon," he stated to the mirror. "We wish to speak with the Tower of Light." He waited, but no face appeared, and no voice issued forth. As before, there was only the bland shimmer of the mirror's surface. Suddenly the spell ended, cut off from the other side. Annoyed, Ingal repeated the spell twice more, once for each of the other great towers. But the Tower of Balance cut him off as well, and the Tower of Darkness simply never answered.

Ingal pounded the ground again, fluttering his wings. *How dare they! Denying us!* Never in the memory had the Towers denied the Gold Dragon's hails.

Energy from the planar wraiths still coursed through his body. Flying madly over the forest and feeding on wild game would normally exhaust him, but not this time. It was as if he were a thousand years younger. He wanted to run and fly again. *If only old Metharcus could see us now!* he thought. The last thing he wanted to do was sit in an underground chamber trying to concentrate. And to think he was near death only a few hours before! Old. Failing. Nearing decrepitude.

It was as if he had been reborn. And at this moment, he felt he could overcome any challenge to the White Lands.

Ingal closed his eyes and ran a serpentine tongue across his teeth. *Concentrate!* He thought. *How are the elves involved now?*

He consulted the memory and focused on the speaker. Two-hundred and twenty years ago, Ingal had visited the Hall of Emeralds for the current speaker's birth. Hundreds of the world's most powerful elves, mages, and dignitaries had been there to witness his coming.

For six hours they waited. Then the expectant mother appeared, bathed in sweat and carried on a laurel-wrapped litter. She was flanked by her mate, the previous speaker and father of the child. On the other side and slightly behind walked the *Eholminal,* a second male necessary to carry out elvish fertilization—a nephew of the mother in this case. The speaker's retinue followed, along with a host of midwives and Padgarun clerics.

Badly fatigued and bleeding, the mother was dying, but she found the energy to hold her child and hear the blessing of the Padgarun. In unison, the clerics chanted the Rite of Noble Birth:

To the spirits of the overworld,
    To the trees, sun, and sky,
We commit this child of elvish birth,
    A newsprung leaf of stars' delight.

To the spirits of the underworld,
    To the iron, gems, and stone,
We commit this child of elvish birth,
    Tender root to pierce cavern thrones.

To the spirits that bind the two,
    And bring balance high and low,
We commit this child of elvish birth,
    To bring control for all to know.

To the sorrow of all in the room, the mother died slowly and sweetly, whispering in her child's ear with her last breaths. As the speaker grieved, the child was passed to the *Eholminal* to raise.

Ingal dug a hole into the sleeping mound with an extended claw. The rite had seemed to him, as to all of his forebears in eons before, to be a simple blessing meant to begin a life in tune with nature. He had also thought of it as a call to the *eshenae*, or spirits of nature, to protect the child. But in light of what he now knew, Ingal reflected on a potential deeper meaning to the rite. A meaning, perhaps, known only to the Padgarun and few others.

Ingal wondered, could the "spirits" actually refer to the three Triumvirate gods? There were three verses, after all: one devoted to the over-world of the elves, like the elvish god of the Triumvirate, one devoted to the underworld of the dwarves, like the dwarvish god of the Triumvirate, and one devoted to the spirits that bound the two, the role of dragons and their god in the early history of Irikara, according to Azartial. This rite was one of many such blessings, performed for time eternal in all of the elvish lands around the world. Could the elvish clerics and nobility have known of the Triumvirate all those eons? Worldwide, even? How deep did this conspiracy go? There was surely none deeper.

Ingal wanted to know. The Speaker of the Hall of Emeralds was the key. How could he manipulate the speaker into revealing the conspiracy to him?

Ingal thought back to the last serious conspiracy he had dealt with. Some thirty years before, an uprising of Namisti militants threatened to stage a coup to take over the state of Namistad and secede from the White Lands Federation. Riots broke out. Extremists took over the Namistad capital, threatening to murder noble families. Ingal called forth troops, and civil war was imminent. With scant time to decide on a course of action, he saw no way to avoid further violence.

When Ingal told a young Metharcus about his dilemma, the new chamberlain offered a word of advice. "My lord," Metharcus had said, "at the summit of our desire, clouds obscure our sight."

Ingal had looked up and replied, "We cannot grant the rebels their desire—independence from the Federation."

"Of course not. But can you not give them a new *vizier*, with greater powers for self-rule?"

Ingal saw his point. It was a clever plan. The prior vizier was painted as a Federation loyalist, and ousted. Ingal worked behind the scenes to make the rebels feel they had an ally in a new, and seemingly more independent vizier, a larger (but more loyal) army, and more lenient trade agreements to make the region wealthier. The new vizier, Navi Janisim, kept Namistad in the Federation. His young general, Udullu Tasami, rounded up the few militants who weren't satisfied with the change. An unsteady peace set in, and the secession was averted.

An ally in disguise. Ingal stood and stretched, wings out. Maybe, he thought, he could use the same ploy with the elves. The speaker was a shrewd player in the most dangerous game the world had ever known. Doubtless the elvish leader needed a strong ally in his plan. One who knew the Triumvirate and their story. An entity great in physical prowess and powerful in magic.

Ingal made a fist and gritted his teeth. He would grant the speaker his desire … and cloud his sight.

TWENTY-SEVEN
Masquerade

Once again, from Ingal's chamber came the swirling reverberations of magical incantations, rising and falling in the dragon's robust voice, slipping through the air like a length of silk ribbon captured by the wind. His doors were unlocked, but Torra feared that peeking in might disrupt the spell. Whatever the incantation was, its casting was powerful enough to stand the hairs on her neck and vibrate along her bones.

She scratched nervously at the rash on her arms and tried to keep her mind on Ingal's spell. Although she couldn't hear all of the enunciations, she nonetheless tried to analyze what she could understand. Here, Ingal increased pitch, but maintained rhythm. There, he maintained diatonic integrity, then changed key within the phrase. He sang a portion in one long suspiration, then lowered an octave and articulated the syllables—it was an *illusion* spell, she realized. The next phrase seemed diffident, then suddenly attacked in a regular rhythm to open the magical aura and pull in energy—this was no small illusion. Finally he raised his voice, changing to a darker timbre, and Torra saw in her mind the movement he may have been making as he increased the tempo and forcefulness, waving his forearms through the air as he placed an accent on the last syllable of each tempo change. Torra had heard this sort of accent before, when a visiting mage to the Taxin astronomy guild had changed water into ale.

The chanting stopped. Torra stood, and the elves stopped their preparations and turned toward the chamber doors.

The doors opened, and through them stepped a dragon, but it wasn't Ingal. Torra gasped and stepped back, tripping on the settee and plopping onto its cushions with a thump, mouth agape. The elves pulled their weapons.

Gogonith! It was the Iron Dragon, by all descriptions she knew, rust-colored with ram's horns and piercing red eyes.

The griffins went mad again and rushed away, flapping down the short hall toward the cavern entrance, banging against the wall. Rethuud activated his magic sword, Ascareth, but his advance toward the dragon showed a cautious comfort.

Gogonith held out a forefoot, palm toward the elves. "Halt, Rethuud. I am Ingal Jehai." It was Ingal's voice. "You see before you only an illusion."

Rethuud stopped his advance. "Prove it. You could have been the Iron since returning to the cavern, or since the battle at the Alsanoos River, masquerading all this time."

The dragon lowered his forefoot and said, "Then we had plenty of chances to destroy you or trap you here. As for proof, we would retell our bargain with you if you wish, or how you held Ascareth to our neck, though it would seem proof enough to see a gold dragon enter the room and an iron dragon walk out."

Rethuud deactivated his sword, but the other elves did not put their weapons away.

Torra knew it was Ingal, but she was speechless. Gone was Ingal's large frame, replaced with Gogonith's slim features and long tail. He was smaller, more agile, and every bit as frightening as she had imagined the Iron Dragon to look. Ingal turned to look at her and gave a smile full of sharp, saw-toothed teeth.

"Why?" was all she could say.

"The speaker has already betrayed our trust. He would likely do so again. It is time to test his loyalties and expose his true intentions, posing as one who shares his goals." He turned back to the elves. "Rethuud, when the prince died, he said the speaker was insane and worshipping strange gods. What do you know of this?"

Rethuud licked his green-tinged lips and seemed to consider his words. "The speaker has been different in the last few years—impulsive, vain, unable to concentrate. Lately, he has spoken openly of gods he calls the Creators, but then hides further information on them. Rethuud paused a moment, then explained, "He sometimes rambles about the legendary First Speaker, Peshiluud, rising from the dead after eons past. The Prince of Mirrors was naturally concerned, but the speaker refused to explain himself, looking upon his son with suspicion for having asked. The prince suspected a deeper plot."

"And the court mage, Ektibal?"

Rethuud nodded. "Ektibal spoke openly against the speaker's delusions. They met in private, and Ektibal stormed away, shouting he would never relinquish 'The Spell' to the Creators. The prince was the last to speak with Ektibal, but shared nothing with me about what was spoken. He said it was too sensitive even for my ears. When Ektibal was killed, we knew we were on the run."

Ingal's brow furrowed. "Of what spell did he speak?"

"I do not know."

Rethuud examined Ingal, stepping in a wide arc around him. "But what does this have to do with your … masquerade? The Iron Dragon has not been seen in Peshilaree for over a century. I doubt his presence, or your appearance as him, would lead the speaker to reveal any plot. I know of no link between the Hall of Emeralds and the Iron Dragon."

"We—*I* am testing a theory," Ingal said, lowering his voice and sounding more like Gogonith. He cleared his throat. "I believe there *is* a link. Both Gogonith and the speaker appear to worship a trio of gods called the Triumvirate—the speaker's *Creators*. Gogonith destroyed Alneri Castle a few days ago, linking him with Ocrin against the White Lands, then attacked you and the prince on your way to Palal Jehai as if he knew the prince's mission. I believe the speaker's goals and Gogonith's goals are the same, and that they are two fronts of a common conspiracy which finds its origins with the Triumvirate. Your Padgarun, Phasgala, was yet another pawn involved in the elvish front of this conspiracy."

At the mention of Phasgala, Rethuud lowered his head, seeming to concentrate. Though she had heard the Iron Dragon's voice muted through Ingal's vest, Torra still gaped at Ingal's masterful imitation. She would never have recognized Ingal.

The cavern grew quiet as the griffins were brought under control again, and there was only the breathing of the dragon. The deep sound echoed, and for one crazy moment it seemed to Torra that the cavern itself was a gigantic lung in the belly of some gargantuan beast.

"Phasgala is a Padgarun," Rethuud said at last, "serving the forces of nature, not the speaker. Why would she assassinate the prince for him?"

"Simple," Ingal answered, a wry smile appearing. "The forces of nature are controlled by the same gods the speaker worships."

Rethuud grunted in surprise. Torra raised her eyebrows. "Yes, that's right." Ingal nodded and pointed a foreclaw at Rethuud. "Your prince was assassinated not at the order of the speaker, but at the order of the Triumvirate, whom both Phasgala and the speaker serve. Any elvish plot against the White Lands is therefore driven by the Triumvirate. And *they* have used Phasgala and the speaker as tools for that plot, along with Gogonith and Ocrin, we believe.

"Thus," Ingal continued, "if we appear to the speaker as Gogonith, he may be more willing to reveal his plans."

Rethuud nodded. "It is a cunning plan, Jehai. You have my respect. But I have yet to see a reason *why* the speaker, or my people, would want to invade the White Lands Federation. An order from strange gods, or even the speaker, would not be enough to convince most of them to jeopardize the life they lead."

"The elves have no need of the White Lands, but the Triumvirate does. I have suspicions as to their target, but I must confirm those suspicions before I speak them aloud. What the *elvish people* have to gain is still unclear."

"If the things you say are true," Rethuud said, "then we should easily find evidence."

Ingal's facial features relaxed. "Excellent. But we must split up. You will fly into Peshilaree apart from us … *me*. I must appear to the speaker alone."

"And what of me?" Torra asked. "You are not wearing your vest."

Ingal turned to look at her again. His eyes blazed with a horrible red light that shook her. "You must go with Rethuud."

Torra glanced at the elf, then back at Ingal. "With them? On the griffins?"

"I am afraid so, Com Gidel."

"I feel uncomfortable, my lord, going with … *them*, without you."

"You must. There is too much at stake." Ingal turned back to Rethuud. "Torra will accompany you. She is knowledgeable in renegade spells and will represent our interests."

Rethuud tightened his brow at Torra, then glared at Ingal. "I do not need a chaperone, Jehai, and her presence will be distracting."

"We insist, Rethuud. Do as we say. She is important in uncovering the conspiracy. Consider it an integral part of our bargain."

"Our bargain said nothing about this mage!"

Ingal took a step toward Rethuud. The other elves stepped back nervously. "You dare counter us on this?"

Rethuud's face took on a bright hue as he clamped his jaw. He narrowed his eyes. "She can ride with me, but if she gets in my way, I leave her behind."

Torra gasped. She was about to retort, but Ingal shot her a dangerous look. She remained quiet.

"It's a deal," Ingal said to the elf. "It is up to you to use your political contacts to find out what you can about this conspiracy. If the speaker's goal is what we think it is, he will need strong magic to achieve it. That strong magic may well be a renegade spell. Ektibal may have had everything to do with the situation, for he was very powerful indeed. And find Phasgala. She must be interrogated. After a day at Ishigana, we will rendezvous at the vale of Tegora'Seima, on the south side of Rishae'Uungi."

Rethuud secured the hilt of Ascareth to his belt and looked back to Torra. She turned away from the elf's gaze, suddenly sick to her stomach. Ingal was placing too much importance on her. She wasn't ready for this, not if she was going to be alone with the elves. Rethuud turned to give an order to his warriors. She looked beyond him to the griffins. Their thick, sallow beaks curved down to a wickedly edged point, strong enough to snap off an arm. Their eyes held no intelligence, only animalistic anger. Riding one of those monsters seemed inconceivable.

Ingal turned back to Torra again. "Stay here while I escort the elves out of the cavern."

The "Iron" Dragon stepped to the cavern entrance and chanted a spell to open it. The mountain shook, and the wall opened, spilling sunlight into the cavern. After elves and griffins exited, he let the doors close again and turned back to Torra.

"Is my voice convincing? Do *I* make a credible Gogonith?"

Torra was shaking. "Yes, my lord, too well for comfort." Then a thought occurred to her. "And what if Gogonith shows up? How are we to tell you apart?"

Ingal chuckled slyly. "*He'll* be the wounded one."

He gestured back toward his chamber. "On a table in there you will find a decanter with a symbol for the twin moons. It will appear empty. Pack it away. Do not open it until you use it. When you arrive at the elvish capital, and it looks as if you will be spotted by other elves, open it and place it to your lips. Inside is an invisible liquid. Drink the entire contents, and you will become invisible as well ... " He waved a forefoot in the air and shrugged, " ... for about half a day."

Torra went to the chamber. She found the decanter on the table amid broken vials and mixed, foul-smelling liquids of various colors spilled on the table's surface. One muddy pool was steadily dripping, upward, in defiance of any natural gravity. She tore her gaze away and found the decanter with the twin circles representing the moons of Irikara. She tucked it away in her pack and rejoined Ingal in the cavern.

The dragon crouched where she left him, watching her with Gogonith's maddened eyes as she came out.

"Have faith that Rethuud will not harm you … but watch those griffins," he said as she approached. "Rethuud knows you are needed, and he will not dare to counter us as long as his men are under guard at Palal Jehai. Remember the potion, but do not use it in haste. Once you have quaffed it, you will be invisible to everyone, including Rethuud, so stay with him." Ingal paused, then quickly added, "Show no weakness. Be strong. The elves will take advantage of your weaknesses."

"I can't do this." She felt like a fraud, and alone.

"You can. You must. It is important for the stability of the *world*, not just the White Lands and Peshilaree … and Taxia."

She lowered her head and nodded. How could she say no to that?

Ingal looked to the cavern entrance, then back to Torra. "On our flight north from Palal Jehai, you mentioned the possibility of finding a renegade spell in Peshilaree."

"Yes, my lord. *Rift Widening.*"

"Initially we felt it unimportant, a curiosity, but now … " Ingal leaned down and looked Torra in the eyes, but she turned away. These illusory eyes were too frightening to look into. "What I am about to tell you," he said, "you must not share with the elves." She nodded. He continued, "We have reason to believe the Triumvirate wishes to destroy the Heartstones of the Towers of Magic, and the Towers around them. Whether or not the elves would be part of that plan, we cannot say. But if they are, they would most likely look for a powerful renegade spell to do it. And where you find one renegade spell you are likely to find two or three. Search it out if you can. It may be 'the spell' Ektibal had mentioned."

Torra nodded quickly. "Destroy the Heartstones? Why?"

Ingal briefly described how the Triumvirate were trapped in Irikara by the Heartstones. When he had finished, Torra could only stand in silence. Ingal nodded with a satisfied grunt, then turned and again chanted the spell to open the cavern, shaking the mountain around them. They emerged into the sunlight as the doors slowly closed. Torra breathed deeply the sudden freshness of the air and the rich scent of conifers. The waters of the Cannosa River rushed past them out of the mountain to their right. The elves and griffins were waiting on the shore just downstream.

"We will all head to the Peshilarn capitol, to Ishigana," Ingal said to them. "I will fly along the Relae'Eshanrol, drawing attention away from you if you make a straight flight for Ishigana. When we … when *I* have finished with the Hall of Emeralds, I will search for you south of Ishigana, along the fields of Corithaan, at the base of the Mountains of the Stars. Expect me in two days."

"In two days," Rethuud repeated.

Ingal gave a smile and nod to Torra. Then, sparkling a deep maroon in the midday sun, he leapt into the boundless aquamarine sky and flew north, disappearing around the austere cliffsides of Mount Guulenen.

Torra sighed and looked back to the elves. They stood next to their griffins, wooden, silently staring back at her as if contemplating the best method for her murder.

Show no weakness, Ingal had said. She strode over to Rethuud and plopped her pack into his saddlebag. "Are we leaving, or are you just going to enjoy the scenery?"

TWENTY-EIGHT
A Dragon in Peshilaree

With clear skies, the exposed sun warmed Ingal's wings. Gogonith's rust-red scales absorbed the heat more efficiently than the gold of his own.

He looked down at the rolling, forested hills passing below, an hour northwest of Mount Guulenen. Somewhere down there was the border between the White Lands Federation and Peshilaree. He was passing over the Elvish Forest, as the humans called it, and into the elves' Senosh'Hori, "Forest of the South". The hillsides became higher, steeper, and almost impossibly arched—like a child's drawing—until all of the land below was a series of tall, forested humps clustered into each other as far as he could see.

Ingal could have known he had crossed into Peshilaree with his eyes closed. The air across the border was sweeter, perhaps from the asmarana vines the elves cultivated throughout their land for food, clinging to nearly every tenth tree in some areas and producing huge, globular fruits. Each breeze wafted through these ancient forests carrying the rich scent of humus and the lush dampness of moss.

There were no tilled fields here, or anywhere else in Peshilaree. No crack of whips driving oxen, or the rattle of wagons. No clanging of blacksmiths. No fireplace smoke in the air, tree cutting, or cleared areas with buildings. No roads, only trails through the forest. From border to border, Peshilaree was a continuous stretch of unbridled nature. Its inhabitants lived in complete harmony with their environment, utilizing what they must and wasting nothing. Every plant and animal was sacred. It was a way of life unknown to humans outside of a handful of primitive tribes and the occasional philosopher.

The final sign that he was over Peshilaree was that the streams now ran north, away from the highest hills that defined the border, and sparkled through the canopy like a hundred silver mirrors.

Already griffin riders had spotted him, taking wing and following a safe distance away and lower down near the trees. *Good*, he thought, and slowed his pace a bit for their sake. He was drawing away the elvish patrols for Rethuud. To his surprise, none of the warriors approached or hailed him. Were they expecting the Iron Dragon?

A brief concern flitted through Ingal's mind: What if Gogonith had fled this way? What if the Iron Dragon were already in Peshilaree? Well, it was a chance worth taking, he figured. And if he ran into Gogonith, it was a good excuse to finish him off.

Ingal reached the upper reaches of the Rela'Eshenrol, "River of Lost Spirits". Following its meandering path, Ingal spotted the first of the signal towers. Each was made of four tall lilum trees grown tightly together so that they formed one combined trunk of shredded red bark. At the top, on platforms reminiscent of eagle nests, lone messengers blew horns to the next tower downstream, and they to the next, and so on, of seemingly random notes that announced the coming of the Iron Dragon, until the message outpaced Ingal toward the elvish capital, Ishigana, in the Emerald Delta far away.

Ingal followed the river and the line of towers for several hours, winging over fantastic waterfalls and foamy rapids. Having apparently heard the horns, elvish villagers flocked to meadows and river clearings below to catch a glimpse of the Iron Dragon as he passed.

As Ingal flew, his mind filled with thoughts of the mission ahead. *How would Gogonith approach the speaker? Gogonith is vain. He thinks he's a living god. He answers to no one, except, perhaps, the Triumvirate, and he doesn't tolerate ceremony.*

He dropped a hundred feet to just above the river's surface, dipping a forefoot into the water and wiping his face, before rising back up. The coolness freshened his mind. *Gogonith would want all of the attention on himself. He craves attention. Shows off. Quick to emotion. It's time for us to make a show of our presence and turn some heads.*

When Ingal reached the Rela'Raeshaenonae, "Rapids of the Lost Army", he landed to drink, then turned northward and flew over some low mountains. The thermals from the south-facing hillsides rose to meet his wings, allowing him to glide and soar —and rest his wing muscles a bit—before continuing north. To the east lay the vast fields of Corithaan like an endless waving sea of chartreuse. For some time he flew over the western edge of the fields before turning northeast over the grasses and heading straight toward Ishigana.

~ ~ ~

The sun was nearing the western horizon when Ingal saw before him the great Emerald Delta, formed where the mighty Aesinirol river split into many channels and flowed into the Sacred Bay, Esha'Noricali. There, in the shadow of Rishae'Uungi, "Mountain of the Stars", were the marshy waterways and complexes of Ishigana, capital of Peshilaree and the nation's only "permanent" city. In its center stood the great green dome of the Hall of Emeralds.

By this point in his journey, a score of griffin warriors flanked Ingal, some of whom had followed him all the way from the Rela'Eshanrol. Many of the riders were Padgarun clerics.

Ingal's wings burned, and he breathed heavily. He may have taken on Gogonith's svelte appearance, but his body was still ancient beneath the illusion. All of the energy granted him by the planar wraiths was long spent.

And he had trouble concentrating on his appearance. This illusion spell was a powerful one, difficult to keep up, yet still he needed to maintain the appearance at least another full day. As he had time and again in the last several hours, Ingal gave a quick chant to buttress the spell's energy. It was against elvish protocol to call on the Hall of Emeralds at dusk; he would wait until dawn to do so.

But he could still announce his arrival. *Time to start the show.* He circled the Hall of Emeralds to attract the most attention possible. Situated amongst the trees, its green-veined windows shimmered, alive and pulsing, in the failing light of day. Elvish guards caught sight of him but did not seem surprised. His coming had long been announced by the watchtowers. A solitary horn announced his arrival.

Ingal dove low among the mossy cypress trees for the nobles to get a good look, then soared up to the nearest peak of the Mountains of the Stars. He landed, spread his wings to reflect the salmon sunset off his crimson scales, and bellowed a long, deep roar into the sky as the sun dipped below the horizon.

That ought to get the speaker's attention, he thought, and settled in to wait for dawn.

TWENTY-NINE

Ascareth

As Ingal soared over the first watchtower of the Rela'Eshenrol, Torra and Rethuud crossed the Peshilarn border. Torra shivered as the wind whipped past her ears and tangled her hair. She was chest-to-back with Rethuud, riding his griffin, with only a thin leatherine saddle between her and the vile beast. The leatherine clung to her, as did the blanket over her shoulders that Rethuud had given her at Chaz Sanooc, but still she latched onto the elf for fear of falling to the rushing canopy below. It had been this way for hours.

The elves flew daringly. Where Ingal had soared amongst the clouds, the elves chose instead to skirt the treetops, rising and falling over the hillsides. She feared Rethuud would crash them into tree limbs and stony outcrops of these bizarre, hump-like mountains.

"You're holding too tightly again," Rethuud yelled to her. She barely understood him for the rush of air.

"Sorry," she said, and loosened her grip ever so slightly. "Could … could you maybe fly a little higher?"

Rethuud didn't respond. She couldn't tell if he had heard at all. She checked to make sure she was still holding the Rod of Translation.

The other two warriors and their griffins flew in formation to either side of Rethuud, and slightly behind. There had been no sight of any other elves. Torra wondered how much farther they had to go.

Her legs were cramping and going numb, and her rash itched terribly. It was her disease. She wanted to scratch, but there was no way she would let go of Rethuud to do so. Instead, she shifted her weight to change the pressure on her legs. The shift caused the griffin to sway dangerously and protest with a loud shriek. It shrieked every time she moved at all.

"Sit still!" Rethuud yelled back. Torra complied instantly.

Rethuud made hand signals to the other warriors, and the three of them veered to the left and closed formation. The hills grew lower now, and farther apart, allowing Rethuud to guide the griffins into a low valley, following a thin river with grassy banks.

Torra's arm itched more than ever now that she couldn't scratch it. The irritation had spread in the last hours to her right shoulder, chest, and left leg. She needed to get her mind off of it. She leaned her head forward until her lips were near Rethuud's left ear.

"When will we stop to rest?"

Rethuud did not answer right away, tilting his head as if that was enough of a reply. Finally he answered, "Not until we reach Hasala Squalma."

"What's that?"

"A squalma is a nomadic village. Hasala Squalma is currently located north of here, at the southernmost edge of Corithaan."

Torra wasn't sure how far that was. She chanced to scratch her arm, but quickly thought twice and reaffirmed her grasp around Rethuud.

Rethuud flew lower in the valley, then slowed as if they were now out of some danger and could relax. With the river surface only about twenty feet below, the air temperature rose to a tolerable level. They passed over cattails and other tall reeds and grasses growing out of the shallow river. Blue herons, white egrets, and blackbirds with orange-striped wings fled from the griffins as they passed, and Torra glimpsed a black bear at the edge of the woods.

Through one clearing in the trees she spied a rounded hut made of large, green leaves, with a pair of very young elvish children playing near its open doorway. One looked up as they passed. He had long green hair, wide, intelligent eyes, and stood in unabashed nudity. Light, green-tinted skin was broken by dark green splotches in patterns along his sides and chest.

"Rethuud," she said, speaking now in a more moderate volume, "do all elves have green spots on their skin?"

"Yes," he replied gruffly. A moment of silence passed during which Torra wondered if she had crossed some taboo line by asking. Rethuud sighed as if he realized her naivete, and added, "The spots serve to absorb energy from the sun, like our hair. Most common elves do not wear clothing or head coverings for this reason."

"From the sun? How fascinating! Like plants."

"Like plants. But like plants, we must still find other nourishment."

Now that they were flying slower, Torra carefully scratched at her arm and chest. Waves of relief washed over her as the itching subsided, but it returned two-fold almost as quickly. She put her hand back around Rethuud and tried again not to pay attention to the irritation.

"Your magic sword," Torra said, "Ascareth. Why haven't I heard of it before? How does it work?"

Rethuud groaned. "It is not my intention to make small talk with you, Com Gidel."

"Of course not." But she needed the conversation right now. Struggling to find an opening, she said, "It's just that my life is in your hands. I'd like to know how you would defend me."

Rethuud did not answer for several minutes. He guided the griffins around a bend in the river, heading northwest, then said, "Ascareth is an ancient weapon of powerful magic, called a Baneblade, forged in the mage-armories of Occultii, ages ago."

"Is it the only one of its kind?"

"There were only four such swords made, each given to the commander of each of the four regions of the Occultian Empire. Ascareth is the Baneblade of the East. No one knows what became of the other three. Likely they were lost when Occultii was destroyed."

"How does it work?"

Rethuud made another motion to the others, and the three griffins banked right and headed northward up the narrow valley of an adjoining stream. "Ascareth's blade is a dimensional rip, able to slice through any earthly material, even stone." Rethuud's voice took on a certain amount of pride. "Each cut transports an infinitesimally thin slice of the material to a random plane of existence as it is slicing."

"Like a dimensional portal."

"Yes, but because it is so thin, nothing can pass through it and live."

Torra shook her head. "A sword that can cut through any material. Amazing. There can be no armor against it."

"No armor from the material world, at least."

Rethuud pulled back on the griffin's reins, and the griffin rose in altitude up and over the valley wall. Ahead, northward, the hills gradually became lower. To the northeastern distance lay a line of high, snow-capped mountains. On the horizon Torra saw a flat area of land with a lighter color of vegetation.

Rethuud continued. "Ascareth has not always been a tool of destruction. For much of its time it has been a symbol of rulership, passed from king to king. At one point it was lost for a couple thousand years, until a sculptor stumbled upon it in the ruins of an ancient mausoleum. For three generations, he and his sons used Ascareth to cut massive carvings out of the sides of mountains. Two of these carvings yet exist, in Ocrin."

A ghost of uneasiness passed through Torra at the mention of Ocrin. "And how did you come by the sword?"

"Long ago Peshilaree captured it in battle from what is now Ocrin. It was immediately passed to the protector of the Prince of Mirrors. And so it has stayed, from protector to protector of each prince or princess down the line … until me." Rethuud grew stiff and added, "But even the best sword in the world cannot protect the prince when the protector fails to wield it." Then, bitterly, "Or kill the traitor who murdered him."

Rethuud was silent for a while. Then, in an apparent attempt to shake off his darkness, he gestured ahead toward the horizon. "Behold, in the distance, the plains of Corithaan. And to the east of them, Unola'Uungi, the Sheltering Mountains."

The air grew colder and the wind stronger as Rethuud forced the griffins onward. Torra fell silent, pulling the leatherine blanket tighter around her shoulders. Her thoughts went back to Taxia, and Master Morikal.

Two years before, following a lesson in spellcasting, Morikal rummaged through a drawer and pulled out a small dagger. The blade shimmered a dim blue.

"Magical?" she had asked. The master nodded, turned the hilt toward her, and said, "It is enchanted with an *Enduring Sharpness* spell; it will never lose its edge or rust, nor be destroyed by any earthly power. It is yours, Torra. Happy twentieth birthday. May it protect you in your travels."

She had taken the dagger and judged its weight, surprisingly light, but then handed it back.

"What's wrong?" he asked, confused. "It was *my* master's, and his master's before him. Aren't you impressed?"

"Yes, master. But I would never use it. The world is violent enough without my help."

Morikal smiled and placed the dagger back in the drawer. "It is here if you should ever change your mind." He placed liver-spotted hands on her wrist and gripped her lovingly. "Your intentions are honorable, Torra, but we cannot always predict how the world sees us. As mages, we manipulate energies beyond the imagination of most commoners. Every spell changes the world in some small way, and we cannot always foresee the consequences. It is a great responsibility. Because of that, others will fear us, or try to use us. One way or another, you will be forced to defend yourself against them from time to time."

She wondered if she had made the correct decision. For all she knew, the dagger was still in that drawer.

THIRTY
Hasala Squalma

After hours of constant flight, the griffins were struggling to stay aloft. Torra could not keep from shivering and had long since stopped paying attention to her surroundings. She closed her eyes and cast a *Warmth* spell. Heat washed over her from head to toes, too hot at first, but quickly cooling. All too soon it was gone and she was shivering again.

When Rethuud called a halt at long last, Torra opened her eyes and saw the Sheltering Mountains looming much closer now, just to the northeast. A number of low, rolling hills built up to a stark precipice spotted with stunted trees, then snow, as it rose to a startling height. How anyone could associate that with shelter, she did not know. Far over the cliffsides circled large birds, which she at first took to be condors. Torra realized they were other griffins, though, when they emitted challenging shrieks which were quickly answered by the three griffins they rode. Torra brushed away visions of griffins swooping upon them, talons out, as they attacked intruders in their territory.

Commanding everything else to the northern horizon was an unending sea of grass waving in the breeze. The fields of Corithaan, she reminded herself. The fields began just north of their position, where the seemingly endless forest they had flown over dwindled to grassland.

Torra wondered where Ingal was. She was unfamiliar with the territory, or Ingal's intended path. But if he flew steadily, he was surely far away by then. Did she wish she was with him? She wasn't sure which was worse: stifled in Ingal's cocoon-like leather vest pocket, soaring over the world, or holding on for her life on the back of a disgusting and dangerous beast, flashing by treetops. On second thought, she decided the vest had been better.

The griffins circled a forest meadow, descending gradually until they landed, hopping along the ground and nearly throwing Torra off in the process. When Rethuud's griffin had stopped, he dismounted and helped Torra do the same. As soon as she stepped down with her pack, the beast went squawking off to the north end of the meadow and plunged its beak into a swift-running stream, raising its head to gulp down the water. Soon it was joined by the other griffins.

Torra fell to her knees. Her legs had gone completely numb and weak, shaking. Rethuud called to one of the other guards. Together they walked her around the meadow, stopping occasionally for her to rub her legs, until warmth returned and she could stand on her own. Torra apologized to the obviously annoyed elves.

It was only then she realized they were being watched. The meadow was ringed with elves of all ages. Most were nude, though some elders were clothed in leatherine. They whispered to each other in Peshilarn, becoming more excited. Almost as one, they approached in curiosity, closing the circle around her.

Torra grasped her Rod of Translation and said, "Please. My name is Torra. I'm a friend … She didn't finish. Speaking in their language only excited them more, and the youngest of them rushed forward to feel her hair, run their hands along her hands, face, and clothing, and tried to peek under her robes.

"Please!" she said, and tried to push through the crowd. *Have they never seen a human?*

Rethuud came to her aid, saying, "She wears plant corpses for clothing."

Instantly the elves backed away, gasping, and making warding signals toward her. Torra was at once relieved and embarrassed. For the first time she wondered if she might be more comfortable if she were naked in public.

"You should walk around more," Rethuud said, "and try to eat and drink while you have a chance. Dusk comes soon. At sunset we will continue across Corithaan and enter Ishigana at night."

Torra nodded. Rethuud continued, "I and my men will speak with the elders. Stay here."

Torra eyed the griffins. "Actually, can I come along?"

"It would be too distracting." Then Rethuud looked around and, apparently sensing her discomfort, said, "Fine, you can come a little way with me. But there is something I must do first."

Rethuud turned to the south and walked several steps through the crowd. An elderly female, bent over with a cane and bald except for a dark green scalp, took a couple of faltering steps toward them, shuffling through the grass. She held in her hand a stone platter with a stone cup, sloshing water.

Torra stepped forward to help, but Rethuud stopped her. "You cannot aid her," he said. "It is tradition that she deliver the Greeting Water. The day she is unable to ceremoniously provide for her squalma's visitors in this way she must step down as its leader and exile herself to the forest—forever."

The elder hobbled to Rethuud and handed the platter to him. Rethuud picked up the stone cup, drank from it, then placed it back on the platter. Another elf came and took the platter and cup away.

Rethuud raised his hand and cried in Peshilarn, "Rethuud of Hasala clan and Ishigana, with warriors of the prince, and with Torra Com Gidel of human lands, mage!"

The elder looked at Torra, then raised a hand partway, stating in a shaking voice, "Hasala, elder, of Hasala Squalma." She paused to lick her lips, again glancing at Torra, then continued,

> Our squalma grants you
> Its trust and its truth.
> We will nourish you and keep you long
> If our squalma is true.
> Take from us as you need,
> And know such gifts are from our heart.

To which Rethuud replied,

> We accept your gifts,
> Your trust and your truth,
> And sup with you as long as we can.
> For we are true
> And take only from need,
> As our heartfelt gift is ourselves.

Rethuud stepped closer to the old woman and spoke with her in quiet tones. Torra looked around at all the elvish faces staring at her. The common elves seemed neither happy nor angry at her presence. Surely they knew of humanity, but it seemed to her that she was a museum piece to them, a figure from an ancient legend now living and breathing. She sighed, realizing that it would be no different if an elf dropped into a human village back in Taxia.

"Torra," Rethuud beckoned, then turned and walked into the forest. Torra followed.

When she passed the elder, the old woman smiled, toothless, and ran the back of a bony hand along Torra's arm as if caressing a sleeping babe. In a voice so old it seemed to shatter, she said, "See before you the past of the world, my child. See before you its future!" The elder cackled as if she had just shared some hilarious secret. Torra hurried to follow Rethuud, glancing back to see the old woman still laughing and watching her, leaning heavily on her cane.

"Rethuud," Torra whispered, catching up, "who was that old woman?"

"Her name is Hasala, leader of this squalma, and one of the eldest of the land. And she is regarded as a seer."

"How old is she?"

"Over three-hundred fifty years, now."

They entered the darkness of the forest. Looking around her, Torra saw that the squalma consisted of a great number of low, domed huts made of live, interwoven vines with broad leaves that had been folded in to fill any gaps. The vines had grown together in most places to form a continuous wall. The doors were either left open or covered by loose vines and leaves draping down from the roof. The forest floor around the village had been worn flat and pounded in places into broad trails, but nowhere else were any trees or understory plants disturbed. Thick, glossy vines curved around many of the mature tree trunks. The vines bore globular fruits, each like a gigantic red grape as big as a grapefruit.

The villagers followed close behind Torra, weaving softly through the trunks like an army of ghosts. The color of their skin and clothing blended them so closely into their environment that she had trouble distinguishing them from one another and the flora around them.

Rethuud stopped in front of a low hut and spoke with an older male. The elf gestured to the hut's opening, and Rethuud pulled the vine door aside.

"Here you may rest undisturbed," Rethuud said to Torra. "Stay here until I come for you."

Torra nodded and entered, thankful for the reprieve from curious eyes. The door fell closed behind her, and she was alone. Dim green light filtered through impossibly thin leaves in the roof. Like the trail just outside, a pounded layer of humus and dark soil formed the floor. A pile of decaying vegetation lay in one corner, steaming in the dimness, giving out low heat and the pleasant aroma of mint. In the back of the hut was a bed made of live, lush moss growing from the floor. A thin, stone bowl filled with water sat next to the bed, along with one of those large fruits.

On a flat, raised mound of compacted earth near the door stood a wooden bowl containing what looked to be a length of leatherine rope and a knife, both completely submerged in a greenish liquid. Torra touched the liquid. It was thick, like sap. Curious now, she reached further in, grabbed the knife, and pulled it out. The knife and her skin came out of the sap with only a slight dampness, seeming to defy the apparently gooey liquid. To her surprise, the knife, both handle and blade, were made entirely of a heavy wood. Traces of green colored it, even, as if it still lived. Testing the edge, she found the blade at least as sharp as any metal knife she had known. She put the knife back in the bowl, and it slowly sank back to the bottom.

Torra heard many elves padding around outside the hut, but none attempted to look in or disturb her. She tried to relax on the moss, rubbing her legs and stretching to get her blood moving again. She resisted scratching at the growing rash. Her chest still hurt from the fight Ingal had with Gogonith. Her buttocks ached from the griffin saddle, and her ears stung from the wind of riding.

She opened her pack and ate some of the rations she had taken from Chaz Sanooc, then, untrusting of the water in the stone bowl, drank from her own waterskin. She remembered the way Rethuud and his warriors had prayed before eating, and briefly wondered if she should do the same now that she was in their land. But the thought was quickly wiped away. *There is no such thing as gods*, she thought. *Food imparts necessary nutrients regardless of prayer.*

Torra listened to the sounds of the squalma around her, expecting to hear elvish conversations, the play and laughter of children, and the hustle and bustle of any village. But none of that was evident. A few villagers spoke in hushed tones about her and Rethuud. There was no laughter or shouting, nor the running footfalls of riotous children. Was it always like that? It was almost as if the village was just another collection of undergrowth in a vast and dark forest, occasionally rustled with the breeze or lightened by the call of songbirds. She sat on the moss bed with her knees up to her chest, feeling alien—a huddled animal in a thicket.

Time passed, and her legs recovered. Tired of waiting for Rethuud, Torra decided she needed to explore the village, and opened the vine door to venture forward. But she stopped. All around the hut stood elves waiting and watching. They weren't menacing, just … blank. She changed her mind and went back inside.

Torra would have sworn that night had fallen by the time Rethuud came for her, parting the vine door and beckoning her to come out and follow. As before, a throng of elves stood watching in silent curiosity, then followed her and Rethuud to the clearing, moving as one like so many ghosts through a quiet and darkened woods. Upon emerging into the meadow from the near darkness of the woods, she found it was still dusk.

Mounting the griffin was easier this time as Rethuud and one of his other warriors held the beast down for her to sit on first, then Rethuud joined her. As before, taking off on the beast was a rough, flapping, running affair that jostled Torra against Rethuud and threatened to knock her off. As they circled up and over the forest, Torra looked down to see the meadow lined with elves again. The decrepit elder woman, Hasala, stood in the dying sunlight, laughing up at her with sparkling eyes.

The high cliffsides of Unola'Uungi glowed ocherous in the failing sunset as Rethuud led the flight northward, flying low to the trees past the last of the forest and then over the growing expanse of Corithaan grasses. Herds of brown-and-white-striped antelope split and ran as they flew over. The griffins tensed and jerked toward the herds as if ready to dive into their midst for a quick meal. She shivered as she pictured griffin beaks rending antelope bodies.

Torra tried to get the thought out of her mind. "Rethuud," she asked over the wind, "did you learn anything new back there?"

He nodded. "As I had expected, Phasgala landed in Hasala Squalma two days ago for food and drink, but stayed only briefly before flying toward Ishigana, as we are now. The other Padgarun clerics of the village flew after her.

"Oddly, Phasgala changed mounts, calling down another griffin from the mountain, after hers nearly died of exhaustion in the meadow. Clearly she was in a hurry to report the assassination."

"I guess that's not a surprise."

"Her direction confirms she is collaborating with someone in Ishigana, and that most likely means the speaker or someone of his court. And the fact that she was in such a hurry tells us that much depends on her success. I would guess that plans could not go forward, or would be in jeopardy, if the prince had been allowed to convey his warning to Jehai in full. The Gold Dragon may have more of an advantage than he thought."

Torra rode in silence for many minutes as the sun sank below the diminishing line of trees to the west. The grasses below changed from green-gold to sullen orange to burnt umber as the sun fell.

"What will you do when you find her?" Torra asked.

Rethuud looked down. "Capture her, of course, and get answers—one way or another."

Torra saw again the wild Padgarun running across the lawn of Palal Jehai, the maddened look, the bloody spear, the melting face of the guard. She shivered. *There's no way anyone could capture Phasgala alive,* she thought, *and Rethuud surely knows it.* Again she wondered how anyone could love such a bloodthirsty creature. Could Rethuud fight, and interrogate, a female he loves? Could he kill her if he had to?

Before she knew what she was saying, she muttered, "I wish I had someone to love." Rethuud jerked. She held her breath. Should she try to qualify her statement—justify it? "It ... it must be tough to deal with her treachery." She grimaced and shook her head. *Stupid. Stupid! Just be quiet!*

Rethuud took many minutes before he answered. His voice, however, held no emotion, and his words were measured. "I love

Phasgala, but I love my nation more, and my culture. Back at the squalma, you caught a glimpse of the way common elves live; in harmony with the world around them. Our borders and culture are secure. Being the aggressor in a war against humanity—even one nation—will lead to loss of that harmony, no matter what gods may interfere. The prince undoubtedly felt the same. I'm certain the elves of Hasala Squalma would as well. Conflicts with humanity have always led to the loss of elvish lands in eons past. The conspiracy must be unveiled and stopped at all costs, and peace must be maintained."

Torra thought about Rethuud's words as she held onto him and felt the buck and sway of the griffin as it flew. Memories of her old love, Taenos, flashed through her mind. She could almost feel the warm touch of his arms around her, his coarse chest hair against the skin of her breasts, his tight abdomen against her belly. She wondered if she could go to such lengths—fighting and interrogating a lover, to the death if necessary—for any one cause. She would rather harm herself first.

Finally she said, "You are braver than I, Rethuud." He didn't answer. She had made her own sacrifices. Taenos refused her love for fear of her magic. There wasn't a time in her life when she didn't feel so alone.

Torra tried to divert her attention away from these thoughts. She settled into as comfortable a position as possible and stared up at the growing darkness of the sky, waiting for the nightly arrival of the only lovers she had left. The stars never lost their shine.

THIRTY-ONE
Ruler of the Ages

The morning sun advanced against the darkness like a traitor, stalking the shadows. Its vermilion eye glowered at the delta through a sullen haze tinged with storm clouds, refusing to cast its heat upon Ingal's barren summit.

The dragon yet stood upon Rishae'Uungi, his Gogonith-wings folded around him like a cloak. He readied himself to release a bellow and fly down for reception. The first dim rays of sunlight glimmered off the dome of the Hall of Emeralds. He opened his mouth to roar.

Horns blared from below. Scores of griffins rose from the cypress swamp. Padgarun riders. Long broad-tipped spears.

A trap! Ingal threw open his wings. But the Padgarun seemed not to notice, flying instead to circle the dome. Soon a distinct ring of griffin riders orbited over the dome. At some unseen signal, the griffins shrieked in unison, accompanied by a massive cry of "Hail!" from their riders.

Ingal tilted his head and watched in amazement. "Who are they hailing?" Ingal said to himself. *The speaker? Not likely. No Padgarun hails the speaker, no more than they would a common elf.*

Neither Ingal nor any of his forebears had seen so many Padgarun in one place at the same time.

He shook his head and reminded himself of his mission. Was Phasgala among those Padgarun? He couldn't make them out well enough from this distance. Then he remembered who he was at that moment. How would Gogonith respond to this?

He wouldn't be upstaged, that's how. Ingal filled his voluminous lungs and let loose a deep and mighty roar, filling the sky with auditory terror.

The ring of griffins broke, many flying off without regard to their riders' panicked efforts. Some threw their riders entirely. Ingal leapt from his towering perch and dove into their midst, further scattering the beasts, laughing madly as he thought Gogonith would.

He didn't see Phasgala among them, but there were so many clerics. He threw out his wings and dropped to the Emerald Hall courtyard like a hawk pouncing on prey, emitting another massive roar.

Why weren't they retaliating against him? By the look of most of the riders, they wanted to. Instead, the clerics tried to get their mounts back into order, circling over the Hall again.

The courtyard was walled in by towering cypress trees. Glimpses through them revealed the ruins of fragile, arching stone structures. A couple hundred noble elves stood along the edge of the meadow, seeming to loiter in expectation of something. Behind Ingal was a stone dock projecting into the Aesinirol river. In front of him rose the massive Hall of Emeralds, as big as his own hall at Palal Jehai. Dark green, a series of concave membranes on its living surface served as windows, with thick, pulsing veins between. A dozen fearsome guards stood at the arched entry, spears and acid slings ready and blocking the way.

"I am Gogonith. I come to address the speaker," Ingal announced. The guards tightened their grips on their weapons.

"Let him through." It was a female voice from behind the guards, her voice measured. The guards parted, revealing a late-aged elvish woman half-hidden in the dim light of the entry. "The speaker will see you now."

"Hmmph," Ingal grunted, and lumbered past the guards. He bent down to go through the arched opening, hoping the elves did not hear his old vertebrae popping as he did so.

The stern-faced woman wore a thin robe made of a single layer of living leatherine, decorated with natural pigmentation of blue and green. Lapis beads were woven into her intricately arranged, fading green hair, indicating that this was a Dendarin graduate, like Rethuud. She turned at Ingal's approach and led him into the dome.

Upon entering, Ingal's magic senses went into a flurry of activity. A great deal of power surged here which had not been present in ages past, but it didn't seem to emanate from anyone or anything in particular.

The interior was bathed in light green, filtered through the living windows above. The light sparkled off emeralds grown haphazardly into the very flesh of the dome's walls. At the far end lay a natural granite outcrop which acted as a dais for the Hall. A massive, gnarled oak grew over and through it, shaped and trimmed over many hundreds of years into a living throne made from its lower trunk and exposed roots. The Throne Tree continued up through the roof of the dome. Vines tangled into intricate knots all over the Throne Tree—trumpet vine, clematis, and asmarana—blooming in bright flowers and loaded with asmarana fruits. But despite the Hall's seeming vitality, an angry heaviness hung in the air.

Servants tended the living walls, pouring liquid nutrients over the woody roots along the base and scattering flower petals over the floor of the dais. Upon seeing the Iron Dragon walk in, the servants quickly gathered their things and left through a back exit. Soon the hall was empty except for Ingal and those on the dais. Ingal closed his eyes a moment and concentrated on keeping up the Gogonith illusion. With the elves so close, they would be more able to pick out flaws.

Staring up past his thick green eyebrows and high, garishly-flowered headdress, the speaker sat in his throne watching the Iron Dragon's approach. He held a long wooden staff, branching at the top with thin leaves. Between the branches sat a wasp nest teaming with the yellow-and-black-striped insects. Ingal knew these weren't ordinary wasps, but lethal mutants able to kill a man with a single sting and able to follow the directions of the staff's wielder.

To either side of the speaker stood advisors and Padgarun guards. Phasgala was one of them. She nodded to the Iron Dragon as if they had met before. Once again, the riders orbiting overhead gave another hail.

The speaker chuckled, looking toward the roof. "Such loyalty!" he said, his voice smooth despite his advanced age. "They've come from all over Peshilaree for their lord." He looked back to Ingal. "Well, Iron Dragon, let's be quick about this so we can get to the event of the eon."

Ingal wondered what he meant, but it was then that the speaker stood, grunting. He raised his hand and stated,

> Granted be the right of trust.
> Granted be the right of truth.
> No time is long
> If the court is true,
> And all gifts given are from the heart.

Ingal remembered who he was supposed to be, and simply replied, "Good. I am Gogonith."

Phasgala tried to hide a sly smile. A number of the Dendarin advisors exchanged annoyed glances. Ingal wondered if he had been too flippant, even for Gogonith.

The speaker stared at the dragon a moment, then put on a smile. "We weren't supposed to meet until the endgame, Iron Dragon." Endgame? Before Ingal could comment, the speaker continued, "But given today's occasion, I am certain my lord and the Creators will be pleased with your presence."

His lord? The speaker has no lord, Ingal thought. Don't become distracted. Stay in character. "There has been a setback."

"Oh?" The speaker walked forward to the edge of the dais and stepped down to the main floor. As his living robes shimmered in the thin light, the pigmented pattern shifted from a random scattering of bright colors to a gray-and-white striped one. "The Gold Dragon?"

"Yes."

The speaker walked up to the dragon, his staff tapping the floor. Phasgala and the other Padgarun guards hurried to stand behind him, followed by the female Dendarin who had led Ingal into the hall. The speaker chuckled, a wild gleam in his eye. "Phasgala tells me of your failure to stop my son on his way to Jehai's palace. She had to do your dirty work for you!" He jutted a finger in the air, saying, "But she succeeded, and Jehai knows only what the Creators have told him. Right?" He stepped even closer, directly beneath Ingal's face. His robes changed again, this time blending in with the floor beneath him. The wasps stopped moving over the nest and stared up at Ingal with their cold, insectoid eyes. "Tell me, Gogonith, what is this … setback?"

Ingal made a fist. "The Gold Dragon would not come around to the Triumvirate's way of seeing things."

"You must try harder. He would be the Creators' best asset." He looked up quickly to the dragon. "No offense, my dear Gogonith. And we need him to carry out our plan." The speaker's eyes took on a murderous gleam. In a conspiratorial whisper he asked, "Did you have to educate him?"

Ingal forced a toothy smile. "We fought, but he lived, crawling off to that palace of his to be babied by his servants."

The speaker's smirk disappeared. He looked over Ingal as if examining him for wounds, raising an eyebrow, but saying nothing. Ingal cursed himself for not thinking to add wounds to the illusion. "That doesn't sound like the Gold Dragon I know," the speaker said. "You should have pursued him. Likely he is formulating a plan against you—and us. I assume you told him nothing of our plans."

"Nothing." Ingal couldn't help adding, "But given the Gold Dragon's formidable intelligence, I imagine he may suspect what is going on."

The speaker shook his head. "Go back to him. The time has come. I already moved up the Creators' plans when Ektibal and the prince decided to counter us." He turned and stomped back to the dais, the hornets buzzing in a cloud around his head, then he turned again and pointed at Ingal. "The Gold Dragon is key, and the code on my dispatch was only the start of educating him. You and the Triumvirate must turn him to our side. Luring his troops away from our goal is not enough to guarantee our success if you fail."

Luring troops away? "You mean, luring the troops to the border with Ocrin."

His brow tightened. The Dendarin woman frowned. "Of course!" the speaker said. "We can't have them in the east where the Tower is." Once again he stomped toward

Ingal. "You arranged the troop movements, right? With that Namistad traitor in charge there? You said you had made the arrangements."

Namistad traitor in charge? Vizier Janisim? "Yes," Ingal said, hoping his anger did not show. "It's all arranged."

The Padgarun riders gave another hail, louder this time. Seemingly annoyed at this, the speaker gave a hand signal to one of his advisors, who turned and left through the back exit.

The speaker seemed to relax. "My ambassador returned from Ocrin with assurances that the Doom Empress is cooperating. Troops have massed along the Federation border and should attack at the Traitor's signal."

Ingal wanted to know what the signal was, but could not think of a cunning way to ask without giving himself away.

The speaker pointed a finger at Ingal and smirked again. "It was a nice touch, destroying Alneri Castle. At first I was angry that you exposed your loyalties so soon. But that strategy will ensure that the Federation generals move more troops to the north of the border, expecting an attack there instead of through Namistad."

So Ocrin will strike in Namistad. The Viziers are falling into the trap! Ingal, trying to respond as Gogonith would, blurted, "That was the idea."

"It probably didn't help convince Jehai to our side, though. Pity." Just then, from outside, a horn blew again. The speaker looked up, then toward the entry. "Here they come." He looked Ingal in the eyes. Gone was the sardonic humor. "I didn't appreciate your stunt. Don't disrupt our cermony again, eh?"

The speaker turned back toward the dais. Ingal ran a long tongue over his teeth. "Wait," he said, tapping the tip of his tail against the floor. Too late to reconsider.

The speaker returned, throwing annoyed glances toward the entry. His robe flashed red, then green.

"I am still unclear on one important point in the Triumvirate's plan," Ingal said. "How, exactly, do you intend to destroy the Heartstone?"

The speaker remained silent at first, bunching his brow and tilting his head slightly. "Haven't the Creators told you the plan?"

Ingal knew he had to maneuver carefully here. The Dendarin whispered something into the speaker's ear, watching Ingal all the while.

"Obviously they didn't tell me that part," Ingal said. Remembering he was now Gogonith, he added, "Perhaps you would risk it all by keeping me in the dark! I am no simple servant! Tell me if you wish my cooperation."

The speaker spoke with deliberation. "Once the Ecimii rise, Peshiluud will cast the spell." He didn't elaborate.

Questions rushed through Ingal's mind faster than he could fathom their answers. *Ecimii. The Great Ones—elvish nobles and heroes sunken in the Lake of Origins, Eshenakaree. Was the myth true? Would they rise from the lake, reborn? And Peshiluud—the mythical First Speaker and founder of Peshilaree, long into the depths of time. Alive? Casting a spell? Which spell? A renegade spell?*

But any pointed question could signal his deception. He chose a roundabout question instead, feigning irritation. "Yes, yes. But how can you be sure the spell will work?"

A large number of elves were entering the hall through the front entry. Noble elves and those Padgarun clerics who had earlier given hails from their mounts.

The speaker's suspicion seemed to wane. "Oh, the spell will work with *Him*." He nodded toward the dais. "But to get it we need the Gold Dragon to cooperate with us." The speaker threw a dangerous glance to Phasgala. Her face flared red in response.

The speaker walked back to the dais, followed by Phasgala and the Padgarun guards. The Dendarin woman also turned, still eyeing Ingal over her shoulder.

Ingal sighed. *So they don't have the spell, whatever it is.* He had to find it before they did. He thought of Torra, hoping she would have a chance to look for her rumored renegade spell. *Why would he need us to 'cooperate?'*

As the speaker stepped up to the dais and sat on the throne, many hundreds of Padgarun clerics filed in around Ingal, each armed with spears, slings, and acid spheres. The hall filled to capacity. Ingal tried not to act surprised or intimidated. One Padgarun was enough to throw his entire palace guard into disarray, he thought. If the masquerade were discovered now, there would be no escape. There were perhaps twenty warriors between him and the dais, but hundreds between him and the entry. He was struggling to keep up his illusion spell against the power of this place. If his true identity were discovered, should he attack the speaker?

A large contingent of aquatic elves entered, still dripping from the river, having come up the delta channels from the Sacred Bay. They were hairless, gilled, and covered over their unclothed bodies with tiny, blue-green scales. Their webbed feet flopped conspicuously on the rock floor of the hall. One stood out among them, their equivalent to the speaker, wearing a crown made of pearls and living, multicolored mussels and a robe fashioned from live kelp. The other aquatic elves were armed with spiky coral clubs and with sea urchins baring six-inch long poison spines—a throwing weapon, he figured. They took a position to one side of the dais.

Then, more exotic yet, a dozen dwarves entered the hall through the rear entrance. Hairless, they stood perhaps three feet tall, skin various hues of brown and gray, bodies squat and smooth like river stones stacked one on the other. Deep Dwarves, from parts of the Deeplands so far below the surface that the heat and lack of fresh air was deadly to most Overworld species. They squinted their wide eyes to near blindness against the dim light of the room. Dressed in their species' most honored and prized clothing, they wore tanned hides made from the skins of their own ancestors, a layer of fine titanium chain mail on top of that, then an outer layer of plate mail shining with platinum and gold melded into the steel surface in elaborate designs. Armed with gem-encrusted ceremonial swords and battle spikes, they carried elaborately decorated helmets under an arm. The most decorated dwarf held in his hand a flawless crystal sphere of quartz—a sign of rulership. They took up positions in the front and stood muttering to one another in their odd, rumbling language.

The speaker rose from his throne and held up his arms, raising his wasp staff high. His robes flashed and sparkled a wide range of colors, matching the floridity of his headdress, yet seeming to enhance the sincerity of his face. The Hall of Emeralds grew silent.

The speaker kept his arms up another moment, surveying the audience before he spoke.

"Today is one of the greatest moments in the history of the world, my children. Irikara quakes for us!"

The Padgarun again shouted "Hail!"

The speaker continued, "We gather to call an end to untold ages of imprisonment. Long have elvenkind lost ground to humanity. Long have we bided our time, preserving what we can of our traditions and culture, and protecting that which is most sacred to us. We are the keepers of the world's origins, patiently waiting through the epochs for omens of rebirth.

"No longer!" Here the speaker raised his staff even higher. "No longer do we wait! Today the world splits to its core. Today, those who made Irikara come forth to reclaim it. And with their efforts, elvenkind and dwarvenkind will be reborn, granted power to take back all that has been lost."

He lowered the staff, then paced the rocky edge of the dais. "Never forget our history! Long ago, three gods created our world, then populated it with species of their creation. But they lost their world to Outer Gods—interlopers—who imprisoned the Creators in the very quintessence of Irikara. It was even forbidden by these interlopers to utter or write the Creators' names, on pain of death. Did they wish us to forget? Since that time we have guarded their secret, built our immortal army, and planned."

Ingal caught a scent in the air of the chamber. It was Torra, he was sure of it—that inexplicable sulfur smell, and the scent of human sweat. He looked around but could not find her. Invisible, he thought. Good. He returned his attention to the speaker.

"But today," the speaker shouted, "today we begin their liberation! Today the Creators will be nameless no more! I call forth their names, unafraid of retribution."

He raised his staff again. "Come, *Dwarn!* God of the dwarves. Maker of stone and metal. Ruler of the Deeplands beneath our feet! *Dwarn!*"

The dwarves looked around in their slow fashion. Thunder clapped, echoing off the distant mountains. The sky dimmed. The audience looked up as one.

"Come, *Draq!* God of the dragons. He who ties the world together and holds it in balance! *Draq!*"

Heavy clouds rolled across the sky, blotting out the sun. Thunder boomed. Chain lightning shot across roiling storm columns and illuminated them from inside.

"And come, *Elva!* Goddess of the elves. Maker of tree and stream. *Ruler of all the Overworld! Elva!*"

Lightning struck the courtyard. Griffins shrieked and fled, flapping to escape. Then a bolt hit the top of the dome, seeming to dance there and sending runners of electricity down the veins of the dome and into the ground, but harming no one.

"Yes!" the speaker shouted. "Yes! They come! And they protect us from retribution. *Here* the Outer Gods hold no power. Let it be a sign of what's to come, when the usurpers' hold on Irikara is broken and they retreat under the punishment of the Creators!"

Ingal's magic senses abruptly overflowed like a torrent through a spring. He went dizzy, threatened to lose consciousness. He couldn't let his masquerade fail. He struggled, muttering a quick spell during a lightning strike to buttress his appearance. When he looked up again, the hall had fallen silent, but none looked to him, only outward. Three immense and sinister shadows surged up the walls—one to Ingal's right, another to his left, and one behind the dais. They loomed over the audience from floor to top and remained there, pulsing and horrible. Lightning continued to strike, but no light penetrated those three shadows. The room chilled.

The speaker stepped to the center of the dais. "Hail the Creators!"

"HAIL! HAIL! HAIL!" came the unified response, "HAIL! HAIL! HAIL!" repeated again and again, resounding, until the speaker held out his arms for silence.

"Guarded all these millennia, let the tale be heard for the first time since the world was stolen!" Then he sang.

> From wind and wave, stream and tree,
> The goddess Elva first formed one
> Then many elves from Eshenakaree
> Beneath the moons, beneath the sun.
>
> Guardians of Nature since first light.
> Mirrored eyes to see the way
> Reflect the stars when in the night,
> Reflect the sun when in the day.

Ingal jolted to attention. *That* was the verse he couldn't place! *That* was the verse that haunted him all these days!

> Verdure was their flowing hair.
> Growing like the leaves of trees.
> Tall and strong they worshipped there
> Beside their loving deity.
>
> Sang they praises to their queen
> And brought her treasures from the woods.
> They built halls from living things
> To house their goddess and their goods.
>
> Elvenkind spread across the land
> And over the wild forlorn sea.
> Wielding power from Elva's hand

Built they nations from wave and tree.

Knew they nothing of war or pain.
No soldier nor miscreant.
Art and science were their gain.
Their tales were long and elegant.

Innocent is the new-sprung seed
When tempests come to wash away.
Even dragons cannot flee
The wrath of gods when they're betrayed.

Came the armies of mankind,
By god-spell dwarves were driven forth.
Raging battle struck heaven blind
And laid waste the jewels of sea and earth.

Greedy were dwarves for the upper world;
For trees and beasts and sunlit seas.
Gods fought, and dragons roared.
Millions died of foul disease.

Fractured nations of elves combined
And to their fore came Peshiluud.
This warrior mage was strength defined,
And led the elves to lands renewed.

Then Outer Gods crept in to steal
The world away from rightful lords.
The Creators fought with endless zeal.
Seas were boiled and mountains torn.

Elva's magic died away,
Trapped in wind and in the ground.
Dwarves retreated without delay.
The human horde spread the world around.

In the region of the Sacred Bay
Peshiluud formed a land apart.
But protecting it a price was paid.
A human arrow pierced his heart.

Elvish eyes mirrored only pain
And elvish souls were sorry
As the hero's corpse was grimly lain
In the calm, cool waters of Eshenakaree.

Beneath the moons, beneath the sun,
Elvenkind, oh here be said,
Remember you and everyone
No noble is truly dead.

No noble is truly dead.
In our future, let it be read.

Peshiluud, arise! Arise!
Champion again your god's return
With verdure hair and mirrored eyes!

The speaker fell silent. Lowering his eyes, he removed his headdress with a shaking hand and stepped away from the throne.

Verdure hair and mirrored eyes, Ingal thought. *The elf from the mural at Chaz Sanooc!*

Rain and wind slammed the hall as if attempting to knock it down. Gigantic trees were heard uprooting and shattering. But the dome held.

The looming shadows closed ranks around the dais.

Suddenly, the Padgarun clerics roared in adoration as a figure stepped up to the back of the dais.

Long green hair. Laurel crown. Dark leatherine clothing. He strode to the speaker's place at the throne, turned, and stretched out his arms in salute to the crazed audience.

"All hail Peshiluud!" the speaker shouted. "Ruler of the ages! Hero to the true gods of Irikara!" He bowed low to the leering newcomer.

"HAIL! HAIL! HAIL!" shouted the crowd. "HAIL! HAIL! HAIL!"

Lightning flashed off mirrored eyes.

THIRTY-TWO

Apprentice

Invisible, Torra sneaked past the entry guards back out of the Hall of Emeralds, exiting into a natural world gone mad.

Lightning struck a tall cypress tree to her right, deafening and blinding her a moment before the trunk fell to the courtyard in a rain of splinters. Torra ducked and raised her hands over her against the thousands of wood shards, then bolted away toward the woods in the opposite direction. The courtyard before her had been filled with griffins when she followed the Padgarun into the hall. Now there were only a dozen beasts left, calling for their masters with pitiful, chick-like cries. Many lay dead where they had been struck by falling trees or lightning.

Already soaked, Torra ran into the ferns and slough of the surrounding swamp. Limbs crashed all around. Her robe snagged as briars ripped through it. Twice she tripped and fell headlong into the foot-deep water, unable to see the placement of her own invisible feet. Finally, she spotted Rethuud where she had left him, between the wide buttresses of a cypress trunk.

"Rethuud!" she yelled over the wind.

He turned toward her voice, then saw where her feet splashed. "Turn visible," he commanded.

"It doesn't work that way. I can't control it. I may stay invisible for half the day."

He grimaced, then jumped as a limb crashed to the water beside them. He backed into the tree. "What did you see? What's going on in the hall? Was Phasgala there?"

"Yes, she was there. Ingal is there, too, in the audience. At least, I hope it was Ingal and not Gogonith." Torra brushed her wet bangs away from her face. "The room is packed with Padgarun clerics. Phasgala is toward the back with the speaker. You'll never get to her past all the Padgarun.

"There's something else," she continued, shouting over the wind. "The reason why they've all gathered, I think."

A massive cypress tree about forty yards away let loose a series of high-pitched cracks then rent at its base, crashing down through the canopy and exploding as it hit the water.

She grabbed Rethuud by the shoulder. "Another elf joined the speaker. It was the elf with reflecting eyes that we saw in the mural. The speaker called him 'Peshiluud', like the legend you told me about back at Chaz Sanooc."

Rethuud's brow tightened. "What? No. You heard wrong."

"He had reflecting eyes and wore a laurel wreath. The speaker called him 'ruler of the ages.'"

His eyes opened wide. "That's not possible! It's just a myth!"

Torra took her hand away from Rethuud's shoulder. "All myths have a basis in reality."

Rethuud's eyes glazed over. "The Ecimii. Will the Great Ones rise again?"

She was about to ask what he meant, but another gust tore into the trees. More limbs crashed around them. And now hail joined the driving rain.

"We've got to hurry!" Torra yelled over the wind. "We have to act now." Rethuud seemed not to hear her, lost in thought. "Rethuud!"

Torra looked around, trying to decide what to do. She had to follow Ingal's orders, find out more about the renegade spell. "Rethuud! The audience is the diversion we need to get inside the elvish palace." She shook him again, and he turned a blank face back to her. "Ingal said something about a mage named Ektibal," she yelled. "He said he may have something to do with renegade magic. Remember? Rethuud!" She put her face near Rethuud's. "Where are Ektibal's chambers?"

The elf took a sharp breath and seemed to snap back to reality. "Go around to the back of the hall. There will be a large number of adjoining structures and a rear entrance. Being invisible, you should be able to slip past the guards. Ektibal's chambers are five doorways down the entry corridor, on the right."

Torra started away as lightning flashed around them. "I should learn more," Rethuud said, rising to go toward the hall. "I have contacts."

"No," Torra said. "You can't. They wanted you dead. Ingal is in there. He'll tell us what he's seen when we meet up with him again in Corithaan. Just go back to the meadow where we landed and wait for me."

"Be careful," Rethuud said in a monotone. "Ektibal had two very powerful apprentices with him in his chambers. I don't know what they would do if they discovered you. Though maybe they have been killed, too."

"We'll rendezvous back at the meadow," Torra said. Rethuud nodded. Satisfied, she splashed through the swamp back to the hall. When she looked back, Rethuud was gone.

The Hall of Emeralds rang with salutatory song, but Torra turned away. Following Rethuud's directions, she skirted the dome and its adjoining structures until she found the back entry.

The back door reminded Torra of a heart valve she had seen in her anatomy lessons years before, gaping open but pulsing as if waiting impatiently to shut tight, and clearly alive.

Five Padgarun guarded the door, their eyes darting this way and that at the falling trees and lightning. Their spears gleamed. Slings and bags full of acid spheres hung at their sides. Torra gulped and circled around them, coming in along the far edge of the entry. Any noise she made was drowned out by the rain and wind. With her heart pounding in her ears, she slipped past them and leapt inside, then looked back to ensure they hadn't noticed her.

The corridor was perhaps ten feet wide and arched with ribs. The thin, living skin of the walls quaked like a coward with every lightning burst.

Torra spotted the fifth door on the right. A warrior stood with sword drawn, guarding the door, tense at the sounds of insane nature filtering through the building's living walls.

Torra paused and wondered what to do. She had no weapon. Could she throw something down the hallway to distract him long enough to enter the room? But what did she have to throw? Nothing. And he probably wouldn't hear it over the thunder. Wouldn't he notice the door opening, anyhow?

What offense spells did she know? Not many. *Force Strike,* perhaps. If she cast a spell, her voice would give her away and he could attack before she finished it.

She was about to try anyway when a massive lightning flash and thunderclap jarred her out of her thoughts. With a deafening percussion, a massive tree crashed through the ceiling just down the corridor. The impact sent ripples of force along the walls, shaking the entire structure. But the rest of the building held.

The guard yelped and jumped back. Rain and hail blew through the gaping hole of rent tissue. Leaves fluttered down the corridor. The guard sheathed his sword and stepped toward the tree—away from the door. Seizing the opportunity, Torra pushed the fleshy door open and entered, closing it behind her.

She waited a moment, listening for signs that the guard detected her. Tentative, she backed away from the door, then turned into the room.

Torra gasped. Bound to large, stone tables were the bloody corpses of two young elvish men. Around them was a wreck of jumbled and broken furnishings, books, glassware, and assorted devices and materials that she could not at once identify. Two leatherine mages' robes lay crumpled on the floor next to the tables. She realized that these elves must be Ektibal's apprentices —what was left of them, anyway.

She stepped closer in horrified fascination. Their mouths gagged so they wouldn't be able to utter spells, it was obvious that the apprentices had been tortured. Their naked bodies were lacerated and burnt to the point of disgust. Each flash of lightning illuminated another dreadful wound. The face of the elf on the left table was frozen in a nightmarish death mask, eyes wide open and unblinking. His gut had been torn open revealing organs half-pulled from the torso. The apprentice on the right was draped across the table with ugly lacerations on his belly and legs where the underlying muscle had been ripped out.

"Horrors!" she muttered, fighting nausea.

Beyond all expectation, the elf on the right moved his head and moaned. *He's alive!* Torra grabbed her Rod of Translation and quickly stepped forward. The floor was sticky nearer the tables. Hand shaking, she removed his gag.

"No more," the apprentice said, his speech slurred by a swollen tongue. "No. No more."

A wave of compassion swept over Torra. Finding a chipped ceramic bowl with water in it, she used her hand to wet the elf's fevered brow.

One eye was swollen shut. The other fluttered open. "You've come."

Torra stopped. How could he expect her? How could he *see* her despite invisibility? Should she answer him at all? "What do you mean?" she finally asked.

His head lolled. He spoke again, his voice as dry as autumn leaves. "I prayed, and now you've come. My spirit."

Spirit? Torra blinked, then reached down and untied the elf's arms, but he didn't try to rise. Judging by his wounds, he probably never would.

"*Eshenae*," he prayed, closing his remaining eye, "Spirits of Nature, carry my soul to Eshenakaree. Make me one with its waters. Let me rest in the cool womb of my people."

For a moment the apprentice lapsed into unconsciousness. Then he gulped and opened his eye again. "You *are* my spirit, aren't you?"

What else could she say? The truth? Neither would benefit from that. And this was her best chance to get the information she needed. "Yes," she said. "I am your spirit. Rest, now, and tell me why they have done this to you."

The elf took a deep breath. "He's here. Peshiluud. Isn't he?" He licked split lips. "We didn't tell her—that Padgarun. We promised Ektibal. We didn't tell her."

"Phasgala? Tell her what?"

The apprentice shivered at the name. "About the spells. The Book of Alasar."

The Book of Alasar! Torra stepped back. *The renegade spell!* Rift Widening. *What does he know?*

"She's close," he said. "She knows the spell's on the mountain. Will soon find it."

Torra knelt by the apprentice. "Which mountain?"

"Rishae'Uungi." *The Mountain of the Stars.*

Torra's heart pounded. "Where? Where on the mountain?" *The spell!*

A shadow passed over the apprentice, and he turned away. Did he suspect her? With a pang of guilt for her deception, Torra poured a small amount of water between his dry lips, then wiped more across his fevered brow. "It's all right," she said, hoping her voice was soothing. "You've done well. You can tell your spirit. I am here for you, now."

The apprentice sighed. "The Book of Alasar … in a cave near the highest peak … behind the red boulder. Connect the Polar Star with the tail of the sleeping dragon." His eyes went wide. He suddenly sat up and reached out. Finding Torra's arm, he grasped it so hard she wanted to cry out. "You must keep the book safe!" he gasped. "Ektibal died for it! All the court mages have guarded it with their lives since Quintominel! It has fallen to me to guard now. To me!"

The guard burst through the door. "You there!" he yelled at the apprentice. "Be quiet! What are you doing without your gag?"

The apprentice pointed at the guard and shouted a *Psychic Whip* spell. The guard screamed in agony, holding his head in his hands, but then the apprentice gasped and dropped his hand, and the spell abruptly ended. In that moment the guard lunged forward and thrust his sword deep into the apprentice's belly.

"Eshenae!" the apprentice screamed. "Take me now!"

The guard decapitated the apprentice with a single stroke. The head and body flopped to the ground with sickening thuds.

Torra fled back into the corridor and to the rear entrance. Guards ran past her to Ektibal's chambers, oblivious to her presence. She burst into the catastrophic weather and ran as fast as she could through the swamp to meet Rethuud.

Images flashed through Torra's mind as she splashed through the murky waters. The first apprentice, gutted, his face a mask of horror. Blood on the floor. The second apprentice's head falling, severed, his lips still moving. *Eshenae! Take me now!*

And if Phasgala learned that Torra now knew where the spell was, how gruesome would her own torture be?

The Book of Alasar. Rift Widening. *A renegade spell!*

She had to reach it before Phasgala.

THIRTY-THREE
Three Voices Speak

Long did the Padgarun audience sing to their hero, Peshiluud, with elegies about his death and legacy, and paeans praising his return and the return of the Triumvirate. The Emerald Hall resounded with their voices, so loud they drowned out the raging tempest outside.

Peshiluud sat in the speaker's throne watching his adoring clerics with unblinking mirrored eyes, a wry smile occasionally playing at his lips.

And over the audience still loomed the three massive shadows. The singing appeared to strengthen and inflate them, color them even, until it seemed to Ingal that they were not shadows at all, but shapeless monsters made of coagulated blood.

Ingal looked behind him toward the entry. A sea of spears stood between him and the exit. The clerics pounded their spear shafts against the floor with the rhythm of their singing. Turning back toward the dais, Ingal wondered if he could reach Peshiluud before the clerics could react. Peshiluud sat there leering at the crowd, but where exactly was he looking? Watching *him*, perhaps?

One good lunge and Ingal could grab the elf, crush him, and put an end to the Triumvirate's plans. But was his own death worth it? And how integral *was* Peshiluud? There were still too many unanswered questions. As if to answer Ingal's thoughts, Peshiluud rose again and held up his hands for silence. The Padgarun grew quiet.

And then Peshiluud addressed the crowd for the first time. When he spoke, it was an amalgam of three distinct voices. One was feminine, the others masculine, and the words did not quite match the movements of his lips. Yet Peshiluud's speech was strong and clear.

"The time has come, my children. Long have you waited. Prepared. Guarded. The Creators have also waited. *They* have prepared. *They* have guarded you, all this time."

Peshiluud grew silent and paced back and forth along the dais edge, scrutinizing his worshippers. At one point he looked directly into Ingal's face and gave a knowing smile, but then looked away.

"The Towermasters and their mages will shake as they witness how sincere the Triumvirate truly is! Tomorrow the other Ecemii will rise from Eshenakaree, fulfilling your most ancient prophesy. Within days will we strike at the Tower of Light, tearing it to its foundation, and the first Heartstone will crumble!"

Peshiluud laughed, an odd cacophony of three discordant exaltations, one low and rumbling, another piercing and quick, and a third that was a solitary "Ha!" The Padgarun roared in excitement.

Ingal thought quickly. So it was true what Azartial had said; the Heartstones were the target. But it would take a renegade spell to destroy them. Who here could be strong enough to cast it? Himself, perhaps … and Peshiluud.

Ingal tensed. He had to remove Peshiluud. He had to do it now! He crouched, ready to spring.

"Gold dragon!" Peshiluud shouted, pointed directly at Ingal. A wave of energy washed over the dragon, and the illusion of

Gogonith was swept away as if a sheet had been pulled off of him. The crowd gasped as one.

Ingal leapt at Peshiluud, roaring, claws outstretched. But instead of landing on the elf, he was suddenly thrust high into the air, tumbling. He slammed against the ceiling of the hall and was held there, spread-eagle, looking down at the chamber and hundreds of angry upturned faces. He could hardly bend a joint against the force of Peshiluud's spell.

"Kill him!" the Padgarun shouted.

"Traitor!"

"Don't let him escape!"

Ingal voiced a *Terror Probe* spell at Peshiluud, but his magic was negated. He tried another incantation, and then another, but his efforts had no effect. Each time the heavy energy of the room surged to quench his magic abilities. He tried to move, but he was pinned. His wings were thrust back against the ceiling so hard his bones threatened to snap.

The shadows pulled closer to Ingal, seeming to studying him. Their concentrated energy flooded over him.

Peshiluud laughed again. He held Ingal against the ceiling by merely pointing. "Yes, Gold Dragon, I could see through your disguise. It is an amusing game you play!"

"You won't succeed, Peshiluud!" Ingal said. "The Towers will have prepared for you."

"Oh? And how would they do that, Gold Dragon? Because Ektibal warned them? Yes, I know about that. All of their magic combined could not equal the power of the Triumvirate. No living human has the ability to cast a spell powerful enough to protect them. Let the mages combine all of their will in protecting themselves, only to see their efforts shatter. What will that level of failure do to them?

"Months they have had, Gold Dragon, since Ektibal's warning to them, and yet not one word have they spoken to you. Am I correct? Have the Towermasters answered your hails? I am sure they have not. They distrust you. Special you are to the Triumvirate, and the Towermasters know it. You are alone. Old and showing your age. Join the Triumvirate, take your place next to your ancient god—next to Draq, your creator—and be a part of their renewed freedom. With you as their champion, victory is assured. Thus will we *all* benefit."

Peshiluud made the slightest bend in his finger, and Ingal moved away from the ceiling, hovering in the air and rotating slowly.

"You'll get no help from us," Ingal shouted. "We won't cooperate."

"And yet," Peshiluud said, "you will. A child of the Triumvirate are you. A special one. It is in your nature to help them, even if you do not realize it. Your part has been foreseen."

"Kill him now, my liege!" the speaker cried, livid with rage. "He can play no part that warrants sparing him!"

Peshiluud glared at the speaker, and the speaker backed away.

The ancient elf looked back up to Ingal, and his unblinking features softened. He motioned toward the entryway, and Ingal floated in that direction. "A wicked child you have been, Gold Dragon, plotting against your parents. But just as a loving parent could not murder his son, so too the Triumvirate spares your life. They guide you even now. Go. Redeem yourself. Little do you know, but your efforts will help father a new hero for the Triumvirate."

"Never!" Ingal said. He was tumbling faster now toward the entryway, and the Padgarun moved aside. He had to stall

Peshiluud, seek out a weakness, and buy time for Torra and Rethuud. Maybe if he played the diplomatic card?

"But a compromise may be possible, Peshiluud," Ingal said in a sincere voice. "If elvish dominion is what you desire, land can be granted to Peshilaree. All of Ocrin can be yours, if you wish. Nations will fight for it in your name. The Tower Mages would grant almost any desire for you. Great magic. Lands and resources. Slaves. Riches. Name your price and they will listen."

Peshiluud chuckled. "A valiant effort for peace, Gold Dragon. But there is nothing we want except the freedom of our Creators. With that, everything is within our grasp anyhow."

"You will fail, Peshiluud. You *and* your gods!"

"Farewell, Gold Dragon!"

Ingal was thrown through the entry and into the pouring rain beyond, released from Peshiluud's hold and tumbling across the courtyard. Instantly he stood and charged at the entry, but slammed against an invisible barrier. He pounded a fist into it. Phasgala stood on the other side staring at him with accusing eyes. From behind her came Peshiluud's odd, triplet laughter. Then she turned her back to Ingal, and the clerics sang again.

Ingal growled. He looked over the Hall's exterior, seeking a way in. Mighty trees had been flung against it by the storm without effect. Their shattered remains lay piled around the base. If they had no effect, what could *he* possibly do? His old, aching muscles could hardly compete.

But the Gogonith ruse had succeeded. He had learned what he had come to learn.

Now he had to find the renegade spell before the elves did. It was the key to the elves' attack. He looked around and sniffed the turbulent winds for Rethuud or Torra, hoping to learn what they had discovered, but found no sign of them.

Grunting, Ingal leapt into the sky, fighting the torrential wind and rain to fly southward to the fields of Corithaan.

THIRTY-FOUR

Lost

Still invisible, out of breath and limping from a fall, Torra was helplessly lost in the swamp. So blindly had she run from the apprentice and his gruesome death that she got turned around in the mire and underbrush. The lashing wind and biting rain had slackened to a shower, yet through the trees she saw no sign of either the Hall of Emeralds or the meadow where she was to meet Rethuud. She couldn't even tell through the glowering clouds which way the sun was.

Searching around for natural clues to direction, Torra spotted a cluster of tiny, brown shelf fungi growing on a rotting trunk. Going on the assumption that this indicated the shadowed portion of the trunk, she decided that south lay to her right. If she could find her way back to the Hall of Emeralds she would be able to recognize how to return to the landing meadow. Picking what she thought to be southeast, she turned and headed in that direction.

There were strips of dry land, but they were typically overgrown with thorny brush and ferns up to her neck. It was quicker to wade the still, black waters. Tiny, four-leaved weeds covered the surface, obscuring anything that moved below. On more than one occasion she yelped and splashed away as something slithered over her feet or brushed her ankle.

Torra rubbed her itching, goose-bumped arms and tried to ward off a bout of shivering. Mosquitoes whined around her in a cloud of hunger. Her invisibility seemed to do nothing to keep the little devils at bay.

Everywhere life abounded. Frogs. Snakes. Birds. But these were not the timid creatures she had known as a child hiking in the woods of Taxia. These animals were large and unafraid, seeming to sense her despite the invisibility, turning their heads toward her with unblinking eyes as she passed. She got the distinct impression that animals were crowding every tree hole and burrow, soundlessly waiting for her to pass and turn her back to them.

The rain finally petered out, leaving the swamp oddly quiet. Mists rose off the water like amorphous phantoms lost in the world of the living. An occasional breeze disturbed the stillness, swirling the mists into eddies and spiriting them away. Gone now was the scent of rain. In its place was the rich decay of untold numbers of decomposing leaves and creatures.

So intent was she on keeping her footing in the murky water that Torra at first failed to notice a significant change come over her. Then, as she stepped into a spot of sunlight that slanted through the canopy, she reached up and wiped her forehead— and saw her hand. Rather, she saw a ghostly image of her hand, transparent enough to make out the swamp through it. The translucence of it pulsed with each heartbeat. She took a step back into shadow, and the image disappeared. She reached out, into the light, and saw her hand pulse back into visibility, then withdrew it and made it disappear again. The Potion of Invisibility was already wearing off. "The sooner the better," she mumbled. From then on she kept as much in the light as possible.

Torra came upon a channel where the water moved with a languid current. No weeds floated there, giving her a better idea of her footing under the surface, so she turned and followed. The water was deeper, forcing her to keep near the shore and climb over woody debris that had accumulated.

The sun came out in full force as she waded into a particularly open area where a cypress tree had fallen. Exposed in the light, she could now clearly make out her arms and tattered robe.

The tree's broken trunk lay diagonally out of the water, having fallen and lodged there from a steep rise to her right. She bent to go under it, then froze. Gasped.

Pitiless eyes watched her from just beneath the surface like reflections of harvest moons.

Torra backed up slowly. The beast's shadowy body and long snout spread out toward her like a dark nightmare. Paddle feet. A mossy, armored back breached the surface.

Torra bolted the other way and leapt to the safety of the shore as the beast splashed behind her. She scrambled up the land like a crab, turning, grabbing for anything to use as a weapon. The beast came partway up the shore, writhing in the mud, snapping with a gar-like snout brimming with needle teeth. Torra gripped a limb and broke it across the beast's head, ripping open one of its huge eyes. The monster writhed and disappeared in a plume of water and mud.

The water settled as Torra crept higher up the bank. The murk under the trunk was slowly washed away by the current, leaving no sign of the beast other than scrapings in the bank and a hint of blood on the cypress trunk.

For many minutes Torra lay there shaking, panting, watching for the monster's return. The enormity of her situation suddenly overwhelmed her. Alone. Lost. An exotic and hostile land. The entire world counted on her to find a spellbook before the elves did. She pounded the mud and looked up to the canopy through tearing eyes. "I didn't ask for this," she cried to the sky. Visions passed through her mind of Master Morikal laughing, her family as they said farewell. Taenos. Handsome, broad-shouldered Taenos.

"All I wanted was to deliver the Stone of Lethori and go back home." But she knew it was a lie. *I didn't have to accept Ingal's offer to come along, did I?*

"I did," she said, surprising herself by saying it aloud. She hurled the limb into the water. "This is my destiny." *Yes, my destiny. We all have a destiny. Mine is to find that spell and ... and ...* She paused, afraid to finish the thought. *Destroy it?* Torra scratched at her itching neck as she processed the question. She hadn't thought about what she would do if she found the spell. Keep it? Find a good use for it to help mankind? She could never be powerful enough to cast a spell of that immense power. Hide it again?

If that spell is necessary for the elves to achieve their goal, it's better to destroy it. But could she do it?

The clouds came again and blotted out the sun. Torra turned invisible once more. She forced herself to stand on unsteady legs. Unwilling to enter the water again, she turned and climbed up the shore into a thicket.

Torra wasn't sure how much time passed as she fought through the undergrowth. She had made little progress when she heard first one voice, then another. She stopped, heard them again, and turned to orient herself. Elvish. Peshilarn. She grasped her rod, but they were too far away to hear distinctly. She checked to ensure she was still invisible, then moved toward them as stealthily as she could.

A moment later Torra parted the brush and nearly cried out in joy at the sight of Rethuud standing in the greensward of a clearing. But the moment of gladness instantly dissolved as she saw who faced him. Phasgala.

Neither had pulled their weapons. In the distance stood two other elvish clerics, both male, looking on in detachment. Through the trees in the distance stood the Hall of Emeralds.

"I understand what you ask," Rethuud said to the Padgarun. "It is the moment of legend. Drastic measures are necessary."

Phasgala caressed Rethuud's cheek. "And are you willing to take those measures, my love?"

Torra blinked back surprise. Phasgala's voice was light and airy, like the jingling of wind chimes, and speaking of love, no less! It failed to match Torra's picture of the cleric as a wild and untamable creature of destruction, killer of Ingal's guards, screaming as she melted faces.

Rethuud placed his hand on Phagala's cheek as well and spoke too softly for Torra to hear.

Phasgala continued. "The prince was to father our child, but even his death was worth ensuring the Triumvirate returns to their rightful place. Help the Triumvirate, and even humans will be empowered with their energy. Within our lifetime, all dreams will be made possible through the magic they grant us as faithful worshippers."

Rethuud lowered his hand from her cheek. "One by one, the ancient legends have come true. You say the Ecemii will rise from Eshenakaree to join Peshiluud. I believe it now."

"Then you will do as I ask? You will bring us the spell if they find it?"

Rethuud nodded. "If they find it."

Traitor! Torra wanted to yell it out, run down and punch Rethuud. Ingal had trusted him!

The elves embraced. "Speed well, my love," Phasgala said. "Bring me the spell, and all will be forgiven."

Rethuud caressed Phasgala a moment longer, then turned and walked deeper into the swamp.

Phasgala's face hardened as soon as Rethuud walked away, then she joined her comrades, striding through the swamp back toward the hall.

Torra stood and took a step to follow Rethuud, but her robe snagged the brush and ripped.

Phasgala stopped and turned. Torra sucked in a breath and stepped back, but she tripped on a root and collapsed backward into the thicket.

When she came to her senses, Torra lay still and tried hard to catch her breath, daring herself not to move. She heard nothing over the beating of her heart. Building her courage, she slowly sat up and peered over the sedges. Phasgala approached up the rise like a hunter, her steely eyes scanning the brush.

And she was placing an acid sphere into her sling.

The clouds parted. Sunlight streamed down. Torra saw her body pulse back into partial visibility. She threw herself back down.

Torra fought the panic rising in her to run. She crouched as low as she could, sending a silent prayer for the clouds to come and cover the sun again so she could turn invisible.

Her prayers were answered. The light slowly dimmed as a cloud passed over, and Torra disappeared. *But for how long?* she worried. Phasgala stalked up the rise toward her, gently swinging the sling. Twenty feet away. Fifteen. Ten.

"I *see* you," Phasgala said, drawing it out in one long breath. Torra's legs tensed to run. Should she dare? Was Phasgala lying?

Phasgala launched the acid sphere. Torra winced. The sphere hit the bushes five feet to her left. The leaves and stems smoked and withered where the sphere burst open.

A thrush fluttered out with a twitter, flapping madly into the misty air, but fell to the water a stone's throw away and thrashed in agony.

Phasgala scanned the brush again. Took a step closer. Gazed at the spot where the sphere had hit. She looked directly at Torra and stepped through the sedges toward her. Scowled. Placed another sphere in the sling. The sky parted again, illuminating the trees beyond Phasgala. The light approached like a predator.

Torra froze, feared even to breathe. Phasgala stepped within touching distance. Looked down at the spot where Torra lay, then up past her. The Padgarun flared her nostrils like a bloodhound, snuffling. The sling's leatherine handle creaked as she tightened her grip.

And then the clouds parted and the sun shone straight down on them from behind Phasgala, silhouetting the elf and creating a halo effect around her head. Torra realized with horror that she lay curled in Phasgala's shadow. She dared not move even a fingerbreadth in any direction or risk turning visible in the sun's rays.

Torra lay rigid in a fetal position. Clenched her jaw. Held her breath against a scream. The assassin lorded over her ready to destroy at the first sign. Mercifully, the clouds closed again. The light dimmed. Phasgala's shadow was lost.

The other elves called out for Phasgala to hurry. She ignored them, peering through the thicket beyond Torra. Slowly, the Padgarun put her sphere back into its pouch at her side, then turned and walked back down the rise with no more apparent concern. But before she joined her comrades, she veered away and picked up the dying thrush. Whispering over it, she cupped her hands and a green fluorescence glowed around the bird. Suddenly the thrush flapped away, healed, into the surrounding brush. Phasgala turned and joined the warriors back toward the Hall of Emeralds.

As soon as she was certain Phasgala had departed, Torra gathered her courage and sneaked down the rise. Constantly watching for Phasgala's return, she quickly followed Rethuud through the swamp back toward the landing meadow.

THIRTY-FIVE

Glen of Peace

Ingal sat upon a flat, overturned stone megalith as large as he was long, an ancient monument whose writing was too faint to read when his forebear first discovered it tens of thousands of years before, now worn completely bare by time. Here, in Tegora' Seima, Glen of Peace, he and his forebears had only ever found tranquility, hidden away in a vale overlooking the fields of Corithaan. Yet there was no peace today.

He tried to meditate, breathing slowly, absorbing the environment around him through his six senses in the way that the ancient So'Chai masters had taught his forebear, eighteen thousand years before.

> Become the green of the leaves and grow with them.
> Converse with the running brook and travel with it.
> Feel the austerity of stone and become stronger.
> Imbibe the evening mist and know purity.
> Smell cherry blossoms and realize beauty.
> And sense the energy flowing throughout.

But no energy flowed through him. Not here. Not this time. He tried again, and again, but the magic wouldn't flow.

And where were Torra and Rethuud? He had to get back to the White Lands. His generals needed to be warned of the traitor's deception—of Vizier Janisim's deal with Ocrin to enter the White Lands unchallenged. He had been a fool to trust the Vizier! But he could not leave Peshilaree until the renegade spell was found.

Ingal shook his head. No, there would be no peace for him as long as he remained in Peshilaree.

And the Triumvirate was stronger now. He sensed their energy all around. It played over his scales like static and sent shivers up his spine. Every shadow seemed alive with sentience.

"We know you're here!" he shouted, looking around. Only the babbling stream answered. "Do you hear us?" He stood and thrashed his tail in irritation. Never before had anyone embarrassed the Gold Dragon as they had, using that reanimated puppet, Peshiluud. Magic of that magnitude had manifested itself only a handful of times in the memory, and Peshiluud had wielded only the tip of the power that had surged through the Hall of Emeralds from the Triumvirate.

"Show yourselves!" he shouted. He had to draw them out, show his anger, destroy the land sacred to them. *Mirrored eyes.* Ingal reached down and grabbed a boulder. Threw it, crashing, into the trees. "We said show yourselves!"

The pounding of spear shafts to the floor. Clerics singing. He lunged off of the monument. Ripped a fir tree out by the roots. Swung it around, roaring, snapping limbs and shattering trunks. *A wicked child you have been!*

Ingal busted the tree into fragments. Reached down. Lifted the megalith with a wild bellow and shaking muscles. Tossed it with all his might. The massive monument fell longways into the stream, shattered into huge pieces with a rumble, splashed water and mud.

Pinned to the ceiling. Like a moth under a child's thumb. Ingal roared, cast a *Fire Throw* spell, scorched the earth around him as flames shot from his claws to ignite the trees and grass, roaring up the lush hillsides. Everywhere was smoke and destruction. The vale that had inspired thousands of years of meditation for his forebears was a burning wasteland, yet he kept incinerating, roaring, destroying.

Special you are to the Triumvirate, and the Towermasters know it. You are alone. Ingal collapsed to the ground where the monument had lain. Gasped for breath. Body ached. Energy spent.

Old! he thought. *Too old for this fight! Too old to make a difference.* This was no feud for an aging dragon. How could he contend with the power of the Triumvirate when his joints popped and his belly dragged? Ingal dug his claws into the soil and squeezed. How could he compete with an enemy stronger than anyone the world had ever known? How could he fight *gods?*

"Why do you deny your birthright, Gold Dragon? Why do you fight us?" Ingal hardly reacted to the voice. At first he thought he had spoken it himself, but soon realized that it was the deep, smooth voice of the ancient warrior, Noc Ang Soon, speaking the dead language of a time long forgotten.

Ingal didn't bother looking up. He knew it was the god again, appearing as he had when he visited Ingal in his sleep chamber.

The power of the glen had not changed. The god had been there all along. "We fight you because you are irresponsible, *Draq.*" Ingal nearly spat the name.

"Gold Dragon, you are a child to us. To *me*, especially, your *Creator.* Would you suffer a child to critique its parents? Would a child be a suitable judge of adult responsibilities?"

Ingal finally looked up. Draq, in the form of the long dead warrior, stood in the flames of burning grasses, untouched, looking just as he had in the vision back at Palal Jehai: dark skin, bronze armor, red and white conical headpiece. Raw power emanated from him, blurring and warping the flames around him and whipping them into a frenzy, blinding Ingal's magical senses. Ingal extended his wings. "Even a child can know right from wrong."

The god stepped closer. "Yet children cannot comprehend the world as their parents do. You must accept our wisdom, Gold Dragon, and obey, for the betterment of all."

Ingal made a fist. "We will not comply. No individual, no matter the species, has the wisdom to wield the power you would give them. Not us, not Gogonith, nor any elf, human, or dwarf. More importantly, the Outer Gods would not allow it."

Suddenly it made sense to Ingal why the Stone of Lethori had glowed. His eyes went wide with the realization. Draq looked on, seeming to sense what Ingal was thinking. "That was the Triumvirate's plan all along, wasn't it?" Ingal said. "Once you're free, you give your power to the people of Irikara, and make *them* fight the war for you against the Outer Gods." Ingal stumbled backward as his mind raced. "Once the Towers were thrown down and you regained your full energy, you would march the people of this world into the heavens and battle. The Stone of Lethori glowed not to warn us against any one person or group, but against all the peoples of the world who would embrace your magic!"

Draq laughed, deep and hearty, and made a fist of defiance. "This is why the Outer Gods fear us, Gold Dragon. Now you see the true strength of the Triumvirate. Before, when we fought each other, when our children fought each other, we were no match for these Outer Gods. But united we can attack and win."

Ingal slowly shook his head. "You would make pawns of us, foot soldiers to leap upon the spears of your enemy so that you may pass unharmed." Ingal pointed a claw at his god. "Well it won't work, Draq. The ancient land of Occultii tried it, remember? Magic thrived. An army of mage warriors the likes of which the world had never seen since, many hundreds of thousands strong, tried to march through a dimensional gate to attack the gods themselves. But they failed, just as you will, and the gods destroyed a vast part of Irikara, leaving in its wake a desolate and spoiled wasteland too immense to cross, decimating Occultii and its citizens. You would have this repeated—worldwide!"

"Not repeated, Gold Dragon. Overcome! Occultii was a *test* of our plan. Do you not see it? We learned the strategy of these intruders, their capabilities. We know our enemy now. When they strike again, we will be ready to counter them."

Ingal licked his lips as he realized the magnitude of Draq's statements. "By all accounts, hundreds of millions of people died in the holocaust wrought by the Outer Gods. In a day, an entire civilization was wiped away, the largest the world has ever known. An inland sea was turned to desert. Mountains rose up. The whole world suffered earthquakes. You say *you* put the Occultians up to it? And you call it a *test*? Have you no regard for life at all?"

Draq grew flushed with anger. "There would *be* no life here without us. And steps must be taken, child! Sacrifices must be made!"

"You are small, Draq!" Ingal said, again pointing at the god. "Petty and selfish!"

Draq suddenly convulsed, shifted, his features melting into shapelessness. The illusion of the warrior dissolved into a darkness that defied the sunlight and grew into a monstrous, dragon-like shape that towered over Ingal. Coldness emanated from it. Thin streaks of sapphire static played around and through the darkness of the god like flashes of lightning.

"See me as I truly am!" Draq commanded. His voice shook the earth around him and echoed off the hillsides. The flames sputtered out. "Remember whom you address! The world we would make is beyond your imagination, child! Question us not. Be a part of its change, and profit from it. Consider the difference you could make for the people of Irikara. Make your decision!"

Ingal staggered away from the god. His legs quivered. His ears rang. He couldn't pull his eyes away from the awesome sight. But he wouldn't give in so easily. "We have decided already. We will not join you."

Draq pointed a forefoot at Ingal. "Then consider this your last option! You have a choice, Gold Dragon—the choice we gave the Iron Dragon, Tellonta, and that he accepted. Surrender your life and be reborn as we see fit, and the human land that you have nurtured for so long will be spared in the destruction to come. Your offspring will have powers that surpass any past generation, and he will fight for our cause as a living god. Touch our energies, and no spell will be beyond his grasp. It is in your *nature* to aid us."

Anger welled in Ingal like lava. "Why not just kill us and take our offspring as your own?"

"It is our limitation as gods that those who follow us do so by their own self-determination."

"You will never get our compliance!"

Draq lowered his gargantuan head to glare at Ingal with eyes that glowed with hellfire. "Refuse, and your beloved White Lands will be *ravaged* as punishment, burnt and cast asunder with your pride. Made a wasteland. Your people will blame you for your defiance and ineptitude."

"Extortion!" he screamed. "You might as well kill us, for we will never give in to such threats!"

The sparks of light within Draq's body flared. His shadowy appendages moved over Ingal, holding him down, rolling him onto his back.

Every fiber of Ingal's body erupted in pain, burning, not from fire, but from ice, as if dunked into freezing water and held there. Ingal felt his throat and lungs freeze. He couldn't talk. Couldn't breathe. He clawed at his throat, but his forefeet had grown numb. His teeth felt brittle enough to break. He clenched against the pain, shivered, thrashed his tail. His head froze to the point that he could feel even his mind numbing. His pulse slowed. Muscles stopped responding. The blood stopped. Fading. Fading. Dimly he felt himself beating the ground in a reflexive spasm as the darkness enveloped him.

Then the darkness lifted. His body warmed. Blood flowed. Air returned to pliant lungs. Muscles shook and twitched. Ingal groaned and rolled his eyes, trying to focus again on the god lording over him.

"I could never destroy you, my child," Draq said. "You are special to me. But if you continue to resist, punishment must be meted." The god stepped closer to Ingal, crushing the ground into sand beneath his feet. "Tellonta forever protected his precious land of Sofon by accepting my offer. Surely you consider your own life less important than hundreds of thousands of your White Lands vassals. What is one sacrifice for their protection?"

"It is everything!" Ingal gasped. His lungs hadn't recovered. "This extortion may have worked to turn Tellonta into Gogonith … but it won't work with us!" He took another sputtering breath. "Destroy the White Lands if you dare, but you will never have us as your champion, and you will never get the tower!"

Draq suddenly shrunk and colored back to the form of Noc Ang Soon, stern of face. He pointed a bronze sword at Ingal. "So be it, Gold Dragon. You have made your choice. The only way to halt your punishment will be to serve me as your kind once did, and to fight for us against the Outer Gods."

And then Draq disappeared without a sound. The sense of power faded. The wind died away.

Ingal was left alone and shivering in the smoldering hot wastes of Tegora'Seima, Glen of Peace.

THIRTY-SIX
Demonskin

Ingal remained in the valley for hours waiting for Rethuud and Torra and thinking over what had just transpired. He sat on the fragmented remnants of the megalith absently watching a smoldering log a few feet away. Embers glowed in its secret core, crackling, sending thin tendrils of smoke into the still air. He watched as they diffused and joined the low haze that had gathered in the air like an army of smothering ghosts. Like the So'Chai masters of old, he attempted to place his own life into those embers, and saw there a reflection of the current conflict. The Triumvirate gods were dangerous, glowing cinders that could spread and grow out of control.

Overhead, occasional flights of griffins flew northeast in V formations like migrating geese, riderless except for each lead griffin, upon which sat a lone Padgarun. Another mystery. But he could not pursue it. He had to wait for Torra and Rethuud.

Where were they? Ingal worried over the many dangerous scenarios they could have encountered. Torra *had* been in the Hall of Emeralds, after all. Was the Potion of Invisibility enough to protect her? Peshiluud had seen through the Gogonith illusion. Could he also see those who were invisible?

Ingal could only hope Rethuud had protected Torra. Together, perhaps they could find some answers to the conspiracy and the renegade spell that Peshiluud intended to cast.

He focused on the smoldering log and muttered the incantation for *Extinguish*. He created a void around it, sucking out the air with a hiss. The smoke stopped. The embers dimmed and went black. Releasing the spell with a pop, Ingal extended a claw and quickly ripped open the wood, placing his forefoot into the cavity. "Your heart is as cold as snow, old log," he said.

At last, as the sun dipped toward the horizon, Ingal spotted Rethuud and Torra flying over the edge of the fields of Corithaan, joined by the two other warriors, making tight rotations in search of Ingal. The dragon opened his wings to reflect the sun and let out a quick bellow. The elves spotted him and flew to the valley. They circled, seeming to examine the destruction, then landed nearby.

When Ingal saw Torra he nearly cried out. Her finely woven tan robes were tattered and muddied, her eyes revealed stark fear and anger, and her posture betrayed exhaustion. But even more alarming was the bright red rash that covered every visible part of her skin. And the smell. Even over the smoke Ingal could detect a sulfurous odor coming from her like a fume, so strong that even a human could sense it. She scratched at herself and frowned, casting dark glances at Rethuud as if he were the cause of the symptoms.

The elf, in turn, seemed not to notice at all, dismounting and striding toward Ingal.

"What has happened here?" Rethuud demanded, jutting out his arms. "What have you done to Tegora'Seima?"

"Be still, Rethuud. It was necessary to draw out the enemy. Much has happened in your absence."

Before Rethuud could reply, Ingal looked beyond him at Torra and said, "Com Gidel, what has happened to you? You are not well!"

Torra did not answer, but merely threw a withering glare at the back of Rethuud in response, then made a wide arc around the elf to stand by Ingal's side.

Rethuud scowled. "She's been like this since we left the Emerald Delta. She's said nothing to explain. I am left believing that some trauma has transpired."

"Some trauma," Torra mimicked, still watching the elf. Then she looked up to Ingal. "He's a traitor, my lord. A *traitor!*" She again glared at Rethuud as he and his warriors stared back. One warrior pulled his sword. "He's in collusion with Phasgala," Torra continued. "He means to turn over the renegade spell if we find it." She pointed an accusing finger at him. "They're lovers. I watched as they embraced each other and made the agreement."

Everything was silent as Rethuud and Torra glared at each other.

Ingal broke the silence. "Is this true, Rethuud?"

Rethuud deliberately closed and opened his eyes in an apparent attempt to reign in emotion, looking up to Ingal. "Which part?" he asked in a measured tone. "Yes, we were lovers. Phasgala still believes I have such feelings for her. Because of this, I was able to lead her into sharing certain key information, including the spell they seek and its general location."

"And you agreed to turn it over to her!" Torra shouted. "I heard you. Admit your guilt!"

Rethuud turned his gaze back to Torra, his elvish features cold and emotionless. "I might agree to many things I do not intend to carry through, if they would help our cause."

Ingal looked down at Torra. Her jaw was locked, her glare firm. "Rethuud," Ingal said, "might you not also give false pretenses to us? If Torra is certain about your expressed intentions, we are willing to believe her."

"I *am* certain, my lord," Torra stated.

Rethuud gave an exasperated sigh. "Fine," he blurted. "Is she also certain that the prince and I, and our men, were not responsible for the death of the court mage, Ektibal, and that the prince was not plotting to overthrow his father?"

"Clearly you and your prince were innocent of the crimes the speaker accused you of," Ingal said. "The blame lies with the speaker, Peshiluud, and the gods they serve. They assassinated your prince to keep him from exposing their plans to us."

"Then the agreement we made at your palace is complete. We have aided you and your mage in this venture and found the answers you sought. Release me and my men, and give word to my warriors at your palace that they are free as well."

Ingal nodded. "Yes, consider yourself and your men released. If you wish, you may send a warrior to deliver the code phrase for their discharge from imprisonment. Have him tell the captain of the guard, 'Ingal sheaths his sword,' and the captain will escort your warriors and your prince's body out of our palace."

Rethuud turned briskly back to his mount, but Ingal stopped him, adding, "Though the nature of Torra's accusation precludes you from being trusted with our search for the renegade spell, we still need you. We are convinced that you sympathize with us against the Triumvirate." Ingal reached out an open forefoot in gesture. "Remain our ally, Rethuud. Together we make a stronger force against these gods."

Rethuud seemed to consider the request, lowering his gaze and working his jaw. "You know *my* thoughts, Ingal," Torra muttered. "I was nearly killed because of what I overheard."

"We shall see, Jehai, if I choose to remain in your stead." Rethuud aimed his gaze at Torra. "But I am true to those who deserve it." Without another word, he turned back to the griffins, mounted, and flew off over the fields with his men, turning south and disappearing below the line of trees.

Torra's shoulders slumped, and she wavered as she stood, supporting herself against the megalith.

"My lord," she said in a thin voice, "I know where the renegade spell is. I learned it from Ektibal's apprentice, before he was …" She closed her eyes against some memory … "murdered. The spellbook is on the mountain, in a cave near the summit. We must go."

In a rush of emotion, Torra related what had happened to her since they had parted, starting with Ektibal's apprentice and what he had told her about the renegade spell and its location. She told of being lost, then finding Rethuud and Phasgala together and how Phasgala had stalked her. Finally, Torra related the trip up from Mount Guulenen and their visit at Hasala Squalma.

"We are impressed, Com Gidel," Ingal said at last. "Finding a renegade spell is no easy feat."

"We must go at once, my lord," Torra said. But her eyelids drooped, and she swayed on her feet.

Ingal shook his head. "Rest now. You are not well enough to travel."

"But we have to find the Book of Alasar. Phasgala is searching for it. She may locate it before we do."

"First you must recuperate. You have ventured far with little rest. And …" Ingal again smelled the sulfur, remembering a talented physician, centuries before, and a patient of his with a bizarre illness. "You have an illness which is more than simple fatigue. We suspect you have known how serious it is for quite some time."

Torra closed her eyes and pounded her fist against the megalith, then threw out her arms in surrender. "What is wrong with me? Do you know? None of the wise men of Taxia can find the answer."

"When first we had asked, you had replied that it was only a skin rash, a reaction to some plant on the trip to our palace. Why did you not tell us the truth and ask us then?"

She averted her eyes. "I didn't want to appear weak to you, I guess, or somehow a threat to others by way of this disease."

He had an idea what her illness could be, but the disease was very rare. "Tell us the symptoms."

Torra sighed. "For the last year I've had cramping in my joints, difficulty breathing, and this itching. I have applied a salve, and took dried herbs, but their effects are only temporary." She scratched again at her arm. "Now those remedies are gone, and my symptoms have returned tenfold."

Ingal looked closely at Torra's features. Bright red hives. A yellowing of the whites of her eyes. This was not from the invisibility potion. He thought back through the memory.

"We know of a disease, Com Gidel, that matches your symptoms." He paused. This would not be easy to tell her.

"What?" she asked. "What is it?"

"One name for this illness is 'brimstone disease,' though this is not its most common name. The great apothecary who named it thus, many hundreds of years ago, found that it was the result of the body accumulating sulfur. His patient had first shown symptoms as a war refugee. It is likely that the stress of this crisis has triggered an attack of the disease, as it did with him."

"Will it ever go away?"

He slowly shook his head. "We're sorry, Torra, but little is known of brimstone disease. Unless a treatment is discovered, it will only get worse."

"How much worse?"

Ingal shook his head. He couldn't bear to reveal to her the horror of what she would face. "This is not the time or place … "

"Tell me!" she insisted, leaning forward until she nearly collapsed. "Don't you dare hide this from me. Not you."

Ingal sighed and nodded. "Very well," he said, and absentmindedly drew random patterns in the ashy soil as he spoke. "As the disease progresses, sulfur will continue to build up in your body. The itching will turn to pain. In time, your skin and eyes will grow jaundiced and dry. You'll slowly go blind with yellow cataracts. Your joints will stiffen. And a strong smell of sulfur will follow you until few will be able to abide standing near." He paused and tapped his tail before finishing, remembering that long-ago patient. "At the end, your hair will fall out, and large flakes of skin will fall off. Each movement will be a torment, you will no longer be able to walk or eat, and you will waste away."

Torra's eyes welled, but she quickly wiped them dry before tears could form. "How long do I have?"

Ingal remembered back to that patient. How his friends and family had cursed him, called him a devil. And when the man had finally died, they had burned his wretched body, marveling at the bright blue flames it produced as proof of an evil, supernatural origin.

"You have perhaps a decade, at this point," Ingal finally answered. "Maybe two. It is hard to say with so few cases to compare."

Torra groaned. Ingal lowered his head near hers in an attempt to console her.

She seemed to gather her strength to her, sat up straight, held her head up. "Is there no treatment at all?"

Ingal shook his head. "Not that anyone has found. But we will search for one. It may be that you could reduce symptoms with a special diet to reduce your sulfur intake and medicines that remove the sulfur from your body."

Torra's eyes reflected red and orange as she looked off into the distance at the setting sun. "You said it had a more common name."

Ingal grimaced. "It's not important. A wives' tale."

"Tell me."

Ingal sighed and looked away. "In more than one region of the world, it is known as … 'demonskin.'"

Torra fell into a brooding silence. At Ingal's encouragement, she lay on the megalith with her head on her pack and fell into a fitful sleep.

Ingal pondered everything he knew about the Triumvirate and their wide conspiracy. Time was running out. Ocrin could invade the White Lands at any moment. Peshiluud was ready to raise the other Ecemii. Phasgala was searching for the renegade spell. And now, with Rethuud gone in anger, an apparent traitor, and Torra sick with this disease, Ingal wondered if he could achieve anything at all.

He sighed, situated himself into a more comfortable position, and once more channeling the old So'chai masters, let himself become the smoke curling up into the starry sky.

THIRTY-SEVEN
The Book of Alasar

Torra awoke face up, greeted by thousands of stars gleaming in the cloudless dome of night. The constellation directly above was that of Corbilla, the griffin. To the west was the constellation of Mantalla and her cub. These had been two of the star patterns depicted on the elvish cube. By their positions, Torra knew it was about three hours past sundown.

She thought back to the words of the elvish apprentice, just before … she didn't want to remember his death. What had he said about finding the Book of Alasar? *Connect the Polar Star to the tail of the sleeping dragon.* Torra looked northward toward the Polar Star, but it was hidden behind the mountain. And the sleeping dragon? The constellation of Corthos. This had been the third constellation on the cube, depicted in mirror image. She looked southward, knowing she could never see Corthos from this far north. She would have to travel thousands of miles to the southern lands to view it.

What did the apprentice mean by "connect"?

Torra put the thought aside for the moment. The sleep had been much needed, yet she was still exhausted. A cool breeze calmed her itching skin. She yawned and stretched, but stopped when the irritated skin burned and bled.

Then she remembered the diagnosis. Demonskin. A wasting disease. Her already wounded spirit dropped again as she thought about the future she must endure.

Torra shook off the thought. Told herself there was no time to dwell on the negative. She knew they couldn't loiter; they must continue on to find the Book of Alasar. She sat up, ignoring the pain in her joints and the discomfort of having lain on a slab of stone, and looked around her at the ruined valley. Smoke still curled up and away, blue-gray in the moonlight.

Ingal lay curled up like a cat forty yards away. Torra watched him for a minute before asking, "Are you awake, my lord?"

One of Ingal's eyes opened, then the other. He cleared his throat and raised his head. Opening and closing his eyes as if to ward off his own fatigue. "Yes. Are you rested?"

"Rested enough, my lord, to be moving on."

Ingal stood and arched his back like a cat, groaning. A series of alarming cracks issued forth from his spine, then still others as he twisted his shoulders and stretched his wings. He took a deep breath and looked over at Torra. Noticing her expression, he muttered, "Old dragon!"

Torra dug into her pack and took out the last of the food from Chaz Sanooc, gnawing on it absentmindedly. Between mouthfuls she described again the location of the Book of Alasar as told to her by the apprentice.

Ingal nodded. "We think we know where a red boulder is located near the peak. It isn't far. We will need to carry you in our arms, though. There is no other way to take you with us."

Torra nodded. Following his instruction, she stood with her pack to her chest as he swept her up with a powerful forefoot and clutched her close to his chest in the crook of his arm. She lay there coddled against his mighty breast, her head to his scabrous scales. Ingal's heart was clearly audible, beating with an unconquerable strength. The warmth of his body threatened to overheat her. And, for a fleeting moment, she imagined herself a baby dragon in the arms of her stalwart father.

But dragons don't have fathers, or babies, like humans do, she thought.

"Hang on," Ingal said, and leapt into the sky.

Torra was jolted back and forth in Ingal's arms with each wing beat as they rose up the moonlit cliffs and slopes of the mountain. She clutched one of his massive digits as best she could against her fear of falling.

The air quickly cooled as they flew higher, rising above the tree line to barren, rocky crags. In no time at all they had scaled Rishae'Uungi, "Mountain of the Stars," to the same altitude as its snowy peak, then Ingal turned and flew east into the wind and snow, then downward along a tortured ridge. The cold and gusting wind buffeted Ingal and Torra up and down and side to side. Shadows played tricks with Torra's eyes, convincing her at times that gaping caverns lurked in flat rock faces, or that beastly creatures followed them in flight.

She watched for red boulders, but in the moonlight there was little accounting for color. Ingal didn't appear to be searching. "How do you know where it is?" she yelled.

"The memory. We know this mountain very well through the generations. There are several large, red boulders that stand out, but only one near the peak. If this one isn't it, we may have to search a bit. It's right up here."

In moments they came to a low saddle in the ridgeline. A round boulder sat off to one side against the mountainside. Fighting the wind, Ingal came to an abrupt landing nearby and lowered Torra to the ground.

A frigid gust nearly knocked Torra off her feet as flurries flecked her clothes and face. Accustomed to Ingal's body heat, she was instantly shivering in her tattered robe. She voiced a *Warmth* spell, but it managed only to make the temperature just tolerable. She pulled her robe close and tried to use her pack to shelter her face from the wind.

Torra made her way over to the boulder. At least forty feet in diameter, it was indeed red, though muted by the darkness, and unnaturally spheroid, with part of its bulk embedded into the stone of the mountain. Its surface was spotted with mica, gleaming in the moonlight. If there was an entrance into the mountain behind it, it was hidden completely by the boulder.

"You say there is a cave behind this?" Ingal asked. He appeared distracted, looking out into the darkness. "Is that what the apprentice told you?"

"That's what he said," she yelled over the wind. She rubbed her itching neck and studied the boulder's surface.

Ingal stepped up and hugged the stone. Grunting, he tried to roll the boulder out of the way. His arm and leg muscles quivered with the exertion, but the stone didn't move. He stopped, then tried again, attacking it with greater effort, but it refused to budge.

"The apprentice mentioned something about the Polar Star and the constellation of Corthos, the sleeping dragon," Torra shouted over the wind. "When I saw the mica in the surface, I thought this might be a star map, like on the elvish dispatch at your palace, but I don't recognize any constellations."

Ingal stepped back and cocked his head. Then he smiled. "Ah, but do you remember how Corthos appeared on the elvish dispatch?"

"Mirror image," she said. "Yes. Imagine if the boulder was hollow and we were looking at the surface from the inside. It would be like looking at the heavens above us." She stepped closer to the boulder's surface and ran a hand along it. She found the constellations of the Swordsman, the Great Tower, and the

Bear in mirror image. She moved her gaze down the boulder to the Sleeping Dragon. "Yes, here is Corthos—and the star at the tip of his tail." She stepped back and looked up toward the top of the boulder. "The apprentice said to connect the Polar Star to the tail of the Sleeping Dragon, but there is no way I could reach both at the same time." She looked to Ingal. "You could, though!"

Ingal reached with a claw on his left forefoot and touched the gleaming spot that represented the tail of Corthos, then reached to the top of the boulder and touched the spot representing the Polar Star at the same time.

Nothing happened.

Ingal stepped back. "This does not make sense, Torra. No elf would have the ability to touch both points at the same time, for elves are little taller than you are."

She nodded and rubbed her chin. "Of course!" she exclaimed and put a hand against her forehead, recalling her astronomy training. "When I hear 'Polar Star' I naturally think of the one I am most familiar with—the *northern* Polar Star. But according to the ancient naval records of Alman, there is a *southern* one as well!"

"Ah, certainly," Ingal said. "We had all but forgotten. But it is not visible from even the most southern reaches of the lower kingdoms. The elves could never see it; only sailors are familiar with the southern Polar Star. Our forebears have only twice ever seen it with our own eyes."

"And yet," Torra said, "here it is—I think." She reached with her left forefinger and touched the lowest gleaming spot on the boulder, next to the ground, then reached up as far as she could and connected the tail of Corthos with the right forefinger.

Instantly the boulder rumbled and moved. Torra and Ingal stepped back as it rolled forward then off to the right, coming to rest in a depression in the bedrock. Behind it was a yawning opening, wide enough even for Ingal to squeeze into.

There's a renegade spell in there, Torra thought, and stepped forward. "Wait," Ingal said. He placed a forefoot in front of her. "There may be traps. Such powerful spells are rarely left unguarded." He cast a *Light* spell on the cave walls.

Through the opening they saw a cave that narrowed as it went back. Rough stone walls and an uneven floor seemed carved not by man or water, but by the forces of nature that formed the mountain itself. Here and there along the jagged walls were streaks of iron deposits and glistening quartz.

Ingal went first, studying the walls and stepping gingerly for fear of setting off a trap. But there was no sign of danger. Ingal had gone completely into the cave before he called for Torra to enter. She stepped in and crept along the wall, squeezing in places to get around him, then moving to the front. Before them against the back wall of the cave was a natural granite shelf. A large book lay on it as if forgotten by some explorer.

The tome was huge—as large as the ones in Ingal's study – and coated in ages of gray dust and debris. A leather strap tied the covers together.

Torra's eyes went wide. "The Book of Alasar! We've found it!" A renegade spell!

Ingal tried to squeeze in further, but the cave became too narrow. "We cannot reach it, Torra. You will have to retrieve the book. But study it carefully for traps—and do not open it!"

Torra nodded and stepped up to the spellbook. She saw no obvious traps. Time seemed to slow as she reached out and placed a hand on it, wiped away the debris from the cover, blew off the dust. Her eyes grew wide at what she saw. She bolted upright as the realization sunk in.

"What is it?" Ingal asked. "You are blocking our view."

The Book of Alasar gleamed golden in the magic light, its surface made of dragon scales—gold dragon scales.

Torra stepped aside and looked back to see Ingal's reaction.

The dragon's eyes widened. He snorted. "By the gods!"

"How barbaric!" Torra said.

Ingal shook his head and seemed to force himself to relax. "It is not the first time We have heard of powerful books and other items bound in dragon hide and scales. It is considered a sign of power. But it does not necessarily mean that the dragon was killed for this purpose; it may have been that our forebear had died by other means, and the hide was taken from the corpse. Shields, armor, ceremonial vestments, even building materials have been the final result of dragon body parts. We have even heard of a ceremonial barge whose construction was fabricated completely of the remains of the Onyx Dragon! Sadly, this is not even the first instance we know of where the Gold Dragon's hide became a book of magic, though it is certainly the most powerful of such books."

Torra blew more dust off the book, revealing faded writing.

"There are runes here," Torra said, "but I don't recognize them. Can you see them from there?"

"No. Hold still a moment." Ingal cast a *Protection* spell upon Torra. "That should help protect you against any magical traps. You may pick up the book and bring it to us, if you please."

Torra spread her arms wide to encompass the tome, leaned over it, and hefted it with a grunt. The book peeled away from the rock shelf, so long had it lain there. It was almost too heavy for Torra, but she managed to struggle the few feet to Ingal. She tried to lower it to the floor in front of him but dropped it the last few inches. The ancient binding split down the middle as it hit the stone.

Torra yelped. "Oh no! I'm so sorry." Stupid! Stupid! How can you be so clumsy with something so precious? "Will it hold together?"

Ingal scowled at her. "Yes, but we had better carry it from here."

Torra scratched at the inflamed skin on her arm and looked back to the writing. "Can you read it?"

"Yes. But it is very ancient." He reached up and scratched at the base of one of his horns as he studied the writing, mouthing the words as he read. "It is Occultian," he finally said. "The noble dialect, late period, to be precise. If we are not mistaken, it reads, 'Within lies the doom of the world, for gods may enter, and mountains will quake and fall.'" He paused to translate, then continued, "'Open not this tome unless ye be he who made it, or suffer death by disintegration. Speak not this magic unless to beckon in a new age of man, for madness is your price.'" Ingal paused once more to translate. "'Thus speaketh Alasar, Mage Superior of Occultii, Suzerain of the Eastern Province.'"

A moment of silence passed as they considered the words. Wind wailed across the cave opening, echoing off the walls as if blowing through eons of time.

"This confirms the legends," Ingal said. "Alasar may have been the most powerful of mages ever to walk the world. He at least was the leading mage of the wealthiest and most powerful land in history. But he was also the key figure in its downfall. It was this spell, *Rift Widening*, that allowed the creation of the great portal to the heavens and angered the gods into destroying his great empire."

"How ironic that we see the same thing happening again."

Ingal gave a sarcastic smile and looked over to Torra. "It is not ironic, Torra, for we have spoken with the Triumvirate at Tegora'Seima. The Triumvirate inspired Occultii to invade the heavens. They may have even aided Alasar in creation of this spell. Is it any surprise, then, that the book has found its way to Peshilaree, where it has lain in wait all these millennia to be used now?

"It is ironic, though, that after all these millennia of waiting for the opportunity, the time came to use the spell, yet the mage entrusted with protecting it—Ektibal—refused to present it in the end. Ektibal and his apprentices must have known what was at stake. They were willing to endure torture and death rather than relinquish the book and plunge their people into a war between gods and man. It is fortunate for us that Ektibal managed to communicate a warning to others, including the Prince of Mirrors and the Tower of Light, before he was killed."

"But we can't open it," Torra said. "It says not to open it unless 'ye be he who made it,' or be disintegrated." Once again a vision flashed through her mind of the palace guardsman hit by the acid sphere, his face melting as he screamed. Torra shook off the thought.

Ingal appeared not to notice. He studied the book, then a smile crept over his face. "Did we not make it?" He looked over to Torra. "The book is literally made of us!"

Ingal motioned for Torra to move back. "We will attempt to open it now." Torra moved as told.

After casting another *Protection* spell on himself, Ingal reached out with a claw and cut the ancient leather ties, which crumbled and fell apart with ease. The sense of foreboding was palpable. Electricity filled the room and made Torra's hair stand on end.

Ingal pulled open the cover. Instantly a thunderclap erupted from the book, ringing through the cave and forcing Torra to cover her ears and yell out. She looked away, afraid of what had become of Ingal, but curiosity overcame her and she looked back.

"That was most unpleasant," Ingal said, shaking his head. His powerful voice was heavily muted by the ringing in Torra's ears, but she was overjoyed to see that he yet existed and in one piece.

Ingal read the first page. "There are two renegade spells in this book!"

"Two!" Torra exclaimed, and rushed forward. Ingal flipped to a marker halfway through the tome, where the binding had split.

"The first spell is *Rift Widening*, as you had suspected, Torra. Do you remember how we wondered why anyone would want it? This spell is practically useless. One can only widen a rift that has been created with *Dimensional Rift*, the only copy of which is long destroyed."

Torra nodded.

"Well, my dear astronomer," Ingal said, shutting the book, "it seems *Rift Widening* is not the spell they sought!"

Torra could hardly catch her breath. "So what is the other spell in the book?"

"*Obliterate Mountain*," he said.

Torra blinked in surprise and mouthed the name. What had she expected? she asked herself. Something more ... explosive? *Decimate Army*, perhaps? *Hurricane*?

Ingal continued, "Any massive body of stone, such as the very mountain upon which we stand, can be reduced to sand and scattered to the winds with this powerful spell. The Triumvirate means to destroy the Tower of Light and its Heartstone as if they were obliterating a mountain. The presence of *Rift Widening* is an added bonus, if you will."

A moment of silence passed as Torra thought about the implications. The tower was said to be one piece, a sculpted mountain, after a fashion. She scratched at her arm and tried to bring herself back to the moment. "Now *we* have it, my lord. What shall we do with it? Hide it? Use it for our own defense? Destroy it?"

Ingal sighed and grimaced as he ran a forefoot over the book. "It is not an easy answer, Com Gidel. Though our first impulse is to destroy it, who is to say that the Triumvirate does not possess other means of attack? Keeping and using these spells for our own defense is tempting, but we cannot guarantee that even we have the wisdom and ability to use them properly. Chances are no one does. And hiding it only delays the decision and adds another layer of worry."

Torra placed her hand on the rough, golden cover. *Did I really suggest we destroy it? A renegade spell? One of the most powerful spells the world had ever known is in my hand!* It was a moment she had always dreamed about. All those years of researching renegade spells and practicing magic in secret. Now to have her hand on not one, but *two* renegade spells!

Ingal bowed his head, his brow tight, frowning. "What's wrong, my lord?"

"This," he said, nodding toward the book, then gesturing around him to the cave. "All of this. There are too many odd coincidences that tie us to this conspiracy. The inverted star pattern outside was of the sleeping dragon constellation, like on the elvish dispatch. The Stone of Lethori finds its way to us. The prince dies in *our* audience chamber warning us. And even the book is made of the hide of one of our *forebears*, with a warning that only *we* can open it! It can't be coincidence." Ingal paused to shake his head and sigh. "The Triumvirate said that it is in our *nature* to help them. Had they foreseen our involvement many tens of thousands of years ago? Is it possible that fate can overcome personal conviction?"

Torra took her hand off the Book of Alasar and placed a hand on Ingal's forefoot. "You are a noble leader, my lord. None can control your fate but yourself. The Triumvirate might have foreseen your involvement, but they cannot control your loyalties."

Ingal sighed. "Of course. Of course." He grabbed the Book of Alasar with one mighty forefoot and backed slowly out of the cave. "But there will be time for musings later, and for determining the fate of these spells. For now, we must take the book away from here to a safer location."

Torra followed. Again she was blasted by the chill wind and flurries at the cave entrance and pulled her robe closer around her. Then she stopped, watching Ingal.

Ingal stood just beyond the entrance holding his head high and sniffing. He dropped the book to the snow.

"What is it, my lord?"

Ingal's eyes opened wide. "Griffin scent!"

Suddenly, the mountaintop became alive with battle. A confusion of many things happened at once. A horn resounded off the ridge. At least three griffins swooped upon Ingal out of the darkness, attacking his face. Talons. Shrieking. Dragon roaring. Claws ripping at feathers. Tail whipping. "Torra!" Ingal managed to yell.

Three Padgarun warriors jumped down at Torra from above the cave opening. Acid spheres. Splattering. Burning her legs and arms. Screaming—*her* screams. Other fighters ran from behind the boulder toward the Book of Alasar.

"No!" Torra cried. "The book!"

She glanced behind her and dodged an acid sphere, then sputtered a *Light* spell into the eyes of one attacker. The Padgarun screamed and threw his hands to his face, dropping his sling. Bright white light streamed from between his fingers as he flailed and ran headlong into a companion.

Another Padgarun swung his spear, narrowly missing Torra's chest. She leapt out of the way and fell backward into a snowdrift.

"*Astoris glumina!*" she shouted, throwing her hands into the air. Her *Force Strike* spell threw the Padgarun to the ground as if he had been slammed in the chest by a war hammer. His spear clattered to the rocks.

Torra scrambled to her feet and tried for the spear, but the Padgarun was already recovering. Instead she ran toward the book.

Bloodied, Ingal grabbed one griffin by its neck and threw it into the mountainside. It hit with a sickening thud and crack and fell limp to the ground. He glanced to the book and whipped his tail into two of the Padgarun trying to reach it, sending them flying. One elf tumbled over the cliffs into darkness.

Torra screamed and fell to the ground as a spear whistled over her and hit the stone nearby. She was mere feet from the book. She turned over just as a Padgarun lunged upon her, stabbing his knee into her gut and knocking the breath out of her. She grabbed his hand as he raised a dagger over her, ready to plunge it into her neck. She fought to stop his arm from coming down, but the tip of the dagger inched ever closer to her skin.

Fostem decrona! she chanted. The elf's clothing caught fire, but the elf was unrelenting. They continued to struggle as the dagger came closer and closer, but then the flames grew and spread, fanned by the wind, and the Padgarun let go and fell away. He rolled in the snow, but the magic flames refused to extinguish. He ran back up the ridgeline, shedding clothing.

The last of the three elves came at Torra. She threw herself to the spear. Seizing it, she wheeled the blade around to face the attacker, but the Padgarun yanked the heavy spear out of her hand, twirled it around, and thrust the blade back at her.

Torra rolled out of the way as it cut through her collar, narrowly missing her neck. She kicked as he thrust again, turning it aside. The elf grimaced and cursed at her.

"Ingal!" she screamed. "Help!"

A forefoot swept through the air over them. The elf reacted in time to bury the blade deep into Ingal's palm and then fall to the ground out of the way. Ingal roared.

In that moment of distraction, Torra threw herself into the elf and ripped the bag of acid spheres from his waist. The Padgarun punched her in the face, sending her flying, then he dodged another blow from Ingal before Ingal was forced to turn his attention back to the griffins.

Torra pulled out an acid sphere and threw it as hard as she could at her attacker. It hit his neck, splattering and steaming in the cold air. His skin and hair melted, blood gushing from the melted arteries and bubbling as it dissolved in the acid. The elf fell to the ground, writhing, screaming, clutching at his neck with fingers that blistered and reddened. Torra's mouth opened wide in horror, and she turned away, hands on her ears against the screams. She staggered to the Book of Alasar.

Ingal roared and threw off another shrieking beast, his claws deep into its belly. Blood poured from its wounds as it rolled over the cliff. The remaining griffin fluttered away, badly wounded.

And then twenty more Padgarun came running down the ridge at them, slinging acid spheres and brandishing swords and spears.

They were led by a screaming female with flailing hair Phasgala!

Ingal moved to protect Torra, tensing to leap into the air, but a dozen acid spheres slammed into his flanks, wings, and limbs, forcing him to fall back. He quickly cast a *Word of Safety* over her, and a thin membrane of shielding energy enveloped Torra just as spheres burst against it and splattered around her. Taxed to its limit, the shield popped out of existence.

The elves swarmed over Ingal as their weapons flashed and whirled. "*Chrosti manius!*" he shouted, and chain lighting shot through them, throwing some of them to the ground in a seizure of electrocution. But others sunk their weapons into him in an organized attack, striking at vital points on his neck, arm joints, and the base of a wing.

Torra turned from Ingal and looked directly into the eyes of Phasgala as the Padgarun ran toward her. Torra backed up to run, but tripped over the Book of Alasar, falling backward on top of it. Her mind raced to find other spells to cast in her defense, but she knew so few! With her remaining magical energy, Torra cast a *Break* spell, snapping Phasgala's spear in two.

Then Phasgala was upon her faster than seemed possible. The she-elf shouted a spell and slapped Torra across the face.

Instantly Torra fell to the ground as fire burned through every nerve in her body. She screamed, balling up into a fetal position and ripping her nails into her own crawling flesh. Her joints froze. Her eyes opened wide as she rolled over to face her attacker through the haze of helpless pain.

Phasgala pulled a sword and raised it over Torra in a death strike, her eyes blazing with murderous glee.

A griffin swooped overhead. A figure fell from the darkness onto Phasgala, throwing her to the ground.

The Padgarun and the figure wrestled, flailed against each other as Torra fought her pain to turn toward them. *Rethuud!*

The two elves wrestled for control of Phasgala's sword, then Phasgala kicked Rethuud away. Rethuud pulled Ascareth and activated its blade as Phasgala swung her own sword at him. He cut her blade cleanly in two with his … and then in a single move, cut through both of her arms at the elbows.

Phasgala's limbs dropped to the ground as she jumped back, too late, screaming. Rethuud kicked her in the chest, knocking her to the ground in a shower of her own blood. "Beloved!" Phasgala screamed in a voice full of panic and disbelief. Rethuud plunged his shimmering blade into his mate's heart.

The next moment slowed to a crawl. The tempest-blown flurries seemed to hang in place. The roar of Ingal against his enemies deepened and lengthened to infinity. And alone over his fallen lover stood Rethuud, his hair whipped out of its topknot, Ascareth shimmering in his hand in a thin line of lethal energy, and eyes glazed over with anguish and loss as if he had looked into the whole of life's suffering and fallen prey to despair.

Then time caught up. Ingal's incantation flashed fire across the sky. Elves cried out. Torra turned to look, but Phasgala's spell finally overcame her, throwing her into a bottomless well of pain.

THIRTY-EIGHT
Parting

Moments of lucidity passed through Torra's consciousness, pierced through clouds of agony in half-believable tones like momentary blue or green flames dancing in a bonfire. Visions of bloody elvish warriors dying in a flash of golden scales. Starlit forests passing far below. Being swallowed alive by the trees. The old elvish woman leaning over her, cackling.

See before you the past of the world, my child. See before you its future. And then the visions dissipated like a slowly rising fog.

It was the very stirring of dawn when Torra opened her eyes and beheld cerulean skies pushing away the nighttime darkness. Her eyes could barely focus. She lay curled in a fetal position under the leatherine blanket that Rethuud had given her at Chaz Sanooc. She was shaking, but not solely from the chill air. Her whole body throbbed with pain, right to her fingers and toes. Her head pounded, and she closed her eyes again.

Something moved behind her, rustling heavy in the grass. Torra opened her eyes again and forced herself to turn.

Torra lay in a meadow. Ten feet or so away Ingal sat sphinx-like and at a slight angle from her, watching her intently. After a moment Torra was better able to focus. Ingal's scales were melted over large portions of his left side, and small wounds crisscrossed his body.

"She is awake," came another voice to the left. Rethuud. Ingal nodded.

"My lord …" Torra had to stop speaking. Her throat was on fire, and the words came out as a croak. She put a hand to her neck and realized that her skin there, and everywhere else, was coated in some sort of slime.

"It is called *manasalum*," Ingal said to her in Taxin, "a plant sap which soothes deep pain and inflammation. You can thank the squalma elder for applying it and bringing you out of your suffering."

"Squalma elder?" Torra rasped. She looked around again and realized she lay in the landing meadow for Hasala Squalma. Two griffins squawked and tapped their beaks at each other at the far end of the meadow next to the stream. One of Rethuud's warriors stood guarding them.

A handful of elvish villagers watched Torra and Ingal from the shadows of the forest. They peered from the undergrowth like a herd of deer, curious and unafraid, but shy enough to keep their distance.

"I don't trust them," Torra said to Ingal.

"Just as you did not trust me?" Rethuud said. "These are *my* people, *my* ancestral squalma. They would not betray me."

Torra realized she was grasping the Rod of Translation in her pocket. She sighed and looked back to the elf. "I'm sorry, Rethuud. I thought …" Torra paused abruptly against the pain in her throat.

"You thought I was colluding with Phasgala. I comprehend your suspicion. But could you truly believe I would still love a woman who assassinated my prince, my friend, my cousin? Love cannot survive such betrayal, such *murder*."

Torra sat up, rasping, "I was wrong to have doubted your loyalty, Rethuud." She paused to swallow against the pain in her throat. "But you *did* still love her. You love her still. I saw it in your eyes as you stood over her." Rethuud turned his head and said nothing.

Torra looked down at her hands and gasped. They were red and raw, cracked like sun-dried mud. The skin had lost its flexibility, making hand movements stiff and painful. A quick study revealed she was like that over large portions of her body.

"What's happened to me?" Torra looked up to Ingal. "What did that—" Torra gave a furtive glance toward Rethuud "—that cleric do to me?"

Ingal rubbed at one of the melted areas on his scales. "During the fight on Rishae'Uungi, Phasgala must have cast a *Disease* spell on you. Did she touch you at all? Was she chanting?" Torra nodded. "It is likely a very powerful clerical spell meant to accelerate your worst ailment," he continued. "What you are experiencing is the brimstone disease, as you would have felt it in perhaps a dozen years."

"Demonskin," Torra muttered. "Yes, she slapped me. When will the symptoms return to normal?"

Ingal's face grew drawn. "Oh, Torra, they may never subside. And it is likely the disease will progress faster than one would normally expect."

Torra wanted to lie down and curl up against the anguish and pain running through her. "I'm sorry, my lord."

Ingal tilted his head. "For what, Torra?"

"For failing you. I'm not much use to you. I'm just an anchor, slowing you down."

Ingal rose and stepped toward her. "Nonsense. You have been a tremendous aid to us." He laid down again with his face nearer hers. "We have the book. You were the one who learned where the Book of Alasar was hidden. And you were the one who discovered how to open the cave. Without you we might not have gotten this far."

Torra wanted to somehow indicate that she appreciated his comments, but she simply couldn't believe she was so invaluable. "It has been an adventure, my lord. But I think I've had all the adventure my body can handle."

Ingal nodded and crossed his mighty forefeet. "The worst is over, but the adventure has not quite ended, Torra. You have one last duty to do. Rethuud has agreed to deliver you and the Book of Alasar to the Tower of Light. You are to hand the book over to the towermaster and explain to him everything that has happened to you since you came to our palace."

Torra's eyes went wide. "Me? You're sending *me* to the tower, to talk to the *towermaster?*"

A smile crept into the dragon's lips. "Well, no one talks directly to the towermaster. The towermaster is one with the tower itself. You will actually speak with a mage called the Voice of the Towermaster. He is quite literally the eyes, ears, and voice of the towermaster."

A moment of adulation passed through Torra like a spirit. It was a great deal of trust and responsibility Ingal was placing in her unworthy hands. The Book of Alasar—*two* renegade spells—would be entrusted into *her* hands to deliver to one of the most powerful mages in the world. "But why me?" she finally asked. "Why aren't you doing it yourself? Wouldn't they *want* you to?"

"We don't think so." Ingal stood again and grimaced as he stretched his wounded flank. "They are suspicious of us right now. And there are other duties to which we must attend. The White Lands Federation is about to plunge into war with Ocrin, and they are likely falling into a trap. As the leader of the Federation, we must fly to the War Council and warn them."

Ingal wiped a forefoot across a cluster of melted scales. The plant sap had been applied there, too.

Ingal sighed. "But there is no underestimating the importance of delivering these spells into the appropriate hands. We hailed the tower early on, before we knew the whole story, but the mages did not reply. As you heard Peshiluud say, they have known for quite some time about the Triumvirate and their intent to destroy the tower and its Heartstone. Because one of the Triumvirate gods created the dragons, and perhaps because of Gogonith, the tower mages do not trust us. Likewise, they probably do not trust the elves or dwarves. Because of these reasons, we must entrust *you* with the responsibility to deliver the book." He paused for effect, then added with a smirk, "Try not to drop it again."

Ingal looked to Rethuud. "As soon as Torra is able to fly, you must take her directly to the tower with all haste. Do not land on the grounds of the tower, but rather just off the grounds, in the city of Taraman. Torra must carry the book to them herself —alone." Rethuud gave a slight bow. Ingal looked back to Torra. "Do you think you can do this?"

"Yes," she said. She would find the strength if it killed her.

"Good." Ingal looked to the sky. The dawn was full, and the entire sky had turned shades of blue, lightening toward the eastern horizon over the trees. "You are in safe hands here, Com Gidel. Rethuud and his warrior will watch over you and carry you to the tower when you are ready. We must depart with great dispatch now. Do not tarry longer than absolutely necessary."

"Don't worry. I don't want to be in Peshilaree any more than I have to."

"We will meet again at the tower, some time after you deliver the book. Until then, Com Gidel."

Rethuud gave a hail, and Torra waved as Ingal leapt into the sky and flew southward, disappearing over the treetops.

Once again Torra experienced that moment of dread at being left alone with the elves. She looked back to Rethuud and found the elf watching her intently.

"Do you trust me now?" he asked.

Torra nodded. "Yes. You saved my life. And there is no doubting your commitment after your sacrifice." Torra looked around the meadow again. "Where is your other warrior?" She looked back to Rethuud in alarm. "Did he die in the battle?"

Rethuud shook his head. "We sent him to the Gold Dragon's palace. There he will deliver Ingal's code to release my other warriors and the prince's body from imprisonment."

Torra lay back down. A cool breeze wafted across the meadow, drying the sap on her skin. The drier the sap became, the more the pain returned. "Where is the Book of Alasar?"

Rethuud motioned back to the griffins. One of them had a huge, leatherine satchel strapped to its side. "Do you feel like riding yet?"

The thought made her nauseated. Simply sitting upright had been painful enough. The thought of flopping around on the back of an undulating griffin was more than she could take at that moment. "Not yet. Do you think the old woman could bring more of the sap, and some water?"

"Hasala," Rethuud said sternly. "The elder's name is Hasala. I will let her know you desire more." Rethuud stepped past her to the edge of the forest, spoke with an elf there, and then returned. Soon more elves showed up at the meadow's edge. Hasala emerged from the shadows, bent over her cane as she walked with faltering steps. In the morning light she seemed impossibly frail, with each bone clearly defined by her paper-thin greenish skin. She carried a small platter with three stone drinking vessels and a leafy packet of some sort.

The walk seemed to take Hasala forever, and the platter bobbed precariously with each of the old woman's teetering steps. Torra wanted to help, but she knew from their first introduction that it would be improper. If Hasala failed in this ceremonial duty, she would be exiled from the clan. Finally, Hasala reached Torra and Rethuud, and the two elves exchanged the customary greeting ritual.

When finished, Hasala leaned over Torra and smiled, the old elf's eyes sharp and cunning. "My child," she said, her voice crackling, "the squalma presents to you this *manasalum*." The elder reached to the platter and handed Torra the leafy packet— a huge glob of viscous green sap wrapped in a very large leaf and tied with a bit of fine vine. "Rub it into your skin as the sun rises, but only then. Any other time of the day, and it will kill instead of heal." Hasala leaned down even further and whispered, "It will reduce your torment, child, for we wish not to see any living thing suffer. It will sink into you and become a part of you, just as you will become a part of it—and *us*."

"Thank you," Torra said, eyeing the green slime.

The elder stood back up and looked to Rethuud. "To you and your valiant companions, please accept our water to quench your thirst for your coming journey." The elder handed each of them a stone cup of water, then she turned and walked toward Rethuud's warrior and the griffins.

Torra sniffed at the water in the stone cup. Smelling nothing out of the ordinary, she started to take a sip. Suddenly, the old woman fell with a shriek, tripping on something in the grass and hitting the ground with a loud thud, the platter and cup flying. Rethuud's warrior was closest, abandoning the griffins and running to her side to help her up. Rethuud ran over, too, as Torra tried to stand.

Then a shadow passed over the rising sun, dark and silhouetted. It roared and swooped over the meadow. Rust-colored scales. Ram's horns. A huge, inflamed wound on its belly. *Gogonith!*

The dragon shouted a spell, and a lacework of webbing shot from his forefoot to settle over Torra and her companions. The webs stuck to their skin and hair and became tangled around them as they tried to wipe them off, then gelled on them like glue. Moving a boot from the ground or an arm from the torso became a sticky battle.

"The book!" Rethuud shouted to his warrior, but no one could move more than a foot against the mucilaginous fibrils. "We have been tricked. Protect the spells!"

Rethuud activated Ascareth and cut through the webs, but he was too late.

The griffins screamed and flapped to take off, but Gogonith grabbed the one with the Book of Alasar with one mighty forefoot and lifted the beast into the sky, shattering its vertebrae with a single squeeze and loud crack. The griffin went limp as Gogonith flew eastward over the forest.

Rethuud threw Ascareth at the griffin. The magical blade cut partway through a strap of the saddle, but the saddlebags remained tied to the beast with the Book of Alasar.

"All too easy!" Gogonith shouted in Peshilarn. "Give the Gold Dragon my fond regards!" Then he was gone into the rising sun, laughing in triumph.

Rethuud cursed and peeled off the gooey webbing. Once he was clear of the webs, he reached a hand to his mouth and made a loud shriek into the sky, repeating the call a couple of times.

By the time Rethuud recovered his sword, the second griffin returned, landing in the meadow and cowering under some trees.

"Come! Hurry!" Rethuud shouted, waving a hand at Torra.

Torra still struggled against the webbing and her own pain. The other warrior helped the elder to her feet, then ran to assist Torra, roughly grabbing her arm and pulling her through the webs toward the remaining griffin.

The elder was cackling again. "Oh, what adventure!" she creaked.

"Hasala!" Rethuud said from the griffin's side. "How could you do this to us? You tripped at just the moment of the dragon's attack. Tell me not that you assisted the Iron Dragon! My own elder!"

Hasala stopped laughing and peered at Rethuud with somber eyes. "It was no conscious fall, my child, but there are no accidents. We are children of our Creators. We have no choice but to assist them."

Hasala turned and looked Torra in the eye, pointing her cane at her. "Remember well, child! No being born solely of this world can deliver you from the Creators. Yet a purely supernatural creature has no stake in saving it. Your savior must be of *mixed blood*, able to choose his own mind for—or against—your cause."

Torra had no idea what the elder meant. All she could think about was how the Book of Alasar had been stolen from their very grasp. After all they had been through, the spells were in enemy hands.

Torra was rushed to the griffin by Rethuud and his warrior and practically thrown onto the beast's back. Rethuud climbed on in front of her, then turned to his warrior. The griffin rider tried to apologize for leaving his post, but Rethuud cut him off.

"Call another griffin from the hills and join us as soon as you can."

Torra hung her head. "They have the book now. There's no way we can catch the Iron Dragon. Ingal is long gone. All is lost. What could we possibly do now? Where could we *possibly* be going?"

"Where do you think, human?" Rethuud said. "Where would Peshiluud be now?"

Torra sighed. "The Lake of Origins—Eshenakaree."

"He is resurrecting the Ecemii, the Great Ones. Gogonith will carry the spellbook to him. So it is there that we must now fly."

Rethuud shouted at the griffin, and the beast reluctantly trotted forward, then ran and leapt into the sky. They circled the meadow once to gain altitude, then flew eastward after Gogonith. The Iron Dragon was already just a dark smudge in the distance.

Torra took one last look at the meadow behind them and saw the lone elder still standing where they left her, surrounded by thousands of silky strands of webbing slowly waving in the breeze.

This time the old woman wasn't laughing.

Torra wondered if Hasala was thinking the same as she: How could a stricken human mage and a solitary elvish warrior possibly reclaim a renegade spellbook from the great Iron Dragon, a mythic elvish leader, and an army of ancient heroes resurrected from the heart of Peshilaree?

They had no choice but to try.

THIRTY-NINE
Firestorm

Ingal had doubts. Doubts about Torra's health. Doubts about the book's safety. Doubts about Rethuud's ability to protect them both. Had Phasgala truly been the love of his life? Elf or not, what would killing his lover do to his ability to focus?

He turned back toward Hasala Squalma, wondering if his worries were warranted.

Ingal sighed as he increased his altitude. *Prudence,* he thought. *Torra is in no condition to travel. And Rethuud has just killed his mate, distracted by her death, with only one of his warriors to accompany him. Too much rides on their ability to get the renegade spells into safe hands.*

Ingal rolled upside down and looped back southward toward the White Lands, then righted himself. He grimaced, mentally running over the argument.

Trust. We must trust in their abilities—and in our own intuition. Rethuud and Torra haven't yet disappointed us. And right now they are with Rethuud's ancestral clan. They need only to fly southward across the border and deliver the book to the tower. Yes. Trust in delegation.

Ingal put more force into his wing beats, picking up speed. *Besides, We are late for the War Council. Our role as the leader of the White Lands Federation necessitates we do our duty to protect it. We have been gone too long in a time of urgent need. Ocrin could attack the White Lands at any moment now, and Our troops have likely been misled to expect an attack from the north of the border. Vizier Janisim will pay for his treachery!*

Ingal flew many hours at his best long-range speed. Things were eerily quiet. No wind. No Padgarun rising from the forest. No sign of villagers in the meadows and forests below. All the world seemed to be holding its breath. Not a good omen.

Ingal had flown to a great height by the time he reached the federation's border just after midday and started his descent for Mount Guulenen. The mountain, with the great cavern of Chaz Sanooc at its empty heart, stood alone over the forest just to the southeast.

The moment Ingal crossed over into the White Lands, the azure skies suddenly grew overcast with puffs of white clouds, then woolpack, condensing from nothingness, turning black and closing out the sun. The roiling darkness inside the clouds pulsed with an unnatural orange and red as if burning from the inside.

Never before in the memory had Ingal and his forebears seen such a strange and surely supernatural display. He flew in a slow circle, watching the phenomenon, then realized with horror that the clouds stopped abruptly where the Elvish Forest began.

The Triumvirate! Draq's warning came back to Ingal in a rush. *Your beloved White Lands will be ravaged as punishment, burnt and cast asunder with your pride.*

As if on cue, a thunderclap resounded across the sky. The clouds caught fire. Nuggets of burning tar fell from the heavens. *Firestorm!*

Ingal threw himself into a dive, speeding southeast. He cast a quick *Shield* spell, but he knew it wouldn't last long. His magical energy was still depleted by the fight on the mountain. He had to reach the shelter of Chaz Sanooc, still many miles away.

In moments, lumps of fiery tar struck the shield at his back, his wings, his head. The air itself seemed to hiss and steam. In moments the shield failed. Ingal roared in pain from hundreds of burning wounds and beat his wings with all the strength he could muster. Below, the forest erupted in a million miniature bonfires and quickly turned into a massive conflagration.

Finally reaching Mount Guulenen, Ingal swooped around its east side. The Cannosa River poured forth as always from the mountain base, and Ingal lost no time diving into it. Instantly came relief from the burning as the tar on his back sputtered and extinguished.

Ingal swam to the river's opening, sheltered by the mountain. Able to breathe underwater like all dragons, he sat on the rocky river bottom and felt the pain of the burns diminish in the chill. He turned and looked downstream through the water at the meager daylight filtering through. It turned dark as the storm intensified, then red as the fires swept over the land on either shore.

The gods have grown more powerful. Now they cast their own renegade spells in the material world! Ingal clenched his fist. *Be you god or not, Draq, We will have our vengeance.*

He turned and swam upstream and burst through the cavern opening, inside the mountain. He spent a moment twisting and turning for a quick inspection of his wounds. Angry black and red welts bulged through the scales on his wings and tail, and, by the feel of it, over all of his back and head. He paused to gather his strength, then lumbered to the doors of his study. Instead of entering, though, he raised up on his hind legs and reached to the gigantic battle scythe over the doorway. Gripping the ebony handle, he slid the weapon off its perch with a ring of the mighty, reinforced blade.

The scythe felt natural in his grip, perfectly balanced from the tip of its gargantuan blade to the twisted handle. How many centuries had it been since last he wielded it in battle? At least three. He tested the edge with a claw. Made of a special alloy by the Deep Dwarves of Sarsa, it retained its edge even after all that time. Ingal wrapped the handle around his right arm and swung the scythe in the air, smiling at the satisfying hum.

Energized by his anger, the dragon again slid into the river and emerged just at the opening to the outside. All around the forest was in flames, but the burning hail had abated. The unnatural clouds were dissipating. The damage had been done.

Ingal dove under and swam to build up speed with the current, then burst into the air and flew southward, scythe at his side.

The forest was aflame for as far as he could see. Everything, that is, south of the elvish border. A wind had picked up, fueling the conflagration and blowing the thick cloud of smoke southward. Ingal shook his head. The extent of the forest fires would wipe out much of that area's economy and threaten at least a dozen villages and towns.

Ahead, already in flames, was the small town of Cannosa on the banks of the river that bore its name. While Ingal needed to get to the western border with all due haste, he had to stop. The village would be lost without his help. He flew low and dropped the scythe into a shallow portion of the river to await his return, then rose up and over the village.

Villagers ran from building to building, rescuing what they could and passing buckets of water to put out the flames. Seeing Ingal circling, they bowed in reverence and prayed for deliverance from the evil sky fires.

"Arise," Ingal shouted. "Arise! We must save your village."

He landed in the water just offshore and overturned a fishing boat. Filling the vessel with river water, he took to the sky and poured it on the buildings, returning to the river to get more.

First he doused the storehouses of grain, then the center hall, then finally the homes until all the fires had been extinguished.

Long they labored until the village had been secured, keeping a careful eye on the forest burning all around. The exhausted inhabitants of Cannosa had gathered in a ragtag group near the hall, raising their hands and singing a song of praise to their lord, but Ingal had no time for flattery. He raised his forefoot in blessing, stating, "I am Ingal Jehai, Dragon of the Federation. May your town be blessed with renewed fertility and recover from the evils of our enemy." He lowered his forefoot. It was then that Ingal noticed there were no men of fighting age among them. He continued, "War has come with the elves. Call to arms your men and women and prepare for battle."

The villagers blinked and looked at each other in confusion. "The elves?" said one. "What have the elves against us?"

An elderwoman stepped forward and bowed low with shaking arms. "My precious lord, I am Genem Sa'Jehai. May I be granted leave to speak?"

"Yes, of course. Please, rise. One of your generation need not bow so low to us." Then he consulted the memory. "Yes, Genem Sa'Jehai of Cannosa, we remember your birth in our palace. Yours was a difficult birthing. Your mother would have died had it not been for our priests."

She stood and gave a quick, exhausted smile, but did not meet Ingal's eyes. "My precious lord, it honors me that you remember, and that you have come to our rescue. Was it the elves who brought forth the fire from the sky?"

Ingal sighed. How could he explain it? "No, elderwoman, it was not the elves, but they fight at the behest of others who are responsible. Allow us to worry about them. It falls to you to guard this stretch of the border. Where are your men?"

"My lord, a messenger from Namistad came yesterday and took them away. He told us of the war with Ocrin, and that our men were needed at the western border."

Ingal gritted his teeth. The viziers had betrayed him and countermanded his orders. The reserves were not to be used!

"We were betrayed, but it was a mistake for which we are ultimately responsible. Fear not, for we shall find your men and send them back. But do as you can to defend yourselves. In time we will return. Dark times have befallen our fair land." Ingal again raised his forefoot in blessing as the villagers bowed. "Lead your village well, Genem, for you bear our name." Then he took to the sky.

In moments, Ingal returned to the river where he had left the battle scythe. He paused to rest there as the fire burned out around him. He lowered his head, coughing in the heavy smoke, and allowed his muscles to stop shaking. This was no time to feel old!

He grasped the battle scythe for support, coughing again. Anger surged through him like an onrushing tide.

He gripped the handle so hard the scales on his forefoot cracked.

~ ~ ~

Ingal had intended to fly straight to the Keep of Casan, reaching the stronghold by midnight, but four times he spotted reserve armies, including Cannosa's, marching westward along the great River Road toward Ocrin.

Each time he landed and spoke with the army commanders, ordering them to return to the elvish border or to guard the Tower of Light. The reserve troops were largely untrained and undisciplined, cowering, bowing, or simply running away at the sight of the Gold Dragon and his massive battle scythe. Even the reserve commanders, who had been lesser officers until the posting, hardly seemed able to command their troops or deal with their own sense of awe at Ingal's presence.

Too much time had been wasted with the reserve armies. Dusk had come. Ingal sent a runner to the Keep of Casan to announce his coming at dawn and to convene the War Council at that time, then he turned and flew northwest into the state of Alneri. The ether hung with the scent of decaying plant matter, the organic gases released from the Marwin Fens stretching out to the east.

The night air slipped soft and cool over his still-throbbing burn wounds. Hours passed as he soared to the northwest beneath a cloudless, starry sky. The fecund ethers of the fens gave way to a faint scent of burning forest: he was now downwind of the fires he had witnessed earlier in the day. He picked up speed toward the western border.

By midnight the moons had risen, and Ingal had nearly reached the object of his diversion—Alneri Castle—a massive citadel built upon a plateau overlooking the border with Ocrin.

He thought back to the final moments of its construction. Five towers rose from its bailey, each connected to the others with sturdy, buttressed bridges. From the highest tower, Ingal had been able to sit and observe a hundred miles of border. The castle was a marvel of engineering in any age of the world. With its creation a thousand years before, Alneri was fortified against Ocrin, known as Zern at that time, and that sense of safety translated into the state's willingness to join the White Lands Federation.

On the day of its completion, he had placed the last stone at the top of the center tower. The day was bright and warm, and the long brown streamers of Alneri snaked and snapped in a moderate breeze. The stone slipped into place, and the Gold Dragon landed at the top, spread his wings, and emitted a long, noble roar. The call was answered by thousands of cheering soldiers and Alnerians crowded in and around the castle below. Horns blew, and days of celebration commenced. The Iron Dragon, Tellonta, his loyal companion, the friend who had aided him in building the castle, joined him at the top, and together they looked over the shining white structure they had created.

No more. The castle now lay in smoking ruins.

And it was the Iron Dragon who destroyed it.

Ingal swooped low over the last hill and turned tight circles as he surveyed the damage in the moonlight. Stone blocks were scattered and heaped over the castle plateau. The highest battlement, upon which he had stood thousands of times, lay broken on top of the heap. Little more than a retaining wall was left intact. As if to add insult, the interspersed wooden remnants had burnt. Ingal flared his nostrils at the fumes. Judging by the faint, fetid vapors, it was the stores of whale oil that were at the root of the fire.

Gogonith. With what renegade magic had Gogonith found the power? An *Earthquake* spell? Perhaps. It mattered little. The deed was done.

And as a result, twenty thousand Federation troops now expected Ocrin forces to charge screaming over the border at this location—thousands of Federation troops that were not posted down in Namistad, where Ingal now knew the real charge would be led. Their campfires dotted the landscape all around the plateau and up and down the border, flickering with the winds of conspiracy.

Ingal looked to the border. On the other side, along the rise of land that ran north-south in parallel, were just as many Ocrin campfires glimmering back at them. Did Ocrin truly have so many troops? He had to find out.

He flew straight west and across the border—a violation of the Treaty of Long March Keep—and winged over the rise. At one point he flew very low over a camp, close enough to look the startled soldiers in the eyes and send them running. The campfires were manned, but only by small squads. They were little more than children, conscripts, and old, crippled reserves. And just over the rise? Nothing. No fires. No troops. No war wagons or siege machines. It was a ruse. There were no armies waiting to rush over the border. Only a force of militia meant to deceive the Federation.

Ingal wasted no further time. Flying back into the White Lands, he found the highest concentration of campfires and landed. Soldiers, caught off guard, announced Ingal's arrival and scrambled to form up in attention. Ingal didn't wait for ceremony. He plunged the scythe blade into the drilling ground and stepped toward a high command tent where the flag of Alneri was posted.

A handful of officers came forward, half-dressed and still strapping on their armor.

"Who is the commanding officer here?" Ingal demanded.

A haggard, elder soldier stepped forward and saluted. "We were relieved to see the arrival of reserves, my lord." A valet handed the soldier a high-crested helmet, which he immediately donned. "Danerel Sanoam, Commander of the Alneri Guard,

Master-of-Arms of Alneri Castle." Then, glancing toward the plateau, he sputtered, "Formerly."

"Commander, time is short," Ingal said, "and we are overdue for the War Council at the Keep of Casan. We must leave immediately, and thus it falls on you to spread our orders amongst the troops here. The generals have been misled. Ocrin will strike in Namistad, not Alneri. The enemy forces you have seen across the border are a ruse, and are smaller than they seem. Small squads of militia, nothing more."

Ingal lashed his tail in concentration. "Coordinate with the other commanders and move the bulk of the armies southward to Long March Keep—double time. Leave here only a holding force of two regiments. Our armies in Long March Valley will, in turn, be moved southward to the Naminari Valley, where the incursion will likely occur. Do you understand?"

The commander acknowledged the order with a nod, repeating it half in disbelief, and started issuing commands to subordinates. By dawn, the troops would be moving. But Ingal doubted it would be soon enough.

Ingal half-turned to leave, then looked back. "Commander, have there been any sightings of the Iron Dragon in the last four days?"

The commander bristled at the mention of Gogonith. "That demon hasn't dared to show his scales since he destroyed the castle, my lord. But you have my word, on the heart of my father, I would see the Iron Dragon dead if he passed over my fires again."

Ingal nodded, then raised his forefoot in blessing. "We wish you the chance, Commander, and may you wield your troops with the strength of *three* dragons." Without another word, Ingal retrieved his scythe and flew southward into the darkness.

Gogonith would have flown this way in retreat after our battle over the Alsanoos. So where did he flee? Did he survive at all? Could he have gone north into Peshilaree? Ingal drove the thoughts from his mind. It was no use speculating. It was enough that Gogonith was out of action.

Ingal spent the next few hours flying southward along the border surveying the Ocrin encampments. Everywhere he saw the same thing. Wherever possible, Ocrin had posted just enough soldiers to seem like a larger force, erecting temporary embankments and structures which could never hold up to a true attack, and moving troops back and forth as if they were subordinate to a bigger army. The scheme was elegant in its complexity and implementation, and likely would have succeeded if he hadn't disguised himself as Gogonith and heard the truth for himself. Clearly the planning for this event went back years. How had his spies failed him?

They had been misled, that's how. Their messages distorted or blocked by connivance. By the traitor in his midst. Vizier Janisim would pay for his deceit!

As Ingal flew southward into Long March Valley, the number of Ocrin troops across the border grew. But these forces were no ruse; these were battle-hardened troops. Ingal looked eastward into the White Lands. Long March Keep, a squat stone citadel with rows of battlements, guarded the valley from Ocrin incursions. Federation armies gathered around the citadel might be enough to hold them off.

Ingal continued southward and along the Alsanoos River. Here, at the opening of the Naminari Valley and within the shadow of Highwatch Mountain, the sweating mass of men and horses was numerous enough to smell even at a great height.

And across the border into the White Lands? There was hardly a Federation force to counter them.

Ingal had seen enough to confirm his worst fears. He turned back and flew northeast back into Long March Valley. The great peaks of the Vigil Mountains curved toward him. At their eastward end was the Keep of Casan and the War Council.

Dawn would come soon, and Ingal was exhausted from his flight. His flight muscles burned almost as much as the tar wounds on his back and wings. With the first moon setting, Ingal winged to the top of a foothill below the Vigils and lay down, curled around an ancient maple tree. He tried to slow his breathing, closing his eyes, but sleep evaded him. His mind spun with plans. Troop movements. Supply lines. But even if he could hold back the Ocrin forces, the Tower of Light would still be open for attack at the other end of the Federation.

Ingal clenched his jaw and growled. He had been duped by the largest of conspiracies. It was the cleverest of plans. The Triumvirate wanted to use the elvish Ecemii, the Great Ones, to attack the Tower of Light, but they knew the tower would be defended by the Gold Dragon and Federation troops. So the elves conspired with Ocrin to have Ocrin attack the Western border. Combined with a traitorous vizier and an attack by the Iron Dragon, the Federation troops were moved west, but to the wrong area, and because he was duty bound as the ruler of the White Lands Federation, Ingal had no choice but to deal with that situation. Now, just as the Triumvirate had wished, the Tower of Light was left undefended except by the mages themselves and local militia.

There was a twinge of concern in his mind, a shadow of doubt.

Ingal once more regretted leaving the renegade spells in the hands of Rethuud and Torra. Though he knew he had no choice. Despite the importance of their mission, Ingal's first duty was to the Federation that he ruled. He had to trust in Torra and Rethuud's abilities.

Right now he wished for Metharcus's counsel. The old human had a way of making even the most dire of circumstances seem less than emergent. Ingal sighed and tried to rest, planning for the coming day. *At least the Book of Alasar is secure,* he thought.

FORTY

Eshenakaree

Torra couldn't stop shaking. But it wasn't from the cold. Not anymore. She shook from the pain of her skin as it cracked and bled from the brimstone disease. Not in gushing wounds, but in thin, crisscrossing lines as if she had fallen through a briar patch, each wound drying within minutes of being formed.

The all-day flight from Hasala Squalma had jarred her up and down and side to side as Rethuud flew after Gogonith, down into valley bottoms to keep from being seen, and generally following the northeastern base of Unola'Uungi up into the mountains until they followed a thin river eastward.

Then there were griffin warriors, and Rethuud would duck their mount down into the woods to hide, sometimes for hours, during the night. The rest periods were welcomed relief for Torra, but all too soon she would be hefted back onto the irritable beast and off they would fly again. All she remembered toward the end of the night was cold wind, the lusty smell of fir trees, and ghostly mountaintops passing alongside and overhead like giant, ominous sentinels caught napping. It didn't help that the griffen didn't want to fly at night and kept trying to land.

Torra dimly noted the end of their journey when they landed on the edge of a high, mountainside grotto and dismounted. She waited impatiently for the sunrise, pawing at the leaf wrapping around the *manasalum* as if the act could will the sun to rise sooner. She fought her inanition with the febrile compulsions normally reserved for addicts. When the first sapphirine glimmer of dawn faintly lit the grotto opening, Torra ripped open the leaf bundle, plunged her hand into the cool, green salve, and smeared the emollient over her raw and scabby skin. The instant soothing made her gasp and pull open her robes in a frantic and unabashed attempt to reach and slather areas that she would normally be too shy to expose in Rethuud's presence.

Rethuud at first turned away, but quickly ran to Torra's side and grabbed her wrist. "You must ration this medication," he said. Torra yanked her hand away, eager to continue spreading the salve, but willpower won out. She wrapped the remaining portion back into the leaves with great reluctance and tried to spread what she had already removed.

Spent by the sudden relief, Torra fell back onto the cold and irregular stone of the grotto and nearly fell asleep, pulling the leatherine blanket over her. The bleeding stopped. The broken skin tingled. All over she felt a warmth that defied the high altitude.

The moment of relaxation quickly ended as a roar echoed off the mountainsides. The griffin, which had pushed its beak under a wing to sleep, squawked awake as Rethuud ran to the grotto opening. "I shall return in a moment," he said. He started to turn away, then added, "There is a short sword in my saddlebags. I recommend you keep it near." He carefully stepped out, disappearing around to the left.

Curiosity won over, but Torra ignored the sword. Such weapons were too barbaric. She gingerly stood and wobbled to the opening. Outside, mountains rose and fell as far southwestward as she could see. Turning, she watched as Rethuud followed a narrow trail up the stony mountainside and disappeared over a ridge. Feeling her courage return, Torra followed. Soon she found Rethuud lying flat on the ridgeline. She lowered herself to her knees and joined him.

What she saw on the other side of the ridge took her breath away.

Below lay a circular lake, deep beyond penetration, and completely still. Its waters quickly colored from cerulean at the edges to a rich cobalt blue in the center. Torra and Rethuud lay at the ridgeline of a ring of mountains encircling and guarding over the fairy-tale scene, with sheer cliffs down to the water's edge. Prominences of stone as large as five-story buildings leaned out over the void from the mountaintops as if straining for an even better view, so much so that some of them looked as if they would topple down into the tranquil waters with the slightest of quakes.

On the eastern edge of the lake was a beach of cobble rock where the mountains lowered to make a valley. There, gathered together in front of a living hall similar to the Hall of Emeralds, was a band of Padgarun clerics. Peshiluud stood in front of them, arms wide and gazing up with eyes that reflected the azure sky. At his side stood the speaker in his iridescent robe and brightly flowered headdress. Behind them all lorded Gogonith with rust-colored wings unfurled, a wound on his chest blistered and infected.

"This is Eshenakaree, Lake of Origins," Rethuud whispered. "The holiest of elvish sites. The place where our kind is said to have been born into the world. You are the first human to see it, as far as I am aware, and would surely be killed ... as would I for bringing you here." Rethuud flashed her a quick look that she could not readily translate. He continued, "Only the Padgarun and nobility are allowed access, and only for sacred purposes. When a noble dies, he or she is dressed in their finest attire and lowered into the water by the Padgarun, sinking into its depths, and takes on the name of Ecemii, the Great Ones. It is said that one day the Great Ones will rise again to fight for elvenkind."

At that moment the first direct rays of the sun shone upon the water, and Peshiluud began to chant. The words were lost to the distance, but were punctuated by ritualistic grunts and stomping by the clerics behind him, their spears raised toward the sky. The air took on a static charge, raising the hairs on Torra's neck. Peshiluud strode the few feet to the edge of the water and waded in to his waist. The chanting increased in volume, then suddenly ended. With a serene smile, Peshiluud lowered his hands and touched the water's surface.

At first nothing seemed to happen. Peshiluud and the clerics remained motionless for many minutes, looking expectantly into the water. Gogonith shifted uncomfortably.

And then, from her great height, Torra saw something move deep in the water.

Rethuud gasped. "*Ecaea Ecimii alu alleia,*" he muttered.

Dim shapes ascended out of the depths. Singly, then in groups, rising slowly up the column of water and toward the beach without needing to swim. When they neared the beach, they slowed and headed for Peshiluud.

And then the first one broke the surface.

It was a woman, a female elf, with a fine, long gown of white flowers, and viridian hair braided into a coronet. She waded through the water until she stood before Peshiluud. They briefly touched hands, then she waded past him to step upon the beach. The speaker reached out and caressed her shoulders, then the two embraced. Arm in arm, he escorted her to the hall.

"That was the speaker's mother," Rethuud said. "She died just after giving birth to him."

Others rose from the surface. One by one, they touched Peshiluud's outstretched hands and filed past him to be greeted by the clerics and walked to the hall. They were dressed in fine robes, or verdant, leafy clothing, or attired with flowers like the speaker's mother. A few were even outfitted with organically shaped silver armor. Every one of them looked vibrant and beautiful as if they had just been on a pleasant swim, not the rotting, shambling zombies that Torra had imagined.

Rethuud named many of the first Great Ones to emerge. Earlier speakers. Noblemen. Renowned warriors. Padgarun clerics. Mages. Soon, though, they grew too ancient for him to recognize. But they kept coming until hundreds crowded the waters of the lake, with many hundreds more rising beneath them.

And all of them had mirrored eyes.

"By the stars," Torra whispered.

Torra turned to look at Rethuud. The elf was spellbound by the site below them, his eyes filling with tears.

"Rethuud," she said, grabbing his shoulder. "Rethuud!" He turned his head, eyes glazed over. "We have to get down there right away," Torra said.

Rethuud blinked and focused, then frowned at her, shaking his head. "You don't seem to understand, Com Gidel. These are the most powerful elves in the world. Going down there would be suicide."

"But the Book of Alasar is down there somewhere. We have to retrieve it. All we need to do is cause a distraction from up here …"

Rethuud pushed Torra away, causing her to slide several inches back down the slope. "Go back to the grotto and await me, Com Gidel. We are finished here."

"Finished?" Her eyes widened with sudden rage. "Finished! After all we've been through? After the battles with Gogonith and at the hall? After *Phasgala?*"

Rethuud grunted and shoved Torra several feet down the slope. He shouted, "You dare to bring her up now!"

Torra balled her fists and flew at the elf, beating his side. "I'm not going to let *you* tell me when *I'm* finished!" She grabbed his shirt and yanked him back down the slope, and the two of them rolled several feet in a slide of rocks and pebbles before Rethuud put a stop to it and held Torra at arm's length.

"Let me go, damn you!" she screamed, arms flailing but unable to reach him.

"Be quiet," he commanded. "You'll alert the sentries!" He looked back up to the ridge.

"So what! Let them come!"

Holding Torra by the shoulder with one clenching hand, Rethuud pointed a finger at her face. "*You* need to realize our situation! Down there is only death and failure. Consider every great warrior, mage, and king your people ever eternalized in legend, and beyond into the mists of time, and then imagine them all coming back to life again in a single day—*against* you. Add a dragon and the dominion of three very powerful gods, and *that* is what we face. That is what I mean when I say we're *finished* here!"

Rethuud released her, and Torra stumbled backward, coming to rest against a boulder.

"Admit it to yourself, Com Gidel. Go back to the grotto and await me. When my warrior catches up from Hasala Squalma, I will fly you back to your human lands."

A roar filled the sky, causing both of them to duck behind boulders. Gogonith soared over the ridge, no more than thirty feet above. The rush of wind from his wing-beats forced Torra to blink against a cloud of dust and debris. But the Iron Dragon never looked down toward them. He kept flying southwestward across the valley and out over the mountaintops. Cautiously, Rethuud and Torra stood up from their hiding places. She turned to face the elf.

"It seems we have one less obstacle now," she said between clenched teeth. "A good omen. We should go right now, before more Great Ones emerge!"

"I don't believe in omens," Rethuud replied, watching Gogonith disappear into the distance. He turned and raised an eyebrow at her. "And don't get any brash ideas. You're badly afflicted, and we are heavily outmatched. I want to see more of the resurrection, then we're leaving when my warrior comes." Rethuud turned to climb back up to the ridge.

"Why, Rethuud?" Torra pleaded. "Why have you changed your mind *now*?"

Rethuud stopped and half-turned toward her, then lowered his head. "I didn't really believe the legend. Now I see it with my own eyes, and I know the true power we face. There is no defeating it. If Peshiluud is any example of their abilities, we are doomed."

Rethuud climbed back up to the ridge and lay down where he could watch the other side.

Torra unleashed a brutal growl as she spun around and huffed back down the mountainside toward the grotto, then slipped and fell to her buttocks just as she reached the corner. The griffin raised its head and snapped at her, but she slapped its beak away. "Behave, beast!" She stood on shaky legs and made her way to her pack.

For many minutes Torra lay with her back against the uneven grotto wall, fuming. Her body ached everywhere. But the pain of her body paled in comparison to Rethuud's cowardice. "I haven't come this far!" she shouted. "Just—You just better—" She suddenly slumped and let out a long, sobbing sigh. But then she shook it off and stood again. "No, damn it! If they succeed in destroying the Tower of Light, I'll have nothing to live for, anyhow. Magic is all I have left."

She turned and dug through the few items left in her pack, then pulled out a decanter with the sign of the twin moons on it—the Potion of Invisibility. She shook the vial and held it up to the light. There was still a half-swallow along the bottom edge. She thought back to how much she had drunk to turn invisible back at the Hall of Emeralds. If that much had lasted her nearly half a day, she figured this little bit should be enough for at least a quarter of an hour—*maybe*. "It will have to do," she said.

Then she looked up at the griffin and tightened her jaw.

~ ~ ~

Minutes later Torra struggled to control the griffin's flight. She had seen how Rethuud steered the beast, but it was far more difficult than she had imagined, especially now that she couldn't see her own invisible hands on the reins. The beast bucked and yawed, squawking, threatening to throw her to the wooded valley far below. It tried to dive, but Torra tugged hard on the reins, pulling it into a flapping circle back up toward the ridgeline.

Rethuud turned and watched from the ridge with a bewildered expression, then raised his hands to his mouth, calling the griffin to him. The griffin immediately jerked toward Rethuud, shrieking, but Torra yanked hard on the reins, pulling the beast to the right and away from him. Rethuud tried again, but the griffin reluctantly obeyed its new master. Torra figured Rethuud had realized what was happening when he flashed a look of anger toward the grotto and ran down the slope. She wished she could see his face when he found the empty decanter.

Torra flew around a curve in the mountain and out of his sight. In moments she steered the griffin along the mountain's outer edge and around toward the beach area where the Great Ones were emerging.

FORTY-ONE
The War Council

Blaring horns announced Ingal's arrival as he circled around the Keep of Casan. He spread his wings and held his battlescythe at a wide angle to accentuate his appearance and roared back in response.

At nearly six-thousand years old, the Keep of Casan was the most ancient stronghold still standing in that part of the world, having gone through many iterations of wartime and peacetime use. Built on a bell-shaped hill, the keep sported a domed audience chamber at the top, peaked with a massive golden spire. A fortified ramp curved up and around the hill to the dome, with battlements all around. Numerous entryways and windows dotted the hill, giving testament to the catacomb of halls and chambers within. On this day the hill was replete with colored streamers from each of the six Federation states.

Soaring, Ingal waited for the procession of viziers, generals, and their guards up the ramp to the audience dome for the War Council. But after many minutes, no one emerged. The keep was silent. No troops moved. No pages ran from level to level. There was only the wind snapping the streamers. Ingal roared again, but still no response. He wondered if they were waiting for him in the audience dome? Something wasn't right.

The audience dome had an outdoor landing, called the Dragon's Balcony, opposite the main entry. Ingal touched down on the balcony, placing his battle scythe on the granite landing, then looked to the huge, ebony inlaid and gilded double doors to the audience chamber. He groaned, wondering what he would find on the other side, and pushed the doors open.

The audience chamber was empty except for the long table set up for the viziers and generals. Empty, that is, save for a lone figure sitting at the far end, his feet on the table just at the edge of Ingal's long shadow. In addition, two figures stood in silhouette at the main entrance on the other end of the chamber. Ingal stepped inside and let his eyes adjust to the dim light.

"Where is the Council?" Ingal demanded. "Where are the viziers?"

The reclining figure snickered and crossed his feet on the table. His gauntleted fingers tapped the surface of a burnished silver battle horn. Morning sunlight glinted off his red and silver armor and red-maned helmet.

"General Tasami, we demand to know the meaning of this."

The incised lines of the general's weathered face creased into a sinister smile. "You are in no position to make demands anymore, Jehai."

"Tasami!" shouted an old man. Ingal saw now that the two figures at the main entrance were a guard and Vizier Navi Janisim. The elderly vizier's miter had been knocked off, and his staff was missing. The guard held a dagger at Janisim's neck. "Halt this treachery, Odullu!"

"Be quiet old man," the general commanded.

Ingal narrowed his eyes and stepped to the end of the table closest to him, his normal place at the War Council. His tail swished heavily on the granite floor. *So General Tasami was the "Namistad traitor" the speaker had revealed, not his vizier.* "We do not like the tone you use, General. Just what do you think you are doing?"

"While you were playing with the elves, Jehai, I was taking care of the future of Namistad." Tasami paused, seeming to savor the moment. "You have a decision to make, Jehai. You can either allow the state of Namistad to secede from the Federation," the smile grew larger, "with me as its sultan ... or you can deny me and, instead, face the entire army of Ocrin racing through Namistad to take over the White Lands."

"What?" Vizier Janisim screamed, then doubled over in a coughing fit, stammering, "That's ... you imbecile!"

Ingal emitted a wry chuckle, echoing off the hall's arched walls and ceiling. "You treacherous fool," he said to Tasami. "What makes you think we won't simply kill you where you sit?"

Tasami picked up his battle horn. "Because, Jehai, with one blast of this horn, or my guard's, I can signal the attack by Ocrin. Eighty-thousand Ocrin warriors will scream across the border into Namistad and, through it, conquer the White Lands Federation."

Ingal crept forward, and Tasami pulled the horn close to this lips. Ingal stopped.

"Janisim," Ingal said, "you played no part in this?"

"None, my lord! Forgive me, for I have been duped as well. And I had no right to have accused you of conspiring with the Iron Dragon when we met at Dragon's Passage."

Ingal started to reply, but was cut off.

"You need not address that feeble old man, Jehai," the general said. "He is no longer in charge of Namistad."

"Bastard!" shouted Janisim.

"Shut him up!" Tasami commanded, and sliced the air with his hand.

In an instant the guard slit Janisim's throat. Ingal lunged, but Tasami raised the horn to his lips in an obvious gesture. Ingal stopped, crashing through the end of the table.

Janisim emitted a gurgle and fell to the floor, writhing and clutching his spurting neck. In a moment he fell still, blood pooling around him and merging with the red of his robes.

Ingal roared and bared his teeth at the general. "We didn't think even *you* could be so savage. We will see you run through for this!"

"You will see no such thing, Jehai. As you must surely know, most of your precious troops are two day's march to the north. The White Lands are at my mercy." He half-turned toward the doorway. "Bring forth the next one." At his command, the guard disappeared around the corner and quickly reappeared with Vizier Entar Misaqi, pushing her forward at the edge of the bloody dagger. The left sleeve of her white robes was ripped.

She gasped and halted at the sight of Janisim's corpse, then shot an accusing look at Tasami. "General! You're a traitor to your people! You've been blinded by your ambition. Whatever oppressive designs you have are doomed to fail, for the people will not bow to you."

Tasami's lips twisted into a sneer. "Please, Jehai, say no to my demand and give me reason to kill her!" The smile vanished. He pounded the table and stood up, still holding the horn near his lips. "The other viziers and generals are imprisoned within the keep. If I blow this horn, not only will you lose your nation, but they will die as well."

Ingal shook his head. "You have no idea what you are involved with, do you, Tasami? You think you have maneuvered some clever coup against us. You think you are using Ocrin as a tool for your power grab." Ingal took another step forward. Tasami stepped back. "The truth is," Ingal continued, "you and Ocrin are being manipulated by powers that are far, far greater than you imagine."

Tasami snarled, "I have the Iron Dragon on my side!"

"You have *no one* on your side!" roared Ingal. "The elves of Peshilaree are gathering to attack the Tower of Light at this very moment."

Tasami's brow tensed.

"Yes, General! The *elves* are attacking the White Lands. They, too, are being used—by ancient gods who want to conquer the world. The Iron Dragon and Ocrin are working toward *their* ends, and *you* along with them. You are but a pawn."

Ingal took another step, mirrored by another step backward by Tasami. "Did Ocrin convince you to move our troops and reserves to the north of here?" Ingal asked. "Did they tell you it was part of a plan for them to march through Namistad and take the center of the White Lands? They lied to you, Tasami. Ocrin conspires with the elves. The elves only wanted the troops away from the tower. And Ocrin wants to conquer the rest, including Namistad!"

"I don't care about your damned Tower of Light, Jehai, or about the elves, or least of all their gods. Let them attack as they wish! I need only care about my deal with Ocrin." Tasami brandished the horn near his lips. "Decide now, Jehai! Declare me sultan of an independent Namistad, or face the destruction of the White Lands and your viziers!"

Entar looked Ingal in the eyes and almost imperceptibly shook her head, mouthing, *They're dead.*

A smile slowly spread across Ingal's face, allowing the double row of razor-edged teeth to show, and lowered his head to look directly into Tasami's eyes. Tasami stepped further back, until he stood in the doorway. The guard gasped and backed out of the chamber.

"Your plan has failed, General," Ingal said with deliberation, scraping his claws across the floor. "We will not be bullied, and we have seen through your scheming. The unity of the Federation will stand, no matter the deaths of the viziers. Our soldiers should reach your borders by noon. The Federation will prevail against Ocrin, just as we have time and time again in the last ten-thousand years." Ingal flared his wings. "Don't think this is the first time a traitor like you has tried to compromise our nation!" Ingal overturned the massive table, shattering it and sending chairs tumbling across the room.

"I'm not bluffing!" Tasami shouted, waving the horn in his right hand. "I'll blow the horn! Ocrin will invade!" He grabbed the dagger from the guard with his free hand and held the blade to Vizier Misaqi's throat. "The viziers will die!"

"Let Ocrin invade!" said Ingal. "Let the viziers die! *You* will die with them!"

Misaqi punched the general in the face and jumped away.

Ingal lunged at Tasami, roaring.

Tasami ran from the chamber out onto the ramp, blowing his horn into the morning sky.

Below, another horn answered Tasami's, then another, and another in a line extending away to the southwest.

The war had begun.

Ingal quickly slammed Tasami's guard against the battlements, shattering his bones and killing him instantly, then leapt into the sky.

Tasami had run some forty yards down the ramp, screaming commands and pulling his sword. Turning the corner, he pushed through a squad of Namistad archers, who immediately pulled their bows at Ingal.

Ingal rolled and dove away from the arrows, then soared upward. Half of the archers turned and ran.

Ingal dove and plowed into the archers, slicing through them with his claws and throwing them over the battlements. But his eyes were on Tasami, who had mounted a horse and was now galloping down the ramp. Ingal dispatched the last of the archers and flew after the general, catching up to him with ease.

"If you kill me, you kill any chance for peace!" the general yelled.

"Too late!" Ingal slammed into Tasami, sending him flying off the horse and rolling down the ramp.

The general stood and swung his sword, striking at Ingal, but the blade simply nicked a scale on his leg and fell clattering to the stone. Ingal clutched the general in a massive forefoot and jumped off the hillside, taking to the air.

"I can still stop them!" Tasami yelled. "Let me go, and the war will end!"

Ingal tightened his grip, bending Tasami's armor and snapping his ribs. The general yowled in pain.

"It's too late for negotiations, General! We know you well. Except for Entar, the viziers are already dead." Ingal flew to a great height, above the mighty spire at the top of the dome. "Now you will join them!"

"No!" Tasami shrieked.

Ingal swept the general through the air and impaled him upon the spire. The general screamed in agony. He slid several feet down, his hands clasping the massive golden spike rising through his gut and armor.

Ingal shot into the sky, then turned and shouted down at the keep, "This man is a traitor to the White Lands Federation. All those who follow his lead will meet a similar fate!"

The general turned his head toward Ingal. Blood dribbled from his mouth. "Your lands will burn," he sputtered.

Ingal had already turned away. He swooped down to the entrance to the audience chamber.

Vizier Misaqi was bent over Janisim's body, arranging it into a more noble position.

"Entar," Ingal said, "are you all right?"

The Vizier bowed. "Yes, my lord. Please forgive us. We did not know Tasami could do this. He led us to believe that he knew what was best for our defense, and that you were too distracted by other matters. He convinced us to send the reserves to the northwest."

"And the other viziers and generals are dead?"

Misaqi looked down at Janisim's corpse. "All dead. When word arrived that you were coming last night, I was in my chambers. The others were dining in the main hall. Tasami and his men surrounded them, slaughtered them, sparing only Janisim. I heard what was happening and tried to escape, but his men captured me just outside the keep." She closed her eyes and grimaced. "Their bodies still lie where they fell."

Ingal extended a forefoot toward her. "There are more weighty concerns now. Was our envoy, our Minister of Arms, sent to Ocrin as we had requested?"

Vizier Misaqi sighed. "Dead, my lord. Ocrin killed Emoch and his entourage almost as soon as he entered their territory. They returned his head by launching it from a catapult."

Ingal grunted. "It seems negotiation was never an option. And were our battle barges ever sent up the Alsanoos?"

"The lifts at Gotala Falls were never fixed, so the barges could go no further toward the border."

Ingal shook his head. "Tasami." He extended a forefoot to Misaqi. "Let us carry you to safety, and then you must secure the forces loyal to us and send them to the front, as well as spread the news of Tasami's deception."

Vizier Misaqi agreed. Ingal held her in the crook of his arm and, after retrieving the battle scythe, flew her a short way west to the nearest outpost of loyal troops. After issuing commands to retake the Keep of Casan, he made a running start and took to the sky.

"Be careful, my lord!" Misaqi yelled after him. Ingal had already started southwest with all possible haste—toward the battlefront.

FORTY-TWO
Thief

After leaving the griffin in a clearing and making her way to the Reception Hall, Torra peered around a tree at the growing host of Ecemii who had left the lake. Crowding in and around the hall, the resurrected elves milled about, whispering in quiet tones as if they had known each other well from their time at the bottom of the lake.

Every now and then Torra caught a glimpse of the Book of Alasar sitting upon a podium within the hall.

She looked up at the sun and nervously scratched at her rash. The shadows had moved on the encircling mountain. Those overbearing prominences of rock leaned out over the lake like sundials. Her time of invisibility was nearing its end.

She had evaded the Padgarun guards easily enough, but the mass of Great Ones was too shoulder-to-shoulder to squeeze through without bumping. She wondered if they would see the book being carried out. And could they detect her with those accursed eyes?

There was no turning back. She had to try. She steeled herself and gritted her teeth, bending to run into the hall …

A groan echoed over the lake, deep and earthy, like the very earth was splitting.

A cry rose up from the Great Ones. They jockeyed for a better position to see, pointing up at the mountain at the far side turning their heads away from Torra.

A small figure danced along the cliff face beneath a major prominence. Glimmers of light jumped with him.

Rethuud!

The mountain emitted another deep groan, and then a boom that could be felt more than heard and a shower of boulders broke off in a small avalanche as the prominence slipped and fell in one huge piece to the lake below.

The elves screamed and ran for the lake as part of the mountain hit the water, crashing like an ocean breaker, crushing hundreds of Ecemii still rising to the surface. A huge wave rose up from the impact.

Ascareth, Torra realized. Rethuud's description of the sword rushed through her memory: 'Ascareth's blade is a dimensional rip, able to slice through any earthly material, even stone.' *And slice through stone it had!*

A dozen Padgarun rushed past Torra toward the lake. She looked back and saw no others. The Book of Alasar was now in plain sight, sitting upon a stone pedestal.

She bolted forward and turned visible in the sunlight. But she couldn't stop now. She ran into the Reception Hall and hefted the massive book to her chest. It was almost too heavy to carry.

Torra stifled a gasp. Directly in front of her, turned toward the lake, stood the speaker of the Hall of Emeralds.

To her horror, the book did not disappear, but turned only a shade transparent. She took a step back, then wheeled and ran out of the hall. And directly into a Padgarun cleric.

Torra and the elf clashed with a thud, both falling to the ground. The Book of Alasar hit hard, pages flapping. The cracked binding issued a loud thwack and split the book into two even halves.

"Thief!" shouted another Padgarun.

The speaker turned. A hundred reflecting eyes turned with him. "The Book of Alasar!" the speaker cried. "Kill her!"

The tidal wave created by the fallen prominence reached the beach and washed over the shoreline and around the hall, carrying many of the Ecemii off their feet. The water drenched Torra as she struggled to gather the book halves and regain her feet.

Torra was clearly visible now in the sunlight. She elbowed the Padgarun in the face, then splashed past him away from the lake.

She dared to look back. The speaker pointed his staff. The swarm of wasps flew from its nest toward her.

Torra closed her eyes and focused her mind. "*Acrinum defozae!*" she chanted, drew in a deep breath, and exhaled sharply. A thick black smoke bellowed out of her mouth, rushing over and around her head. The taste of it made her gag, breaking her concentration and the spell. But the wasps became lost and soothed in the smoke and returned to the speaker's staff.

Behind the speaker were dozens of Ecemii chanting spells. She ran faster than she could have dreamed against the pain from the Brimstone Disease. Blood pumped in her ears, pounding with her footfalls as she darted between trees. Electricity shot past her. Energy missiles struck tree trunks, bark flying. A Padgarun spear narrowly missed her head and buried itself into the soil ahead of her.

A part of her mind planned ahead, imagining her jumping onto the saddle of her griffin and flapping away.

Torra ran through a thicket to the clearing where she had landed. The griffin was gone. "No!" she screamed, stopping momentarily, looking around as if the griffin were hiding in the grass.

A Great One, a male in armor made of bark, leapt out of the thicket behind Torra and threw her to the ground. One half of the book went flying.

Torra cast a *Light* spell in the elf's eyes. He screamed, but did not let go until she bit his arm.

A Padgarun and two more Great Ones ran into the clearing.

Clutching half of the Book of Alasar, Torra hurried to retrieve the other half.

Someone shouted a *Push* spell, throwing her to the ground nearly ten feet away.

Furious, Torra scrambled to her feet and faced what was now a dozen Padgarun and Great Ones between her and the other half of the book.

"Torra!" someone cried from behind her.

She turned. From the air came Rethuud and his warrior on a wounded griffin, its beak partly shattered. They swept down into the clearing and leapt off, swords drawn. The warrior was bleeding badly from his head, and Rethuud's arm had been sliced.

"Run to the griffin!" Rethuud commanded.

"The book!" she yelled. "They have half of it!"

"Come! Now!" he shouted, and started slashing. Ascareth cut through a Padgarun's chest, then lopped off the legs of a Great One. The sword's dimensional blade warped the air around it, pulling at Torra's hairs like static.

An acid sphere grazed Rethuud's right arm, rupturing only slightly, but enough to set his leatherine armor smoking and dissolving.

Torra ran to the griffin, then cast a *Combust* spell on the vine clothing of a nearby Great One, engulfing him instantly.

More Ecemii entered the clearing.

Rethuud's warrior screamed and writhed, dropping his sword. The scream became a liquid gurgle, then his entire body melted like wax as a Great One pointed at him, leaving only a bubbling clump on the grass.

"But the book!" Torra yelled. "The other half!"

"Leave it!" Rethuud yelled back. "Get on!" Torra did as directed, then cast a *Darkness* spell over the face of an approaching Great One.

Rethuud retreated back to Torra, cutting down two more Great Ones as he jumped upon the griffin to sit in front of her. With a shake of the reins from Rethuud, the beast ran and jumped into the sky.

But not soon enough. Torra's ears popped. The air evacuated her lungs and throat with a gasp. She wanted to raise her hands to her throat but refused to let go of her half of the spellbook. Lights popped in and out of her vision. Mouth agape. Chest heaving. Couldn't breathe. A *Strangle* spell.

Rethuud grabbed his throat. His head lolled. But the other hand shook the reins harder. In moments they were out of range of the spellcaster, and air slowly returned to Torra's lungs.

She gasped for breath as she looked back at the clearing. Peshiluud stood there pointing at them, the speaker and Ecemii by his side. It had been Peshiluud who had cast the *Strangle* spell. He bent to pick up the other half of the Book of Alasar. His head tilted back, and Torra heard a deep laugh issue through the growing distance.

And then she and Rethuud flew around a mountain, and the clearing went out of sight.

Torra allowed a momentary sense of relief, but it was short-lived. Rethuud dove the griffin and then swung it back and forth, glancing up and to his right. Torra followed his gaze and saw four mounted Padgarun flying toward them.

An acid sphere missed Rethuud by mere inches. Another sphere went wide.

"That book had better be worth it!" Rethuud yelled to her.

Torra looked down at the half of the book at her chest. As they dodged and yawed, the first few pages opened and closed. She loosened her grip ever so slightly, allowing the pages to open further. She read the arcane title of the remaining renegade spell. *Rift Widening.*

It was the wrong spell! Peshiluud still had *Obliterate Mountain*, the spell needed to destroy the Tower of Light. Torra flipped to the back. The first spell ended at the last page. The other spell was gone in its entirety, almost as if by design.

No! she mouthed. Only a low moan issued from her lips. She could only stare at the spell's title, practically oblivious to the action around her. *I've failed. I've damned us all!*

Rethuud pulled the griffin into a steep climb and turned sharply, then flew directly at their pursuers. In one deft move he activated Ascareth and sliced through the reins of the lead griffin and cut through the side of its rider, then cut through the tail of another griffin, sending it and its rider into a chaotic dive. The third pursuer, a Padgarun, flew after his companion.

Rethuud pulled their mount down into a gorge and through a winding set of valleys. For the moment it seemed they were free of pursuers. But Torra couldn't think about it. All she could imagine was the tower crumbling before her—a brilliant white mountain of a building falling to dust and cobble—the source of one-third of Irikara's magical wisdom.

"Did we get what we needed?" Rethuud asked, half-turning toward her. Torra didn't have the heart to answer. She only shook her head.

Rethuud abruptly pulled hard on the reins and gained altitude. "More Padgarun," he said, and nodded to his right. Torra impassively turned to see two more of the clerics flying toward them. She clutched the remaining spell to her chest, imagining her attempt to explain her failure to Ingal.

Some dragon's apprentice I turned out to be, she thought, and tried to hang on.

FORTY-THREE
Battle at the Murder Plate

At his fastest speed, it still took Ingal three hours to fly from the Keep of Casan to the battlefront. A strong headwind had blown in from the southwest, unusual for this region, and reeking of supernatural energies that irritated his magic center.

By the time he soared over the river and into the Naminari Valley, the clash of armies had already occurred. From his great height he saw that the forces were engaging each other between the northern base of Highwatch Mountain and the Alsanoos River, at a shelf of land dubbed the Murder Plate, scene of countless battles over the past ten-thousand years. Fortifications had risen and been destroyed over and over again in that time leaving shattered walls, towers, and foundations throughout the area. The bastioned city of Carnathon lay within sight to the east, ancient and crumbling, home to soldiers and veterans, once the thriving and beautiful capital of a nation long gone, but not forgotten.

The sounds of the battle were all too familiar to Ingal: the clang of metal upon metal, screams of men and horses, the pounding of the earth. The smells of blood and sweat permeated the air, even at that altitude.

Ingal estimated that a mere six-thousand Federation troops were struggling to hold back nearly fifty-thousand Ocrin soldiers. There were so many Ocrin forces that the bulk of them were still stuck on Ocrin land, unable to squeeze into the relatively narrow strip of land that defined the Murder Plate. Ocrin forces had wave upon wave of cavalry, swordsmen, pikemen, and archers. Huge, upright battle drums sat on platforms carried aloft on the backs of slaves. Muscular priests were beating out a marching cadence on them in adoration of their living "goddess"—the Doom Empress.

Ingal surveyed the battle strategy. To the Federation soldiers on the ground it surely looked as if Ocrin were using a wedge formation. But from the air Ingal clearly saw that the formation was a ploy, that it was backed with a right flanking maneuver which would imminently push its way through one side of the Federation line.

A cheer rose up as the Federation troops recognized Ingal. "Fight, men!" Ingal commanded them. "Today we will be victorious and repel the Ocrin hordes! Fight and stand your ground at all cost! You have our blessing of triumph!"

"Hail!" the troops shouted as one. "Hail!"

Ingal dipped into the dusty air toward the command platforms in the rear. "Commander, bolster the left flank!" he said. "Send a cavalry unit from the center."

Ingal recognized their commander, a rising star in the Army of Oelistad. The commander signaled his understanding and gave the order to the trumpeters, who then blew a cadence for a particular cavalry unit, then the cadence for "left flank." It was a holding move. Alone, the Federation forces could never win the day. But now they had the Gold Dragon. They raised their long battle standards high, the oriflamme of each state fluttering and snapping in the wind.

"Commander," Ingal continued, "your vizier and general have been betrayed and murdered by General Tasami. We hereby grant you a field commission. You are now General of the Army of Oelistad." The commander paused a moment, then bowed low to the dragon. "And General," Ingal continued, "there will be no retreat until our reinforcements arrive."

Ingal sized up the change in strategy and watched as Ocrin sent in a unit of pikemen in response. It was time he went into action. He rose to a great height, then secured the battle scythe in his right arm, blade out and ready for the harvest. He dove straight down, gaining incredible speed, leveling at the last moment to shoot over the heads of the Federation troops. Just across the battle line he swept the blade through the clustered bodies of the Ocrin warriors like a farmer mowing his crop, roaring, slicing through man and mount, killing and maiming many dozens of the enemy in a single thrust before rising again into the sky with another roar. The ground ran red with a river of their blood.

Scores of enemy soldiers broke and ran. The Federation army cheered in triumph. Ingal rose and dove again, slicing through the enemy ranks, opening long swaths of land to be defended by the Federation. At the end of the last sweep, Ingal latched onto one of the massive battle drums and raised it into the air, ripping it to pieces and raining it down upon enemy heads.

The Ocrin forces had prepared for the dragon's intervention. At a drum signal, a long line of cages were opened, and hundreds of trained bloodhawks were released. Swift and agile, the birds of prey rose through the sky and flocked past Ingal. They swooped upon Federation troops with shrieks of fury, dug their poisoned talons into the exposed arms and necks of their targets, ripped at eyes with curved, carnivorous beaks, tore out chunks of tissue. There was little Ingal could do against bloodhawks, and the Ocrin generals knew it. The best he could do was to cast a *Darkness* spell over some of the hawks to calm them.

A phalanx of archers shot a cloud of arrows at Ingal. Many bounced off his hide, but some found their mark and punched between scales. Ingal roared in pain and dove again. He grabbed an Ocrin war wagon in his free forefoot and threw it at one of the archer squads. The wagon crashed into the men, shattering and sending the squad into chaos. Of more concern were dozens of scorpion catapults, each shooting at him with three-foot long bolts. He dodged most, but two of them punched through the scales on his right flank, and he roared in pain.

Ingal spotted a breach in the Federation defenses. Down by the river, the line of infantry had buckled and fallen under a brutal assault by Ocrin heavy cavalry who had proceeded to try to encircle the Federation forces. Ingal flew into the fray, cutting man and beast with the scythe.

But a blast of light momentarily blinded Ingal. Dazed, he pulled away. It was a spell. The cavalry unit had a mage in its midst.

Ingal activated his magic sense and scanned the unit, dodging arrows. He didn't have to scan long. The fool of a mage cast another spell, *Firefling*, and the ball of fire narrowly missed Ingal.

"*Chrosti manius!*" Ingal shouted, and lightning shot from his forefeet, arcing to the ground and electrocuting the mage and all of those near him. They shook in a dance of death before falling to the ground with their horses. Ocrin's cavalry retreated, and the Federation line reformed.

It continued for hours. Ocrin kept breaking through, only to be pushed back by Ingal. Occasionally, another low-ranking mage would show up to be quickly defeated by Ingal, or more bloodhawks would be unleashed, or large bolts would be hurled by scorpions at Ingal. But despite Ingal's involvement, Federation troops continued to be killed, and Ocrin slowly gained ground.

Exhausted by the fight and wounded by innumerable projectiles, Ingal flew high above the battle and soared, giving himself a moment of rest. He stretched his neck, wincing at the cracking of his vertebrae, then massaged his sore shoulder muscles. He absentmindedly pulled arrows out of his scales.

Looking north, beyond the Naminari Valley, he still saw no sign of the reinforcements he had commanded to be sent from the Alneri border. Had they been stalled by battle? He had to buy more time.

Ingal brandished his battle scythe and prepared to dive again but stopped as a deep roar thundered across the sky from far to the northeast. Ingal turned to see a distant figure flying toward him at an impossibly fast clip, growing larger by the minute. Gogonith had arrived.

But the Iron Dragon stopped his approach and began circling, just within easy sight to the east. He presented a strong face, but Gogonith couldn't hide how winded and tired he was. He had clearly flown hard and fast.

A cheer rose from the Ocrin army as they saw the Iron Dragon. They knew he was on their side. This had been planned.

Ingal watched and waited, pondering his options. He wanted to confront Gogonith, but that would require leaving the battle below. If he left, Ocrin would break through. Gogonith surely realized this, flying just out of range, tempting Ingal to pursue. Ingal chose to keep his eye on the Iron Dragon but continue fighting Ocrin.

Again and again, Ingal dove and reaped more enemy lives, until the scythe's blade and handle were drenched in blood. But the enemy kept coming. There were spells he could cast, but Gogonith still circled to the east. He had to save as much of his physical and magical energy as possible to face him. But his options were growing limited.

Ocrin broke through once more with another cavalry charge. Ingal circled low and activated his magic center, chanting, "Slinia mestoc tostemia!" Nearly half of the cavalry riders slumped and fell from their mounts, fast asleep, forcing the others to retreat. Ingal flew behind them, cutting down the stragglers until archers forced him back. Federation infantry moved in to defend the line and kill the sleeping enemy riders.

No sooner had Ingal plugged the break on the right flank, when the left flank collapsed. The new general ordered troops to fill the breach. Then a wedge of Ocrin swordsmen attacked the center, overwhelming the exhausted Federation troops and breaking through.

The Federation line collapsed. In moments the battle would be lost.

Ingal groaned. He glanced toward Gogonith, then back to the rampaging Ocrin army. He closed his eyes, then summoned all of his magical energy while raising a forefoot over his head. He began a low staccato chant, then raised it to a roar. The air around him glowed with a blue fluorescence. Waves of radiant energy condensed layer upon shimmering layer over his forefoot, coalescing into a ball of brilliant light in his palm.

Ingal concentrated harder, forcing the magical energy to flow through his body to his forefoot. He felt the energies moving through him, flowing like rivulets down unseen magical corridors like blood through his veins. He deepened his chant to a hum and tightened his muscles, cueing his mind to pull the last vestiges of energy from him to the shimmering sphere in his palm.

With a final, emphatic pronouncement, Ingal opened his eyes and threw the ball into the midst of the charging Ocrin forces. The sphere of energy hummed as it fell, then struck the ground with an ear-rending boom. Blue glowing shock waves shot from the impact in all directions. Friend and enemy, human and beast, were disintegrated for two hundred yards around the impact. Nearly everyone else on the Murder Plate was thrown to the ground, deafened and blinded. The sound of the explosion echoed off Highwatch mountain like a hundred thunderstrikes and into the surrounding valleys. Then everything fell silent.

Ingal couldn't catch his breath. His body slumped, and his wings could hardly keep him aloft. He flew to the steep cliffs overlooking the Murder Plate and fell to the ground, gasping. His head ached from the exertion of magic.

But the move had worked. The Ocrin forces made a hasty retreat. Federation lands were secure … for the moment.

But the cost was high. Ingal estimated that perhaps only three-hundred Federation troops remained, and most were horribly wounded. How many combatants, Ocrin or Federation, had his *Energy Strike* spell killed? Many hundreds, for sure. Perhaps even a thousand. Guilt washed over him for the loss of life. But it was a necessary sacrifice. The tide was turned.

Friendly trumpets sounded from the north. With an exhausted smile, Ingal beheld a long line of galloping Federation cavalry rounding a far bend of the Alsanoos. At long last, the first of the reinforcements he had sent from Alneri had arrived.

And then Ingal heard deep and scornful laughter from the east. Gogonith left his position and flew toward Ingal, his rust-colored scales and jagged smile shining in the late afternoon sun.

FORTY-FOUR

Faith in Humanity

Weak as he was, Ingal readied himself for Gogonith's attack. His scimitar would have been a better weapon against the Iron Dragon than the battle scythe, but the scythe would have to do. He controlled his breathing, summoned the pitiful little magical energy he had left. But Gogonith slowed his approach and turned lazy circles around Ingal's position.

Ingal nodded at the inflamed injury to Gogonith's belly. "Nice wound. We thought we had killed you a few days ago. It's a wonder you survived."

Gogonith's eyes flared. "*You're* looking good, Gold Dragon, save for all the arrows and bolts protruding from you. You don't show a sign of our last encounter at all." Gogonith squinted. "And are those acid burns on your side? Funny, I don't remember seeing *those* before." He chuckled between gritted teeth.

"You've manufactured quite a distraction."

Gogonith glanced down at the battleground. "A compliment, to be sure. Thank you. It was *my* idea to draw you away from the tower. The Doom Empress was more than willing to gain some new territory, and your dear General Tasami was just power hungry enough to play along. After all, wouldn't *you* like to rule a nation of your own?" Gogonith put a hand to his snout. "Oh! I guess you still do—*for the moment!*"

Ingal tightened his grip on the battle scythe. "We already executed the traitor, and we have stopped Ocrin's invasion."

"For now." Gogonith winked. "I saw your traitor impaled on the Keep of Casan. Very sporting. Much better than, say, a wind vane." Gogonith looked down at the battlefield again. "Looks like you—"

Ingal launched himself off the cliff and flew eastward. He had to gain more time to build back his magical energies. Otherwise he didn't stand a chance. Putting distance between himself and Gogonith would help.

Gogonith caught up quickly, flying just behind and to Ingal's left. "Where do you think you're going, Ingal? Is the Dragon of the Federation running away?"

"What do you want, Gogonith? If you're here to kill us, then do your best! If not, then get out of our way. We have much to do!"

Gogonith laughed. "Oh, I'm here to kill you, all right, even though the Triumvirate told me not to. It was Draq, as a matter of fact. Spoken to him lately? He said he could never condone the killing of his children." Gogonith swatted at Ingal's tail like a cat playing with its prey. "But I have no such mercy."

Ingal spun around and slashed with his battle scythe, but Gogonith was too fast. The Iron Dragon dodged, then grabbed the scythe with one forefoot and, turning, elbowed Ingal's shoulder with the other arm. The strike caused Ingal to release his grip, and Gogonith yanked the weapon away from the Gold Dragon.

Ingal seized Gogonith's arm, but the Iron Dragon pulled himself free. Turning, he swung the battle scythe and struck Ingal in the head, glancing off Ingal's horn. Shards of ivory showered away. "You've gone and dulled your blade with all the armor you sliced down there, Ingal."

Now weaponless, Ingal flew harder. He still had not recovered enough magical energy.

Gogonith laughed. "You and your weapons." He caught up again, then swung the scythe a couple times. Ingal heard the blade hum. "I am faster, stronger, and more powerful than you, Ingal. I can cast renegade spells at will! And you think you can kill me with a blade weapon?" He laughed again. "You are old and weak. Too old to make a difference. What have you got for me to be scared about?"

"We have the love of our people."

"Oh! Please, Ingal, don't let your puny humans attack me!" Gogonith flew ahead of Ingal and tried to block his way, but Ingal dove and went around him. "They weren't very effective at Alneri Castle."

Ingal bristled at the reference. "Your arrogance will be your downfall, Gogonith."

"And faith in humanity will be yours!"

Ingal could feel his energy returning. Just a little more time! "Tellonta would never have conspired with the Triumvirate."

"Ah, but he *did*," Gogonith said.

"What do you mean?"

"I never told you how Tellonta died, did I, Ingal? You see, the Triumvirate offered him a deal. Watch his precious land of Sofon be destroyed by natural disasters, or commit suicide and allow his offspring to be a hero to the Triumvirate. He chose suicide."

"Impossible!"

"Have I ever lied to you, Ingal, in any generation?"

Ingal stopped flying eastward, and the two dragons circled each other, high over the city of Carnathon.

"It's true," Gogonith said. "Tellonta flew to the top of Copper Mountain and shoved a lance through his ancient heart. If the Triumvirate had granted my powers to him, he would have gone insane—just like the Amber Dragon once did. An older dragon cannot take it. They needed a dragon from birth. And thus here I am, reborn as a demigod to govern the Triumvirate's world!"

Ingal snapped out of his disbelief. He felt his magic center reactivating. "It doesn't matter. The Triumvirate won't succeed in destroying the Tower of Light."

"Oh, *really?*" Gogonith said with a smug tone. "Why is that?"

"Because *we* have control of the renegade spell they need."

Gogonith laughed with a sound that was unexpectedly honest and gleeful. "What's so funny?"

"Do you mean the Book of Alasar? *Obliterate Mountain?* Why, I stole the spell from your little friends yesterday morning! It's in the hands of Peshiluud, now!"

Ingal's heart skipped a beat. "You're lying."

"No, honest! Cross my heart and hope to be reborn. Again, have I ever lied to you, in *any* generation?"

"No." Ingal fumed. *How could we have been so stupid as to leave the book with them? Could Gogonith be telling the truth?* "You better not have harmed them."

"Oh, I wouldn't think of it!" Gogonith smirked and shook his head. "You see, Gold Dragon? There's no winning, now. The Ecemii have been resurrected. Perhaps as soon as this evening they will attack the Tower of Light, and Peshiluud will destroy the Heartstone. You've *lost*, Ingal!" Gogonith lowered his voice to a sinister tone. "You should have taken the Triumvirate's offer. Now I get to kill you, and your White Lands Federation will be destroyed, too! By the time you are reborn, new gods will rule the ..."

Ingal shouted a *Paralysis* spell. Gogonith tried to counter it, but his wings froze and he tumbled toward the ground. Ingal dove after him.

But Gogonith recovered with a *Negate* spell, ending the paralysis in time and swooping away. Ingal grabbed Gogonith's leg and tried to turn his rear claws toward the Iron Dragon's face, but Gogonith roared and flung Ingal off of him.

The Iron Dragon slashed with the battle scythe. The bloody blade hummed through the air and sliced through Ingal's right thigh.

Ingal roared in pain and fell back. "*Ominum tes gorup tackard!*" he chanted, pointing at the scythe. The weapon burst into flame, handle and all, and Gogonith dropped it.

Ingal dove to retrieve the battle scythe, magically extinguishing it and catching it just before it hit the city below. When he turned to defend himself he found Gogonith still high above. Ingal was at a strategic disadvantage and began circling upward.

"This is great fun, Ingal. I will miss having a worthy competitor."

"Is it possible to miss things when you're dead?"

Gogonith laughed. "Tell me, Ingal, when you cast that *Energy Strike* spell on the battleground, how many Ocrin warriors do you think you killed?"

"As many as necessary."

"And how many of your own soldiers did you kill as well?"

Ingal growled, increasing his rate of ascent. He had to close the distance faster. "We did what we had to do to protect the Federation."

"So you're saying some sacrifices had to be made?" Gogonith shook his head. "And to think you scolded me for destroying Alneri Castle! Well, Ingal, it is time to end this little discourse with some poetic justice."

Gogonith raised a forefoot over his head and started chanting. Ingal recognized it immediately. Another *Energy Strike*.

Ingal used the last of his magical energy to cast a *Shield* spell, for what little good it would do, and flew at Gogonith as fast as he could manage. He watched the Iron Dragon as blue waves of energy coalesced over his hand. Then Ingal came to a realization: if Gogonith threw at him and missed, the energy sphere would hit the town below.

Ingal closed the distance. Three-hundred yards. Two-hundred. One-hundred. Gogonith culminated the spell, a huge blue sphere almost complete in his palm. He grinned and reared back his arm to throw.

Ingal threw the scythe. The battle scythe tumbled end over end at the Iron Dragon and cut cleanly through the base of a wing. Gogonith roared as the wing fell away, losing concentration before the spell was finished. The energy sphere exploded.

Ingal's world erupted in a blinding flash of pain and light. He'd been too close. He was falling, falling. He reached out with his wings, hoping to catch the air, but was too oblivious to feel anything at all, unsure even if his wings were outstretched.

And then vision returned. Just in time to see the city rise up to meet him. Ingal's wings caught the air, but it was too late to stop completely. He crashed through slate-shingled roofs, then rolled through a stone wall, collapsing the buildings around him, and everything went black.

When he awoke, Ingal tried to move, but the pain was too extreme. He was on his back. How long had he been out? Did he break any bones? He couldn't tell. He lay there until the dust cleared and the initial shock began to wear off. He heard men's voices in the buildings surrounding him.

Looking around, Ingal found that he had come to rest at the edge of a plaza. He tried to move again. He could flap his wings, at least. Apparently he had remembered to tuck them at the last moment. He tried to raise his right rear leg and yelped. Broken, most likely, and bleeding badly from the battle scythe cut. He rolled over onto his belly and groaned in pain. His right arm buckled. At least a couple ribs broken, too.

The walls behind him exploded. Stone and chunks of mortar rained over Ingal. A clawed forefoot grabbed Ingal by the broken leg and tossed him into the plaza with a roar.

Gogonith was alive.

The Iron Dragon stepped into the plaza, knocking aside the remnants of the buildings around him. His left wing was gone. The other hung limply. The rest of his body was blackened. Gogonith's neck and chest were exposed and throbbing, the scales completely blasted away, the recent chest wound reopened and bleeding.

"That was unpleasant," Gogonith said, his voice guttural and wet, and flecks of blood dribbling out of his broad mouth. He picked up a length of stone wall and threw it at Ingal. It burst into pieces against Ingal's good arm.

Before Ingal could recover, Gogonith stood over him, punched him in the head from the left, then the right. Ingal tried to rise, but Gogonith shoved him down and headbutted him with his ram's horns. Ingal nearly passed out again. Sounds came to him as echoes.

Gogonith sat on Ingal's chest and wrapped his forefeet around Ingal's neck. Ingal reached up with his good forefoot, but was no longer strong enough to push Gogonith away. He couldn't breathe. And there was no magical energy left in him to cast a defensive spell.

Gogonith's eyes burned a fiery red. "Time to die, Gold Dragon!" Ingal thrashed to release himself, but he was too weakened to throw Gogonith off. The Iron Dragon's forefeet remained locked around his throat. Ingal instinctively opened his mouth, demanding air that wouldn't come.

And then someone blew a trumpet. Voices. Shouts. A man called out, "Our lord! Our lord is dying."

"We have to do something!"

"He's killing him!"

"Get him!"

"Attack!"

Gogonith loosened his hands a moment and looked around. "What's this?"

From every corner of the plaza came running citizens of Carnathon. Old veteran men. Some women and teens. Armed with pitchforks, knives, and the occasional sword, they ran at Gogonith, hurling stones and screaming in fury.

"What is this nonsense?" Gogonith spat. He roared at the crowd and lashed his tail, but the attackers paused only a moment, then lunged with renewed vigor. In moments they leapt upon the dragon, attacking him like a swarm of bees defending their hive.

He released a forefoot to swipe at the attackers. Ingal took a breath. Gogonith growled and tried to turn his attention back to Ingal, but was quickly forced to defend against the citizens.

In that moment Ingal summoned his last strength and threw Gogonith to the side. He wrapped his arms and legs around his opponent in a sleeper hold. Dug claws into him. Pulled Gogonith's arms back.

"The belly!" Ingal yelled out. "Strike him in the belly!"

Ingal opened his jaws and bit down into Gogonith's neck, sinking his teeth deep into the roaring throat.

The citizens attacked with renewed fury, hacking and stabbing their weapons into Gogonith's bloody torso. Gogonith retaliated, kicking them away, crushing them with his tail and arms. Dozens died. But they kept coming.

Gogonith thrashed against Ingal's hold. He kicked and bit and whipped his tail at the attackers. He cast a *Lightning* spell, but without concentration, the bolts went astray. As more of his blood was spilled, his attempts to defend himself became weaker and weaker.

At last, as Gogonith faded, Ingal released his hold and pulled the Iron Dragon onto his back. He waved away the citizens and put his good forefoot at Gogonith's neck.

Gogonith watched Ingal through half-closed eyes. Their fire was gone. With a weak voice, he said, "The Triumvirate will prevail. Other dragons will fight for them."

"It doesn't matter about the dragons," Ingal replied, "or the elves, or the dwarves. The world is ruled by humanity, not us, and it is humanity that will make the final choice … as they did with you."

Gogonith merely hissed in response. Ingal released his grip and pulled his arm back. "Goodbye, Iron Dragon." In one quick move, Ingal plunged his claws into Gogonith's ruined chest and ripped open his heart. Gogonith shook, mouth agape, then his body relaxed, and the last of his breath escaped his jaws.

The Iron Dragon's corpse suddenly glowed a brilliant white. Then, in complete silence, the energies that played over him shot to the center of his body and formed an oblong sphere before growing dim and dissipating.

And thus the egg formed, with its adamantium shell, inside Gogonith's corpse, waiting to hatch the next generation of Iron Dragon.

Ingal stood staring down at Gogonith with eyes nearly swollen shut, then he turned and looked at the crowd of ragged survivors. Noticing his gaze, they lowered their heads and bowed to him.

Ingal spread his wings and raised a bloody forefoot in blessing. "You have aided your nation and your world in more ways than you know. Rise. We salute you as heroes, and grant you our most sincere gratitude for your courage and sacrifice."

And then, to their further shock and amazement, Ingal bowed to the brave people of Carnathon, citizens of the Federation.

FORTY-FIVE
Respite

Torra and Rethuud had been on the run all day, constantly diving into valleys, winging between cliffsides, rising and falling with the lay of the land. Just when Torra thought they had eluded their hunters, the Padgarun always appeared around a hillside to chase them anew. Rethuud and Torra fought for their freedom, casting spells and dodging weapons, occasionally taking the offensive and charging the Padgarun.

They had intended to fly southward, directly to the White Lands and the tower. But the elves had anticipated this and tightened the net. Instead, Rethuud found it necessary to fly ever southwest, back toward Mount Guulenen and the cavern of Chaz Sanooc, to get around them. But every mile westward delayed getting the warning to the tower. In time they reached those odd, humped hills Torra had seen upon first coming into Peshilaree. They couldn't be far from Mount Guulenen now.

At last, a couple hours after sundown, the griffin could take no more without rest. Mighty though the beast was, it had been wounded several times, and its energy could only last so long carrying two riders. With no indication of pursuers at that moment, Rethuud swung the griffin into a tight circle toward shelter, between tall rock outcrops with a natural spring. "We should be safe here," Rethuud said. "It is a place the prince and I had found."

Torra dismounted and fell to the earth, trying to ignore the various pains, then half-crawled to a recess in one of the rocky shelves.

She inspected her aching body. The rash was back and gaining momentum. Already her skin was cracking and bleeding. Thin cuts crisscrossed her arms and legs from her chase through the forest at Eshenakaree. At some point, probably during the chase, the back of her robes had been burned. Most likely a spell from a Great One.

She allowed a quick, improbable chuckle. This adventure had been a real challenge for her wardrobe. Her outer robe had gone for dressing a dragon's wound. Her inner robe had been ripped, cut, muddied, bled upon, stained green with *manasalum*, and burned. She would be lucky to make it to the tower clothed at all, at this rate! She cast a *Clean* spell, but it did little to improve the sullied clothes.

Torra accepted a scrap of vegetables from Rethuud—the last of their food supply—then drank from the spring. Rethuud started to mutter the usual prayer for eating, but he stopped abruptly. His face took on a look of abandon, and he popped the vegetable into his mouth, chewing as if in defiance. No prayer was said. Torra figured what he was thinking. If the elvish Creators—the Triumvirate—were the spirits he prayed to in the old Padgarun fashion, then why pray to gods he had just betrayed?

Rethuud bandaged his recent wounds—lacerations mainly, with some acid burns. The two didn't speak to each other. Torra, at least, didn't care to waste the energy. There was nothing positive to say, anyhow.

Rethuud placed a leatherine hood over the griffin's head, in part to help the beast sleep, and in part to prevent it from hearing a beckoning call from the enemy to lure it away or give away their position. The poor beast tried to drink at the spring with its shattered beak. When Rethuud inspected the griffin's wounds, he pointed out to Torra that its right leg had been withered to infirmity. Had the spell been meant for her? she wondered.

She forced it from her mind and managed a light, dreamless sleep while Rethuud took watch. All too soon, though, he woke her for her turn. Though the moons had shifted, it seemed she hadn't slept at all. "Wake me as soon as the moons have passed over," Rethuud grumbled. Torra struggled awake as the elf nestled between rocks and quickly fell asleep. The griffin, too, placed its head under a wing and curled up against the cliffside.

It was a somber night. No nightbirds called. No breeze. Even the spring seemed hesitant to sing its tinkling song. The air, which had everywhere else in Peshilaree carried a humid and vibrant smell, now seemed stale and desert-like.

Torra desperately wished for a campfire to keep her company, keep her awake, keep her mind off of her failure.

I had the spell in my hands! She wanted to scream it into the night. *I failed! And the Tower of Light will be the cost!*

She held her head in her hands and told herself it wasn't her fault. She had done her best. It was more than anyone could have expected of her against the strength of the Ecemii. It was a miracle she escaped with even one of the renegade spells.

She looked up to the starlit sky. Master Morikal would hardly believe her tales when she returned to Taxia. And what would Taenos say? Knowing her bravery, would he take her back? Or would she be even more of a threat to his beliefs? She frowned. Yes, a greater threat indeed.

And then another thought occurred to her: There would be no going back. Even if she lived and the tower was saved, she could never go back. She had been changed by the last few days. The old life she had led, the old choice of future, was forever lost now. The other astronomers. Taenos. Even Master Morikal. She would not be the same to them, or them to her. She had only one choice now, and that was to pursue her magic with Ingal, or the great towers, or on her own if she had to. She had gone too far to turn back from … what? Greatness? The thought was vanity, but she couldn't shake it. Legends came of these sorts of adventures —and heroes. Such a thought was vanity.

Time passed as Torra sat staring up at the sky, lost in thought and fighting the urge to sleep. She was nodding off when she suddenly bolted to attention. Had she imagined it? No, there it was again. A distant shriek. Then she recognized it as a Padgarun trying to call away Rethuud's griffin. Probably from a neighboring valley. She looked over her shoulder at their mount. With its hood on, it didn't hear the call. Rethuud still slept.

Torra hunkered down against her leatherine blanket and searched the sky for the enemy.

She couldn't find the one who made the call. But far to the southwest, looking down the valley and between hills, she spotted something moving in the sky. Glints of moonlight flashed off its surface. This was no lone Padgarun on a griffin. Fearing Gogonith had returned, she stepped over to Rethuud and whispered, "Rethuud. Wake up." He didn't move. She gingerly shook his shoulder, then jumped back, fearing the warrior would awaken with his blade at her throat. But the elf calmly opened his weary eyes.

"Is it time already?"

She pointed out what she had seen. Rethuud groaned as he stood, then stepped forward for a better view.

"Is it Gogonith?" Torra asked.

Rethuud shook his head. "It's a formation of griffin riders. See how it is V-shaped, like geese in flight?"

"Flying *into* Peshilaree from the White Lands?"

Rethuud's eyes widened. "It seems Ingal held his part of the bargain. Those would be my warriors, freed from their captivity at Palal Jehai. And with them would be the body of my cousin, the Prince of Mirrors. They are likely heading back to the Hall of Emeralds."

"*Your* warriors?" Torra grabbed Rethuud's arm. "We should fly to them! Allies to help us gain safe passage to the tower!"

Rethuud sighed and pulled away from her. "No." He turned and strapped his pack back onto the griffin.

"No? Don't you still command them?"

Rethuud shook his head. "They wouldn't understand."

"Understand what?"

Rethuud looked back at her, his eyes full of anger. "I have defiled the most sacred heart of elves everywhere. Attacked our fabled leaders. Betrayed the speaker whom I am sworn to serve! Even the faith we practice!" He turned his back to the griffin warriors. "I am a traitor to my people! They would never follow me again knowing this."

Torra watched the formation as it passed over a hilltop. "But they were there when Phasgala assassinated your prince." She squinted, then pointed upward. "Look!"

A number of other griffin riders converged on the formation from various directions.

"They are in parley," Rethuud said. "See how they circle each other?"

In moments, though, the orderly circling broke up. Even from her distance, Torra could see that some chased others.

"They're fighting," Rethuud said.

"Should we help them?"

"No. But they serve us still." He shook his head in disbelief. "Perhaps you were correct, Torra. They may not have lost faith in me. Or perhaps they refuse to believe what the Padgarun have said, and defend my honor." Rethuud pulled off the griffin's hood and grabbed the reins. "Quickly. Get on. This is the distraction we need to get away." Torra did as told, gathering her pack and her half of the Book of Alasar.

The griffin had difficulty taking off on its withered leg, but in moments Rethuud and Torra were on the wing and flying low, south around the conflict and crossed back into the White Lands Federation.

FORTY-SIX

No Rest

Ingal moved as quietly as a wounded dragon could through the south gardens of Palal Jehai. Metharcus was sitting on a bench beneath a thin-leafed maple, fast asleep. The crisscross pattern of shade played over the old human's gray robes. His hands lay limp upon an open book on his lap—the Holy Writ of Jonaatha, his god of worship.

The chamberlain had grown pale in the days Ingal had been gone. His robes looser. His breathing shallow. Ingal saw in his mind Metharcus as a young boy when they had first met, all those years ago, and recognized the same fragility circling back into the life cycle. How fleeting was the human life!

A languid flutter of pallid eyelids. A palsied movement of hands. Metharcus awoke in slow motion and turned to look at Ingal. "You look horrible," the old man muttered.

Ingal started to laugh, but the pain of his broken ribs stopped him cold, turning the laugh into a groan and wheeze.

Metharcus shook his head. "What happened? I don't think I've ever seen you looking so haggard and wounded."

"You're one to talk! We broke a leg and some ribs, but our priests have fused the bones and sealed the lacerations." Ingal massaged one leg with the other forefoot. "It has been a difficult mission for us, *decauna*. Battles with armies, run-ins with elves, and ... the Iron Dragon."

"Dead?" Ingal nodded. "Is the border safe against Ocrin?"

"For now."

Metharcus closed his eyes and swayed. Just as Ingal was about to ask Metharcus how he felt, the chamberlain said, "And what has become of that young mage you flew off with?"

Ingal frowned. "It is hoped that Torra is with the elf, Rethuud, and safe in his care. We fear we have put her too soon into the fray. Despite her arcane knowledge, she is still young in the ways of magic."

"*Torra*, is it? Not 'Com Gidel'? You've really taken to her."

"She has a great, untapped magical energy."

"For good *or* evil." Metharcus gave a thoughtful look. "If I may say so, you are a good judge of character, my lord. You would not have taken her along if you didn't feel she were capable."

Metharcus tightened his lips. "It's about time you had a thorough adventure. But it's good to see you back home, my lord."

Ingal allowed a quick smile. "It is good to be back, but we must allow only a brief rest. The endgame is soon to come."

"You met with your advisors, I take it."

Ingal nodded. "Very disturbing news is filtering in. From all over the region, priests are having visions and prophesies of a coming holy war. Planistad and Marnistad are closing their borders. Trade has been disrupted by the war with Ocrin. There is even a report of battle between the Emerald Dragon and the Pearl Dragon in the Kingdom of Ongo. Yet, despite all that has happened in the last few days, the Tower of Light has not responded to our hails."

Metharcus rubbed a shaking hand across his face as if wiping away spiderwebs. "I assume the Council told you of the floods in Homineri, the forest fires in Aestistad, the earthquakes in

Oelistad and Octunommed. Somehow Palal Jehai has been spared."

"It is no coincidence." Ingal paused to think of the easiest explanation, then simply said, "Ancient gods wish to punish us by destroying the White Lands, but sparing us personally."

Metharcus started to say something, but broke down in a string of feeble coughs. Ingal waited patiently until Metharcus recovered. Metharcus finally said, "Are these the 'Triumvirate' who wish to destroy the Tower of Light?"

Ingal nodded, then leaned closer to the chamberlain. "How is the heart, *decauna?*"

The human waved him off. "Please, my lord, do not worry about me. Look at you! The only thing you need to worry about right now is taking care of yourself—and your nation. One little old man with a bad drum in his chest is hardly worth worrying over."

Ingal shook his head. "You mean more to us than that!"

Metharcus' face sobered, and he looked out to the distant mountains. "My lord, why is it that you fight these Triumvirate gods?"

"They wish to destroy the great Towers and grant magic to every living being. Few in this world are responsible enough to wield magic at any level. It would be like ... putting a sword in the hands of a babe." He held back from adding, *And once they are armed with magic, they would be made into soldiers to march upon the Outer Gods.*

Metharcus rubbed a shaking hand across his gray-stubbled chin. "Sooner or later all babes must grow up. Having grown older and wiser, I have learned my strengths and limitations. I've gained wisdom and knowledge from my mistakes." He rubbed his hands to warm them. "Civilizations are no different. I don't need a dragon's memory to know that. They grow and mature over time, each generation adding to the wisdom of the next, in fits and starts."

Metharcus turned his sunken eyes back to Ingal. "Even with my own sons I have passed on a bit of wisdom. They don't always listen to me, of course." He chuckled. "But at least they have avoided some of the mistakes I have made and tried to lecture into them. Maybe the Triumvirate should be defeated, my lord. I do not doubt your wisdom for a moment. 'May the light of Jonaatha shine for all the world, and pierce all evils,'" he quoted from the Holy Writ. "But, perhaps, it would be a growth experience for our world to have a taste of responsibility."

Ingal didn't reply. He hoped against hope that Metharcus was right. If Gogonith was telling the truth—if Peshiluud now had the *Obliterate Mountain* spell—then he would find out all too soon if humanity was ready for the responsibility of magic and could resist the Triumvirates plans for enslavement. If not …

If not, the world may well meet the fate that befell the ancient empire of Occultii—a wasteland of spoiled earth and empty ruins.

Perhaps sensing Ingal's distraction, Metharcus returned to reading his book, squinting and holding it at arm's length. He whispered the words as he read them, so quietly that even Ingal barely heard him.

"It came to pass that the demons of the earth cast their long shadow over Man, though still they be chained, and confused Man from the Sunlit Path. And in his folly Man challenged the gods, and Jonaatha heard their blasphemies. When Man pulled his sword and rod against her, she cast her fury upon the Land, and all was burned and cast asunder."

There had been a time when Ingal could have read it from his distance, so sharp had his vision been. But no longer.

Ingal could think of only one book at that moment, the Book of Alasar. What was its fate, and the fate of Torra and Rethuud? If Gogonith had told the truth, that he had stolen the book from Torra and Rethuud and delivered the spells to Peshiluud, likely all was lost.

He had only one possibility left. The Celestials. Swordsmen of the Gods. The words of the demon-dragon rang through his memory. *Find a way. Bring the Celestials to Irikara, Gold Dragon, or the Heartstones will fall, along with the towers that guard them.*

He had to summon Azartial again.

~ ~ ~

Ingal limped past the audience hall to stand at the doorway of his sleeping chamber. The warm mud of his sleeping pit called to his aching muscles and joints. The soothing lilac smell of the room made him long to lie down and sleep—just for a short time—and forget his exhaustion and wounds.

But there was no time. With a sigh, he continued down the corridor and past the doors to the Egg Chamber. Finally he came to the once-hidden doors that led down to the cavern. Tracing arcane symbols, he opened the doors and lumbered down a ramp to the subterranean cavern beneath the palace, magically locking the doors behind him.

Lighting the braziers with a *Word of Command*, Ingal ignored the glowing riches of the cavern and continued into a side passage. He came to a set of heavy bronze doors, cast the intricate spell to unlock and open them, then sealed them once he was inside the Summoning Chamber.

Ingal situated himself in the largest circle of protection, drew small changes in the circle's design, and stopped to clear his mind.

When he was ready, Ingal began the *Summon* spell with barely a whisper. Moment by moment, his intonations grew louder and more forceful. He raised a forefoot to direct the energies. A mist developed around the circle, deepening into bright reds and blues as Ingal's chanting rose from a speaking tone to a yell, from a yell to a roar, from a roar to thunder. The continuous incantation became more complex with its crescendo, straining Ingal's energy and lungs.

Shadowy figures peered from the fluorescent clouds as the spell neared its booming climax. Gods. Demons. Entities he could not identify. Instead of the usual few, this time they crowded to look upon him, whispering amongst themselves, jostling for a better position. Ingal couldn't spare the concentration to think about it. He delivered the final, crashing apex of the spell, and all grew silent. The supernatural audience reluctantly backed away and disappeared into the roiling mist, and Ingal was alone.

He commanded, "Come, you footman of the ether. Appear before us, for your name is Azartial, and you are a servant of the Draconii forever!"

The demon stepped forward. Slim and dangerous, his glossy blue body was alive with flames. His thin, amber wings jutted out like swords. Azartial licked his snout with a blue, serpentine tongue and swiped at the circle. The protective barrier sizzled at his touch. Ingal felt the disturbance tax a part of his magic center, so weak was he. He tried to hide the weakness.

Azartial's prismatic eyes sparkled with mischief. "What do you command, Gold Dragon?"

"A question you will answer. Where is the Book of Alasar?"

Azartial leered at him, tapping his talons together. "You don't look so well, Ingal. Getting too old to dodge the arrows and acid spheres?"

"Answer the question! It is my command!"

Azartial stepped along the outer edge of the protective circle and swiped at the barrier again. Ingal shivered against the strain before he could hide it. Azartial's snout curled in a sinister smile. "Worried, Gold Dragon? Wondering if the Iron Dragon lied, are you?"

Ingal didn't have the strength to punish the demon. He had to play the demon's game. "Yes. Did he deliver the book to Peshiluud?"

"Indeed he did," Azartial said, his smile widening to show fangs. Ingal's hopes faded. "But you didn't allow me to answer your first question," the demon continued.

"Oh? Why do you say this? Is it not with Peshiluud now?"

Azartial shook a finger at Ingal. "Tsk! So many questions! In your weakened state, Gold Dragon, your mind is wandering."

Ingal growled. He couldn't keep up the protective barrier. He needed answers right away.

"Your book is with Peshiluud," Azartial said, "*and* it is with your young mage."

Ingal grimaced. "Is she Peshiluud's prisoner, then?"

Azartial whipped his tail through the bright blue and red clouds. All around the circle, tall, ghostly figures stepped forward in unison. *Celestials!* Robed in pearly shrouds of energy, the figures held long, starlit swords. Their faces were featureless save for the gaping mouths and shimmering, golden hair falling around and to the shoulders.

"Not her prisoner, Gold Dragon, for they are half a griffin's flight from each other."

Ingal didn't understand. "If they both have the book, but they are a day's flight apart ... " Ingal paused, but he had trouble thinking and holding his concentration on the spell at the same time. " ... then the Book of Alasar is in two parts!" *The binding had broken on the mountain.* "Did Torra retrieve one of the two spells?"

Azartial snickered and nodded.

Ingal strained to keep up the barrier. He was visibly shaking. "*Which* spell?"

Azartial dug a talon into the barrier. Bright, blue-white sparks jumped from it as it burned. Ingal shuddered. The demon sighed in ecstatic pain before slowly withdrawing his digit and licking it. "You know that casting renegade spells is forbidden by the gods."

"Which spell did she retrieve?"

Azartial inspected his talons. "*Rift Widening.*"

Peshiluud got his spell. Ingal groaned. *But all is not lost.* He had a plan. "The Celestials must be ready. When the elves attack, We shall open a portal for the Celestials to enter the material plane."

The Celestials raised their heads and howled. The sound filled the chamber, polyphonic, shatteringly high-pitched and deeply resonating at the same time. The entities exploded in a golden glow that painted even Azartial's cobalt flames.

Azartial grimaced at the disturbance and waved them off as if shooing a fly. "They will be waiting, Gold Dragon, if you are capable. And be sure to bring that young mage of yours. I have foreseen her crucial role in your attack."

"You are dismissed, demon!" Ingal commanded.

Azartial muttered, "As you command," then bowed and backed into the clouds, looking up with an impish smile as he vanished.

Ingal began the reverse of his incantations, shouting the chant and gradually lowering in tone and complexity. Slowly the Celestials and their howling disappeared, the vibrant red and blue clouds dissipated, and the chamber returned to its previous somber state.

Ingal collapsed in a heaving mass within the circle, unable to catch his breath. Sweat dripped from his body. His heart pounded. But he couldn't rest. There wasn't time. The elves could attack at any moment.

Suddenly, he knew he wasn't alone. The energy in the room changed, charged with electricity like flying through a thunderhead. He felt watched. Had Azartial found a way through the barrier?

Ingal stood on shaking legs and tried to activate his magic center. But his well of magic was gone. He was nearly defenseless.

And then he recognized the energy. The Triumvirate was there.

"Gold Dragon."

Ingal turned toward the bronze doors and gasped in surprise. General Tasami stood there, silver horn in hand. But Ingal knew better. "Draq," Ingal said. "Why do you again invade our presence, and in the form of this traitor, no less?"

"Isn't a traitor the best form to take now?" Draq said, his voice the same as Tasami's. He stepped forward in armored boots to stand at the edge of the circle. "Are you no less treacherous toward your Creators than he was toward you?"

"It isn't treachery if we were never allied with you."

"A child is *born* in alliance with its parents."

Ingal twitched his tail in annoyance. "When last we met, at Tegora'Seima, you nearly killed us. Then you acted to destroy our nation with fires, earthquakes, and floods. Hardly an alliance!"

"You confuse punishment with treachery, my child. And now you have killed your own brother rather than support us." Draq stepped slowly around the circle.

"A fellow dragon, yes, but Gogonith was no brother to us."

"And still you plot to undo our aims."

Ingal pointed a claw at Draq. "Your elvish zombies will fail to destroy the tower for you."

Draq shook his head. "Don't you see, Gold Dragon? We have said it before." He stopped and looked Ingal in the eyes. "You are my special child. It is in your *nature* to aid us, even as you attempt betrayal. This is why the human mages distrust you."

"You speak nonsense." Ingal lumbered toward the chamber doors. "We have no more time to parley."

Draq pulled Tasami's sword. Ingal stopped and looked back.

"Then I shall watch you at the battle, my son." Draq pointed the sword at the entrance. The heavy bronze doors unlocked and swung open, soundlessly.

Ingal turned and stepped through, refusing to look back. When he shut and locked the doors behind him, Draq's energy dissipated.

Ingal struggled to stay focused against his fatigue. He still had to fly to the tower. Find Torra and Rethuud and stop them before they handed over their half of the spellbook to the Tower of Light. Then, against all odds, he must open a dimensional portal with the renegade spell.

No one had done so for more than forty thousand years. And he knew it would likely kill him.

FORTY-SEVEN
The Tower of Light

Torra hardly believed her eyes. After reading and hearing about the fabled Tower of Light for so long, now she was seeing it for herself. She leaned to the side to get a better view around Rethuud.

Surrounded by the city of Taraman, the Tower of Light shot into the sky like a mountain, dominating the landscape. No, not a mountain. A needle. Alabaster white, gleaming, and seamless, it rose at an impossible angle, coming to a sharp point at the top. Regularly-spaced balconies and thin minarets studded its sides.

"It's a single piece of bonerock from top to bottom," Torra said.

Rethuud half-turned. "The Tower?"

"Legend says that a thousand high-level mages with Lyres of Building sang their spell in unison, day and night, for years. Inch by inch, the tower rose with their incantations." She paused to watch the structure as they approached. "It's said that it is drenched constantly in light. The translucent walls let in sunlight in the day, and the Heartstone lights it up at night from the inside, causing the entire tower to glow."

Rethuud didn't respond.

"Have you ever seen it before?" Torra asked.

"No. It is *Asmanguulee*, a site of ancient evil, just like Mount Guulenen and Ingal's cavern. My people are forbidden to go near."

Torra shook her head. "Silly superstitions."

"Elves do not act on silliness. Our warnings are based on our history." Rethuud pushed the griffin into a slow descent. "I shall land on the edge of the tower grounds, but I shall not enter."

The closer they got, the more beautiful the tower seemed to Torra. It looked like a long, straight, ivory tusk pointing to the sun. The city buildings around it, only two or three stories high, were puny in comparison. The tower's base was nestled in a huge park of green lawns, gardens, and arbors. In every glade and lawn there were bonerock statues and rock formations.

Rethuud settled the griffin down at the north end. Separated by a cobblestone paved, tree-lined avenue, they were directly across the lawns from the main entrance.

Torra dismounted, wincing against the pain of her disease. Already her skin was cracking and bleeding. She followed the tower up with her eyes until she leaned her head all the way back. The top was too high to see clearly, and she was forced to lower her gaze against vertigo. She readied herself to grab the renegade spell and walk to the entrance, but stopped.

"Something's wrong," she said.

Rethuud blinked and looked again.

"The Tower of Light is renowned for its openness," she said. "Mages from all over the world flock here. Citizens of Taraman picnic on the grounds. Children play in the gardens. And the main doors are always wide open. But not today."

"Not today. They know what is coming." Rethuud stepped off the griffin and leaned to Torra's ear. "I recommend you do not yet give them the renegade spell."

Torra turned sharply. "What? Why not?"

"It is wise to hold on to your advantage. You do not know their motivations. If Phasgala was any example, we have seen how these powerful spells can change people. Visit with them first and get an impression of their intentions."

Torra huffed. "These are our allies against the Triumvirate, and Ingal himself told us to hand it over." But a part of her agreed with Rethuud. Things were too unsure, and Ingal had said the tower had rebuffed his hails.

Rethuud spoke in an even more hushed tone. "I recommend you leave the spell here. You can always come back to get it."

Torra started to agree, but then she realized she would be leaving it in Rethuud's hands. She trusted him, right? He had killed his lover for the cause. And there was what he did at Eshenakaree. And even if he were trustworthy, the last time she left the Book of Alasar in someone else's possession it was stolen away. Such powerful spells had a way of twisting the minds of their possessors.

But Rethuud had sacrificed too much not to be trusted. He had saved her life, as well, and could have killed her at any time. And what were the chances the spell could be stolen again with him on guard?

"Very well," she said, "I will leave it with you." But for good measure she added, "Don't go anywhere."

Out of nervous habit, Torra found herself trying to smooth out her robes and pat down her hair, only to realize the robes were shredded and stained beyond any reasonable appearance, and her hair was matted and dirtied. She quickly cast a *Clean* spell on her robes again, but it still did little against the mess they had become. She sighed. "Wish me luck," she said, and started down the drive.

"Wouldn't *luck* be a 'silly superstition'?"

Torra smiled and kept walking.

But the smile quickly faded when two figures materialized in the path ahead of her. Not *materialized*, really, as much as *unfolded*, like looking at a sheet of paper from the side then turning it to see its face. Torra wondered how many other sentries were hidden around her.

These were Tower mages, one male and one female, dressed in the featureless white robes of the Tower of Light. "Halt," the female commanded, making a "stop" motion with her hand. The sign of the tower was branded on her palm—an inverted V with rays emanating up and away from it. "None are allowed entry to the tower at this time. Turn back at once." The other mage looked past Torra, clearly examining Rethuud with suspicion.

"I am Torra Com Gidel, Third Astronomer of Caranamere, Taxia. I must speak with the towermaster. I have information about an invading army of elves, due to attack at any moment."

"What kind of information?" the mage asked with a stern voice.

Isn't that enough? "I have battled them in Peshilaree, I know their origin, and I have witnessed their leader. Now, please, we haven't much time."

"One moment." The female sentry bowed her head, then looked back up to Torra. "The towermaster has agreed to speak with you. Please follow me."

Torra's heart skipped a beat. Not only was she going to enter the fabled Tower of Light, but she was going to speak to the towermaster himself! She followed the mage as the other sentry took up step behind her.

As they neared the entrance, the mage leading the way raised her arms and made a motion as if parting curtains. At that cue, something massive moved ahead of them, camouflaged against the background to the point of being nearly invisible. It was large enough to give even Ingal a challenging wrestle. It wasn't quite invisible, but translucent enough that Torra couldn't exactly make out the shape. Whatever it was, she distinguished tentacles flailing out of its broad back. Apparently guarding the doors, the beast stepped aside to let them pass.

The entrance to the tower was composed of two massive doors, also made of bonerock, that were shaped to match the curvature of the tower's base. At least four levels tall, they were decorated with the tower symbol in the center and intricate fretwork radiating away from it. Despite that the tower dated back to the time of ancient Occultii, tens of thousands of years before, there was no sign of weathering or erosion to the fine stonework.

At their approach, the doors opened smoothly and silently.

Revealed inside was a huge central hall … and the Heartstone.

Torra stepped in and gawked. The Heartstone was as tall as the doors, smooth, and conical. Made of bonerock like the tower, it rose to a smoothed apex. It was featureless and glowed with a soothing white light that was brilliant without being blinding.

Around the Heartstone was a great hall that echoed with every sound. Looking upward, Torra discovered that the space above extended as far up as she could see, probably to the very top of the tower, with balconies at every level. Mages in white robes were everywhere. Many came to the lower balconies to watch her entry.

The doors closed behind her. A contingent of a dozen mages greeted her just inside. Most were old and wizened. Several looked her over with a sense of alarm at her condition. Torra noted that all of them, including the sentries, were barefooted.

Which is the towermaster?

A mage with salt-and-pepper hair and sunken eyes stepped forward, his face pallid and wrinkled. Torra's escorts stepped aside.

"I am the Voice of the Towermaster," the mage said with a surprisingly young voice. "The towermaster is aware of your request for an audience. What is it you wish to say?"

"I think this information should be presented to him directly."

One of the other mages grinned and looked at another.

The Voice smiled blandly. "The towermaster is one with the tower itself. He hears and sees everything within its grounds. But to interact with you, he must speak through me. None may see him in person except those at the highest levels. Thus, you may say what you wish to me."

Torra looked around at the other mages. "Here?"

"Here." His slight nod and demeanor suggested that all listeners could be trusted.

"Very well." She wondered where to start. For a moment she feared she would freeze up, unable to speak at all. "I am Torra Com Gidel, Third Astronomer of the Astronomer's Guild in Taxia. I come to you at the behest of the Gold Dragon, Ingal Jehai, with whom I have traveled to Peshilaree in recent days. I come with dire warning of an impending attack by the elves."

The Voice shuddered, and his eyes glazed over, unblinking. His tone of voice had previously been unremarkable, but now it came out as a deep baritone, resonating as if heard through a long tube. "The Gold Dragon is long our ally, but we cannot afford to trust him in our current ordeal."

Torra blinked in surprise. "Why not? He went to great lengths and personal danger to uncover the threats now bearing down upon you, as have I!"

"The tower means no disrespect, but because we are battling the very gods who gave him life, we cannot take the chance that he may turn against us in our time of greatest need. So pervasive and compelling is the enemy's power, the Gold Dragon may not even realize the true outcome of his actions, however honorable they may seem."

Torra's mouth hung open in disbelief. "I have always believed that the towermaster of the legendary Tower of Light would be one of the wisest people on all of Irikara. I still hold that belief, but in this matter I firmly believe you are wrong. I vouch for him personally. You haven't seen how he fought the Iron Dragon. You haven't heard him stand up against the resurrected elvish leader, Peshiluud. And you haven't seen him battle the elves themselves for the renegade magic they need to destroy you!"

The mages shot glances at each other at the mention of renegade magic. The Voice of the Towermaster seemed to blink out of his stupor a moment, then he returned to a glazed appearance.

"Of what renegade magic do you speak?" the Voice of the Towermaster said.

Given their reaction to Ingal, Torra decided to follow Rethuud's advice and keep some information to herself. "Peshiluud now has the renegade spell called *Obliterate Mountain*. He intends to use it to destroy the Tower of Light and its Heartstone to free ancient gods called the Triumvirate. He has raised the Ecemii from Eshenakaree to form a vast army of long-dead elvish leaders. They could attack at any time."

"We know of the Triumvirate and the Ecemii's return. But we were not aware of the renegade spell. How do you know this?"

"I was there and saw it for myself." Fearing she would have to reveal her role, she quickly added, "I saw it in Peshiluud's hands at Eshenakaree." *Not a lie, really. Just an omission of facts.*

"How did Peshiluud come to possess the spell?"

"His minions found it in a cave on top of the mountain called Rishae'Uungi."

"How many Great Ones were there at Eshenakaree?"

Torra shook her head. "Many hundreds, at least. They were still rising from the depths of the lake when I escaped."

The Voice of the Towermaster was silent for a long moment. "Thank you for your warnings."

At a cue from the Voice, the sentries touched Torra on the shoulder and gestured back outside.

"We appreciate your troubles, Torra Com Gidel," said the Voice, "but your further assistance is not requested. You must now leave. We ask that you deliver the tower's thanks to the Gold Dragon, but that we wish him to please keep his distance and not involve himself in this conflict."

Torra wanted to argue, but it was clear the towermaster wanted nothing more to do with her. The Voice of the Towermaster slumped as his eyes refocused. He gave a short bow then turned and walked away. The escorts stepped up to Torra and motioned toward the doors. She took one last look at the tower's striking interior, then turned and walked with the escorts back through the doors to the outside.

It had been a sunny day when she entered. Now storm clouds were rapidly moving in over the tower from every direction.

Rethuud still stood at the far end of the avenue, tending to the griffin's withered leg. When she had walked the length to Rethuud, the escorts suddenly disappeared in the same enigmatic way they had appeared.

Rethuud turned at her approach and seemed to try to read her face. "Either it went well or it went terribly."

"Let's go," Torra said. She climbed onto the squawking griffin, feeling to make sure the renegade spell was still in the saddlebags. It was, which both relieved her and made her feel a pang of guilt for not completely trusting Rethuud.

"Where are we going?"

"A safe distance away where Ingal can find us," Torra answered. "There's nothing more we can do here." Soon they were airborne. In moments Torra pointed to a three-story stone building with a flat roof, not far from the tower. Rethuud landed the griffin on top.

As they landed, Torra looked back and saw soldiers emerge in rank and file through the buildings, encircling the tower grounds. But their coordination was sloppy, and many of them wore civilian clothes.

"Troops of the White Lands Federation?" Torra asked.

Rethuud squinted. His sight seemed sharper. "Yes, see how they turn their backs to the tower as if guarding. But these must be reserve soldiers. Many are very old, and they lack the order of experienced warriors. They appear weary from hard marching." He shook his head. "They will not last long against the Ecemii." Rethuud turned to look at the griffin saddlebags, then to Torra. "You didn't give the tower the renegade spell."

Torra shook her head. "I went with your instincts, Rethuud. The tower doesn't want my help, nor the Gold Dragon's. I'll let Ingal give the spell to them if he feels it is best." She looked around at the darkening horizon. "Where is he, anyhow?"

The words had hardly left Torra's mouth when, turning, she saw the first wave of elves fly over the northern horizon in flights of V formations. They darkened the sky with their numbers.

Roiling over the elves, and moving with them, were dark and brooding cloud-like shadows in recognizable shapes: two were humanoid, the other dragonlike.

FORTY-EIGHT

Battle for the Tower

Ingal watched as the elves flew in, but he didn't attack. He couldn't. The flight from Palal Jehai to Taraman had been almost more than he had been capable of. He lay upon a distant hilltop, heaving for breath. His wing muscles ached. His eyes were raw and strained. His leg and ribs burned where they had been broken then hastily fused back together.

Gogonith's words came rolling back to him from the encounter over Carnathon. *You are old and weak. Too old to make a difference. What have you got for me to be scared about?* "What, indeed?" Ingal muttered. Faith in humanity had saved him then, he thought, but that faith could not now blow air over his wings or bring a burst of energy into an old dragon! And there was no Vitanomicon to revitalize him here. There was a spell or two that could help, but he needed every last bit of magical energy he could muster to bring the Celestials to the material plane and defeat Peshiluud.

He couldn't stop now. It was too late for rest. Already there were hundreds of elves on griffins circling the tower, and hundreds more arriving by the minute. Dark, supernatural clouds had converged over the tower. They glittered internally with multicolored lightning. Any moment Peshiluud could begin casting the *Obliterate Mountain* renegade spell. Ingal had to find it in himself to carry on.

He hefted up onto his legs again with a pained grunt, stretched his wings out to their greatest width and grimaced. He dug his claws into the hillside, building up his resolve, then leapt into the air with a roar.

As he neared, Ingal saw that the sides of the Tower of Light shimmered with a light blue wave of energy. On every balcony and window stood a tower mage, arms raised, chanting in unison. Many hundreds of them. Their combined *Shield* spell would repel almost any physical or magical attack. They spoke with one voice, hollow, the voice of the towermaster reflected in many hundreds of slight variations.

But could the unified *Shield* spell be powerful enough to repel a renegade spell?

Ingal flew closer, but his target wasn't the elves or the tower. He was looking for Torra and Rethuud. Had they made it? He scanned the elvish riders, but saw only mirrored eyes staring back at him.

Ecemii. The Great Ones watched his approach but made no effort to confront him. Ingal kept his distance. He couldn't take them on right now. He had to save his energy.

Ingal recognized many of them. Legendary leaders and nobles from millennia back into his memory: Gornibal, the great elvish mage who repelled an Ocrin invasion over four thousand years ago; Hanathuud, the elvish sea captain who destroyed the Royal White Fleet of the Ja'Zhameel, twenty-eight thousand years ago; Antangala, the majestic elvish noble lady who first introduced the healing *granaldelum* plant to the human world, back at the early ages of the memory, some thirty-thousand years ago; and so many more. But for every one he recognized, there were at least ten he didn't. Some actually wore metal armor, unheard of by today's Peshilarn elves, while others wore the leaves of plants that had been extinct for most of his memory.

Some of the reserve troops had made it back to the tower, but they were too few and too ill-trained. Most broke and ran when the elves attacked. The others were badly outmatched, dying in droves and retreating to the relative safety of the city blocks.

And then a movement caught his eye. Torra stood on a distant rooftop waving her arms, Rethuud by her side. With a sigh of relief, Ingal swung down. The building was made of stone—a magistrate's office. He landed gingerly, slowly lowering his bulk onto the building's edge. The roof groaned but held his weight.

The griffin shrieked and fluttered at Ingal's approach. Rethuud struggled to keep it from flying away, chasing it across the roof and fighting to hold its reins. Finally it settled down.

"My lord!" Torra said. "You're wounded. Was it battle with Ocrin?"

"Please, Torra, do not fret over us, for we are well enough. We are relieved to see you and Rethuud alive. We were afraid Gogonith had killed you." Ingal paused to place a forefoot around Torra in a sort of hug. "Ocrin is under control, for the moment, and Gogonith is dead."

Rethuud exclaimed, "This is good news indeed, Jehai. One less concern."

Ingal gave a nod. "Yes, but it was a diversion which has weakened us and—"

A long, low trumpet blast echoed over the city. Ingal looked back over his shoulder toward the Tower of Light. At the horn's blow, the elves flocked around the tower and increased their speed. One by one they dipped toward the tower walls, attacking the balconies where the tower mages stood chanting their unified *Shield* spell. Each attack tested the tower's shield, wavering it over the mage being attacked. The elves then moved on and tested another, then another.

"Finding chinks in the armor," Ingal said.

"That must be Peshiluud," Rethuud said. Ingal followed his pointed arm. A mass of griffin warriors and Ecemii had landed at the north end of the tower grounds. A pitched battle erupted. Even from their distance, Ingal saw flashes of light and heard the cries of the dying. Great beasts moved there, one moment attacking the elves, the next disappearing and regrouping.

"What *are* those monsters?" Torra asked.

"They are called noru'uncu, beasts of the Veldtlands." Ingal looked around the rooftop and saw the griffin saddlebags. "Do you have the renegade spell with you?"

Torra cast her eyes downward. "Well, I have to admit …"

"We know, Torra. You only have one of the spells."

Torra looked up in surprise. "How did you know?"

Ingal shook his head. How could he quickly explain Azartial? "It doesn't matter. Which one do you have? *Rift Widening?*" Torra nodded, eyes wide. "And Peshiluud has *Obliterate Mountain?*" Again Torra nodded. *So Azartial had told the truth,* he thought. "All is not lost," Ingal continued, "but we must work quickly."

Thunder shook the building. Lightning shot from the clouds to the tower, striking a mage and throwing him to the ground far below. The lightning strike was answered by a massive explosion on the ground at the north end, sending noru'uncu flying. The Ecemii closed ranks.

And then the voice of Peshiluud rose into the air, clear and menacing, chanting. The air crackled with electricity.

Ingal's magic senses suddenly activated, dizzying him with their energy. Peshiluud had begun his renegade spell.

Ingal looked back to Torra and Rethuud. "Torra, bring us the spell at once. We haven't a moment to spare."

Torra raised an eyebrow. "But, my lord, the spell is useless. It is meant only to widen a dimensional rift that has already been made. Even you surely don't have the power to open a portal!"

Ingal cracked a smile. "We don't need to. We already have a dimensional rift in our presence!" He looked to Rethuud.

The elf nodded. Turning to Torra, he pulled forth the hilt of Ascareth and whispered the command to activate it. Instantly the thin, shimmering blade extended—a blade made of an infinitesimally thin dimensional rift.

"Of course!" Torra exclaimed. She turned and ran for the spell, shouting over her shoulder, "But an open portal for what? How will a dimensional portal help?"

The voice of Peshiluud grew louder, more urgent. At the same time, the Ecemii increased their attacks on the tower, converging on weak points. Mages fell from their balconies under the assault. Lightning streaked from the clouds to the tower, striking and killing a mage near the top—surely one of the most powerful mages in the tower. The protective shield flickered and wavered.

"We must call forth the Celestials, entities of great power to fight for us," answered Ingal.

He turned to Rethuud. "You must plunge the activated sword into the stone of this building. Then you must mount your griffin and prepare for the attack."

"Attack?"

"The elves will sense our spell, but we will be absorbed in the casting of it, unable to protect ourselves. It falls to you and Torra to protect us."

"And yet I will not have the use of Ascareth!"

Ingal nodded, watching as Torra hefted the book to him. "Do your best, Rethuud. The fate of the world's magic rides on it."

Rethuud hesitated. "It is my solemn duty to maintain control of Ascareth at all times."

Ingal frowned. "Solemn duty? Your oath is hollow given what has happened. Your prince is dead. Your leaders have betrayed your trust by waging war against us. And you have betrayed them in turn by countermanding their plans for conquest. The only way you can return our nations to peace and maintain magic as we know it is to prevent your leaders from succeeding. There is no duty left to be honor bound."

Rethuud grimaced, then plunged his sword into the stone of the building. It sank to its hilt with no effort at all.

Torra placed the torn half of the Book of Alasar in front of Ingal. "I'm sorry, my lord. We weren't able to protect it intact. Gogonith ..."

"It's all right, Torra. We know. You can tell us more at a later time. But do not despair, for all is not lost." Ingal looked down to the book and used a claw to open to the first page of the spell.

"What do you require of me?" Torra asked.

"You must assist Rethuud in protecting us."

Peshiluud's voice rose again through the air. The ground vibrated as if a great force were rising up through the earth. The tower shuddered, swaying at the top.

The population of Taraman had gathered at windows and on rooftops around the city to watch the battle, and they voiced a common cry of awe at each explosion, lightning strike, and spell.

"Once we have begun the spell, under no circumstances are we to be disturbed," Ingal said, "and you must do all that you can to ensure that we finish our spell before Peshiluud finishes his."

"What happens if you are disturbed?" Rethuud asked.

Torra answered for him. "Once begun," she said, "the spell cannot be interrupted until it is finished. If a renegade spell is disrupted midcast, at the very least the caster could go insane. At the worst, we could see a citywide explosion."

"The caster is likely to go insane, anyhow," Ingal added, "or die outright from the strain." He turned his attention back to the book. "Now, bother us no more! We must begin."

Ingal closed his eyes, meditating on his magical energy. He felt it thrumming through his limbs, his torso, his head. He massaged that vibration, shifted it, formed it into cohesive waves that swept back and forth through his body in a regular motion. Then he focused it at just the right moment, felt it flow through his veins, skeleton, and tendons, then into his mind. It congregated there, all of it, shaking through his soul, ready to burst forth in a blinding blast of energy.

With a detached composure, he opened his eyes and began to read the spell aloud.

FORTY-NINE
A New Energy

Torra withdrew as Ingal started the incantations. She watched the venerable dragon read from the crumbling text, a forefoot raised in the air, his voice rising above the tumult that was the battle for the tower. The syllables he spoke filled the ether with electricity, standing the ends of her hair and causing her body to shiver.

As she stood transfixed, she became aware of an abrupt change in and around her. Energy flowed through the building like an ocean wave, crashing into her in stages, rolling up her body to her mind. Energy was drawn to Ingal's spell, but diverted to her for some reason. Suddenly she *felt* the magic, not just mentally, but *spiritually*. It coursed through her deeper than any trifle spell she knew. Rather, it commanded her, touched her mind at its core. She shut her eyes hard against the strangeness of it—the fiery tendrils infiltrating her mind.

And then she realized the feeling. It was like waking from amnesia and rediscovering an identity that had been there all along. It was the energy that had rushed through her at Chaz Sanooc, transforming the innocuous *Darkness* spell into an incantation that shrouded the entire cavern.

She opened her eyes and saw before her a world that mirrored the changes in her mind. Gone was the everyday world she knew, replaced with a glowing, vivacious replica. Or was the world she knew the replica? This one seemed more *real*. Every line burned with vibrant coral and orange. She was actually seeing magical energy. And it was part of everything. Ingal's body shimmered with opalescent waves that coursed through him like blood through veins. Rays of bright white shot from Ingal's claws, arcing through the air to Ascareth's blade, which in turn resounded with an ever-growing charge of power that throbbed, sphere-like, around the artifact.

In answer to his vocalizations, a column of iridescent energy welled up from deep in the earth to Ascareth, adding to the power there.

Torra turned toward the Tower of Light and gasped. The tower was like a white sun, dazzling without blinding, alive on its surface with overlapping waves and boiling hot spots. Raw energy rose from the bowels of the earth like a volcano of radiance as wide as the base of the tower, then hit the Heartstone and shot out at every angle, through the tower, to infiltrate the world beyond. But the waves faltered everywhere the Ecemii attacked, shimmering and losing coherence moment by moment.

And on the north end, where a pitched battle was taking place on the ground, another great white luminance was growing sphere-like, pulsing with energy, fed by the intonations of Peshiluud and a column of energy of its own from deep in the earth. *Peshiluud.*

"We have attackers coming," Rethuud shouted.

"I see them," Torra said. A dozen of them, right from the tower. "They must sense Ingal's renegade spell."

"Get ready," Rethuud said. He reached to where he normally kept Ascareth's handle, then turned and pulled a short sword from his saddlebags. "I will take to the air to attack them. You focus on protecting Jehai from here."

Torra looked again toward Peshiluud, then back to Ingal and Ascareth. Peshiluud's spell was stronger, larger, its energy sphere greater and more focused.

"No," Torra said. "You have to trust me. I can see the enemy's magical progress. Peshiluud is further along in his spell." She stepped to the griffin and mounted it. "We have to divert Peshiluud's attention. Otherwise he will destroy the Heartstone before Ingal is able to widen the rift."

"What about the Ecemii headed this way?"

"Just get on. I have a plan." She lied. It was more of a *feeling*, but she trusted it.

Rethuud glanced back toward the tower, then leapt onto the griffin and ordered it aloft. Torra took one more look at Ingal. He was straining. Though his roaring voice still commanded, warbling and growing in tempo, the channels of energy were growing thin. Already wounded and fatigued in appearance, his body quaked with every exertion of his voice.

Torra concentrated on the Great Ones flying their way. She began to chant a spell—tendrils of the renegade energy shot from Ascareth and hit her like lightning. She went into a seizure, nearly falling off the griffin. When the shock wore off, she knew she had been changed. Her body quaked and vibrated with dynamism. Looking back toward Ascareth and Ingal, she found that she was connected to the energy there, like an ethereal umbilicus.

"Torra!" Rethuud yelled back to her, but she couldn't answer.

The energy of the renegade spells had invaded her, pulled forth this strange power coursing through her. But it was chaotic, threatening to overwhelm. She struggled to control it, channel it, form it into a cohesive wave as she did for lesser spells, but she was unable. The power of it struck fear into her as if it were a charging beast.

And then the Ecemii were upon them. A spear flew inches from her face. A fireball exploded ten feet away, singeing her hair. The griffin shrieked, slamming into another griffin in a cloud of feathers and ripping talons. Torra struggled to hold on as Rethuud fought with the other rider, a female Great One wearing a catalpa leaf robe and sporting a platinum tiara. With a primeval scream, Rethuud plunged his sword into the Ecemii's neck, and they broke free.

Five more Ecemii circled down upon them.

Torra could hold back the energy no more. "*Ecrem sai toraclama!*" she screamed, neck craned, and slashed through the air with her outstretched hand. At once it seemed as if her innards had exploded out through her arm, emptying her body in a blinding flash of salmon light. The Ecemii and griffins screamed, high and piercing, falling, flailing, as their bodies disintegrated from the inside out. There was nothing left but ashes by the time their remains hit the ground.

It was a spell she had never learned or heard of, yet somehow knew. Torra slumped against Rethuud, spent, but already the powerful energies were welling up inside her again, filling like a tub, threatening to overflow and flood her mind if she didn't empty them again.

"I can't control this!" she screamed.

"Control *what?*" Rethuud asked. "The spell you cast?"

But she couldn't put words to the feeling. She could only grab Rethuud's shoulder and struggle to master the expanding power in her. It tightened her muscles into spasms, pulling her skin taught. The Brimstone diseased skin cracked and bled over her arms, her face, her belly.

Rethuud pointed toward Ingal. A half dozen Ecemii had flown past them toward the dragon and were nearly in attacking range. "We have to protect him."

Ingal stood upright, wings outstretched and eyes focused on the spellbook at his feet. His voice shook the air around him, wavering the sphere of energy surrounding Ascareth. Tiny bolts of electricity danced around the sword. The Gold Dragon seemed oblivious to the enemies bearing down upon him.

Rethuud turned his griffin toward Ingal's attackers.

"No," Torra said. She dug her nails into his shoulder. "Turn away! Back! Back to Peshiluud. I will handle them from here."

Rethuud hesitated but did as she said.

The Ecemii were within striking distance of Ingal, and two of them cast their magic. A *Silence* spell seemed to have no effect at all, but the other incantation produced a glimmering sphere that the Great One lobbed into the air. It fell upon Ingal's back, exploding in green and blue flames. But Ingal's concentration did not waver. He continued with his incantations as the flames burned out, leaving behind charred and fused scales.

The other attackers were chanting, nearly finished.

Torra felt the energy in her unleash, exploding from inside her. "*Accorae sint bosidona!*" she shouted. Her bones popped, her body tensed, and she vomited forth a ray of energy that shot forward and slammed into the first Great One, then danced to another, and another, until all six were jumping in their saddles in a dance of death, stopping their hearts.

Torra blacked out, falling sideways. Dimly she heard Rethuud say, "I've got you."

When she awoke, she was lying against Rethuud, her arms around his body and held by him with a free hand. Her mouth was on fire. Her eyes felt as if someone had dug their thumbs into them. Her body burned with pain. Her robes were red with her own blood where her skin bled.

Lightning struck the tower again, so strong as to break apart a balcony, then struck once more at the battle below Torra, so close that she felt the electricity raise her hair.

Torra looked around in a daze. She and Rethuud had nearly reached the battle at the north end of the tower. To her right and overhead, Ecemii circled the tower, attacking the mages casting the unified *Shield* spell. Many balconies were empty now. Bodies of both sides littered the ground at the tower's base.

Below, the battle raged. A protective sphere of elves on foot and on griffin shielded Peshiluud, somewhere within. A front had formed between him and the tower grounds. There she saw three noru'uncu attacking, mages in white robes all around. The noru'uncu were no longer invisible. Like huge mastadons, they trampled elves beneath them. Long, toothed tentacles from their backs lashed out and wrapped around the enemy, delivering the unlucky victims to a waiting, serrated proboscis and gnashing jaws. Half a dozen more beasts lay dead, along with a growing pile of dead elves, Federation soldiers, and tower mages. The line of attack flashed and shimmered with spellfire and airborne weapons.

Peshiluud's voice filled the air and seemed to order the very substance of it. Torra's new magical sight beheld powerful currents of magic flashing around the fray, rolling and jumping. With a momentary exclamation in his chanting, a bolt of energy shot forth and slammed into the base of the tower. The tower emitted a deep clap that Torra felt in her chest, followed by thunder. A huge crack shot up the tower wall, rending balconies and throwing stonework to the ground. To her magical sight, the tower glowed with a sudden, unrestrained light.

"The Heartstone is cracked!" went a cry from the ground.

Cracked! "We've got to hurry!" Torra shouted.

And still Peshiluud continued casting. The spell wasn't yet complete.

A contingent of griffin-borne Ecemii turned and flew toward Rethuud and Torra.

Torra looked back toward Ingal. Though distant, his golden scales glinted with sunlight, and his sphere of magical energy had multiplied in power. More Ecemii were headed his way, but she couldn't help him. She had to stop Peshiluud.

The magical energy in her had built up again, stronger and more chaotic. This time it strained at her body, pushing her apart from the inside. She struggled to control it. As soon as she made one part cohesive, another jumped out of her mental control. She had to release it.

Rethuud half-turned to her as he dodged to evade attacks. "We can't get to Peshiluud. There are too many Ecemii guarding the way."

Torra shook her head against the dizzying magic trying to take control of her. "Fly into them—*now!*"

Rethuud dove into the attackers. The Ecemii wheeled around and encircled Torra and Rethuud, chanting and rearing to throw their weapons.

At that moment, Torra flung out her arms and straightened her body, eyes wide and staring up at the torrential skies. She yelled, "*Alua vendamenta!*" then screamed in pain as every tendon and vessel in her body seemed to rip asunder. Raw energy detonated from her in an expanding sphere that enveloped and burned to ash all those around her for hundreds of feet. Even those fighting below were thrown to the ground.

Torra went limp, gasped, fought the urge to pass out again. Already the energy was building up again, filling like a torrent into a bucket.

Rethuud shook his head, looking around them with his mouth open in awe. "We have a clear path to Peshiluud," he shouted.

Peshiluud stood in the middle of a circle of Ecemii guards. The elvish speaker stood by his side, pointing up at Torra and Rethuud with his hornet staff. Peshiluud ignored him, concentrating on casting his spell, the copy of *Obliterate Mountain* open before him. With a sudden gesture at the tower, the energy boiling around him shot out again to slam into the tower wall, rending another crack in its side. A minaret broke off and slammed into the ground in a hail of bonerock and cloud of dust.

The Heartstone cracked again, echoing off the surrounding city buildings.

"Fly closer," Torra commanded.

Ecemii pointed toward them, beginning to cast their spells.

"Torra?" Rethuud shouted.

"One moment!" she said. The energy in her flowed through her mind in uncontrolled currents. Torra gritted her teeth against the pain of it. She had to try to control it enough to combat the strength of Peshiluud's energies. She closed her eyes hard and fought to order the chaos.

Dozens of mounted Ecemii were turning, coming at them. Rethuud dodged a *Lightning* strike, then flew through a sphere of *Darkness*. Spears came close to reaching their height.

"Torra! Whatever you're planning, do it now!"

She couldn't stop what was coming even if she tried. With a spasm of her body, Torra screamed the words to the *Strangle* spell and pointed at Peshiluud.

She heard a sucking sound and a high pitched pop. And then … silence. Peshiluud continued mouthing his spell, so intent was he, but no sound came forth. The speaker, standing at his side, looked around in sudden confusion, then twitched and fell to the ground, his hands at his throat, gasping for air that was no longer there.

Torra struggled to control the magic flowing through her, trying to sustain the vacuum around Peshiluud. Ecemii attempted to *Negate* her spell, but hers was more powerful than theirs and they failed.

Peshiluud stopped mouthing and shook his head. He shot alarmed glances around him, his mirrored eyes dancing left and right, then looked to the sky in anger. Their eyes met. Peshiluud stopped struggling and stared at her with a vehemence that was as much an admission of defeat as a demonstration of anger.

The speaker turned and lunged as far as he could, then crawled, gasping, to put as much distance between himself and Peshiluud as possible. Torra lost sight of him behind Peshiluud's Ecemii guards.

Torra let the spell end. She had stalled Peshiluud's progress —at least. "Get us away from here," she said, resting her head against Rethuud's back. Rethuud turned the griffin and flew back toward Ingal with as much speed as he could get from the exhausted beast.

Peshiluud heaved for air and tried to continue the spell. But Torra saw the magical energy around him vacillate. He tried to pull it together, but lost control. With a sudden rush of ethereal current, the spell collapsed around him. He screamed, "Creators!"

but the gods didn't listen. Still screaming, he fell to his knees, his hands clenching his head. In slow motion his body pulled apart in every direction, defying gravity, his blood forming spheroids and floating off. Eyes rolling in their sockets, Peshiluud's head finally cracked and burst in a sickening cleavage that caused Torra to turn away.

The energies from Peshiluud's *Obliterate Mountain* spell dissipated. The Ecemii fell into disarray for a few moments, then regrouped and focused all of their energies onto a few weak points. The tower once again shook as the cracks in its side widened.

"We stopped Peshiluud," Rethuud said. "Is the tower not safe?"

"Safer, certainly. But it seems the Ecemii are capable of finishing for him!"

Ingal was under attack. Ecemii had swooped upon him. His body was blackened and punctured. And yet, despite their attempt at distraction, his voice didn't waver, growing to a roar as he reached a climax. The sphere of magic around Ascareth had grown to encompass the entire building, fending off many of the Ecemii's attacks.

Rethuud flew back, attacking the Ecemii. Torra barely noticed. The energies had grown again, flooding through her body, overwhelming her mind. She pressed her hands to her head and screamed in agony. Unable to be controlled, the energy rushed through her body like a geyser and shot out of her mouth and eyes. The beams obliterated all they touched. They burned through Ecemii, griffins, and buildings. Everything she laid eyes on was obliterated. It was all she could do to keep from incinerating Rethuud or Ingal.

FIFTY

Endurance

Ingal was caught in an onrushing, maddened current of magic, struggling to keep his attention on the seemingly tiny pages of the spellbook and the necessary vocalizations of the spell.

To Ingal, it was like being dunked into river rapids and trying to hold himself in place while violent waters rushed over and around, threatening to dislodge and drown, freezing right down into the core of his being.

A new phrase of the spell came, and Ingal raised a forefoot to guide the magic's flow. But raising the forefoot brought no sensation. He willed the body, but he couldn't tell if it responded. There were no senses other than those necessary to speak and to read. But the spell continued, and as far as he knew, he wasn't yet insane or dead.

Something happened out there—out there in the world beyond his spell. To his body. Something painful. A shudder rippled through his being. A momentary sense that could have been a pinprick or an amputation, for all he knew. But the spell remained, and he with it. He continued.

The energies rushing through him to Ascareth weren't like any spell he had known. This wasn't a condensation of the life force around him. This was raw. And it was sentient.

He was drawing away anima from someone or some thing, like possessing its soul and then passing it on. *The Triumvirate.*

The thought shook him, and he almost lost the rhythm of the spell. The magic shuddered in response, tearing at a part of his mind. He actually _felt_ it, like a claw reaching into his brain and clenching. But he caught the rhythm again, went with the flow of the rapids, and the claw unclenched. Yes, he was pulling away anima. But not all of it passed though. Some of it was inserting itself into him, pushing away part of him that went out to the sword in its place.

And with those new pieces came odd memories, flashes of sight and smell and sound, strange and fascinating. Names. Languages. Creatures. They weren't in the memory, and yet they were part of him. Part of his lineage.

But he didn't humor them with curiosity. He had to stay focused. He wanted so badly to stop the madness. Shut his eyes. Reclaim himself. To at least put his forefeet to his head and roar in anger and pain. Catch his breath.

But he didn't. He couldn't. He didn't dare. And even as his brain was being taken over, bit by bit, he continued reading, building and building, roaring out the words and turned the last page.

FIFTY-ONE
The Final Spell

Torra heard Ingal shout one final line of incantation, trilling the last syllables and making a parting motion with his forefeet.

At that movement, the sphere of energy imploded into Ascareth and sent the sword whirling upwards. With a thunderclap, the infinitesimally thin blade shot outward in a shimmering plane of light as wide as a building.

The energy coursing through Torra shut off like a door had been slammed shut. The destructive power stopped surging, and her sight returned. She slumped against Rethuud. "Land us," she beckoned.

Ingal held a single, long note, seeming to sustain the gate in its open state. The glowing portal hummed back in response, then wavered and warped as hundreds of angelic beings rushed forth from it. Celestials!

Tall, glimmering entities in white flowing robes. Their golden hair fluttered back from blank faces with gaping mouths that howled in a piercing victory shout. Wielding long, starlit swords that burned with nearly invisible flames, they flew toward the Tower of Light with astounding speed.

In moments the Celestials reached the Ecemii and their mounts. The supernatural beings slashed without mercy or hesitation. No spell the elves cast seemed to have any effect against them. No spear, no acid, no sword did any damage at all.

And because the Celestials were not from this plane of existence, they could not die. The elves were on the run.

And then something else emerged from the dimension gate. A dragon, but smaller and slender. Its scales were glossy blue. Blue flames danced over its body. Amber wings shot out from its back like dagger blades, but did not flap; the beast flew with some form of levitation. It narrowed its malevolent eyes and turned its jagged snout toward Ingal, starting toward the Gold Dragon.

"No!" Torra screamed, then reached around Rethuud to grab the reins. The griffin shrieked and dove toward the demon.

The demon dragon stopped its approach and looked up to Torra. Their eyes met. And its hellish gaze softened. Lightning jumped in the demon's pupils and fell silent. "You!" it said, its voice surprisingly smooth and urbane. "You're the One ..."

The One? she mouthed. The two of them remained locked in their gaze. She was drawn into those eyes; felt as if she were right next to the demon. Her fear and defensiveness faded away, replaced with curiosity and awe.

"The One from the Nexus," the demon dragon said without explaining. He hovered a moment longer, flew backward several feet without looking away, then turned and slowly flew westward away from Ingal and the tower. Torra wanted to follow, get an explanation for its utterance.

And there was power there. There, in its eyes. It was different from the magical energies coursing around her. It called to her. She wanted it. She wanted to *control* it. To roll it around in her being as if it were a curious bobble in her hands. Play with it. Mold it. Make it hers.

It was instantly addictive. Ingal's voice wavered, weakened, then fell silent. Torra tore her eyes away from the demon and looked back to the portal. One last Celestial flew out as the dimensional gate collapsed. Ascareth deactivated and fell, its hilt

clattering to the stone in front of Ingal. Ingal, in turn, closed his
eyes and dropped to his side with a crash that shook the building
and collapsed part of the roof.

Torra's magic sight faded away. The wild energies playing over
everything disappeared, leaving the world mundane again. Torra
looked back toward the demon dragon, but it was gone. She
looked back and forth trying to find it in vain.

Rethuud landed the griffin next to Ingal, and Torra
dismounted and fell to the slanting rooftop. Rethuud helped her
to her feet, and together they stepped over to stand in front of
the dragon lord.

The Book of Alasar had nearly disintegrated. At their feet,
all that was left was the dragonhide binding and a pile of flaked
pages blowing away with the wind.

Ingal was still alive. His burned and lacerated body shivered
and twitched. At Torra's approach, he opened his eyes to look at
her. One pupil was dilated, the other constricted. His breathing
was erratic. His claws scraped over the stone.

Rethuud picked up Ascareth's hilt. He muttered the
command to activate it, but the sword didn't respond. It never
would again.

Torra placed a shaking and cracked hand on Ingal's expansive
jaw. "My lord, tell me what I can do for you."

Ingal tried to raise his head but managed only a couple feet.
"The Celestials," he rasped. "Elves. Peshiluud."

Torra withdrew her hand and looked back to the Tower of
Light. The Celestials had flown around the tower, killing and
chasing away the remaining elves. The Celestials' howls filled
the air like a lingering nightmare. The Ecemii retreated over the
northern horizon.

"You've done it, Ingal." She turned back to him. "The Celestials have ended the attack. The battle is over. Peshiluud is dead. The elves have retreated."

"And the Heartstone?"

"The Heartstone is damaged, I … I can feel it. And the tower is damaged, but both yet stand."

Ingal closed his eyes, a smile playing at the corners of his mouth. "Then I was not too old to make a difference." His head fell back to the rooftop.

"Ingal?" Torra said. She placed her hand back on his jaw. The scales were cold to the touch. "My lord?" Ingal exhaled in a long, exhausted sigh.

"Ingal?" The Gold Dragon did not reply. He hardly breathed. And in those suddenly quiet, helpless moments, Torra watched as the ancient and mighty ruler slipped into a coma.

FIFTY-TWO

Funeral

Torra stood shivering on the South Portico steps as black funerary streamers snapped and popped in a chill wind. She huffed on her hands and slid them into the pockets of her new white robes, longing for the ermine stole she had left in her quarters. Winter had come early to Palal Jehai, mirroring the solemn occasion. The drab trees and overcast skies cast a morose tone to what had months earlier been a gay expression of life. Ingal's beloved palace gardens.

Torra leaned against a pillar and ran her hands along its smooth surface. Despite the weather, the cold stone felt good against her inflamed skin. She closed her eyes, reliving for the millionth time the battle for the tower. Though it had been two months, she felt herself both reviling the event and longing for a part of it to return—the excitement, the power. Yes, that was it, she thought, the power. The vast, unbridled energy that welled up with the renegade spells … and from the demon dragon.

She pushed her palm tight against the pillar's surface. She searched for any hint of that magical vibration she had felt, running through everything around her. But the stone of the pillar was dead. No magic vibrations made their way to her hand. She opened her eyes again, hoping to see surging energy through every edge and shape. The vibrant oranges, reds, and blues. The flow of magic as spells were cast. The sense of … *connection* to the world around her. For that brief time, at the battle, the world's energy flowed through her so strongly she couldn't control it.

Now she felt powerless again, diseased and bereft. The palace doors behind her opened as Rethuud stepped through. "At last I have found you. The funeral cortege is about to start, and the priestess of Jonaatha has started the final rites."

She shook her head. "I'm not going. I don't feel I knew him well enough."

Rethuud took a position standing next to her, following her gaze out over the gardens. "Apparently Metharcus was very dear to Jehai. It would honor Ingal if you paid homage to his chamberlain and friend." Torra started to reply, but she stopped and nodded.

From through the open doors came the lumbering footfalls of the Gold Dragon. Torra thought back to the first time she had heard that sound, back in Ingal's audience chamber. How frightened she had been! *Was that only three months ago?*

Torra turned and watched as Ingal pushed the doors open the rest of the way and stepped out onto the portico. The dragon saw Torra and Rethuud and smiled. But one eyelid drooped, and the legs on his left side dragged slightly when he walked. The left wing would not fully extend. Though he had awakened from the coma a month before, it had clearly left an unremitting effect on the dragon's physical—and mental—state. And the horrible wounds he had sustained left permanent scars.

But the renegade spell had left something else behind. Ingal was more powerful than ever. Torra could feel it. Wanted to be near it. And though the dragon denied it, she knew the spells came to him far easier. He hardly needed to speak the words, now, to cast them.

"Ah, Irana. You have not taken your morning scones," Ingal said, looking at Torra.

Torra grimaced and looked down to the portico floor. "My lord, I am Torra Com Gidel, not Queen Irana. She died over a thousand years ago."

Ingal blinked, then seemed to shake out of a daze. "Of course. Of course. Please excuse us." He cleared his throat. "We want to spend some time with you before you leave."

Rethuud turned to Torra. "Are you returning to Taxia?"

"No." She rubbed her hands to warm them, but they slid together with a rustling sound as the dead and dying skin flaked off. She needed to lotion them again already. Chagrined, she quickly shoved them back into her robe pockets. The disease hadn't let up. "I sent my bodyguards and my servant, Olos, back to Taxia a week ago. Ingal has arranged for me to apprentice with the Tower of Light."

Rethuud's eyes widened. "You are to be a tower mage, then?"

Torra flourished her white robes, the attire of a mage of the Tower of Light. Then she raised her right hand, palm out, to show the branded symbol of the upturned V with radiating lines from it, still inflamed from the ritual of branding she had endured.

"How could they refuse her?" Ingal said. "She saved the tower and its Heartstone from destruction."

"I only helped, of course," Torra quickly added. "Your good word is greatly appreciated. And they need to replenish their numbers."

Ingal lowered his head to look her in the eyes. "You have a great gift, Torra, for you possess both a knowledge of powerful magic and a talent for channeling it. But if you wish to control it you need training that only the towers can provide."

"Thank you, my lord." Torra gave a sidelong look at Rethuud. "And what is to become of you, Rethuud?"

The elf fingered the hilt of his new long sword, a gift from Ingal from his stash of treasured artifacts in the caverns beneath. "I do not know. Perhaps back to Peshilaree to continue the fight? There has been a call for my execution. Banished from Peshilaree, I am without a nation, a traitor to my people … in most of their eyes."

"A hero to others," Ingal pointed out. He slid his tail across the stone portico floor. "In time they will realize the wisdom of your actions. You are always welcomed in our lands, and we need an elvish advisor. Consider Palal Jehai your home for as long as you wish."

Rethuud gave a nod. It was the closest elves ever came to bowing. "I will be honored to serve, Jehai, now that the tower is out of danger."

Ingal's eyes widened. "The Tower of Light may now be guarded by Celestials, but the danger has not passed. This was but an opening skirmish in the Triumvirate's plans. There is a world to conquer, and two other Towers of Magic and their Heartstones to destroy. The Heartstone of the East yet stands in the Tower of Light, but it is cracked. Even that crack has increased their power. Soon they will find more allies in the battle for the other towers, including other dragons. I … " Ingal shook his head, " … *We* must be diligent. The Stone of Lethori still glows, meaning that the Outer Gods are watching closely for Triumvirate activity. If the gods feel threatened enough, they may still destroy the world. It makes me worried."

Torra had heard Ingal use singular pronouns many times in the past couple weeks, and he was catching himself less and less.

"And what about the demon dragon? Azartial?" Torra asked. She saw again the flaming blue scales, the serpentine body, the piercing, iridescent eyes. *Yes, those deep, powerful eyes. That magical power!*

"As we have told you, Torra, it is distressing that he came through, but we do not know his motives. Remember, he is a servant to dragonkind, for good or evil. We still command him. And it is his duty to serve the Outer Gods as well."

Ingal straightened his back and rose to a nobler stance. "We may count our blessings, Torra. Though the Speaker of the Hall of Emeralds yet lives, Peshiluud is dead. Those renegade spells are destroyed. The Iron Dragon will not be reborn for centuries —unless the Triumvirate somehow speeds it up. And the Tower of Light, for now at least, seems to be beyond the reach of the Triumvirate. We are witnessing the birth of a new world, Torra, however this ends. Let us hope it will be a world of responsibility and freedom."

Torra shivered again and pulled her robes tighter. "Let us go inside, Torra," Ingal said, starting to turn back into the palace. "I am very soon starting the memorial service for Metharcus."

But Ingal paused, seeming to linger on a thought. "Dear *decauna.*" He shook his broad head, then looked back toward Torra. "One of the last things he expressed to us—right out there under that maple tree—" Ingal pointed a broad claw toward the garden, "—was a thought that the world's civilizations need this latest crisis to mature and pull together, to grow in wisdom as children do." His eyelids sagged, and the old dragon seemed to age further. "We did not agree at the time, believing that the changes brought by the Triumvirate could only be negative. But now we feel he may have been correct." Ingal shook his head and snuffled. "If we truly were a living god, as Gogonith had thought himself, perhaps it would be in our power to do more to help the people of Irikara grow toward that wisdom.

"But then again," he continued, "perhaps we are all gods in our own right, sculpting the world as we see fit—like children, changing their parents' world as the parents seek to shape their offspring. With each action we bring forth the birth of a new reality, however small or large it may seem." Ingal's worn face softened and broadened into a warm smile. "Somehow the thought makes us feel *young*, again, yet wiser." He stood still a moment and seemed to savor the concept. With one last glance to Rethuud and Torra, Ingal turned and lumbered back inside.

Rethuud tightened his sword belt and followed Ingal into the palace, but Torra lingered a while longer on the portico, alone, listening until Ingal's steps faded into the background and all that was left was the mournful hum and wail of the wind over the mountain crags.

Yet again she thought about the events of the past few months. Ingal had changed, but so had she. That power rushing through Ingal was in her, too, in residual form. But after all they had been through, she almost didn't need it anymore. Dragons. Elves. Renegade magic. Gods, even.

Gods? she thought. Utter nonsense. There was no such thing as gods. Just more powerful entities with a scheme for power. She scowled at the thought of sitting through the funeral rites for Metharcus as the Jonaathan priestess chanted and wailed. She shoved the thought aside.

Once again Torra rubbed her hand along the pillar and closed her eyes, searching for that familiar magical vibration. The one she had called forth at Chaz Sanooc. The one that had nearly destroyed her at the Tower of Light. Was it there? Was it hiding, just beneath the cold stone and the beat of her heart?

And then it *was* there, so strong she thought she shivered again. She removed her hand to be sure it wasn't her, and then returned it to the pillar. The magic was still there. Suddenly, a tendril of energy shot through her arm to her mind, blazing her magic sense to life.

She yanked her hand away and saw, just for an instant, a humanoid shadow dodge between trees in the garden. But she was alone, and there were no shadows in the gray light filtering through the clouds. Torra backed toward the doors, then turned and strode inside.

The Triumvirate could keep their magic today.

Acknowledgments

A special thank you to my friend, Adam Breashears, whose generous patronage paid for the original cover art.
You can contribute, too, at: ko-fi.com/worldskilgore

And my everlasting thanks to my writer's group, the Peeps of Corvallis, Oregon, past and present, who critiqued every word and helped me take my writing to the next level.

Chapter One from *Footman of the Ether:*

Book Two in the Heartstone Series—Coming 2024

In all the worlds and all the dimensions Darilos Velar had known, Irikara was unmatched for its fine balance between scorching and freezing, chaos and order, blandness and flamboyance. Irikara was a world of contrasts and compromises, making it rich in energy. Little wonder the gods fought over it. Does fighting over this world threaten that valuable balance, or does it accentuate it? He gave a wry smile. Yes, he decided, it accentuates it. Peace, after all, is so very boring.

He stood on a hilltop absorbing the sunny, late-autumn morning, just past sunrise. A light breeze, chill with the promise of winter, rustled the dry grass at his feet, yet the heat from the sun warmed his blond hair. Below him lay a valley adorned with changing oaks and elms. The vale seemed on fire with the vermilion and canary yellow of dying leaves, their host trees pulling away the life essence through each fragile petiole until all that was left was this brilliant display of sorrow. In the center of the valley was situated the town of Caranamere, of the nation of Taxia. Its sleepy streets and somber stone buildings bespoke simplicity and harmony with the setting. A bell tower rang the hour, its deep toll echoing off the edifices of the Astronomer's Guild at the town's heart, then out to the surrounding hillsides and beyond into the bright cerulean sky. Two small children ran down the flagstone-paved main street playing "tag the orc." Goodwives fetched water from the town fountains. A baker pushed a small wagon filled with freshly baked loaves and called out for customers. Thin trails of smoke wafted over the town as townsfolk awoke to light hearth fires.

"How pastoral," Darilos muttered. "Pastoral?" asked Apostle Agnon at his side—one of seven mages standing on the hilltop with Darilos. "Let us not wax poetic when destruction is at hand." The high priest of the Brotherhood of Blood, with his six Disciples, were all dressed in the Brotherhood's crimson vestments. Darilos was not of the Brotherhood, and his garish red and orange traceried robe to set him apart. "Pastoral," Darilos repeated. "It's a shame we must disturb such simple beauty." Agnon narrowed his eyes at Darilos. "You had better deliver on your promise. I've staked everything on this, Outlander."

Outlander, Darilos thought, a suitable alias he had given himself—one of many—for tasks like this. An alias of an alias. Darilos followed Agnon's gaze off to his left. A massive, iron-reinforced oak chest sat on the hilltop with them, a long metal bar arcing over the chest like a giant handle. Even with the help of magic, it had taken all night for the disciples to lug the chest up the hillside on a strained wooden litter. Bright yellow light streamed through the chest's lid, so bright it defied the morning sun. Strapped to the side of the chest was a long, slender sword—the Key of Otemus. The key featured a gleaming, silvery blade and a two-handed hilt, yet the blade was oddly carved with squared pits and curious projections. Darilos could just take the sword now, by force if he wanted to, but a contract had been made. He had to wait for the task to be completed.

Contracts, oaths, and promises were perhaps the only things he held sacrosanct. One of the fisciples, a man with a cherubic face and eyes so blue they could only be described as ultramarine, stepped up to Agnon. "All is readied, Apostle." "Thank you, Immolatos." Agnon then turned back to Darilos. The apostle's stark green eyes contrasted with his ashy, pock-marked face. "Your dragon is late! He was supposed to strike at dawn." "Mordan does as he must, Apostle," Darilos replied, but he sensed the dragon nearby. He didn't need to look. Its energy was blazed like a brilliant star on a hilltop behind them, to the west and behind a low hill. Evidence that he'd been infused with the power of the Triumvirate gods, so-called "terrestrial energy," which made up nearly all magical energy in the world of Irikara.

But Darilos couldn't usually feel it unless it was very strong, since he was not of this world. He knew that the Triumvirate, the three gods who created the world of Irikara and now were imprisoned in it, would be reaching through the bars that morning, so to speak, endowing their energy into Mordan. The Emerald Dragon had been there in the distance all morning, watching, calculating. The Brotherhood mages can't feel it.

Pitiful. "Why must we be so far away, Outlander? I can hardly see the Guild towers from this distance. It must be half a mile, at least!" This peevish cultist whines like a child, Darilos thought. He didn't bother to answer Agnon. He could see farther than these humans. They would need every cubit they could spare during the spectacle to come. Darilos felt the dragon's energy shift. Mordan was on the move, silently swooping down into the neighboring valley toward them and the town.

"Apostle, if you have doubts about continuing, now is your last chance to stop this," Darilos said. "Of course, I have no doubts!" At that moment the Emerald Dragon roared over the hilltop behind them, scattering the disciples. Agnon ducked and yelped in surprise. Treetops swayed with the cyclone from his wings. Darilos stood unfazed. One of the largest of the twelve dragons, at around eighty yards in length including the tail, Mordan's body bulged with muscle, covered with scales gleaming like emeralds, and crisscrossed with scars. His back was armored with shining steel bars like a metallic exoskeleton of overlapping bones, with a skeletal metal helmet to match. He turned his broad head to look back for a signal. One-eyed from an ancient wound, with wide lateral horns like a water buffalo's and a mouth lined with serrated fangs, the dragon's visage was a glimpse into terror. Darilos pointed down at the Guild compound—a sign that the mission was to proceed. The dragon roared again and swooped low over the town, gaining speed, then shot up past the resplendent hillsides to an incredible height, almost out of sight. The bell tower rang out in chaotic tolling. Faint screams and shouts of villagers echoed into the sky. They knew the Emerald Dragon's reputation. Darilos leaned forward. This should prove interesting, he thought. Figures moved on the fortified walls of the Guild compound. The mages there harmonized their spellcasting, creating a shimmering *Shield* spell, one of the strongest he'd seen, over the center of the buildings.

Darilos chuckled. A *Shield* spell would be little protection against the will of a dragon. Apostle Agnon called his disciples to him, then brought forth a leather wineskin. Reciting a quick prayer, he poured out the blood of three virgin youths—two boys and a girl sacrificed just before they came up the hill— coating his right hand and the right hands of each of the disciples. The disciples knelt and bowed their heads, raising their blood-stained hands in the air.

"Oh, great Triumvirate," Agnon chanted, "to you we give the promise of the future. Take from us the shreds of our jaded past. Correct our ignorance. Deliver us to your great powers. See before us a symbol of our dedication to you!" Darilos paid little attention to the mage's prayer, even as he felt the energy of the hill beneath him magnify, welling up from the core of the world. The Triumvirate had come to bear witness. All three gods, creators of this world, Irikara, trapped in its energies by the Outer Gods. Agnon finished his prayers and shouted, "They are here! We are in the presence of the Triumvirate!" The disciples each gave a hail of praise. Agnon searched the sky for the dragon. Darilos looked as well and found Mordan now but a speck in the blue. The Emerald Dragon finally stopped his ascent, pausing a moment at the suffocative roof of the world. Then he shot downward toward the town, his descent reaching an astonishing speed.

"He'll kill himself!" Agnon gasped. Darilos smirked. *He still underestimates the dragon!* Mordan pulled in his wings and rolled himself into a tight ball. He barked a one-word spell. The syllable thundered across the sky. He burst into scintillating green flames and multiplied the speed of his descent to the point of blurring. Mordan struck the Astronomer's Guild like a meteor. A fireball of blinding white plasma exploded from the point of impact, instantly enveloping the town and shaking the valley. The wind and heat of the blast shot up and over the hillsides, leveling trees, hitting Darilos and the others with a massive wall of force that threw the others to the ground, temporarily deafening them with a grinding roar of destruction. Darilos stood motionless. The heat radiated raw, magical energy. It swept through him, energized him, sent his senses into rapture. He laughed openly into the blast, feeling the heat sting the back of his throat. It was the most thrilling sensation he had felt in millennia.

The valley below was a hellfire. Smoke and dust exploded in a billowing cloud half a mile into the clear sky. Flames raged up hillsides in infernal tempests. The mages' *Shield* spell had had no effect against such powerful magic, as the dragon's spell had been "renegade magic"—an incantation of immense power, forbidden by the Council of Mages. *Bombard*, Mordan had called this one, in his last message. Darilos and the others were just out of range of the fires on their distant hilltop. The men were now struggling to their feet. "Gods!" Agnon gasped. "Did he have to destroy the entire valley?" Darilos turned and leered at the apostle. "My dear mage, what do you expect when you hire a dragon as mercenary?" He glanced at the Key of Otemus, still strapped to the chest.

"Now, Apostle, my payment please." Hardly taking his eyes off the destruction, Agnon gave a nod and gestured to one of his disciples, who unstrapped the sword from the chest and carried it to the apostle. Agnon unceremoniously handed it over to Darilos. Darilos held it up, marveling at the lightness of the metal and the poetic nature of the valley's flames playing on the long, silvery, reflective blade. The apostle raised an eyebrow. "I don't understand the significance of this weapon to you, Outlander. It is of valuable metal, some platinum alloy, but much of the treasure we brought is of greater value and power. It is magical only in its ability to remain sharp and untarnished."

Darilos stabbed the blade into the ground before him. "Its value to me is of no concern to you." He looked back at the destruction and pointed. "Behold!" Seeming beyond possibility, a giant figure rose from the impact crater. Shadowy and warped to Darilos' sight by the heat and distance, Mordan winged up and over the smoke and dust. "Your mercenary comes for his payment," Darilos proclaimed to Agnon. The apostle waved his disciples away from the great chest. But Mordan was in no hurry. The soot-covered dragon orbited the valley a couple times before closing in on their hilltop. The dragon was visibly exhausted, but Darilos knew he was likely still powerful enough to give a good fight. When the Emerald Dragon had flown near enough, Darilos hailed him and gestured at the chest.

"Mordan, your payment is here." But Mordan maintained a distance, circling the hillside. "We feel your energies now,

Outlander." He spoke in Taxin, accented with the speech of the Northlands. "Or rather, the lack of them. You are not as you appear." He flew a bit closer and hovered in place for a moment, an act not easily performed for a dragon of his size, sending gusts from his wings. Darilos waited, amused at the game. Then Mordan's good eye opened wide with recognition. "Yes! We know you now! It has been a long time. Shall we state your true nature to your friends, so that they may fear you? Or perhaps we should order you to do our bidding, footman?"

Darilos frowned. The dragon would go and ruin a good day, wouldn't he? "I would consider it a breach of contract, and gladly melt down the chest and your payment with a word. Go now with your reward and trouble me no longer." Mordan stopped hovering and flew backward. "That sword before you—the Key of Otemus—yes, We recognize it. Is this your feeble payment as their middleman? You know it's useless to you. You cannot wield it, and the lock is long lost." "It is of no concern to you, dragon."

Quickly gathering speed, Mordan circled the hilltop and gained altitude. "Hmm. Perhaps you have found that lock, then? Very well," he shouted. "We shall leave you to your fate and whatever fool's errand you embark on with that artifact." Mordan shouted a spell. An explosion heaved up the hilltop, throwing the disciples off their feet again in a shower of soil and rock— propelling the Key of Otemus high into the air. Darilos stumbled sideways, trying to catch himself. Mordan caught the Key midair and stabbed its blade through Darilos' torso, impaling him and throwing him to the ground. Darilos let out a bestial roar of pain, clutching at the weapon and arching his back. In moments the dragon was gone, carrying the massive chest with his forefeet and disappearing, laughing, into the northern sky.

Apostle Agnon crawled over to Darilos. "Outlander!" he yelled. Darilos growled, sitting upright. He coughed out a strained chuckle as he watched the dragon's retreat. "Cheeky bastard," he muttered. Mordan had known perfectly well that the blade wouldn't kill him. Wrapping a hand around the handle of the key, he yanked the sword out of himself, emitting an inhuman bellow. Agnon stood and stumbled back, drawing in a harsh breath. "By the three gods!" Darilos winced as the bloodless wound closed. It's pathetic how fragile human bodies are. Of all the forms I could have chosen! He stood and stabbed the Key of Otemus into the ground once more. Agnon gave Darilos a sidelong look, eyes wide, shaking his head. "How did you survive that wound? Outlander, why did the Emerald Dragon call you 'footman?' Why would he think you should do his bidding, but then deal you what should have been a mortal blow?" He backed away from Darilos. "What are you?"

Darilos ignored him, scratching his chest through the cut robe where the wound had been. He looked down upon the burning valley and the crater at its heart. Nothing more than rubble remained of the institution of magic that had been the "Astronomer's Guild." Magic was illegal in Taxia, and yet, this secret society and its annexes in other towns had its tendrils in every facet of this region, right up to the throne of Taxia's king. The Brotherhood of Blood had paid for a major political coup that would shake this part of the world, and, they thought, take care of a potentially powerful enemy of the Triumvirate. But using the Nexus, Darilos had seen enough of the future to know that the Guild could have gone either way in this fight. There can be no neutrality in battles between the gods. Darilos didn't care about all that. A minor loss for a greater gain.

His mission was to find the Convergence, a mysterious object of such incredible power that its potential worried the Outer Gods. The mages of the great Towers of Magic would investigate the destruction of Caranamere, and Darilos would use them to retrieve this powerful artifact. Whatever form this Convergence took, it would be the focal point for control of the world's magic. The Outer Gods knew it. That was why he was here. That was why he had traveled to the material world. But does the Triumvirate know about the Convergence? he wondered. The Key of Otemus seemed to mean nothing to the Brotherhood, so perhaps the Triumvirate they served didn't yet know.

And another notion remained at the forefront of his thoughts as he watched the conflagration spread up the mountainsides. A notion that kept him from rest, no matter where he had gone in the past few years. The woman. That human mage he had seen at the battle of the Tower of Light riding astride a griffin, at battle with the elves. She was the One who was always at the Nexus of futures in the Ether. She was the one he had foreseen before coming to this world, and then again, in person for a brief moment. The one named Torra Com Gidel. So rich in energy was she that it filled his senses just being near her for that brief moment. She would be the one he needed to implement his plan.

According to the scant information he could find about her, the burning valley below had been where she had been raised and learned the ways of magic. That certainly was no coincidence. The Tower of Light would surely send the woman with their expeditionary mages. And he would be with her, at last. Darilos trembled at the thought.

"Answer me, Outlander!" Apostle Agnon shouted. "What you?" Darilos shook off his thoughts. He had almost forgot about the Brotherhood. "Something more formidable thar

Emerald Dragon." He looked again at the destruction below. "It is time for you and your disciples to leave," Darilos continued, his voice measured. "Our business is finished. Do not record it. Discuss it with no one. If you should see me again, do not reveal my role in this, no matter what the circumstances." He turned to look at the Apostle and narrowed his eyes. "And do not stand in my way. Defy my demands and in your last moments you will find out exactly what I am." The Apostle scowled, but replied, "Whatever that sword may mean to you, you are still a hero to the Triumvirate. May the Triumvirate bless you for your assistance in their cause. But do not stand in our way, either!" He raised a bloody hand in salute, spared another look of horror at the destruction unleashed in the valley below them, then turned and fled down the hillside with his disciples.

Darilos gazed again on the flaming valley and mused on the contrast of the burning hell below against the blue heaven of the skies above. It was a fitting symbol for his methods, using the Triumvirate's followers to achieve the goals of the Outer Gods. Yet another compromise in a world of compromises. Darilos smiled. What was he? If only the apostle knew! He looked back to make sure they had gone. In exaltation of his true identity, Darilos dropped the masquerade. His human body disintegrated into ash. From its shell burst the giant, serpentine body of a demon. Sapphirine skin. Blue flames dancing. Slim amber wings jutting out like dagger blades. Talons that he held out to clack the air in front of his long, rippled muzzle. He stretched to full height, joints and tendons popping, muscles shaking. ptured, he roared into the burning valley like the thunder o estruction. He was once again his true self ... he was A2 Demon dragon. Footman of the Ether.

ABOUT THE AUTHOR

Jason A. Kilgore is a multigenre writer in speculative fiction, including horror, fantasy, and science fiction, as well as poetry, scientific publications, and essays. By day, he is a scientist with a global biotech company specializing in microscopy and cell biology. He lives in Oregon and when he isn't writing, he loves hiking and camping in the mountain wilderness areas and the Pacific coast.

Thank you for reading *Dragon of the Federation*. If you enjoyed this story, recommend it to a friend or leave a review.

Sign up for news about the Strange Worlds of Jason Kilgore to receive updates on Jason's scribblings, get cool links to speculative fiction stuff, and more: https://mailchi.mp/a9205da52dab/worldskilgore

Visit and follow the author's web and social media pages:

Author website: https://jason-kilgore.com/
Blog: https://jasonkilgore.blogspot.com
Twitter: https://twitter.com/WorldsKilgore
Facebook: https://facebook.com/WorldsKilgore
Instagram: https://instagram.com/WorldsKilgore

More Books from GladEye Press

The Time Tourists
The Yesterday Girl
Sharleen Nelson
Follow the adventures and missteps of time-traveling PI Imogen Oliver as she recovers lost items and unearths long-buried stories and secrets from the past in this exciting series!

Tripping the Field: An Existential Crisis of Ungodly Proportions
Ian Jaydid
Empiricist scientist, Professor Michael Huxley tumbles, stumbles, strides, and crawls through the jungles of South America, the mountains of Tibet, and the backwoods of Colorado in search of enlightenment and the hope of saving the world from a religious cult that has discovered a dark shortcut to the power of quantum realities.

Dye. Run. Don't Die: A Love Story
K.G. Kolsen
Chased by shadowy figures, Winnie and Jimmy reunite somewhere between Oklahoma and Colorado and embark on a wild ride filled with disguises, stolen vehicles, murders, truck-stop perverts, a sex-cult, deadly shootouts, and rediscovered love.

Faith, Hope, Dying
Patricia Brown
Eleanor, Angus, Feathers, and the coffee club friends are back! When sisters Hope and Faith return to the small coastal village to settle their preacher father's estate, rumors swirl and the truth about a decades-old mystery leads to a fresh wave of murders.

All GladEye titles are available for purchase at
www.gladeyepress.com and your local bookstore.

Dying to Win
Patricia Brown
Even a bucolic beach town has its skeletons. When the newly wed husband of the area's richest heiress mysteriously disappears, Eleanor and her friends find themselves entangled in dark secrets involving bullies, racists, murder, anonymous love letters, and more!

Under A Dying Moon
Patricia Brown
When a young girl washes up on the beach, there is no doubt murder is once again the topic in town. Two more brutal murders bring the town to the edge of panic. Are the newly arrived young swingers involved or the cute retired couple? And what is the deal with the gnomes scattered around town?

Dying for Diamonds
Patricia Brown
When a mean-spirited mystery writer visiting her sleepy coastal town is murdered, Eleanor Penrose, her retired detective friend Angus, the coffee club ladies, and Feathers, the irascible African grey parrot, work to solve the puzzles without becoming the murderer's next victims.

A Recipe for Dying
Patricia Brown
The old people are dying in the small coastal town of Waterton, but no one seems to notice—after all, that's what old folk do, isn't it? Eleanor and her delightful assortment of friends, most whom are getting up in age, set out to discover what is going on. Is it a series of mercy killings, or murder, and is their investigation putting them in danger?

COMING 2024 *from*

Footman of the Ether
Jason A. Kilgore
Revisit the rich landscape of Kilgore's Heartstone series in the second book in this high stakes fantasy adventure set in a world inhabited by dragons, malevolent gods, a magical cult, and a powerful renegade spell-wielding mage.

The Fragile Blue Dot—Stories from Our Imperiled Biosphere
Ross West

Veteren science-writer and journalist Ross West's collection of award-winning short fiction touches on the human aspect of living in a world on the brink of ecological disaster.

The Risk of Being Ridiculous: A Historical Novel of Love and Revolution
Guy Maynard
Join 19-year-old Ben Tucker for a passionate, lyrical six-week ride through confrontation and confusion, courts and cops, parties and politics, school and the streets, Weathermen and women's liberation, acid and activism, revolution and reaction.

Watch for *Trial,* Maynard's second book in the series, coming later in 2024.